CW00866015

BY THE GODS'S EARS

CHANSON DE GUERRE BOOK 1

CHRISTOPHER FLY

Copyright (C) 2021 Christopher Fly

Layout design and Copyright (C) 2021 by Next Chapter

Published 2021 by Shadow City – A Next Chapter Imprint

Edited by Fading Street Services

Cover art by CoverMint

This book is a work of fiction. Names, characters, places, and incidents are the product of the author's imagination or are used fictitiously. Any resemblance to actual events, locales, or persons, living or dead, is purely coincidental.

All rights reserved. No part of this book may be reproduced or transmitted in any form or by any means, electronic or mechanical, including photocopying, recording, or by any information storage and retrieval system, without the author's permission.

To A C
You are my Claire

CHAPTER ONE

THE UNRELENTING DROUGHT plagued the Prince's hunting party. After a long struggle to catch anything with little appreciable success, the Prince declared in the fading evening twilight the entire endeavor a failure. They would make camp and return to the city of Darloque in the morning. As the other hunters unsaddled their horses and made arrangements for the night, the Prince trod off into the thickening darkness alone. No one dared follow him.

When the twilight gray of morning had given way to the first tinges of sullen orange, the solitary figure of the Prince returned from the wilderness, his mood substantially lifted from the previous evening. As his men moved about in their morning rituals, he greeted each one warmly, congenially slapping his hand on backs, and speaking to them with bright and encouraging words. Each man watched the Prince warily, waiting for the punishment he did not merit. When no random act of punishment came, the wariness shifted quickly to apprehension and then to outright fear. The Prince mounted his saddled horse with a cry of, "Home men! Onward to Darloque!" The others followed dutifully.

The hunting party made quick progress across the open plain, the stubby, drought-stricken grasses offering little resistance to the galloping horses. Shortly, they came upon the road to Darloque. An argument was escalating within a small group at the rear of the hunting party. After much contention, a rider reluctantly kicked his horse faster and drew up alongside the leader and addressed him.

"My Prince, you appear in much better spirits than last night." The rider spoke in a dreary tone, which barely veiled his trepidation.

The Prince kept his eyes forward, seemingly ignorant of his lieutenant's address.

He cleared his throat and was about to repeat his statement when the Prince spoke, his eyes still forward, a small smile forming on his lips.

"I know the men are concerned about my sudden cheerful mood." He turned to his lieutenant. "Does my sudden cheerful mood disturb you as well, Jean-Louis?"

The lieutenant kept his composure, showing no response to the jab. "You have your reasons, and I do not question them. The men merely notice a sudden change from the previous night. Such changes, as they have come to learn, usually foretell an unfortunate experience for one of them."

The Prince threw his head back and brayed laughter.

"The men fear the coming storm of your hidden rage," the lieutenant said flatly. "But I know you all too well. This grand mood of yours is genuine, and I wish to know its source."

The Prince ceased his laughter. His face dropped, and his eyes lit with hellish fire, seemingly perturbed that his lieutenant could judge his moods so well. He leaned over to the lieutenant and whispered just loudly enough over the thunder of their horse's hooves: "This grand mood of mine is indeed genuine, for soon I shall make my greatest achievement which will etch my name in the great book of history."

The lieutenant pressed his lips together tightly. He could think of no response to this fantastic pronouncement.

"We have no time for details now. Let us make haste for the city, I will give you and the men the specifics when we reach the castle." The Prince kicked his horse faster. The other men, seeing this, kicked their horses as well, endeavoring to keep up with the pace. The lieutenant gradually slowed his horse, and then reined it to a halt in the middle of the road.

"This bodes not well," he said quietly. "I do not know the meaning of this yet, but still it bodes not well." After a moment of silence, the lieutenant kicked his horse into a hard gallop after the Prince and his entourage.

The Prince stayed far ahead of the others for some time. The lieutenant intentionally held his charger back behind the main group, wishing the time alone with his thoughts. He looked up to see that the Prince and the other men had disappeared around a bend in the road. Tall but rangy stalks of corn grew across a field all the way up to the edge of the road blocking the lieutenant's view of the hunting party. He rounded the bend to find the entire group stopped in the road watching the Prince as he engaged in conversation with a young farm girl. A very young farm girl.

The lieutenant pulled his horse to a sharp halt and shook his head sadly. "By the gods's ears," he muttered under his breath.

He had caught up with the Prince in the middle of his pitch, but the girl seemed not to be buying any of it. The lieutenant had to smile a little when the girl gave an impertinent flip of her chestnut hair. She stood back from the road amongst rows of pathetic cornstalks, a basket of small, shriveled ears of corn at her feet. The lieutenant shook his head again, but this time at the mean harvest the girl had been collecting.

The Prince did not notice the girl's lack of interest at all. What he did notice was her pert, budding breasts and deeply tanned thighs. The heat was already oppressive just past dawn, and the girl had apparently loosened her collar and hiked her skirts up around her waist in order to work more comfortably. The Prince recited a well-used speech he had given to countless other young farm girls across the country. The lieutenant, unfortunately, had heard it so often he knew it by rote.

And now he shall tell her how far he has traveled, he thought.

"And, my lady, I have seen the White Forests in the North, traveled the lands beyond Ocosse in the vast Eastern Steppes, climbed the magnificent Silent Mountains to the South, and sailed on the Great Western Sea—"

The girl broke in. "You have seen the sea?" She took a couple of quick steps toward the Prince.

Momentarily thrown off his pace by her interruption, the Prince's face dropped for the briefest of moments and a look of uncertainty flashed in his eyes. Only the lieutenant noticed.

"Why yes, my lady," the Prince answered after the moment had passed, "I have been to the sea, but its beauty pales in comparison to yours."

A few snickers behind him. The Prince did not notice; he was focused upon his prey.

"You must tell me what it is like!" the girl cried. She had completely missed the Prince's compliment, focused entirely as she was upon the subject of the sea. She did take another step toward him though.

"Describe the sea? It would be like trying to describe your beauty to a blind man. Words could not contain it." The Prince was off his script, but he was displaying a rare moment of creative inspiration. "Describe it, I cannot, but I would gladly take you there."

The girl's eyes lit up and she took another step forward. She was almost upon him now. "You would?! Oh! I would so much like to visit the sea!"

More snickers from behind. Still, the Prince did not notice, nor did the girl.

"I would with much delight show you the brilliant blue of the Great Western Sea." The Prince leaned down from his horse. "Ah, there is nothing like standing in the lustrous white sand watching great foaming whitecaps crashing onto the shore. The sounds of the waves and the wind, the smell of the salt in the air! C'est magnifique!"

The lieutenant shook his head sadly as he saw the girl's eyes light up and he realized yet another innocent was caught in the snare.

"Oh, you must take me! Please!" Her eyes were wide and wild, her voice pleading.

"Oh yes, my lady, I certainly will." The Prince looked across the field. "Your house," he said, indicating the small stone structure at the end of a cart track. "Your parents are there, are they not?"

"Yes!" the girl replied eagerly.

"Well, I must ask their permission to take their daughter on such a long journey." A broad rapacious grin spread across the Prince's face. "We must respect their wishes."

More snickering came from behind followed by a couple of guffaws that were immediately shushed by the others. The Prince was completely oblivious to the men, enthralled as he was with the catch.

"Oh yes! Oh yes!" The girl exclaimed brightly. "But they shall say yes! They shall! They shall!"

The Prince said his farewells, promising to return for her soon, and kicked his horse into a gallop down the cart track toward the farmhouse. The men followed suit, ogling the girl as they passed, and laughing with each other.

Only the lieutenant remained. He stared at the girl sadly and heaved a mournful sigh. The girl regarded him curiously. For a moment, their eyes locked. The girl suddenly could feel the heavy burden the man carried. She felt the weight in her heart and a longing to ease his pain grew within her. The rider broke his gaze with her, reined his horse around, and slowly rode after his comrades. Just as quickly as the feeling had come upon the girl, it was gone.

———

Murielle froze when the unexpected staccato of furious knocking came at the door. Her eyes darted nervously about the room. *Where is Gilles?* she thought, a slow panic rising in her. "*Non, non,*" she whispered, trying to calm herself. Gilles was working the fields and an unfamiliar knock at the door of their home could be nothing more than a traveler seeking rest. Their home lay on the main road to Darloque, and quite often weary pilgrims stopped to find rest and repose from their travels. Never had they regretted taking a stranger in. They lived by the maxim "Welcome a stranger and be rewarded manifold." Gilles had engraved the motto in ornate script on a plank, which hung over the door.

"But why so early in the morning?" she said, louder than she intended. The knock came again, full of foreboding. *This bodes not well*, she thought, this time holding her tongue should Gilles suddenly enter. The words over the door mocked her in their simplicity, their naïveté. The staccato came again, ever more urgently. Murielle moved hesitantly toward the door, reminded of another tenet: "One cannot turn his back on Fate."

As she drew in breath slowly and held it, she pulled open the door. *Let us dispense with this quickly.* At the doorway stood a tall burly man with an unfamiliar face, a man she had never seen before in her life. *Oh, thank the gods,* she thought automatically, *it is only a traveler seeking repose on his long journey.*

"Good morning, Madame," said the stranger, thickly.

"Good morning, *Monsieur*," she returned with a heavy sigh, "What has brought you to my humble home this fair morning?"

The stranger stood wordlessly for a moment, a constrained look on his face as though he were attempting the arduous task of collecting his thoughts. Suddenly he burst out, "Madame."

"Yes," she replied.

"*Bonjour,*" he began, as though attempting recitation of an ill-remembered speech, "It is my pleasure...um...to present to you...um...His royal highness...um... the Prince." The burly man stepped aside, offering an awkward bow to the Prince who had been standing behind him.

Murielle's blood froze. The Prince strolled indifferently past her into the house. "You must forgive my new man he has not quite gotten that memorized yet. He is otherwise particularly useful and came highly recommended."

By the gods's ears, Murielle thought, her relief returning to panic, *where is Emmeline?*

The Prince strolled casually around the small stone cottage wrinkling his nose at the simplicity of it. "What a simply charming home you have here, Madame." The Prince offered his compliment flatly with just a hint of veiled distaste in his voice.

"Ahh..." was all that Murielle could offer in response.

"Well Madame, I am sure you are very busy this morning so I will come to the matter directly." The Prince paused at a chair in the center of the room as though he might sit then changed his mind. "I have seen the most beautiful girl up by the road who tells me that she is your daughter."

Emmeline! NON!

The Prince turned to face Murielle.

Murielle's head began to spin. For years she had heard the stories of the Prince's appetite for young girls. At first, she had dismissed the stories as just that, stories. *Rumor volat, as the priests say,* she thought, *rumors fly.* But as time passed and the Prince became more brazen in his pursuit of young girls, even the most outrageous stories became believable.

Why me, she asked herself, *why us, why Emmeline?*

"I would like to ask for your daughter's hand in marriage." It was more a command than a request.

As a woman and a mother, Murielle had pitied the families the Prince had touched with his lechery. Deep inside, however, she had convinced herself that such things only happened to other people, not to her and Gilles. She was sure that it would miss them because they were isolated and watchful. Foolishness, she told herself now, foolishness and vanity to think that they were immune from the Prince's sickness. But it was here, now. The madness had touched her, the sickness was upon her, and her daughter was gone.

"I assure you, Madame, your daughter will want for nothing," the Prince recited. "She shall be my queen, and I her loyal consort." He walked abruptly toward the door and announced, "I am worn and weary from my hunt, I shall return for your daughter this evening when I am refreshed."

The Prince exited the cottage with a flourish of his hunting cape. The burly man at the door offered a mechanical bow as he passed. Murielle watched blankly, her mouth agape, her breath coming in short, panicked gasps. The burly man offered her an unsettling wink as he pulled the door closed, a large humorless grin spread across his face, a grin that was more hungry than menacing.

Murielle snapped out of her torpor and rushed to the door. She threw it open with a bang and gazed upon the assemblage outside her home. The Prince was just mounting his horse while a large group of men chatted amongst themselves on their mounts. All the men with the Prince were large, burly, and menacing characters like the first one. Save for one.

He was older than the rest, about her age. Although slightly slumped in the saddle of his horse, his frame carried a look of strength and power. He wore his hair to his shoulders in the fashion of a knight of the Old King–the style her father had worn. His horse was a large, dark, fast-looking charger with a fiery eye and a muscular build brought of fine breeding. *Yes*, she thought, *I do not know much, but I do know the appearance of one of the Old King's true knights.* Her eyes locked on his. *So, what are you doing with this sorry lot?*

Murielle's heart softened as she gazed into the knight's eyes. Despair dwelt in those eyes, and it washed over her, melding with her own sadness. He carried a heavy burden, the weight of the world– and then some, perhaps–upon his shoulders. He was not broken, yet, but he was very well near the point of breaking. Her eyes pleaded desperately with him. *Please, I know you can stop this.* Murielle felt her eyes welling with tears as she appealed to him across the gap. A single tear slipped down his cheek. *I am sorry,* he mouthed before he reined his horse around and rode up the track after his associates.

"Hurry up, Jean-Louis!" the Prince shouted, and this brought uproarious laughter from the other men.

Murielle closed the door on the fading drum of hoof beats and pressed her head against the rough-hewn wooden frame. She sighed heavily. *By the gods's ears.* She rubbed her forehead back and forth against the coarse surface. *Pourquoi? Why, why, why?* With her head still pressed to the doorframe, she turned her eyes to the altar near the door. "You could not even protect us from this," she reproached the god. "What good are you?"

Of all the hardships they had endured in their lives, nothing compared to this. How would she tell Gilles? That was difficult enough, but how would she explain it to Emmeline? She was just an innocent girl of only twelve seasons who knew nothing of the world.

As if on command, Emmeline burst through the back door of the house with a basket in her hands. She looked eagerly about the room, then her eyes settled excitedly upon her mother. "Mama, mama! Did you speak to him?!"

Murielle turned slowly to face her daughter, and her eyes drifted idly to the basket the girl held. The drought, now in its third season, had again reduced the crop to a mere shadow of its once glorious bounty. The crop had long since diminished beyond the point of producing enough to sell at the market, and now it was incapable of supplying enough to feed them through the winter. Murielle turned back to the altar. *First the drought and this pitiful harvest, and now you put this new scourge upon us.*

She regarded her daughter again. It occurred to her that the girl seemed to have grown overnight. Emmeline's face had slimmed; nearly gone was the chubby roundness of childhood. Her hair now had a silken sheen to it. And her skin, tanned from working in the sun, had a certain luster to it. Murielle could see curves on Emmeline where there had previously been none.

With a sudden shock, Murielle realized that Emmeline had taken down her long hair, so it hung to her waist. Her daughter's skirt was hiked up almost that high, and her blouse was open, offering a glimpse of the womanhood developing beneath.

"Where did you pick these?" Murielle asked, her eyes narrowing.

Emmeline gave an impertinent flip of her silky hair, the long, lustrous hair of a young girl barely touched by time, and replied, "Out by the road."

Murielle balled her hands into fists. "Child!" she hissed through clenched teeth, "How many times have I told not to work by the road and if you must, tie your hair and wear your breeches!"

"Mama!" Emmeline began to protest.

"Girl, I do not tell you these things simply to hear my own voice. I have reasons for what I tell you to do!"

Emmeline huffed.

The elder woman groaned and pointed to the altar, "You pick this terrible harvest that this ineffective god provides us, dressed like that, and now..."

Murielle trailed off. *And now what?* She began to pace anxiously about the room, wringing her hands. *And now what? What do I tell her? That her life is over?*

"Mama," the girl resumed, "it is barely after sunrise, and already it is sweltering. Breeches are too hot!"

Murielle opened her mouth to say something then reconsidered, choosing silence as a better option. She merely swayed her head in a slow pendulous arc. Emmeline gaped at her mother in curious disbelief. The sound of silence slowly filled the room.

A loud cry broke the uncomfortable tension as the man of the house burst through the back door proclaiming, "Family, behold the bountiful harvest the Lord Aufeese has provided for us!" Mother and daughter both turned to see the same withered ears of corn spilling out of his basket that graced Emmeline's. Gilles gathered up four of the best-looking ears and arranged them in a shallow trough before the altar. Then placing the fingertips of his right hand to his forehead, he kneeled in veneration before the altar and prayed aloud. "*Merci beaucoup* for this great harvest O Golden Child of Mava, although we are not worthy of your great benefaction."

His wife snorted in disgust. His daughter rolled her eyes.

Gilles stood and turned quickly to Murielle. "Do not mock the Golden Child! We must be thankful for all that he gives us no matter how great–or how small." Murielle noted the faint tone of despair in those last three words as her husband defended the god of the harvest. It still awed her that even in his frustration, Gilles remained faithful to his god.

Gilles continued to scold. "It is not for us to know the intentions of the gods, for their ways are far beyond our comprehension. We must have faith in the knowledge that what they do is always for our benefit."

Murielle snorted again. *And exactly how is the Prince's lechery for our benefit?*

Gilles jabbed his finger savagely in the direction of Emmeline. "I am so disappointed that your lack of faith has begun to infect our little one. Already she has fallen out of the habit of daily prayer and refuses to make offerings to Lord Aufeese."

Emmeline huffed indignantly at the accusation. Some days she did forget to pray to the god, but she did make an offering just yesterday–or maybe it was a few days ago. She could not remember. Anyway, she was not as cynical about the gods as her mother was. Although, she did think it a waste of time to make offerings to a god that did not seem to be listening to their prayers. The rains fell further and further apart while the crops continued to suffer despite her father's constant prayers. The Lord Aufeese never brought the needed rain, nor did he give them anything they could use to help keep the farm thriving. There was a belief deep inside Emmeline– growing as a corn sprout in fertile soil–that her father wasted his time praying to a deaf god. That is, if he were even there to hear the prayers at all.

A red flush had been slowly creeping up Murielle's face. It was a condition Emmeline had often seen in her mother when she was very angry with her father. Her anger seemed to come more quickly and frequently in the last few seasons. Quite often her mother and father argued belligerently over the subjects of religion and faith. More specifically, they argued over his faith in the gods and her faith that there were no such things.

"Fine," Murielle burst out finally, "would you like to know what your faith has brought unto us now?" Spittle flew from her lips as she unleashed her fury. "Let me tell what *your* god has let happen to his most faithful servant." She told Gilles of the whole encounter, and Emmeline's jaw dropped as the tale began to unfold.

CHAPTER TWO

"B-B-B-BUT," Emmeline sputtered, "I do not want to marry anyone." She shook her head back and forth and flailed her arms about uselessly. "H-h-h-he just said," she sputtered again, "h-h-h-he only said h-h-h-he would show me the sea!"

Murielle nodded in grim affirmation. "So that is what he told you?"

"*Oui*, Mama, *oui*," she spit out, "*Oui*. He said he would show me *la mer*. That is all. *Oui*."

A low moaning drew their attention to Gilles who was sinking slowly to his knees, his face buried in his hands. "No, no, not my little girl!" he sobbed.

With a loud, agonizing scream, Gilles tore his face from his hands and without a glance to his wife and daughter he scrambled on his knees to the altar, clouds of dust swirling up around him from the dirt floor as he went. "Oh, great Golden Child, please hear my prayer!" Gilles pressed the fingertips of his right hand firmly on his forehead and began mumbling inaudibly.

Murielle rolled her eyes and sighed heavily in disgust. "Yes

Gilles, that will help very much," she spat sarcastically. "The god who cannot bring the rain will deliver us from this."

"Mama!"

"You disagree, child?" she snarled with nary a glance to her daughter.

"N-n-n-no," she stammered, "but there must be a misunderstanding with the Prince."

"There is no misunderstanding, Emmeline," she rounded on her again. "The Prince intends that you will be his bride." She paused a moment, watching her husband still muttering his foolish prayers. Then she added with a low sigh, "Whatever that means to him in his sick and twisted mind."

Emmeline shook her head and flailed her arms again. "What... whatever do you mean, Mama? We... we will tell him that there has been a... a... mis... misunderstanding!"

"Emmeline! It is only you who are misunderstanding!" Murielle wrung her hands and began to pace in a tight circle. Emmeline opened her mouth to speak but Murielle cut her off. "Jul...." Murielle paused briefly and took a breath. "Many travelers have told me stories of the Prince."

Emmeline looked at her mother blankly.

Murielle swallowed hard. "Let me tell you but one story."

Emmeline huffed and flipped her hair.

"On a hunting trip in the West," Murielle continued unabated, "the Prince came upon a small, isolated tenant farm. The couple there had a single child, a daughter. A very young daughter. She was about the age you are now, pretty, and she possessed a head of long flaming red hair. Jocelyn was her name. When the Prince saw her, he immediately requested her hand in marriage. Jocelyn's parents were thrilled at the prospect and allowed the Prince to take her back to Darloque.

"A few people remember seeing her enter the city and the castle—the red hair marked her easily—but then, she was seen no more."

Emmeline's brow furrowed. "What do mean by 'seen no more' Mama?"

"She was never seen again—at least not in Darloque. After a long time with no word from their daughter, Jocelyn's father made the journey to Darloque, and inquired at the castle as to her status. After a lengthy wait, the Prince himself greeted the farmer. 'I have no idea where your "thieving bitch" daughter is,' he told the man. He continued, saying that a few days after bringing her to the castle he had returned from a hunting trip to find her gone and several pieces of gold and silver missing, as well as a small chest of his deceased mother's jewelry.

"The farmer was beside himself. He replied that his daughter would never do such a thing. He added that she had not returned home, she was too young to be on her own, and where would she have gone?

"The Prince flew into a rage, shouting and cursing. After screaming at the man that he had made a grievous error trusting the daughter of a serf, the Prince then ordered his guards to throw the farmer out of the castle. Pulling himself from dust, the farmer wandered throughout the city, seeking his daughter, and crying to anyone who would listen about his missing daughter and the treatment he had received at the hands of the Prince. He even went so far as to return to the castle and attempt to attain an audience with the Old King. The guards stood silent, ignoring his pleas. After some time of this, one of the guards with nary a word, placed the tip of his spear on the man's chest. The farmer ceased his cries and left in the slow trudging step of the defeated.

"It was quite some time later, perhaps the following season, when a group of travelers from Darloque claimed to have seen Jocelyn in the far Southern town of Alzenay. They said they saw her in the... in the... in a bad part of town. The flaming red hair was unmistakable. They also said she was... well... in a bad state. Not one of them believed the young girl could have come to that place on her own. The Prince most certainly had sent her there."

Emmeline stared sadly at her mother, her mouth agape. "Did Jocelyn ever return home?" she asked quietly.

Murielle inhaled deeply and released a long sigh. "When he heard the story, the farmer traveled as fast as he could to Alzenay. He inquired about the town and eventually found a woman who remembered the girl with the fiery red hair. She told him that the girl had been... that... that a group of soldiers, mercenaries, had taken her away. But that had been almost half a season previous. When the farmer questioned her as to where the mercenaries had gone, she shushed him and told him that she could find him another red-haired girl much prettier than that one. He pushed the woman aside and continued with his frantic search. But he never found Jocelyn."

Murielle released a long, weary sigh. "I have said too much," she muttered under her breath.

Emmeline's mouth had gone dry. She rasped her tongue across her lips. "What shall we do now," she said in a hoarse whisper.

What shall we do now? Murielle asked herself. *Keep your wits,* she heard her father's voice insist. She needed to calm herself and clear her head. *Every problem has its solution,* her father had always told her, *and one merely has to discover it.* Murielle knew that with reason she could find the solution.

Gilles was still on his knees before the altar to Lord Aufeese, fingers to forehead, muttering inaudible words of prayer. When Murielle had first met him, his devotion to the gods–Lord Aufeese in particular–seemed quaint and added to his rustic charm. Now, so many seasons later, his devotion had grown annoying. He seemed to think that Lord Aufeese, Mava's golden child, could solve anything, even though it was evermore clear that he would not, or could not.

If he even exists at all, Murielle added. In all the length of her life, she had never seen any sign that the gods were anything more than flights of fancy created by the ancients and supported by the superstitious masses seeking any easy path out of their problems. In none of the ubiquitous temples to the various gods she had visited had she ever seen one of the gods. Since she had come to be with Gilles, she had visited the Temple of Aufeese in Darloque more times than she could count. The building itself was impressive: a massive, intricately designed facade fronted by immense stone columns reaching into the sky and a grand stained glass window featuring every color of the rainbow. Inside, a towering white marble statue of the Golden Child himself stood behind the altar. Daily, the faithful prostrated themselves before the altar beneath this grand statue of Lord Aufeese. Priests hovered about, assisting the faithful in their devotions: helping with sacrifices, instructing novices on prayers, and doing what good men of religion should do.

Yet, regardless of her feelings toward the gods and religion in general, she could find no fault in the good priests she had met at the temples. The memory of Emmeline's first trip to the Temple of Aufeese in Darloque sprung into her mind unbidden. She was still young and had never been away from the farm before. The High Priest welcomed them warmly and approached the little girl first. He was kind looking, an older man with streaks of gray in his long hair and beard. He squatted before Emmeline, his eyes level with hers, as she tried to hide behind Murielle's skirts. He spoke with the soft voice of a man who possessed a vast experience with young children.

"What a pretty little girl," he exclaimed, winking at Murielle and Gilles. "Have you ever been to the Temple of Aufeese before?"

Peeking out from behind Murielle, she shook her head nervously.

"I believe that if Lord Aufeese were here now he would be jealous because you are so pretty."

This elicited a smile from the girl, but she still hid behind her mother.

"Will you let me show you the altar," the Priest asked in his gentle manner, extending his hand to her. "I do not think Lord Aufeese will mind if you look at it."

Emmeline looked nervously from her mother to her father, then her eyes turned to the Priest. The Priest's blue eyes sparkled, and he winked. "I think there may be some candied figs up there too."

Emmeline broke into a huge toothy grin, stepped from behind her mother's protective skirts, and took the Priest's hand. He led her up to the altar, telling her about temple and the statue as they walked hand in hand. He launched into a well-worn tale of Lord Aufeese and his exploits with the Wild Hares while Emmeline stood with him before the altar, transfixed by his every word. At last, he reached into his robes and withdrew the promised treat, a huge, candied fig. Her eyes lit up with delight as she reached for it.

The Priest held out his other hand, stopping the girl. "Always remember that Lord Aufeese loves you," he said, pointing to her. "He always wants the best for you, and he is always watching over you," he added, tilting his bright blue eyes toward the statue behind the altar.

She nodded very seriously, her eyes transfixed on the fig. With a great flourish he gave the treat to Emmeline. "Will you come back to visit me again?"

She hesitated briefly then broke into another huge grin, nodding furiously while clutching the fig in a death grip.

"Good! I am very much looking forward to it!" With that he let her run joyfully back to her parents, clutching the fig in her tiny fist.

Murielle had never met a temple priest who was not a good man. Even outside the confines of the temple, each was kind and giving. *Good men*, she thought, *wasting their time serving a fantasy*. A fantasy indeed. Gilles was a good man as well, and his faith and prayers had come to naught. She had long hoped that just a little of his faith would one day come into her heart, but his faith had only hardened it. Murielle had finally settled on the belief that all things were random and generated by some callous machine of the universe–impartial and unfeeling, incapable of being swayed to move in any direction by the feeble pleas of the victims locked within its gears.

Emmeline waited for her mother to say something, anything. She desperately wanted her to tell her that this was some kind of joke, an elaborate hoax perpetrated on her to teach her a lesson for not obeying her parents. The deep pain in her mother's eyes told her this was not the case. There was no punch line to be told, nor any deceit to be revealed. Her father's muttered prayers offered at a fevered pitch told her this as well. He was a religious man, a pious man, who took his obligation to the gods very seriously. But when he prayed with this intensity, Emmeline knew the situation was particularly dire. And it scared her. Soon her mother's fearful silence and her father's fevered muttering were too much for her to bear. Emmeline had to speak, to say something, anything that would break the spell that had come over their household. But before she could get a word out, her father leapt to his feet with a shout.

"Oh, blest be Mava's many litters, I have it!"

Murielle and Emmeline awakened from their reveries and turned to Gilles. "*Que?*" they asked in unison.

Gilles raised his hands to the rafters with another shout, startling the two gray doves Murielle had been trying to shoo from the house for the past several days. "Oh, great thanks to you Lord Aufeese! Oh, thank you Mava's golden son! You have saved this poor man's daughter from a terrible fate!"

"Gilles!" Murielle cried, "Why in Mava's name are you shouting so?"

"Because," he exclaimed, staring though her with mad, distant eyes, "Lord Aufeese, the Golden Child, the god you mock, has blest me with his great knowledge! He has given me the answer to our dilemma!"

Emmeline gave her father a disdainful look which quickly turned hopeful. "He has?"

"Yes, my sweet girl he has," he replied. He swept across the room to her and took her face gently into his hands. "He has indeed!"

Murielle looked at her husband and crossed her arms across her chest. Her expression was more doubtful than Emmeline's. "*S'il vous plait,* what has your great golden god told you that we should do?"

Gilles turned on his heels to face his wife and jabbed his finger at her. "Lord Aufeese loves you despite your scoffing," he said with a mad gleam in his eyes. He looked at her, but suddenly Murielle doubted that he saw her at all.

And why, she thought to herself with a sigh, *if he loves me so much, does the great god himself not deliver the message to us in the flesh?* It seemed to her that the solution to such a dire problem required a visit from the Golden Child himself. In all her life Murielle had never seen a single one of the gods. Of course, she had heard stories of people who had encounters with the gods. Even some of her childhood friends had claimed to have seen the gods. One friend had even boasted that she had personally spoken with a god. But they were children and what did they know? Murielle's father was a knight, so her childhood home contained a perfunctory altar to the war god. As a little girl she had made up her mind to pray at that altar. Every day she tried to pray. She soon focused on one request to the war god: *I wish to meet you.* Every day she was disappointed when no answer came.

Then she met Gilles, the son of a freed serf, who prayed fervently to Lord Aufeese. Still harboring serious doubts, Murielle offered prayers to this god, thinking that perhaps she had offered her allegiance to the wrong god. She never saw him. Gilles had never seen him either. But he prayed nevertheless, and his faith grew stronger while hers withered and died and her heart grew colder.

Now what she wanted was for the great Golden Child of Mava to show himself. *Enter through that door right now*, she thought ruefully, *and I will believe once and for all; I promise I will believe.* In her mind's eye she could see him burst into the room, smashing the door from its hinges. He would squeeze through the doorway and stand before them. The Lord Aufeese would not be able to straighten to his full height, for the low rafters would prevent it. Towering above them, nevertheless, he would spread his front paws wide as if to gather them all in a deep embrace. In a booming voice he would announce to them all, "I, the Lord Aufeese, am here! You are under my protection, and no harm may come to you!"

Murielle opened her eyes, and all she saw was Gilles's beaming face and that mad gleam in his eyes. Her heart sank but not by much. Not to have faith in something means not to be disappointed when it does not come true. The gods were myth, fairy tales told to children.

Gilles was speaking again. "But we have little time. If it is to succeed, we must perform our task before the chariot of the sun has left the sky."

"Well," Murielle snorted.

Ignoring her, Gilles laid out the plan. Murielle slowly nodded her head as she took in what her husband was saying. She had never heard such a well-thought plan come from Gilles. Whatever madness had seized him, it was a clever madness.

Emmeline would have to run. She would set out alone to the east for Ocosse, travelling cross-country, avoiding the roads and anyone who might be looking for her. Once across the border, she was to find a tavern called The Wild Hare. The tavern was easy to find. It was located at the crossroads of the two major trade routes. Once there, she would wait for Gilles and Murielle to join her. In the meantime, Gilles would travel to Darloque and seek an audience with the Old King, supplicating for protection from the Prince's lascivious intentions. By then the Prince would be on the way to their farm to collect Emmeline. Murielle was to stay behind and delay the Prince and then, after a sufficient amount of time, let it slip that Emmeline, refusing to be married to the Prince, had run away to the south. Gilles having convinced the Old King to help, would collect Murielle at their home and then follow Emmeline to Ocosse and The Wild Hare where they go into the protection of the Old King's guard.

Murielle pondered what Gilles had just said. The plan was not perfect. Success depended largely upon the mercy and indeed, the availability, of the Old King. But certainly, when the Old King was presented with another story of his son's misanthropy, he would intervene in their favor. The essence of the plan was good. Once Emmeline crossed the border into Ocosse, the Prince could not touch her without risking the peace that existed tentatively between the two kingdoms. At the very least, their ruse would allow Emmeline the time to get across the border. Murielle felt that the plan was good enough to work, but it needed one change to make it perfect.

"I should be the one to go to the Old King," she said flatly. Gilles fixed her with that same distant look, seeing her, but not seeing her. "For he would hear the pleas of a woman sooner than he would hear them from a man." Thus, it was well reasoned that Murielle should be the one to appeal to him.

Gilles agreed, but his nod of affirmation was slow and distracted. Emmeline would run to The Wild Hare, Murielle would travel to Darloque to petition the Old King, while Gilles would stay at the house and send the Prince in the wrong direction when he returned. As Gilles and Murielle moved to make preparations, Emmeline however, simply stood fixed on the floor staring blankly at them.

"Emmeline, we must pack you some food and water and then I will tell you how to get to The Wild Hare," said Gilles mechanically as he turned toward the pantry.

Emmeline gave no reply.

"Emmeline?" Murielle looked at her daughter as Gilles busied himself collecting food and placing it in a small piece of cloth.

"Emmeline?"

The girl began to shake her head. "*Non, non, non, ce n'est possible.*"

Murielle took her by the shoulders as if to shake her. "Emmeline, you must try to understand what trouble we have here. Please–"

"*Non!* No Mama," she shouted, pulling back suddenly from her mother's grasp. "*You* do not understand! I will not marry anyone!"

Emmeline paused briefly, then folded her arms emphatically across her chest as if the matter were settled. "And I will not run away." Another brief pause then, "I am free; I am a slave to no man!"

Murielle had heard Gilles utter that phrase innumerable times in their marriage, but it shocked her to hear it come from her daughter, especially now.

Gilles dropped a small baguette which rolled across the floor and stopped at Murielle's feet. She picked it up and brushed it off methodically as she spoke.

"You have no choice but to run," she said, turning the bread over in her hands.

"*Non, non,*" the girl said less fiercely. She fell back into shaking her head weakly from side to side. "*Non.*"

Gilles came over from where he was packing supplies and took his daughter in his arms. She allowed him to embrace her but continued to shake her head against his chest.

"You must understand," he said softly, the familiar warmth returning to his voice. He cupped his rough, calloused hand under her chin and gently tilted her face toward his own. "Lord Aufeese has shown me the way. You are in serious danger here, but the Golden Child has shown me what we must do to keep you safe."

Emmeline pulled back from him a little. A look of deep stubbornness slowly set in the girl's face like stone. It was a look that Gilles had seen many times in her mother's face.

"Besides," he said, smiling at her, "my father always told me that the greatest gift a free man possessed was the right to choose whether to stay and fight or to flee and fight another day." Emmeline's face brightened as he added, "And it is truly a wise man who can choose correctly."

Gilles gently stroked the girl's soft hair, his eyes locked into hers, her face open and completely absorbed in the words he spoke. Emmeline's racing heart began to slow, and she grew calm as she stared into his eyes. She knew what she had to do. She still did not understand why the Prince was to be feared, but she knew that her father believed she was in danger. He believed she was in danger, and so she would do as he wished. Never mind that he claimed his idea came from the god of the harvest. If he believed that this plan of his would keep her from harm, then she would follow his word. She would follow the plan, and all would be well. She was sure enough of that now.

Emmeline pressed her head against his chest as her father's

strong arms pulled her into his embrace. She felt their strength, their solid farmer's strength. These were the arms of a man who lived constantly in the life of honest manual labor. She inhaled his musky, sweaty smell. This was not the smell of a laborer but the comforting smell of love. The strong smell of her father comforted her in a way that nothing else could. He was the one person who always had time for her no matter how worn he might be from the day's grueling work. He was a constant in her life, a steady rock, a bastion of protection.

Emmeline recalled the time he and her mother had taken her to the Temple of Aufeese for the very first time. The High Priest had been kind to her. He had been old, his face wrinkled but with smiling eyes set deep into those wrinkles. His hair had been long and graying. She thought that he was precisely what a grandfather should look like. He spoke to her in soft, gentle tones like she imagined a grandfather should have. As he took her up to the altar and showed her the statue of the golden child, she listened to him, entranced by his voice. It was not so much the words he spoke as it was the tone of his voice which captured her attention. In fact, later, she could not remember a word he had said. She just remembered that gentle, soothing voice washing over her, taking her away. He had given her a candied fig, she recalled. With a great flourish he pulled it out from his robes and presented it to her. She knew that grandfathers were always supposed to have treats for their grandchildren. At that moment she wanted to stay right there with him forever. She wanted to climb into his lap, listen to his voice, and eat figs. She had held the sweet in her hand and looked into his eyes again. She felt safe.

This was how she felt about her father, but far more intensely. She longed for his security. Emmeline did not want this business with the Prince. She wanted to crawl into her father's lap, listen to the sound of his voice, feel his strong farmer's hands stroke her hair, and tell her that everything would be alright. More than that, she wanted him to make it right. She did not want to have to do anything except sit in his lap and let him make everything right. Is that so difficult? she thought. Why must I run when I should be able to sit in my father's lap as he makes it alright? Certainly, her father had the power to do that. There was no need to involve the gods. There was no need to run away. If she could just sit in her father's lap, listen to his voice, and feel his strong arms around her, then everything would be right.

But another voice was coming into Emmeline's head–a stronger voice, a voice older and stranger. It was the voice of the adult she was becoming. *Do not be silly*, it said, *that will not make this trouble go away*. For deep in the center of her being she knew that her father was right. She knew she had to run. To stand and argue with the Prince was foolish. All those men–those ferocious looking men who rode with him–could seize her by force and take her away to only the gods knew where. To try and hide in her father's arms was simply childish. He could not protect her from this by simply holding her in his lap–not now, not ever. It would indeed be wise for her to run to Ocosse. Still, she longed to curl up in a ball and wish the bad men away. But the ever more present adult voice–ever more annoyingly so–told her this was a wise plan. Yes indeed, it was the best course of action for her to follow to protect herself and the people she loved the most. Yes, it was indeed very wise. The older voice won out, and Emmeline looked up into her father's eyes, those brilliant blue eyes that had been such a comfort to her all her years.

"*Oui*, Papa," she said, "Yes, it is prudent sometimes to run. And now it is prudent for me to run."

Gilles smiled broadly at her, his brilliant blue eyes welling with tears.

"And perhaps," Emmeline added, "we will fight another day."

CHAPTER THREE

EMMELINE MOVED ABOUT with grim determination, although ghosts of self-doubt still haunted her. She finished packing some bread and cheese into the small bundle her father had started, and then filled a jug with water. As she filled the jug from the bucket, she felt the whining voice of the child welling up inside her again. Emmeline suppressed that voice, albeit with a great deal of difficulty. *Why must it be so hard*, she thought as she reached for some dried meat, *to keep the voice of reason?* Since the previous season she had found it increasingly difficult to keep her mind focused on the tasks at hand. This did not disturb her greatly, but it was terribly bothersome to begin a task again and again before finally completing it because her mind had wandered off.

And to where exactly had her mind been wandering? Nowhere. She thought about nothing that could be considered a concrete idea. Nothing at all. She slipped away, musing on thoughts she could not later recollect, coming to herself a little later no wiser than when she had left and sorely behind in some chore. The dreams were equally bothersome. She would awake in the morning, the faint mist of some dream dissipating around her, ethereal and untouchable, the memory of it agonizingly out of reach. The most unsettling were the occasional nights when she awoke suddenly in the dark. The dreams which awoke her at those times were more emphatic and urgent, but nevertheless just as untouchable and unknowable. She awoke, bathed in sweat, a powerful stirring from deep inside her fading rapidly as she broke into consciousness. Her skin prickled in a way that was not altogether unpleasant yet at the same time shamefully uncomfortable. A strange sensation of embarrassment, nay guilt, grew in her as she became aware of her parents' slow, deep breathing in the bed next to hers. After awakening from these dreams, she felt as she did when, as a little girl, she was caught sneaking sweets out of the pantry, yet these dreams engendered a greater guilt than those simple childish crimes. Although she could never remember them, these wispy mists of dreams still spurred the most arcane feelings in her.

"Emmeline, pray tell me, how long do you plan to be gone?"

"*Que?*" Emmeline looked down at the mound of dried meat heaped upon her bundle. "By the gods's ears," she cursed under her breath and scooped handfuls of the meat back into the larder.

Gilles smiled, but Murielle frowned with worry. The plan was good, but so many things could still go wrong. *No good plan is ever truly perfect*, her father had always said. If Emmeline made one foolish error....

"Little one," she called out, "that is enough food, change into your breeches now." She watched as the girl distractedly laid the paquet on her bed and slowly began to change. "Make haste, child. Hurry, Hurry!"

Murielle turned her gaze to the ornately carved beds sitting side by side at one end of the room, one for Emmeline and another larger one that she and Gilles shared. Most freemen of their status did not have beds, only pallets arranged on the floor at bedtime and stowed away during the waking hours. *By the gods's ears*, she thought, *many noblemen do not even have beds as fine as these*. Gilles was a veritable wizard with wood. Indeed, many who saw his crafts claimed that the god of the wood had certainly endowed him with the mastery of woodworking. So, why was Gilles even a farmer at all? The beds were masterpieces. The altar by the door with its wooden relief sculpture was as fine a piece of art as any she had seen in the Temple of Aufeese. Why would Gilles waste such a gift?

But that was Gilles. He loved tilling the soil, working the land, and reaping the produce of his labor. He never seemed truly alive until after he had labored vigorously under the blistering sun or in the drenching rain. Even when his labor yielded nothing, he seemed more alive than when he was at rest. The woodworking, however, was effortless to him. Murielle had watched him work, intricately carving organic swirls and animal imagery into the pieces of wood he had brought home from the Market, which became the headboards, footboards, and frames of their beds. It seemed of no more effort to him than waving off flies on a lazy summer's afternoon. It was merely natural to him. He worked the wood simply because he could. He worked the land because he loved it.

At last Emmeline had changed and was ready to embark upon her journey. With a glare from Murielle, the girl sulkily pulled back her long hair and tied it into a bun. Gilles brought her the small water jug. Emmeline slipped it inside the paquet then slung the bundle over her shoulder. Gilles gently took her face in his hands and stared into her eyes, saying nothing.

Murielle tapped her foot impatiently. "Gilles we must hurry."

"I know, I know," he replied.

Gilles took his daughter's hand and led her to the back door which opened to the barnyard. He paused a moment, then Murielle joined him at his side. She shifted nervously from one foot to another. She was not as anxious now to have Emmeline rush off.

Gilles took his daughter's face in his hands again. "I am sorry you must make this journey alone. You will be safe. Believe that." He paused a moment closing his eyes, trying to collect his thoughts. "Lord Aufeese has promised me. You will be safe; he will protect you."

Murielle looked away at that. Emmeline looked doubtfully at her father.

He opened his eyes again and looked down at his daughter. "You must believe that if you believe anything."

Emmeline caught her father's hands in her own. "Yes," she replied into his eyes. If he believed it, then she would try very hard to believe it herself.

At this, Murielle stepped in. "Gilles, if she must go, she really must go now. The day passes quickly."

"*Oui*...yes, it does," he started as if awakening from a trance. He took Emmeline's hand again and led her into the barnyard. "You must hurry now. Do as I have told you. Travel due East, avoid the main road, and keep out of sight."

Gilles looked up toward the sun rapidly rising higher in the sky. He motioned to Murielle to take his other hand. He bowed his head and offered up a prayer.

"O great Lord Aufeese, O great Golden Child of Mava, hear my prayer. I beg you to come in your magnificence to protect my daughter." Then turning his face to the burning sun, he said, "Oh, Great One, true owner of the sun, hear your humble servant's plea; may we be chosen among the worthy who receive your beneficence."

Gilles gathered his daughter into his arms one final time, then reluctantly let her go. Emmeline turned to her mother and embraced her. Murielle whispered into her ear then tearfully chided her to hurry on her way. Emmeline waved a last farewell, promised to see them soon, then she dashed around the corner of the barn and disappeared from their sight.

As she came around the side of the barn, a loud noise made her stop. It was Jacques, their mule, braying at her from the stable door. She went over to him and scratched his ears. "Oh Jacques, you know I am leaving and thought I would not say goodbye!"

Emmeline set down her paquet and went through a side door. She reemerged a moment later, and offered a handful of oats to the mule, which he devoured greedily. She wiped her hands on her breeches and returned to scratching his ears. Stroking his nose gently, she looked into his eyes and spoke to him in a calm voice.

"Jacques, there are very grievous things coming to pass today," she said seriously. "None of your stubbornness today! I am placing you in charge of the barnyard; ensure that everyone behaves well."

The mule returned Emmeline's serious look, nodding his head in agreement to these terms, and he returned to the cool shade of the stable. Emmeline glanced around the barnyard. All the animals had retreated into shaded areas to find relief from the already growing heat of the morning. All but one. A bright red rooster arrogantly strutted around the dusty barnyard.

"Cocque," Emmeline cried, "you are too full of yourself! No one cares about you in this heat!"

The rooster clucked and strutted about the dusty barnyard stopping occasionally to preen his glossy feathers. But not even the fine-looking Cocque could tempt the hens out of their cool retreat in the barn. And so, he strutted, unaffected by their indifference to him.

"Cocque, I think you strut about so because you do not know how to do anything else!"

Emmeline watched the handsome bird make another circuit of the yard, then dropped her paquet and gave chase. The rooster clucked frantically as it dashed about, just out of her reach. Emmeline stopped in the drifting dust stirred up from the chase, hands on her knees, panting. She mopped the slick sweat from her brow with the back of her hand and looked at Cocque. A little duller from the dust they had stirred up, he strutted about panting. His red tongue bobbed back and forth from his open beak. Soon he stopped and preened the feathers which had been so unjustly ruffed by the unwarranted pursuit.

"You," Emmeline panted, "are such... a vain... bird!"

Cocque clucked in agreement.

Emmeline caught her breath. The dust had settled down in the barnyard again. She looked up at the ascending sun, remembering her important journey, and realized that she was wasting precious time. She looked about, panicked, suddenly afraid that her mother and father had seen her chasing the rooster instead of proceeding on her journey.

"I have been foolish," she said, shaking her head.

Cocque clucked in agreement.

"I do not need your help, you silly rooster!"

Emmeline walked over and picked up the paquet where she had dropped it in the dust. Brushing it off with quick strokes, she looked again at the sun.

"I must take this journey seriously," she mused aloud. "It is very important that I follow my father's plan."

Setting her resolve, she threw the paquet over her shoulder and strolled over to the edge of the corn field.

"If it is East I must go, then to the East I will go."

There was no wind, which had allowed the dust to completely settle in the barnyard, serene and empty save for Cocque who had resumed his strutting, still vainly hoping to draw out the hens. The ground on the far end of the yard shimmered in the already oppressive heat. Emmeline took one last look at the barnyard, turned, and disappeared into the corn.

———

When Murielle moved toward the back door to begin the next phase of the plan, Gilles grabbed her by the arm, a bewildered look upon his face.

"Where do you go, Murielle?"

Murielle looked at her husband narrowly. "To the barn. To saddle the horse, so I may ride to Darloque and save our daughter."

Gilles heaved a deep sigh. "The vision was very specific," he muttered.

Murielle heaved her own sigh. "We agreed. I should go to Darloque because a woman's tears will move the Old King more than a man's pleas."

"The vision was very specific," he said again. "I am to ride to Darloque."

"But I can do it better, Gilles." Murielle turned to go, and Gilles grabbed her arm again.

"The vision was very specific," he said once again and began to walk toward the door. He was almost to the door when Murielle seized him by the arm.

"Why must you be so stubborn," she said, the impatience apparent in her voice.

"Woman..." he began, then fell off. She knew he was beginning to get angry now as he refused to call her by name. He drew a long breath and began again.

"Lord Aufeese has given me a vision in which I journey to the Old King and am able to convince him to stop his son's lecherous intent with our daughter." He held his hand up to stop her protest on the viability of the Golden Child. After years of Murielle's acidic criticism of his god and his faith, this was an automatic gesture. He was no more aware of it than of his own heartbeat. "Although you mock the god of the harvest and his vision, it is unquestionable and unalterable. I am to do this part myself. Lord Aufeese will make the way for me, he always has."

Murielle fumed. "You stupid, stupid man! If you would only see reason, you would realize that I am the more logical choice to see the Old King."

"That is exactly the idea," he retorted, the fury rising in his voice, "I do not see logic! I do not see reason! I live by my faith in my god, and he guides my every decision!"

Murielle balled her fists tightly in anger. "Your god fails you!" she screamed through clenched teeth, "Over and over and over again, your god fails you! All the gods fail you!" Spittle flew from her lips in her sudden, ravenous fury. "When will you see that your god does nothing to help you; none of the gods do! There is absolutely no one to help you!" She threw her head back, screaming in fury, "We are utterly alone in this world and no one will save us ever!"

She brought her fists up to her chest and let out a violent, guttural scream to the rafters, driving the doves into a frenzy. Gilles drew back wide-eyed, shuddering at this unprecedented tirade from his normally peaceful, though willful, wife. His own rage was gone, stifled by the madness raging before him. She dropped her head and broke into choking sobs. He stood helpless a moment, then he took her into his arms. She trembled violently, her fists still held in front of her. Gilles said nothing for he could think of nothing to say. He simply held her and stroked her long hair as she choked out loud sobs. *Murielle's and Emmeline's hair are so much alike*, he thought idly. Gradually, Murielle let herself be held. She dropped her hands to her sides and slowly unclenched her fists. As her weeping slowed, she wrapped her arms around her husband. Gilles continued to hold her, still unsure of what else he should do.

"*Sois calme*," he whispered, more to himself than to her.

Murielle pulled back a little from Gilles, her arms still around him. She looked into his eyes. Hers were wet, red, and sorrowful. He looked down and saw that the front of his tunic was soaked with her tears.

"*Je suis désolé*," she whispered, dabbing at the wet part with the tips of her fingers. She continued to brush at his tunic with her hand as if that would dry it, although it had little effect.

Gilles did not know what to say. He could only stand there by the door and gently stroke her hair as she lay her head back down on his chest. Soon Gilles relaxed a little. He could feel Murielle's heartbeat soft in her chest and could hear her breathing broken only by an occasional sniffle. Before he realized it, he was gently rocking her back and forth in his arms. At that moment he thought he could feel her soul touching his.

"*Je suis désolé*," she whispered again. "I *am* sorry. I do not know..." She trailed off.

Gilles knew what he should do, although it went against everything he believed was right. Lord Aufeese had given him a vision of how to save their daughter. He was sure that a vision from a god must be followed implicitly. But here was his wife, completely distraught over the entire matter with their daughter. Certainly, this was difficult on her. It was difficult enough for him. He had prayed every day since he had first noticed Emmeline's first steps into womanhood that she would be spared this indignity. As time passed and the stories grew more disturbing, he prayed ever more urgently. He had heard stories in Darloque at the Market, stories beyond merely disturbing, stories which reeked of sickness, horror, and madness. Every day the terror grew inside him, and still he prayed. He prayed to Lord Aufeese to deliver his daughter past this dangerous age and safely into her maturity where the Prince would no longer be a threat to her.

Gilles was certain of one thing. He was as sure of this as he was sure that the sun would rise in the East. This was the bargain. Although Lord Aufeese had never spoken to him about the matter either face to face or in a vision, he knew that the drought had come in exchange for his daughter's safety. Every day his daughter avoided the eye of Prince Henri was another day without rain. Another day of peace was another day of struggle on the farm. He had wondered why the Golden Child was making him choose. Either way was death. He could not imagine the humiliations the Prince might bring upon his daughter, instead preferring to think of that path simply as death. She might avoid the dishonorable advances of the Prince, but she would starve to death in the process.

And he would die either way as well. No matter how his daughter died, Gilles would die of grief. When the midwife showed Emmeline to him for the first time, Murielle seemed somewhat ashamed that she had not produced for him a male heir. When he saw the pink wrinkled skin of his daughter, her tiny fists balled up against her little head, he forgot all about the legacy of a male heir. Then she opened her eyes, those bright brown eyes, the same eyes as her mother, and he fell in love. That was his little girl there in the midwife's arms. This one would be his favorite no matter what other children came along after this, male or female. Emmeline did not cry, she just looked around with those brown eyes, seeming to take in the great world she had just entered.

"Would you like to hold her, *Monsieur?*"

Gilles was only barely aware that the midwife had spoken. "*Certainment*," he replied absently, still locked on those tiny brown eyes. He reached for his newly born daughter, completely unaware of anything else in the room.

Emmeline was wrapped in an old fraying mantle. Gilles took her gently into his arms, careful to support her head–he was a new father but not totally ignorant of babies–as those brown eyes sought out his. Still, she did not cry, but only made the softest of cooing sounds. He held her silently.

"You are not displeased?" Murielle asked weakly from the pallet.

Gilles remained silent for a long time. He stroked the girl's head, played with her fingers and toes. He chuckled softly when she caught one of his fingers in a tiny fist.

"I would have no other," he replied after a time.

If that was the bargain Lord Aufeese had given them, then so be it. The gods worked in ways which were beyond the understanding of men. What made this all bearable for Gilles was his deep and consummate faith in his god. Even though he could not now under-stand, or ever hope to understand his divine motives in the slightest way, Gilles believed at the very core of his being that Lord Aufeese had nothing but the best intentions for him and his family. In the end, he knew in the very fiber of his being that only good could come from all this suffering.

Gilles hooked his finger under his wife's chin and raised her eyes to his. "No, dearest," he began," it is I who am sorry. I should have listened to you in the first place." He sighed and continued on, desperately hoping he was making the right decision. "You are correct, and I know it. The Old King–may he live long–will listen more to the pleas of a mother than another man. The gods have given women that gift to move men's hearts with tears when no other thing may move them. You will move him to action where I cannot."

Murielle's wet face beamed at him.

Gilles heaved a nervous sigh. He offered up a silent prayer that the Lord Aufeese was not specific on who should ride to Darloque. *Perhaps,* he thought with a wistful hope, *he was only making a suggestion.*

He gathered his wife in his strong arms and hugged her. Murielle let out a grunt at his strong embrace.

"Go. Go now, before I reconsider," he said. "I will pray that this is the correct path."

Murielle pulled away from her husband to draw water from the barrel then quickly made her way through the back door and into the dusty barnyard. Gilles followed and squinted in the bright light. Shadows were rapidly disappearing in the barren yard, shrinking it seemed, in the very heat of the growing day. The day was passing quickly.

Gilles followed his wife across the barnyard, watching her feet stir up eddies of dust which drifted slowly in the still air, then casually settled into the ground, as she moved toward the barn. Murielle walked swiftly and with purpose.

Gilles slipped behind his wife's quick pace a little, as she opened the barn door and entered the darkness inside. Once inside the barn, it seemed to take an eternity for his eyes to adjust to the gloom. It was still cool in here. He shivered slightly as he waited for his eyes to recover from the brief, but intense, beating the sun had given them. Gradually he could make out Murielle's shape working diligently to ready the horse. She had not wasted any time, apparently, for the bridle was already on, and she was moving with the saddle. Gilles walked over to Murielle and cinched the saddle tight after she had placed it on the horse's back. He tried to take her hand, but she shook it off and moved away from him, checking the fit of saddle and bridle. He offered her the flask of water. She took it mechanically, pausing a moment as their eyes met, and hung it upon the saddle.

Gilles tried to speak but could not. The reality of the situation weighed down hard upon him now. Everything that had transpired this morning came crashing down with brutal force. More so than with his daughter's departure, the imminent departure of his wife made it all the more real to him. Gilles looked at the saddle mounted upon the horse's back. He had always been impressed with Murielle's strength. And, while most women were content to let a man saddle the horse and then help them up to ride, Murielle preferred to do that herself.

Gilles had discovered this when they went riding one day shortly after they met. He moved to saddle the horse for her, as he had done for ladies countless times. Murielle politely brushed him off and proceeded to saddle the horse herself. Gilles was still trying to recover from this departure from womanly privilege as they rode across the meadow when she suddenly winked at him and kicked her horse into a gallop. She raced across the meadow, displaying keen horsemanship as she reined her mount through tight formations. Murielle then aimed for a small copse of trees, weaving through them at a speed that a younger more reckless Gilles would never have attempted. When she returned, both she and horse were winded. Gilles knew that this flamboyant little demonstration was clearly meant to impress. *Now*, he thought, *if she can cook as well as she can ride then I will have to marry her.*

Gilles took Murielle's hand and looked lovingly into her eyes. He could just see her eyes in the gloom, they blazed with intensity but behind that intensity he could see that they were weary and care-worn. Over the years he had learned to read her emotions well. Try as she might, there was nothing Murielle could hide from him. Gilles suddenly became aware of the sounds of the barn–the clucking of chickens, the lowing of their milch cow, the breathing and impatient shifting of the horse. He was aware of Murielle's breathing and the sound of her feet shifting restlessly in the straw. Without another word he helped her check the cinch strap again, then led the horse into the barnyard.

They both squinted and tried to shield their eyes from the glare and gasped at the return to the oppressive heat. Gilles led the horse to the center of the yard and halted. Murielle stepped into the stirrup and pulled herself easily into the saddle. Gilles looked up to her, unsure what to say next, well aware that time was quickly passing. Instead, he addressed the horse.

"Cheval, carry my wife well to Darloque. She has important business there to save our daughter."

Murielle smiled sadly down at Gilles.

"Go now Cheval. Travel with the blessings of the gods."

Murielle leaned down and kissed Gilles. "*Je t'aime*," she said quietly. "I love you, too," he returned.

Without another word, Murielle kicked the horse into a gallop, reining him toward the main road. Gilles remained there in the barnyard until the hoofbeats faded in the distance. He stood watching the dust slowly settle back to the ground. In the fields around the barnyard, dry corn stalks stood mutely in the dead air that was heating rapidly as the chariot of the sun rose ever higher in the sky. Gilles thought for a moment that the Wild Hares had brought the sun closer to the ground than they had ever brought it in his life. Certainly, this summer was the hottest and driest he could remember. *Ah*, the thought to himself, *to have lived in the time when Aufeese drove the chariot straight and true.* But that was not his time and it did little good to wish for something that could never be. Each man must handle the Fate he is dealt and handle it as well as he can. His rumination in the dead silence broke as the clucking of Cocque floated across the barnyard. No doubt the rooster was trying to coax the hens out from the cool shaded areas. Shaking his head in amusement, Gilles walked back into the house.

Now Gilles would have to wait for the inevitable return of the Prince. This was the hardest of all the tasks in his plan. Waiting would give him plenty of time to think. Too much time, perhaps. He had no idea what he should tell the Prince upon his return, but he had time to prepare. He paced anxiously around the large room of the house. Time passed slowly, and the chariot of the sun rose ever higher in the sky.

CHAPTER FOUR

MURIELLE TURNED onto the main road to Darloque and kicked Cheval into a hard gallop. Cornstalks rose above her on either side of the road, obscuring her view of the surrounding landscape. The road rose on a gradual incline bringing her above the crops to a small promontory. She dared not pause for even a second to take in the countryside spread out around her, and she continued hard down the soft slope back beneath the crop line. Although she did not pause, a slight glance to the left and then to the right revealed the green landscape around her. This was not the lush, fresh, green of spring, nor was it the patchy brown she expected to see in this brazen summer. Instead, the hard green of summer farmland returned her glances. Brown sprinkled the scene, but the swarthy green valiantly fought on, revealing an obstinance that only comes from plants driven to not only thrive, but determined to beat back the tyrannical sun.

Murielle continued down the main road at a hard gallop. The road was empty, and all was silent save for the drumming of her horse's hooves upon the hard-packed dirt. Cheval was in his element, and after a long spring as a plow horse, draught horse, and general work horse, he was quite happy to run. After a short struggle with stiff muscles, he had regained his ability and now galloped on with hardly a heavy breath at all. Murielle was in her element as well. She loosened her hold on the reins and let the horse open up his gait. As they raced on, the dry, stale wind blew back her hair and fluttered her skirts behind her. Back on the farm the dusty air was oppressive. Here the same stale air in the same summer heat was refreshing. She inhaled and thought it was the best thing she had ever breathed. Yes, it had been far too long since she had ridden like this. For a few moments she let go of the dire circumstances that had forced her on this ride and relished the ride itself. Murielle filled herself with the pure symbiotic relationship between man, beast, and nature.

Lost in her thoughts, she came quickly upon a fork in the road at the top of a small incline. She reined Cheval hard to the left onto a narrow path just wide enough for the horse. She pulled back on the reins slightly to slow down the animal, but still maintained a good gallop. This was the Straight Road to Darloque. The road she had been on was a wide cartage road that wound around the increasingly steep foothills to give large wagons with heavy loads an easier way into the city. It was a longer way but easier on heavy wagons larger caravans. The road she was on now was the Straight Road, but it was built upon steep slopes and sometimes mountainous climbs. Besides being steep and dangerous for heavy wagons, it was far too narrow for anything but the smallest cart to travel. However, a single horse or pedestrian could make the trip to the city much more quickly than by the cartage road–provided the horse or walking man were energetic enough to climb the steep hills. *The one who travels speedily by the Straight Road,* she recalled the old saying, *easily passes the one who avoids it.* Murielle plunged down this road at a high rate of speed, well aware that if she came over a hill or around a curve upon another traveler she would have nowhere to go. That was a risk she had to take for she was certain that a party as large as the Prince's would not have taken this road, but stayed on the main cartage road, and she could speed down this road and make it to Darloque well before them despite her late start.

Murielle patted the horse on the neck. "Cheval be my eyes for me and–" She looked up just in time to see the low hanging branch and was able to narrowly avoid being knocked from the horse. Nevertheless, it did snatch a few strands of hair from her head. Rubbing the spot on her scalp she said, "Very well. You shall watch the road and I shall watch all that is above it."She hurtled down the Straight Road into increasingly denser forest. Branches whipped at her as she flew down sweeping slopes and charged up steep hills. Aside from lightly bruising her shoulders, they did little damage. She would be sore later, but that was a small price to pay for the sake of her daughter. Gradually, as she and Cheval grew more accustomed to the road's uncertainties, she let him have more rein, and he increased his pace. The hot sun disappeared from view as the forest canopy grew denser, and a chill passed though Murielle. She shivered just as a thin branch of a willow slapped across her right shoulder with a sharp sting. She touched the spot with her other hand and immediately felt the welt rising beneath her blouse. Cheval, his energy stoked by the cool shade, charged down a steep bank unaware of her pain.

Despite the pain in her shoulder, her nervousness about what might lay unseen over the next rise, and the sense of urgency to get to Darloque quickly, Murielle felt an exhilaration flooding over her. She had not ridden like this in many years. *Too many years*, she thought to herself. Not since her father had been alive had she ridden like this. Although Gilles had been quite impressed with her horsemanship when they were courting, he was clearly not as adept on horseback as she. He was competent rider and could handle a horse well enough, but he seemed to take riding as a means of getting from one place to another. A horse was a tool, and riding a horse brought him no more joy than walking or riding in a cart. But for Murielle, there was a great thrill in the riding itself. It was the wordless communication between rider and horse; a slight movement of the rider told the horse more than two humans could tell each other in a thousand words. The horse spoke back as well with a subtle language of its own that only the experienced rider could understand. It was this communication she lived for. It was this communication between man and beast that she had missed for so long. And the fast pace felt good as well.

If she had lived, Murielle's mother would have wanted to shape her daughter into a young lady of the court. Unencumbered by such restrictions, Richard de Conquil had put his daughter in the saddle before she could even walk. Some said that it was his firm desire to have a son, and his insistence upon making Murielle into that son that drove his aspirations for his only child. Richard denied these allegations vehemently. "I will not," he said simply and evenly when confronted, "have a daughter who is dependent upon a man or a temple for survival." For he believed that a woman's choice of marriage or a nunnery–the only two valid choices for a woman in the present society–was the choice of one kind of slavery over another.

Richard de Conquil had driven his daughter from an early age to be self-sufficient. Horsemanship was the first lesson in her education. "If you can learn to handle a horse," he said looking deep into her young, dark eyes, "you can learn to handle anything that comes at you in life." He insisted that she learn to guide the horse without using the reins. "*Porquoi*, Papa," she asked, "is that not what the reins are for?"

"There are reasons for everything," he said with a somber look in his eye, "but we cannot always see them."

Murielle looked at him quizzically.

"Trust me when I say that you will need to know this later."

"*Oui*, Papa."

Richard put her up on the saddle, then climbed on behind her. Reaching around her, he took the reins and nudged the horse into an easy walk. As they rode out across the pasture Murielle thought more and more about how silly this idea of her father's was.

"Now," he said laying the reins on the pommel, "watch my left leg." She looked down and watched as he pressed his left thigh into the side of the horse. Slowly the horse began to turn to the left. Richard released his leg and the horse straightened out. Murielle gasped in amazement and turned to look at her father who smiled back with a boyish grin.

"Do it again!" she cried.

This time Richard pressed his right thigh into the animal, and it turned to the right. He kept the pressure on until they had turned around and were going back the way they had come.

"Now," he said with the same boyish grin," would you care to do it at speed?"

Murielle turned back at her father and grinned. Richard took up the reins. With a shout he kicked the horse into a gallop. The horse raced across the open pasture, hooves drumming the soft turf. Richard laid the reins down upon the pommel again then pressed his leg into the horse's side, and he banked slowly to the right. He pressed his other leg and the horse banked to the left. He alternated this several times making the horse weave and loop around the pasture. "Now, watch this," he whispered in her ear as he steered the horse toward a copse of trees. The horse bore straight down upon a large oak at a fast gallop. Murielle gasped, then instinctively covered her eyes when it seemed certain that they were headed for a terrible collision. Then she felt her father's leg push hard into the animal's side and she felt them bank sharply to the right. She felt him press hard into the horse's other side and they steered left. Murielle put her hands down and opened her eyes to see them threading through the trees as her father steered with just alternating pressure from his legs. Murielle squealed with delight. It was the most exhilarating feeling she had ever had in her life. They burst through some light brush into another open pasture. Richard kicked the horse into a hard gallop. Murielle watched as grass and little field flowers flew by, and the copse fell far behind. She closed her eyes and took in the rushing air. She felt so free now. She spread her arms wide. She was flying. Behind her, Richard spread his arms and flew along with her.

Murielle was only minutely aware that Cheval had lowered his head. She came out of her reverie in time to see the large fallen limb hanging over the Straight Road suspended by the net of tree boughs on either side of the trail. The broad limb hung about chest level and was thick enough to knock her from the horse and inflict serious damage. She barely had time to register the danger, but in an instant, she threw herself over the horse's side, holding tightly to its neck as they passed narrowly under the limb. Murielle quickly righted herself, panting nervously as she did. This close brush with danger had immediate effect–her adrenaline rush abated, and nervous fear grew more present. *What in Mava's name am I doing?* she asked herself. Gradually she slowed the horse from its precipitous gallop until Cheval ran slightly faster than a canter. Her mind began to race as the horse began to slow. Doubts and uncertainty tore at her. *One slip,* she thought, *one wrong move, and all is lost.* She grimaced at the thought. *Emmeline is lost.*

The trees opened up on the left to reveal a large shimmering lake caught between two rows of mountainous ridges devouring the southern horizon. Cheval, now barely at trot, began to steer toward the blue water.

"So Cheval, that is what you want, now is it?" she asked with a trembling voice. "I agree. I need some water too and perhaps a moment to calm my swift heart." The horse slowed to a walk, leaving the cool shade of the road, and entering the hot glare at the lakeside. The heat took Murielle's breath away at once. She could feel Cheval take a sudden sharp breath as they came into the sun. The shade of the road had wiped her mind clean of the summertime heat and now it hit her like an old forgotten enemy, waiting for the appropriate time to strike.

"But only a little time," she scolded him as she gracefully dismounted and led the horse to the water's edge. The lake met the sandy shore with barely a ripple. She loosened the bridle and allowed Cheval to take a drink. He began taking in water in great noisy gulps. "*Non!*" she said sternly, stroking his neck, "Not so fast or you will make yourself ill!" He immediately slowed his rapid gulping. Murielle reached into her pack tied to the saddle and pulled out a corn cake. She turned back toward the lake and looked out across its expansive surface, admiring the view. The flat water made a perfect reflection of the two mountain peaks situated at its distant, opposite shore. Deep rich green climbed into gray craggy rocks which in turn climbed steeply into brilliant white snow caps. She chewed thoughtfully as she admired the pristine peaks. The chariot of the sun hung over them with blazing fury but seemed to have no effect on the delicate snowy tops.

Snow. It was hard to imagine anywhere that snow could exist under that blazing sun. A bead of sweat rolled past her temple and down her cheek as a reminder of the heat. If only she had some snow now to get some relief from this heat. Murielle had to laugh at herself. How many times had she wished for summer's heat in the midst of a frigid winter? A memory bloomed in her head, taking her back to one particularly cold winter long ago.

———

The air had been still as evening came on. It was cold, more so than any other winter's night, and the air felt thick and moist. Dense, dark clouds had moved in before dark, obscuring the sun on its downward slope into the West. She and the house servants slept in a ragged circle around the fire in the center hall since it had become far too cold for the braziers to keep the bed chambers warm. Murielle remembered lying on her back on the overstuffed pallet, her nurse Angélique's arm wrapped protectively around her, both of them covered in a thick fur mantle. She watched the smoke drift up in slow circles through the hole in the high ceiling wondering if she would ever fall asleep. She closed her eyes but for a moment and opened them again to find only a wispy gray stream rising lazily upward toward the high ceiling. Murielle turned her head to find the dying embers barely smoldering in the gloom. She back to the black hole in the stone ceiling. A few stars shone brightly through, twinkling in the clear, early morning air.

It was still dark inside the manor house. She could hear the servants breathing quietly nearby. Somewhere in the room slept her father. She guessed it was some time before sunrise and the commencement of the day's labor. Murielle carefully slipped out of Angélique's arms and the fur garment. The nurse stirred slightly, drawing her empty arms close to her, and gave a small shiver but did not awaken. Murielle shivered in reply and adjusted the mantle over her nurse. It was cold, bitingly cold, and the warmth Angélique had provided her was quickly evaporating. Murielle's breath puffed out in great white clouds, swirling and drifting upward. She watched it for a few moments, the vapor drifting upward slowly and dissipating in the early morning gloom. She grasped the nearby iron and stirred the embers back to life. A small fire erupted in the pit over which she held her hands over to warm them from the stinging cold of the frozen iron. A sound like dried corn husks resounded lightly through the hall as she rubbed her dry, chapped hands together.

She looked about the room; small shadows danced on the walls from the tiny reddish flames. Wood lay in neat stacks against the near wall which Étienne had spent the better part of the week splitting. The stack against the wall was but a mere fraction of the wood Étienne had split, the rest being in the shed out by the kitchen. Étienne was burly man of seemingly boundless energy who set upon a task joyfully and did not cease until had done twice what was required of him. As a result, they now had enough wood to last through this winter and perhaps well into the next.

Murielle crept silently over to the stack, selected a few reasonably sized pieces, and carried them back to the fire which was rapidly losing its strength. One by one she placed the pieces of wood on the fire, arranging them as Étienne had taught her, while casting nervous glances over her shoulder for any sign that Angélique had awakened. She had not. Murielle sat down and watched the flames slowly consume the wood, growing in intensity, and casting yet stronger light about the room. As she rubbed her frigid hands in front of the growing fire, a violent shudder swept through her as she slowly warmed from the cold. She prodded the burning wood with the iron

46

once more then looked around the room. The fire was now large enough to cast orange light throughout the hall, illuminating everything. Angélique had pushed the fur mantle down a little in response to the renewed fire. Étienne snorted in his sleep and rolled over away from the fire, while tugging at his own cape. The light danced on the high ceiling and she regarded with interest the dark ring around the hole made from years of fires in this hall. Smoke rose in dark clouds to the black hole, obscuring the few stars which she had previously seen there. She could see no other light in the hole, so she reasoned that dawn must still be some time away.

I am fully awake now, Murielle thought at once, *so what shall I do?* A younger Murielle would have pestered her nurse until she awoke and either sang her to sleep or carried her away from the others and entertained her. But she was no longer that Murielle, the babe Murielle who needed to be cajoled into sleep or given treats to behave. She was older now and able to entertain herself if necessary– much of the time, anyway. But far more importantly, she was embracing the responsibilities placed upon her by her father.

There were chores to do, and if she was awake then she might as well get right to work. Murielle found a candle, fit it into a sconce, and lit it. Then gathering her cloak around her with her free hand, Murielle walked toward the door, her feet shuffling through the rushes scattered on the floor as her candle's flame lead the way. She gathered her cloak more tightly about her shoulders as she left the fire's warmth and approached the door.

Her first steps into the courtyard were normal. Her boots scraped along the cobblestones as they always had. She even felt the raised stone that Étienne was always too busy to repair. It wobbled slightly as she put her weight on it. She paused to rock it a little and passed on. A few steps later however, she felt a crunching under her feet as the cobblestones gave way to a something entirely different. Startled, Murielle jumped back and felt a cold spattering of light powder on her legs. She lowered the candle, curiosity flaming in her mind. The light fell upon her footprints in a deep white powder on the ground.

She gasped, and with her free hand she tentatively scooped up some of the powder, gazing intently as it sifted between her fingers. Murielle held the candle aloft and beheld the covering of white on the ground over the entire courtyard. She ran to the gate, scattering the stuff as she went. She was able to undo the latch with her free hand and pull open the heavy gate. She rushed outside and scuffed into the snow.

Innumerable stars lit the countryside with their clear, gentle brilliance. The gray-tinged eastern horizon was not yet bright enough to diffuse their light. All around, as far as Murielle could see, the country was covered in a deep white blanket. The road leading to the gate was covered so completely she could not discern it from the surrounding landscape. She could follow the slope of the hill downward, however, to where the road emerged from the woods below. In the pre-dawn darkness, the trees were lost and only the white stuff piled on their limbs stood out against the black sky.

It was calm and peaceful here. No wind blew, and the candle's flame flickered not a bit. All was silent except for her occasional breath which steamed from her mouth and dissipated lazily in the chill air. Murielle looked up again at the stars, their brilliant gleam in the black sky dwarfing the light of the candle she held in her hand. She knew some of the constellations. Immediately she spotted Lord Aufeese at the harvest, riding low in the sky, for his season was over. Over there were the Sisters. After a bit of searching, she found the Three Heroes. She searched for others but only found two more that she knew.

Murielle looked back at the footprints she had left in the snow. Back at the gate they began as neat little impressions in the powder but became more ragged as she had progressed into deeper snow. She glanced around and found a line of tracks leading south across where she thought the road should be and angling down toward the woods. They were not human. She shivered slightly, but not from the cold. After a few moments she was then aware of a new sound. She looked around and at once realized that it was the chattering of her own teeth that she was hearing.

"I must get back inside," she told herself aloud as she watched the candle quiver in her grip. Nevertheless, she remained, staring at the strange footprints in the white powder. "The gods are afoot on this clear night," Étienne would have said. Her eyes closed; she imagined his voice so clearly in her mind that she jumped thinking she had actually heard it. She switched the candle to her other hand, gathered her cloak more tightly around her and trudged back toward the gate. Once back inside the courtyard, she pulled the gate and latched it solidly. A couple of good shoves to ensure it was fast, and she headed toward the barn. The snow was thinner in the courtyard and walking on the hard cobblestones made her realize how cold her feet were from standing in the deep snow. Her boots were warm enough, but they were simply no match for the snow.

Murielle pulled open the barn door and immediately a cow began to low. Another followed, and then another, until there was a small low chorus resounding inside the barn. It was warmer in here; the warmth of huddled bodies made it almost comfortable. If not for the smell, she would be happy to bed down in here every winter's night. She pulled the door to and loosened her cloak a bit. As she entered the barn the candlelight reflected the dozens of expectant eyes in the dark. Cattle, sheep, chickens, and others in the menagerie watched her, waiting for what she should do next, for it was earlier than they were accustomed to seeing anyone. The lowing stopped after a time, and all eyes turned to her curious, and waiting. Murielle walked silently past the stalls, straw sticking to her wet feet as she went. She stopped at one cow and gave it a pat on the neck with her free hand. The warmth of its body felt good on her frozen skin. The cow craned its neck to get its nose under her hand and she gave the muzzle a good hard rub.

"I know it is early," she explained," but I am certain you will give milk just as well now as you would give it at the normal time."

She passed by each cow, petting it in turn. She did not forget the sheep and received a bleat of contentment from each that she patted as she passed. Nor did she neglect the goats. The hens sat on their nests protectively guarding their eggs only giving Murielle the most casual of glances now that they were certain she held no feed. The roosters, ever more hopeful, eyed her eagerly from their roosts as she passed them one by one. One last pat for each of the two donkeys and Murielle arrived at her destination in the barn.

She stood before another door, the entrance into what Étienne called his "court." Murielle unfastened the door and entered, holding the candle before her. The warmth of the animals's bodies ended here, so she pulled her cloak tighter against the cold. Étienne's "court" was actually a storeroom in the back of the barn. Across one wall hung a long row of tools he used in the day-to-day operation of the farm. Shovels, picks, hammers and the like hung in neat rows on wooden pegs. A long scythe hung menacingly on the wall beside these. A table stood further down with a thick coil of rope on it and propped beside it was a broken wheel from the mule cart which Étienne was in the process of repairing. Neat stacks of grain sacks lay on the floor here. At the far end of the storeroom Murielle found what she sought. Several wooden buckets stood stacked atop one another. She took the topmost one, inverted it, and peered inside tilting the candle so she could see better.

"This one bucket shall be good enough for milking this morning," she said to herself.

She turned to leave when the candlelight fell upon the place where Étienne held "court." A pallet lay in the opposite corner next to a simple wooden chair. There was a table here with several sprigs of holly and small branches of evergreen. This was where Étienne normally slept, but in recent years father had given him leave to sleep in the manor house when it was too cold. There was no hearth here, nor was there a brazier. Father would not allow it. He said that he had seen too many barns go up in flames because fools put fire where it had fodder aplenty.

As Murielle turned with her candle, the light fell upon the altar.

Murielle could never recall having seen this particular altar before, so it must have been a fairly recent addition to the "court." She brought the candle closer and gasped when she beheld the delicate details carved into the wood. The main section of the altar was a sculpture of the wood god holding his quarterstaff while standing with one foot propped upon a log. Murielle had seen Étienne pose in this stance many times, and she thought of it as a typical woodsman's pose. The god stood before a relief sculpture of a woodland scene. Holding the candle closer, she examined the detail of the sculpture. Étienne had carved nearly a dozen different trees, each in great detail right down to the texture of the bark and the individual leaves. She thought it was incredible woodwork. She could think of no better disciple of the wood god than Étienne.

She turned her attention back to the carving of the god itself. It was very realistic–the sculpture looked ready to jump out at her. She brought the candle as close as she dared to the altar. She did not want to drip wax or commit the terrible sin of burning it. Never mind Étienne's anger, the god himself should be angrier that such a great likeness should be deformed or destroyed.

The look upon the god's face was puzzling. Murielle pored over it again and again, mindful of the candle, but still, the god's expression confused her. The wood god was known as a jolly fellow with a boisterous personality. In the tales, he delivered serious moral messages with a hearty laugh and never had a condemnation for anyone, even his worst enemies. But the look Étienne had carved upon the face here was serious, if not grim. She did not understand it. She had seen other sculptures of the god in Darloque. His visage there was as jolly as he appeared in the tales. Surely Étienne could not have forgotten.

At the base of the altar was the shallow trough in which to place the offering and on either side of that were candles. She took a length of straw from the floor and lit it with her own candle and proceeded to light to two on the altar. Father saw little harm in candles in the barn though he did not trust them entirely. He admitted that people could not go around in the dark, but he did warn his family and servants constantly—to much rolling of eyes—on the perils of fire in a barn. The candles flared to life, illuminating the altar, and revealing even more of the beauty of the sculpture. The face of the wood god appeared even more grim than it had before. Murielle pinched out the flame on the straw and placed it on the table where it could do no harm. She set her own candle there too and gazed at the altar again. Étienne had placed a sack of grain beneath the altar for use as a kneeler. She knelt on it now, and bowing her head, she touched the tips of her fingers of her right hand to her forehead. Having paid her proper respects, she gazed at the sculpture again. Étienne was taller than she, so she had to look up at it. *Pourquoi*, she thought, *why do you look so grim?*

She jumped as the door flew open with a loud crash, revealing a large and dark figure framed in the doorway, the pre-dawn light straining into the barn from behind him.

A loud splash broke Murielle out of her reverie. Ripples cut across the water from a center point only a short distance from the shore. She peered closely at the water, and she thought she could discern a shape slinking beneath the surface; something moving just out of sight. Suddenly, it all felt wrong. This entire endeavor was simply wrong. She should not be out here making her way to see the Old King. She should be back at her farmhouse. For one moment it felt like sheer, stubborn vanity to be out on this trail and it was exceedingly important that she should be home protecting it, protecting her family. *Je suis mal faire*, she thought. This was all wrong.

Cheval nudged her arm. Rested and refreshed he was ready to continue the journey. Murielle shook her head. She looked at the horse as if she had never seen him before. Just as suddenly as the feeling of wrongness came upon her, it was gone.

"You are correct, my fine horse," she said, ruffling his mane. His ears perked as he realized she was ready to ride again. *"Non, non,*

non, I am on the right path; I am on the only path that can save my daughter from evil. The best path." Cheval looked at her quizzically. He nudged her again, this time harder, eager to ride again.

She cinched the bridle and mounted the horse. Reining him back toward the trail she leaned down and spoke into his ear. "Ride true now, and no stopping until we reach the city."

With that she kicked the horse into a gallop and disappeared down the trail, leaving only a cloud of dust slowly dissipating in the hot, dry air.

CHAPTER FIVE

EMMELINE MADE her way through the field, following the rows of corn eastward. The cornstalks rose high above her head though they offered little protection form the rapidly rising sun ahead of her. She trudged down the row, the plants rustling dryly as she passed. She could not help but marvel at them though. It seemed like no time at all since spring had first come, and she and her parents were rising in the still cool mornings to plow the fields. She and mother with Cheval, and father with Jacques, turning the rich soil to prepare it for these very plants.

But how long ago did they plant this crop? It seemed like it was only a day ago that she was working her way down each row, putting seeds into the ground, and covering them with rich, dark soil. She could remember getting up in the morning, still needing a cloak because of the chill, and looking out over the field as the sun rose over the small plants breaking free from the soil. Now it was summer, oppressively hot, and the plants rose high over her head. Far over her head.

Where had the time gone? Only a short time ago it seemed, the three of them were huddled by the fire waiting for the winter to break. At least it seemed that way. Lately, time was moving faster for Emmeline. When she was a small child the spring and summer lasted forever. She would watch the first green buds sprouting on the trees and the grass begin turning from the sickly brown of winter into lush green. Slowly, the green crept across the fields and spread over the trees as she passed the time busily at the simple chores her parents set out for her. The days slowly grew warmer, and her desire to shy away from her chores and sneak in more play grew as well.

But the green took forever to spread across the land back in those days. It never was fast enough to suit Emmeline. Likewise, the crops never grew fast enough. The corn took an eternity to grow high enough for her to become lost in it. Granted, back then it did not have to be as high to become lost in it, but once it was high enough, she spent days and days dashing through the rows, hiding from imagined pursuers, and lying in wait for foreign invaders. Of course, the chickens made great quarry as she imagined them the foreign invaders and herself as the daring young knight bent upon saving his country from attack. She became quite good at sneak attacks, surprising the unsuspecting hens who unleashed furious cackles when attacked from behind and taken prisoner.

"Aha! Thou art mine madame hen!" she shouted in triumph when she had seized the intruder, "Thou wouldst do well to stay out of my country!"

She passed the days of summer in an endless stream of invasions and repulsions. The only breaks came when mother or father found her neglecting her chores and chided her. Grudgingly she did, warning the hens that they had a short reprieve in her country. Every day the Wild Hares would slowly take the sun far into the west, and night fell subtly. She remained out in the fields attacking and capturing foreign soldiers until mother called her to come into the house. "You've done nothing all day but play in that field," she admonished from the door of the house, "come in now and eat what I have prepared for you." Emmeline was never hungry in the slightest, but she found herself gobbling down double portions before collapsing into her bed.

And thus, passed the days of summer until the corn stalks became too brown and withered to hide within. As the summer matured there came work and more work. Her days were filled with the harvest, though they seemed as endless as the idle summer. Summer meant harvesting corn. Later, as autumn was ushered in, there came the harvesting of other crops in their season that would help sustain them through the winter and hopefully leave a little extra to sell. Beans and other legumes, grains, and a few fruits for good measure, were gathered and put away. But she did enjoy this work. Side by side with her parents, singing work songs and making games of the tasks made it more amusement than actual work. It seemed an eternity before winter came again, and she was huddled by the fire waiting for the spring once more.

A rustle somewhere deep in the rows of corn caught Emmeline's attention. She stopped, shifted the paquet on her shoulder and listened, her head cocked to one side. She turned around slowly several times, unable to determine from exactly which direction the sound came. It was not repeated, but she continued to hesitate. Several times she opened her mouth to call out, but nothing came. "Who is there?" she finally asked in a small, weak voice. There was no other sound except for her own breathing. No other sound in the dead silent heat.

Emmeline resumed her eastward trek down the corn row but at a slower pace than before. She listened carefully for another sound over the whisk of the shriveled corn leaves as they brushed against her shoulders. No further sound came, which made her all the more uneasy. All the business with the Prince had unnerved her. She still did not wholly understand what she was doing out here. She had neither met nor even seen the Prince before today. How could he want to marry her? She remembered her mother's story of Jocelyn. The girl had gone to marry the Prince and then disappeared. But surely there was reasonable explanation. Mother was always touting reason over everything else. Nothing ever happened that did not have a rational explanation. Reason is truth. *Vérité avant tout*, she had said over and over: *truth above all*. Reason would reveal the truth. It was the task of the rational mind to discern truth from primitive superstition.

She thought back to when the Prince had greeted her earlier this morning. She had been disgusted at the woeful harvest they were having with the corn. Emmeline had started close to the house, but finding nothing worth picking, she moved further and further out until she had found some reasonably adequate ears by the road. The plants were stricken terribly by the drought and it was doubtful that they would survive much longer without rain, which seemed less and less likely as the days progressed. So, she took the poor fruits they bore, as sad as they were. She was aware of the pounding of hooves long before she saw the horses, but she paid them no mind. They lived by a well-traveled road, the major road into Darloque, so it was quite common to see many passers-by traveling on it in the course of the day. The sun not yet risen, and it was already uncomfortably hot, so she had loosened her blouse and hiked up her skirt to get relief from the early morning heat. Ridiculous. Off in the east, the orange glow of the cloudless horizon was just beginning to brighten to yellow. The chariot of the sun had not yet risen but the brightening sky told her that it would be very soon that the Wild Hares would begin their skyward climb with the chariot of the sun.

When the Prince addressed her, her heart fluttered despite her misgivings. He was a handsome man, his hair cut short in the style that the soldiers wear nowadays. The stubble on his face accented a strong, squared jaw line. His broad, squared shoulders betrayed the muscles hidden beneath his loose hunting tunic. His thick, muscular thighs stretched taut the fabric of his breeches. He sat tall in the saddle but could not be considered an overly large man. Emmeline was drawn back to his face again. His blue-green eyes smoldered with the intensity of a confident man who always gets what he desires. This last part she knew from somewhere deep within her. How she knew it she could not tell, but something in her could feel his need. The need to possess, the need to conquer. And somewhere inside her she felt a need to be possessed, to be conquered.

Yet, she was wary. Another part of her advised caution. Though he was a stranger, and that alone demanded caution, his smoldering look and confident posture warned her to approach warily. There was a danger, but she did not know what it was, she just knew that it was there. She was drawn to those piercing blue-green eyes. *Good day, sir*, she had said to him. She knew the words came from her mouth, but they seemed to her to come from someone else a long distance away. Likewise, her answers to his questions came from afar. She was not even sure what he was saying and had no idea what she herself was saying in response. She could only focus on his face and his smoldering look.

Then he mentioned the sea. *La mer.* She snapped out of her dream state. She had wanted to go to the sea ever since her father had told her stories when she was little. The god of the sea sounded as beautiful and as dangerous as the sea itself. Since the city was land-locked, Darloque did not have a temple to Lord Merinwar. Having no sculptures or paintings to form her vision, she created her own. So, she imagined him large and fearful, his beautiful dark eyes full of danger and malice. She imagined him as an imposing figure at once drawing the eye to him and yet causing one to look away immediately. She remembered in some of the stories that when the god of the sea was displeased with a mortal–which was quite often–he would appear in all his terrible, furious glory to show his displeasure to the one who had offended him. It always ended badly for that mortal. Emmeline had always been of the opinion that if she ever went to the sea that Lord Merinwar surely would find no fault with her. That was when she was a little girl though. She was older now and such thoughts seemed childish to her. Although her faith in the gods had waned, her fascination with *la mer* had only grown.

Though it appeared that she would remain a farm girl for the rest of her life, barely traveling beyond her homestead, she harbored a deep desire to visit the sea. *Une fois*, she had told herself, just once. So, when the handsome stranger who stirred strange feelings deep inside her mentioned *la mer*, she rudely brushed aside all the warnings and approached him, hopeful that this might be her one chance to fulfill her desire. But she would have gone with the Lord of Death himself just to get a glimpse of the sea.

As she approached the stranger, the odd feeling within her intensified. There was a force pulling her closer to him and destroying the last vestiges of her trepidation. So, she approached, pulled along by the unseen force, compelling her along, compelling her to get nearer to the stranger. She stroked his horse's mane and asked him about the sea. But now that she was right next to him, looking up to him on the horse, the sea was the last thing on her mind. She felt it deep inside her; it was a primitive need like a large lumbering creature creeping forward slowly and purposefully toward its home. A need to be near the stranger, a need to look into his eyes, a need to be within those eyes. But it was more than that. How much more she could not say. She could not put a precise name on the need. It was there, nonetheless. *Is this Lady Blanchefleur's power at work?* she finally asked herself. Her mother had spoken to her only this spring about Lady Blanchefleur and her powers. Though she could not fully name the need she felt deep within her now, it seemed remarkably similar to what little her mother had told her.

"*Adieu, monsieur,*" she had said, "please return soon." she could remember saying that. It pained her greatly to say and it pained even more to watch him go. She felt as if something vital and necessary had just left her and gone with the stranger. As she watched him go and pondered the strange new feelings inside, she turned back to discover that one of his party had remained behind. The man's forlorn appearance drove all the strange feelings out of her in an instant. The man had appeared haunted. That was the only word that fit. He did not just carry a heavy burden, that burden weighed him down and drove all the vitality out of him. He was a man of misery, the sorrowed man, a man so encumbered by his burden that he had little else to live for. What kept him going she did not know, but he was a ghost of his former vibrant self. He appeared ready to speak to her but did not. He opened his mouth, but no words came out. When he hung his head and reined his horse after his comrades, she started to go after him. Emmeline wanted to reach out to him; she wanted to help him ease his burden. The man looked older than her father's age by his appearance, but she suspected that his burden had aged him unnaturally.

Suddenly she knew. How she knew, she was not certain. Just like how she knew of his misery, the knowledge came to her unbidden, the knowledge manifesting itself in her mind out of seemingly thin air. Yet she knew this and more. She knew that he had a girl, a daughter her own age who needed him and needed him to be whole again. It was imperative for her that he be whole again. Emmeline started after the man; she opened her mouth to speak; she *needed* to reach out to him, to ease his burden. But the image of the handsome stranger and the image of the sea came crashing back into her mind like a stampeding bull. These and her own self-doubts conspired against her. She was probably wrong about him. Besides, the handsome stranger had promised to take her to the sea. And this was pleasing to her, the idea of the stranger and herself together watching the sea. Then the stranger was gone, and it was just herself and the sea. And this was pleasing as well.

A sudden rustle of dry leaves from within the corn rows broke her from her thoughts. She turned back to the rows, listening carefully, head cocked to one side, her eyes wary. The sound was not repeated so she went back distractedly to her own thoughts, images of the sea playing in her head.

Emmeline found that she had stopped. It was hot. The sun was in her face. Her breeches clung to her, wet and sticky from the sweat she had worked up on this walk. She looked back the way she came. The farmhouse and the barn were gone, lost in the high rows of corn. All she could see was rows of cornstalks stretching into infinity. A look forward to the east revealed the same.

Suddenly, she was angry. Angry at herself, angry at her parents. The entire situation was ridiculous. The Prince had only promised to take her to the sea. He had never mentioned marriage to her. She was not half-witted; she knew what he had said. She would never agree to such a thing. Despite the feelings the handsome stranger had aroused in her she had no intention of marrying him. Go with him to the sea, yes. Marriage, no.

But the look in her mother's eyes told her differently. Her mother was scared, truly scared. Her eyes were wide, her hands trembled, her voice quavered as she told Emmeline what had happened. She had never seen her mother so frightened in her entire life. She thought now how her mother looked like a small animal in a snare, no way out and Death fast approaching.

And the story of the girl named Jocelyn. Certainly, her parents had told her stories that were not true. Starving children in other countries when she would not eat; the Demon will get her when she would not go to sleep. All tales to get her to behave in the way they wanted. But the look in her mother's eyes when she told the story of that poor girl was convincing enough. Possibly the story was not true, both her parents had warned her of rumor and its savage appetite. But the horrified look on her mother's face as she told it convinced Emmeline that she at least believed the story. Emmeline did not understand what had happened to Jocelyn, and Mother was loath to explain any further. But she did understand that the Prince had taken Jocelyn away, and Jocelyn had disappeared.

So, the handsome stranger had lied to her. He had promised her the sea and had no intention of taking her there. She sighed heavily. She felt crushed and betrayed. Why would someone promise what they have no intention giving? A person should live by their word. *A man's word is sometimes all he has*, her father had told her. *Live honesty or do not live at all*, he had also said. So, the handsome stranger was a man who could not be trusted. Emmeline sighed despondently. She had wanted to visit the sea.

Emmeline's parents frustrated her with their rules and old-fashioned ideas. But to lose them entirely? *Non, ne jamais.* Never. Despite their sometimes-foolish behavior, she loved them more than anything and would not want to lose them if she could help it. For that poor girl in the story to lose the people she loved the most, it probably made her the most miserable wretch alive. Emmeline did not want that to happen to her. Her blood boiled at the thought. She hated the handsome stranger, this Prince, for what he had done to her and for what he had done to that poor Jocelyn. Emmeline had stopped again in the cornrow. She cursed herself. Time was of the essence. The chariot of the sun was rising ever higher, and she was still far from her destination. This Prince was a dangerous man who lied and divided families. It was of the uttermost importance for her to make it to The Wild Hare before sunset. She could not lose her family because of this base and false Prince.

A rustle somewhere in the corn startled her. This noise was closer than the last one. She turned around looking, listening. Her mouth ran dry. She tried to speak but nothing would come. The rustle came again. This time it sounded even closer, but she could not tell from which direction it came. Panic began to build inside her. Slowly she backed down the row toward the East, her head buzzing. Another rustle came and this time she saw the top of a plant move just four rows over. Panic built to a crescendo, and she turned and bolted down the row. The rustling followed her though the corn. She turned and saw plants moving behind her; the thing chasing her was drawing closer. Her mind screamed in panic, and the panic gave her more speed, but the invisible pursuer drew ever closer. The rustling filled her ears, she knew that whatever it was almost upon her. There was no more speed in her. She was running as fast as she was able. Tears welled in her eyes and ran back into her ears. She was gone. She knew it. The pursuer had her. She did not want to lose her mother and father. Goodbye, goodbye–

And then it was gone. The rustling ceased like a candle being snuffed out. Emmeline slowed and then eventually stopped. She looked back. There was nothing but dried corn hanging desperately onto sickly stalks in neat rows. She bent over, panting, watchful, ready to run again should the pursuer return. It was gone. Blood pounding in her ears and her panting breath were all she could hear. Not a sound, not a movement came from the corn.

Emmeline turned around. She was standing at the edge of the cornfield looking out over clear pasture covered in short grass. She stuck her head cautiously out past the last stalks to look across the rows of corn where they butted up neatly against the pasture. The rows stretched out in even lines as far as she could see. The field's neat carpet of green stood in stark contrast to the corn behind her. The grass here was green and doing well despite the drought.

Emmeline was slick with sweat. Her breeches stuck to her like a second skin. She checked her paquet. If only she had smuggled a chemise or something better than these breeches into her bag she could change and be a little more comfortable. In spite of the heat, Emmeline pulled her hair out of the bun and let it fall down her back. Immediately fresh sweat broke out on her neck. She hated the heat on her neck, but she hated having her hair up more. She had become quite fond of it and thought she looked better with it down.

She looked out across the pasture again. There were no animals grazing on it now. They were all back in the barn and there they were likely to remain until hunger forced then out into this heat. She crouched down and ran her fingers over the grass, neatly trimmed by the teeth of hungry animals. Here and there were small patches of brown where the grass was not doing as well as the rest. Emmeline ran her had across the soft grass again. "I despise this whole business," she muttered to herself.

Her father would not like it if he knew that she knew, but it was rather obvious that they were in trouble long before the handsome stranger had come along. She picked the same crops that he did so she could not help but notice the pitiful produce. How they had managed to fill the storehouse these last two seasons was a mystery to Emmeline. Father pretended that this was not the case, and he did a very good job at it, but one ultimately could not deny the evidence before their very eyes. And he prayed to Lord Aufeese every day. Even though it was clear that the god of the harvest was not listening to him, still he prayed. Day after day he prayed for rain and none came. He prayed for relief and none came. He prayed for a sign that all would be well, and none ever came.

Add this new misery to these already present ones. Emmeline saw his face when mother told him what had happened. He had turned white. The deeply tanned face of the farmer had paled to an ashen white in terror. He had been able to mask his fear concerning the crops and the weather and at least put up the semblance of normality, but not to this. He was as transparent as the lake whose water was so clear that one could see all the way to the muddy bottom. That was why she was here right now standing on the edge of this field stroking the dry grass. It was her father's fear that had impressed upon her the true severity of the situation. His ability to mask his fear in a crisis was probably his greatest attribute. His unwavering hopefulness in the face of adversity, his optimism when it seemed that all was lost, was what kept her calm. Even though she was unsure of the outcome herself, the simple fact that *someone* believed that all would be well was a great comfort to her. That was why she was here. Her father believed that this was the right thing to do, and if Father believed this was the right course of action, then she was going to follow through with it.

She had stopped. But was it the right course after all? His face, her father's face in that moment when mother told them what had happened. The strong, tanned farmer's face that offered confidence during hard times was suddenly gone. His face betrayed his true fear. A clear lake all the way to the bottom. In that moment she saw his fear; she saw all his fear. It was not just the handsome stranger who threatened to take his daughter away; it was the drought, the crops, and the overall misfortune that had plagued their family for some time. He had prayed and yet no relief had come. He was faithful in his sacrifices to Lord Aufeese and the god had given him nothing.

"His faith was all for nothing," she said aloud. "I think mother is right, the gods do not exist."

A new sound came at once. Emmeline stood quickly, tucked her hair behind her ear, and listened, her head cocked to one side. At first it was not clear; a faint sound like distant thunder rolling across the prairie. She looked up. The sun stung her eyes, but she could see not a single cloud in the sky. The sound however was continuous, not at all like brief rolling thunder but an ongoing growing rumble that sounded more like...

"Hoof beats!" she cried aloud.

The sound grew in a rising tide from the west. It was the sound of many riders. The sound grew more distinct, and she was sure that it was the hoof beats of many horses, at least as many as was in the handsome stranger's party. *They decided to come for me early!* Panic rose swiftly in her again at the idea that she might end up like Jocelyn, lost and alone, somewhere far from her family. She had to go, she had to run.

The sound grew louder and more distinct. She looked across the open field. It spread out in all directions open and empty. Further across the pasture in the distance was another field of crops. The Wild Hare lay in that direction. But panic seized and held her there at the edge. The pasture was large and open and would leave her exposed to her enemies, but if she could get to The Wild Hare, she would be safe. She knew this; father had said so. The drumming of hooves grew louder, and she could count the number of horses. *Un, deux, trois,* she counted in her head.

RUN!!!! her mind screamed at last, and she shot out across the open pasture. She pushed herself without mercy. She knew what was after her this time. If she could not get away, then she would never see her parents again. She would be taken far away and never see them again. Her feet drummed the turf as she raced across field. She could hear her own panting, her own heartbeat, and the drumming of hooves growing ever louder. *By the gods's ears, they have seen me!* She dared not look back. She knew that if she saw her pursuers, she would lose her footing, and they would surely have her. Emmeline pushed herself into an even faster run. Blood pounded in her ears like it never had before, and her breath came out in sobbing gasps. "I do not want to go," she cried, "I do not want to leave my home!" The thunder of hooves on the turf drowned the out other sounds. Now she thought she could hear the horses's breath in her ears as they galloped across the field after her. *Non, non, non, NOOOOOO!!!*

CHAPTER SIX

STRANGELY, Emmeline found herself thinking about the last time Father had taken her to Darloque with him. It was after the last good crop they had gathered before the drought came. When they had filled the storehouse with enough food to last them until the next harvest, they loaded the remainder into the cart and headed into the city. Father had given the task of pulling the cart to Jacques. He was more capable of pulling heavy loads than Cheval, and besides, her father liked the donkey despite his often-stubborn disposition.

There were many travelers on the road that day. A throng of horses, carts, and humans jammed the main road into Darloque. The Market Days had come, and the city would be filled with farmers selling the fruits of their seasonal labor. In addition, other vendors would be there to sell their wares to the farmers who only came to the city once a season. After they had sold or traded all the crops and bought the merchandise they needed for the farm, Father would always have a little left over to purchase one small gift each for his wife and daughter. Emmeline dreamed about what she might get.

Traveling was slow, but the weather was fair. The chariot of the sun was in an agreeable position this day as it rose ever higher in the sky. A gentle breeze blew in from the West bringing with it a trace scent of rain from the clouds assembled along the horizon. Trees lazily dropped their multicolored leaves which drifted down onto the road. The slow grind of feet, hooves, and wheels upon the dusty road mingled with the myriad voices engaged in pleasant conversation. From somewhere behind floated the sound of the bleating of sheep. Cows lowed, horses snorted, and chickens cackled. Somewhere a baby cried.

Before Emmeline and her father realized it, they had finally reached their destination.

"Darloque," said Emmeline's father. "The City of Light–"

"*La Cité Éternelle*," finished Emmeline, "The Eternal City."

A massive stone wall rose to a dizzying height and extended in either direction as far as the eye could see. The road led right up to and through the monumental timbered gates braced with thick iron, thrown open wide today for the occasion of the Market. On either side stood dozens of intimidating guards at attention, all holding long, menacing spears. They stopped no one, they questioned no one, they simply stood at the gates, mute and serious.

"It is all for show," Emmeline's father whispered to her, leaning across the donkey's neck, "to let everyone know they will tolerate no misbehavior during the Market."

As they passed though the opening, Emmeline stared at two large crests, one high up on the center of each gate. Both crests showed the profile of Lord Portiscule. *May the great Gatekeeper protect this city forever*, read the inscription on each crest.

The city's wall was thick and impenetrable. No army had ever taken Darloque in siege and no one ever would. Emmeline had heard her parents say this many times. They passed through a second set of gates, less substantial than the first, but still large and imposing. It was dark here in the portcullis, and it took Emmeline a moment for her eyes to adjust. She caught the other travelers gawking at the massive entrance, pointing out the huge ancient stonework which made up the wall and the heavily fortified gates through which they passed. Finally, a third gate–a web of crisscrossed iron bars suspended by thick iron chains, hanging high above them, ready to crash shut at a moment's notice–and they walked past the inner wall and into the streets of the city bathed in golden sunlight.

Innumerable people packed the streets of Darloque. Living on a small farm, half a day's journey from the city, Emmeline had become accustomed to her rather solitary existence. Granted, their farm was on the main road to Darloque, so they saw a fair share of passers-by and regular travelers. So, despite her country upbringing, Emmeline considered herself somewhat worldly and her once a season trip to the city made her feel just a little superior to the unsophisticated people of the deep country who never saw other human beings until they came here to the Market. Nevertheless, being surrounded by so many people in one space was just a little unsettling.

The main road continued through the gates of the city where it changed into cobblestones. The stones, worn smooth over time by countless human and animal feet, felt rough on Emmeline's feet, sore from the long march into Darloque. The street snaked its way through the city, making various twists and turns, narrowing here, widening there, until it passed through the West gates and into those lands beyond. At the city's center was the crossroads where the main East/West road intersected with the North/South road. This road proceeded in either direction, snaking its own cobblestoned way through the city to the Northern and Southern gates. Four gates for each of the four points of the compass. Truly, it is said, that one can get to any point in the world from the crossroads at the center of Darloque.

The Market originally began long ago as a small gathering of farmers at the crossroads. In the present day, however, there was not a road, street, or alleyway in the whole city that was not lined with booths. Those who could not find a space for a booth had trans-formed themselves into roving vendors selling a variety of wares from carts or baskets. Astute individuals discovered over time that they could show their wares to a broader audience and thus increase sales by taking their wares through the city and shouting advertisements to the throng. Men and women roamed the streets of the great city selling things from food and beverages to balms and herbal remedies to holy relics and souvenirs.

Emmeline gazed about in amazement as they progressed down the main road, deeper into the city. "Father," she said in a raised voice so to be heard over the crowd, "there are so many people here and so many already set up on the street, we shall never find a place to set up our booth."

"Patience, little one," he replied, giving Jacques a little tug. "The gods will reveal our space in the proper time."

The congenial mood of the main road all but disappeared when they turned down a narrow side street. Buildings rose high on either side of them, in some places blocking out the warming sun and sending a dark chill through Emmeline's body. All around her people scowled. Grumbles from impatient travelers rolled through the crowd of people and animals making their way slowly through the jammed street. Occasionally, the rumble was broken by a shout from some disgruntled traveler whose breaking point had been reached. Curses rolled out on someone or some animal for being too slow. Emmeline felt her own convivial mood eroding away in the mass of impatience and ill will that surrounded her. Her father trudged on, seemingly unfazed by shoving and shouting. She wondered how he could push through the crowd with its ill-mannered behavior and not be brought down by it. Jacques had laid his ears down in a show of irritation, but her father led him on. Emmeline was just beginning to wish she had never come when they poured out of the narrow side street onto a broad thoroughfare.

Emmeline's eyes grew wide with awe as she beheld the magnificent sight before her. "The Temple of Aufeese," she whispered breathlessly.

Immediately the dour mood of the crowd began to lift as one by one, travelers broke out into the brilliant, golden sunlight. The slanting morning sun shone down from the east onto the massive double-towered facade of the Golden Child's temple. All the doors in the triple portals were thrown open to receive the influx of offerings from those who had most benefitted from Lord Aufeese's generous grace. There was nothing Emmeline could think to say except, "Beautiful!" But it came out as a low whisper, barely audible even to herself, as if to speak louder would break the spell the grand temple cast upon her.

High upon the facade, the great, round, stained glass window reflected the sunlight in a glorious rainbow of blue, red, and green. Captivating Emmeline, drawing her eyes ever upward, the facade reached ever higher into the sky, finally capped with two towers disappearing into the deep, blue morning sky. She thought that if she could climb to the top of one of those towers, she would be able to touch the dome of the sky itself. And perhaps, if she could climb at the right time, she might be able to capture the chariot of the sun and finally bring the Wild Hares home to their master.

She fixated upon this fantasy for some time, then dropped her eyes to the complex detail of the sculptures which flanked the portals. On each of the jambs stood sculptures of men, so lifelike that they seemed as real as the people in the street. These were statues of important men. Emmeline knew that much, although she could not remember their names or why they were considered important enough to be enshrined on the Temple of Aufeese, save for one.

The noble-looking statue to the right of the central portal was Senus the Poet. He was the first human to ever commune with the Golden Child, and he composed the bulk of poems which told the god's story. Although others have been fortunate enough to see and even speak with the god, it was Senus who repeatedly met with him and was given special favor. Eventually, the great beauty of the god caused him to become blind–although others would tell a different story on the cause of his blindness.

Nevertheless, Senus continued to praise the Golden Child, telling how fortunate he was to have gazed upon the god though it caused his blindness. *To gaze upon that beauty for such a short time and to be able to hold that memory with me, is apt reward for a life of darkness.* It was after his blindness that Senus composed his glorious poems praising the deeds of Aufeese. *Some might call this blindness a curse,* he wrote, *I instead call it a blessing, a gift that has truly enabled me to see the pure glory of the Golden Child.* Emmeline was not sure what to think about that, but she felt that if she were to gaze long enough at the beautiful facade of this temple, she might very well be struck blind herself.

The slow rattle of the cart upon the cobblestones brought Emmeline back to herself. Her father led Jacques to a line of other carts parked in a wide area in front of the Eastern facade. Bringing the cart to a stop, he then pulled a small wooden bucket from the cart, filled it with water from a nearby cistern and offered it to the hard-working animal who gulped it greedily. Her father ruffled Jacques's mane saying, "We will be but only a short time."

Emmeline watched this dumbly until her father turned to her with a quizzical look.

"*Venez,* little one," he said. "We must go make our offering so the Golden Child may be pleased with us."

She nodded slowly. Her gaze rose up the facade once more, passing the spectacular stained glass window and moving up the towers that stretched ever upward toward the sky. With a sigh, Emmeline pulled a small basket of corn from the back of the cart. Her father, carrying a larger basket, turned to her briefly.

"It is spectacular." His eyes rose slowly up the facade just as hers had.

Her father turned toward the entry, and Emmeline followed, her small offering in her hands. As they drew closer, Emmeline's eyes were drawn again to the statue of Senus on the central door jamb. The sculptor had clothed the Poet in a simple monk's robe with a rope tied at the waist. His feet were bare, and his hair closely cropped. Like the other statuary which framed the portals, it looked remarkably lifelike, as though it could and would walk right out of the column it was carved into. Senus leaned out from the column a little, one foot ahead of the other, his hands held out in front of him in an almost pleading gesture. His head was tilted back and his mouth open, his eyes stared out in the vacant stare of the blind man. Overall, the impression was of a man caught in the act of singing. *Singing about Lord Aufeese, no doubt,* Emmeline thought. It was the most life-like and realistic of all the sculptures here. Emmeline closed her eyes, and she could hear Senus singing–singing hymns of the Golden Child.

They entered though the center portal into the temple, the inside of which was no less spectacular than the outside. The nave stretched out indefinitely, disappearing into darkness. Light filtered in from the great stained glass window, creating a spectacular rainbow glittering and dancing on the worn stone floor before them. Columns stretched in two straight rows down the length of the temple separating the nave proper from the two side aisles. Emmeline smiled. *If only I could plant rows of corn this straight.* Light filtered in weakly from the smaller stained glass windows on the sides, breaking up the dark with brief patches of multicolored light. Her eyes followed the columns upward into the dimness to the arches which capped them. Up Emmeline's eyes went, past the triforium to the majestic rib vaulting of the ceiling standing at an incredible height. One could stand outside the Temple of Aufeese all day and be amazed at the sheer size of the structure, but it was not until one glimpsed the interior that one really saw its true massive size.

When Emmeline's eyes had finally adjusted to the cool dim of the temple interior, she looked at her father and saw him as awestruck as she. She adjusted her basket in her hands and cleared her throat.

"Incredible," she said meekly.

Her father said nothing for a moment, eyes wide in amazement, like someone seeing the temple for the first time instead of one who has visited since before Emmeline herself was born.

"*Magnifique,*" he replied in a barely audible whisper. He shook his head slowly from side to side, still staring at the distant archwork of the ceiling hanging impossibly high above them.

"*Magnifique*," he repeated but louder this time. He turned to Emmeline and looked at her, smiling. "I have come to this temple ever since I was a young boy, and it still amazes me. Every time I come here it feels like the first time." He paused thoughtfully, considered what he said and then added, "And in a way it is like visiting for the first time for I always see something new, some aspect I had never noticed before."

Emmeline smiled back at her father.

"Come little one." He hefted up his own basket and motioned to her. "We must go make our offering, and when we have satisfied the Golden Child, I will show you some interesting aspects of this temple." Emmeline grinned wide and followed her father onward toward the altar.

It was a long walk to the altar, or so it seemed. Entranced by the astounding architecture, Emmeline plodded along slowly, dropping back several paces from her father. She would have to jog to catch up only to drop back again as she got lost in the beauty of the temple. After a short time walking, she was aware of a sound ahead of them. She realized with a start that she had not imagined the voice of Senus singing out from the temple facade but had heard the choir singing a chant and organum composed to glorify the Golden Child:

Behold, the harvest has been gathered in
The Golden Child glows as the sun
It is right to thank the god of the harvest
His beauty shines on us all
Baskets overflow with his generous bounty
We are blessed as he shines on us
The harvest he provides nourishes us
His light will feed our souls

Emmeline walked with her father this way, engrossed in the beauty of the architecture, enraptured by the chorus of lilting polyphony filling the seemingly unfillable temple. It was not until they had progressed halfway up the nave to the altar that she realized that there were others here. Here and there, scattered throughout the nave and side aisles, people came together in fellowship. Even the most buoyant conversation failed to rise higher than the voices of the choir.

However, it seemed to her, as her eyes finally became adjusted to the dim light filtering though the myriad of colored glass windows, that there should be more people gathered here in the temple after a glorious harvest of crops. Scattered here and there was only a dozen or so people, chatting discreetly amongst themselves.

The choir reached the end of the chant and the absence of its multitude of voices left the temple in an eerie pall. Emmeline could hear their footfalls on the worn stone floor echoing through the temple, her small, light steps mocking the heavy, solid ones of her father. It was a rather dreary sound, dry and empty, and it sucked away rapidly the good cheer the temple created in her when she had first seen it from the street. Then she was aware of the voices, the whispering of the acolytes holding secret conversations in the dark recesses of the temple aisles. She could not hear their words, their dark whispers discreetly hidden behind hands bothered her, and the way they stared at her made her uncomfortable.

Much to Emmeline's great relief, the choir began a new chant. This piece of music she recognized at once. It was a simple chant, a two-voice organum, praising the great beauty of the Golden Child and exalting his great benevolence. She knew it well as it was the first song her father had taught her to sing. She found herself humming along as she walked, her footsteps picking up the pace as she felt the warmth and peace return to her, the dreary echo of footsteps and the voices of dark whispers banished now to the shadowy places from whence they had come. Her father looked at her now, smiling evenly as she hummed the tune. She could not help but to smile back. All was well as they approached the altar.

The Temple of Aufeese offered so much in the way of beautiful and majestic architecture that one usually failed to notice the altar until one was right upon it. This was how it was with Emmeline; she was so enthralled with the temple that she did not see her father stop. She carried on a couple of steps past him until a sharp hiss from her father brought her to an awkward halt. An ear of corn tumbled from her basket to roll haughtily to the base of the altar itself. Her eyes followed it to the base, leaving the errant ear to gaze upward and ever upward to the true glory of the temple.

The altar itself was a simple tabular form but carved out of the purest white marble. The lines were clean and exact. She could hardly believe that any human could have carved it. The edges were lined with the purest gold, accentuating the clean lines, and giving off a sharp radiance even in the dim light of the temple. Her eyes roamed over the surface, examining every sharp angle, reveling in the richly carved stone fit for the service of a truly glorious god.

The beauty of the temple and everything in it paled in comparison to altar, and the altar paled in comparison to the great statue which stood behind it. Sculpted from the same pure white marble as the altar, the immense statue of the Golden Child made the statue of Senus look like the product of a poor child's attempt at sculpture. Emmeline's jaw dropped open in awe. The statue of Lord Aufeese stood in an open gesture of welcome. His head tilted slightly downward as if to acknowledge his humble subjects worshiping at the altar's base. His eyes had a gentle appearance to them. His posture suggested warmth and welcome, his face exhibited peace. On his head, a laurel wreath wrought of pure gold rested lightly, enhancing his gentle look with an air of nobility. For the god himself was gentle and noble, the gentlest and noblest of all the gods. His beauty was incomparable.

Here at the transept of the great temple, the vaulted ceiling soaring high above, light streaming playfully through the stained glass windows, as the choir sang joyfully their simple song of the glory of Lord Aufeese, this immense marble statue stood out as a bright beacon to all who would seek the god's favor. Emmeline felt that she could believe; she felt that this was real. She could put away the negative comments her mother made about the gods. Emmeline could brush away all negativity. The dark whispers were gone, banished forever, never to return as long as she stayed here at the altar, in this god's presence. All was peace; all was well.

"Greetings to you both on this fine day!" Emmeline jumped and barely suppressed a yelp when the curly-haired man appeared suddenly before her. "May the blessings of the Golden Child be upon you both!" Emmeline clutched her basket tightly to her and backed away from the stranger. He wore the golden robes of a High Priest, but his beard had barely come in and to Emmeline he looked too young to hold such an office.

The High Priest turned to her father. "Ah, Guy is it? Yes, Guy, I see you have brought a splendid offering to Aufeese on this first day of the Market."

"Gilles, Holy Father, it is–" her father began in a quiet tone.

"Ah, yes, Guy, you have brought a splendid offering. The Lord Aufeese will bless you greatly today because of it." The High Priest's eyes lit up with youthful excitement as he gesticulated wildly.

"Truthfully..." her father began.

"And this must be Murielle," he cried turning to Emmeline. "I am so pleased to finally meet you! Guy has told me so much about you!"

"Well, Holy Father, no–" Emmeline tried to explain.

"Here, put that down," he said motioning eagerly to the basket of corn she held. When she had placed the basket at her feet, he immediately took her hands in his own. His hands were cold and clammy, and they trembled with the energy of his enthusiastic speech. Emmeline wanted to let go immediately but his grip was firm and sure.

"I must say, Guy," he said giving her father a wink that made Emmeline suddenly uncomfortable, "she is much younger than I thought she would be." The High Priest shook her hands roughly. "I am so very glad to meet you finally, Murielle!" Emmeline wished that he would let her go.

"No," her father said pensively, "this is..."

"Ah, yes I see," the High Priest burst out as he winked again, "I understand completely."

"Well, yes... uh, no..."

"You have brought us a fine offering, Guy," continued the High Priest, changing the subject effortlessly as though Emmeline's father had said nothing. "Come now, kneel and accept the blessing of the Lord Aufeese."

The High Priest placed a clammy hand on each of their foreheads. "O magnificent Lord Aufeese, please accept the great offering these, your two humble servants have brought to you. May you grant them full lives, prosperity, and contentment."

She barely contained her sigh of great relief when the High Priest finally pulled his hand from her forehead. Emmeline could see the tiniest bit of revulsion in her father's eyes. His glance at her was brief, then his eyes turned their attention not to the High Priest but to the great statue of Lord Aufeese. He rose without a word, lifting his basket with great care, as if it were filled with precious breakables rather than corn. With great solemnity he placed his basket at the foot of the altar. Emmeline followed and placed hers alongside his.

Emmeline looked at the other offerings lined at the foot of the altar. There were a few baskets of corn, wheat, barley, and other staples around the altar in tiny baskets. Indeed, the baskets here were all smaller than the one she herself had set before the altar. She thought about the various people she had seen milling about the temple as they had made their way in. There were far more people here than baskets. She took a closer look at the tiny basket of corn next her own basket. It was full of dry, underdeveloped ears, the rejects of the crop, the kind not even fit for animal fodder.

As if reading her mind, the High Priest spoke glumly, "The harvest is plentiful, but the offerings are poor."

And the harvest was excellent this year, Emmeline thought. Her family had gathered in more corn than she had ever seen. Her father's basket was large and full of the best ears they could find in the harvest. Her own basket, a larger one than last season because she could carry more now, brimmed with her own golden offering of large, perfect ears. *Should Lord Aufeese not be insulted?* she thought. *Why should he stand there mutely, benignly welcoming those who have insulted him with pathetic offerings?* It perplexed her that the god of the harvest would not immediately strike down those who had made this demeaning offering. But he stood their mutely while they blithely carried on their carefree conversations in the dark recesses of his temple.

"But you, Guy," the High Priest began abruptly, "you have brought the Golden Child a fine offering." He turned suddenly to Emmeline as if noticing her there for the first time. "You and your *amie* here have both brought fine offerings." He winked again at Emmeline. She fought off her revulsion.

"This is my daughter, actually," Gilles spat out. Emmeline could not help but to let out a heavy sigh of mixed frustration and relief.

"Oh yes, certainly," the High Priest replied distractedly. His eyes glazed over, and a dark pall crossed his face. "Oh yes, Guy, Lord Aufeese finds favor in your offering today. You are not like the others. You give the best to the one who provides and save the leftovers for your own table. Not like the undeserving who have laid these pitiful offerings today." He swept his arm dreamily in the direction of the other baskets.

"Oh no," he continued in his trance, his voice slow and deliberate, "those who have made these offerings have offended the Golden Child and will live to regret their neglect and carelessness. They will. Oh yes, they will." He slammed a fist into his open palm with a sharp smack which made Emmeline jump. She looked at her father and saw him staring forlornly at the stone floor as though he had something to be ashamed of.

A smile returned to the young High Priest's face and he came back to them. "But you have nothing to fear, Guy, and neither does your *daughter* here. You are both blessed this day." He placed his hands on each of their foreheads again. Emmeline felt that revulsion was winning the war within her mind and beginning a campaign toward her stomach. She thought to herself that if she were truly blessed then Lord Aufeese would pull this man's sweaty hand off her.

————

Emmeline could feel hot, humid breath of a horse bearing down on her neck as the thunder of hoofbeats filled her mind again. There was no escape, there was no hope, all was lost. The open field stretched out around her on all sides, offering no place to hide. As the panic raced through her mind, the end of the field came more closely into view. But she realized with a curious wonder as it became clearer that she was rapidly approaching a vast field of golden wheat. *Odd,* she thought idly in the midst of her panic, *we did not plant wheat this season.* It was wheat nevertheless, and the feeling grew inside her, abating her panic slightly, that if she could make it into the wheat, she would be safe. No matter how close her pursuers, she would be safe inside the wheat. *Safe inside the wheat, the wheat holds safety.* With a final burst of speed–all she had left in her–she closed the gap between herself and the vast wheat field stretching out into seeming infinity. Just as the sound of hoofbeats and the harsh panting of many horses was about to drive her mad, she made a giant, desperate leap and tumbled roughly into the wheat field, rolling violently before landing in a heap on the ground, stalks of golden wheat crushed beneath her.

Emmeline lay there for some time before her breathing settled enough for her to realize that the horses were gone. She rolled slowly over onto her back, flattening more wheat beneath her as she did. She listened, and there was no sound, not even the twittering of birds. Above her the sun rose steadily on its sharp incline. It did not seem as hot to her now as it had been before. Certainly, it was much less oppressive. Strange, considering that she had just run across a great span of open pasture to get here. Stranger still was the sedate stillness surrounding her. There was no heavy breathing of panting horses. No soldier's voices. No sound at all. Horses were not that quiet, especially after a good run. They breathed, snorted, and stomped their hooves impatiently. There should be the jangle of bridles and the creak of leather saddles, but there was no sound at all. She waited. She waited for what seemed an eternity but there was still no sound. Surely some horse would make a noise, or some man would give his position away. She had felt them right on top of her, pressing her in pursuit. She could not have lost them that easily. *But certainly, they must be gone*, she thought, though she was still wary to raise herself over the wheat and have a look around. So, she waited.

After another length of time, she still had not heard a sound but was still afraid to move. Emmeline closed her eyes and shook her head back and forth making a small rustling noise as her head rocked back and forth on the crushed wheat. *Ridiculous*, she thought, stopping her head. *You silly girl, they are not here. They have lost you and have moved on.* She sighed heavily and opened her eyes to see a brilliant pair of blue-green eyes staring back at her.

"Well, hello there!" the owner of the brilliant blue-green eyes exclaimed.

Emmeline screamed.

CHAPTER SEVEN

GILLES PACED AROUND the empty room. This truly was the most difficult part of the plan. He began to think idly that he should have not given in to Murielle and gone to Darloque himself. At least he would have something to occupy his time and keep his mind focused. He considered. There would also not be the feeling nagging him deep inside his heart that this was not the right thing to do. It bothered him further that he had let his wife's stubborn willfulness win out over his own better judgement.

Again, he added. She had her own mind and as long as he had known her, she was not afraid the argue with him. Even when they were courting, she showed her own mind. Many women, he had observed, put on a good act of complacency before clamping down on their young husbands. In some cases, it was a gradual encroachment, a slow wresting of power from the man until he suddenly awoke one day to find himself devoid of any decision-making ability in the household. Others clamped down with the ferocity of a wolf before the last echoes of the vows had died away, and the last of the white petals were still falling.

Gilles chuckled to himself. "As if I would have her any other way."

In his day he had seen just as many women who were cowed by their husbands. He had seen them on the roads, in the streets of Darloque, at the Market, in the fields. They were easy to find. They usually followed a good four of five steps behind their husbands with a look of watchful expectancy on their faces. They were happy to go wherever their husbands led them. At the Market one never saw them argue, disagree, or offer any thought contrary to that of their dominant spouses. Those women were difficult to speak with, always looking to their husbands for the answer to some question. Some were unable to even tell what their husbands expected, so fearful were they that they might cross his wishes even though his wishes had been set in stone long ago.

No, Gilles had decided long ago that when he married, he would not take a woman like that. He wanted one with her own mind, with her own opinions. In this matter he was alone. As a young man, his friends thought him daft to wish that upon himself. Most expressed the desire, nay, the expectation, to marry a woman who would serve his every whim and look upon him as though he were a god. "The woman I marry," boasted a young man Gilles knew through another, "will have no mind but the one I give her. And if she does not–" he concluded the statement with the sharp smack of his fist into his empty palm. The last Gilles had heard, the young braggart had married a terrible shrew of a woman, and he was often seen wearing a black eye.

Gilles chuckled to himself again. Yes, he would not have Murielle any other way. She was willful and stubborn. She had never hidden that from him. If fact, she had argued with him on the first day they met. Perhaps that was what endeared her to him. She was willful and stubborn, yes, but she was also open. She did not hide it or try to justify her behavior with banal excuses.

The smile faded from his lips as his pacing slowed to a stop. Oddly enough, Murielle's manner frustrated him as much as it pleased him. For each time he could think of that her stubbornness humored him there was another time in which it irritated him. Surely it was good to have her express her own opinions. And certainly, many times her view of a certain situation was better than his own, and he was thankful for her insistence.

One instance sprang into his mind. During one particular harvest, long ago, before Emmeline was born, Murielle suddenly stopped picking corn and stared blankly into the clear, blue sky, still and silent like an animal locked onto a scent. Gilles watched her for a few moments, then ceased picking himself to ask her what in Mava's name she was doing. Before he could ask, she spoke. "A storm is coming." She said this and nothing more, continuing to stare, unblinking, into the sky.

Murielle suddenly shook her head, and looking to the corn with a curious expression, resumed picking at an accelerated rate. Gilles looked to the clear sky and asked Murielle if she were daft. She ignored him, picking the ears swiftly and deftly as Gilles had never seen her do. He began to argue with his wife, but she ignored him and continued her rapid picking. He tried to convince her that no storm was coming, but she would not hear it. Gilles gave up his argument, and they continued to pick corn well into the night using lanterns to guide their work. As they put the last of their harvest into the storehouse, large drops of rain began to patter to the ground in earnest. Gilles looked up in confusion and then to his wife. Murielle smiled weakly.

The two, exhausted from a day and a night of labor, huddled together in the dark house as the storm rattled the rafters. They both desperately wanted sleep, but the violence of the storm made them too fearful to chance it. The storm raged through the night without pause or falter. It was not until the first glint of morning sunlight shone through a break in the thatch of the roof that they realized the storm was over. Tentatively, cautiously, they both moved toward the door to get their first look at the damage wrought by the storm.

The landscape they saw was not the one that had been there the previous day. The land around the house lay open as far as the eye could see. The cornstalks which had been there the previous day were either laid flat or removed completely. Across the soaked ground of the farmyard, thatch, wood, and garbage was strewn about. Rivulets of water wove their way around the destruction, converging into larger streams which snaked their way into the fields. The violence awed them to silence. There was nothing to say, nothing that could be said.

But Gilles had a thought. *A sign,* he said to himself, *Murielle was given a sign from the gods.* He let this thought roll around in his head as they picked through the remains of their farm. The barn was destroyed. The few animals that did not lay dead on the sodden ground wandered listlessly around the barnyard. The storehouse, however, was still intact, and the contents unharmed.

"You received a sign from the gods," Gilles said finally.

Murielle wheeled on him with a violence of far greater intensity than that of the storm. She vehemently denied having any such vision, insisting instead that her human senses had picked up the change of the weather in advance. Gilles continued to insist that she had received a vision until the threat of bodily violence convinced him to cease. For years afterward, Murielle denied any divine involvement in her weather prediction. But Gilles knew better.

Murielle had never come around. And Gilles was jealous. While she refrained from open mockery, her disregard for the customs and traditions associated with the worship of the Lord Aufeese made it truly clear her belief—or lack thereof. Her distrust of the Golden Child and of the gods in general had transitioned into outright atheism. Yet, she had received a vision. And Gilles, the patient and faithful servant of the Lord Aufeese, had received nothing. He prayed often and made abundant offerings, yet Murielle, his faithless and unrepentant wife, had received a gift of the gods.

Gilles stopped his pacing at the small wooden altar by the door. But today he could take heart. The vision for which he longed had finally come, today, in front of this very altar. It should have been a happy day for him. Yet, the circumstances which surrounded it squelched the joy he should be feeling.

It was so ordinary the way the vision had come to him. He had thought that when he received his vision that it would be something more spectacular. He had been kneeling at the altar and praying while Murielle and Emmeline argued about the situation. Gilles knelt on the dirt floor, his hand pressed firmly to his forehead, repeating the same words over and over. *Please Lord Aufeese, hear my prayer*. He was so frazzled by the news that he could not put his request into words or even make a coherent thought. He repeated the only words he could form in the maelstrom of his mind.

Gradually the sound of voices faded. He felt momentarily like he was falling, not quickly, more like floating down on a current of air as a bird might. He opened his eyes and realized that he was no longer in his house. He was standing now–not kneeling–in a corn field. Was this his own corn field? He could not be certain. The sun rose high and hot in the pale blue sky. The rows of cornstalks stood still and silent in the heat that Gilles could not feel. The stillness was broken by the drumming of approaching feet on the dirt. In the next row he saw Emmeline run past. She was dressed in breeches and her hair was pulled into a bun. She carried a paquet in one hand. She ran by, oblivious to her father standing in the next row.

"That was Emmeline," he found himself saying aloud.

Yes, it was, a voice replied that seemed to come from everywhere, but yet from nowhere. Gilles was not surprised to hear the voice. It sounded like his own voice, yet he knew somehow that it was not his own.

"Where is she going?"

She is going to the East.

"Why is she going to the East?"

It is the only way.

"The only way to what? What is in the East?"

The tavern called The Wild Hare and safety. She will be safe in the East at The Wild Hare.

Gilles found himself floating again, drifting on some unseen current. A gray mist surrounded him. It did not upset him, on the contrary he found it quite comforting. It was soft and warm, caressing him tenderly. He found himself back inside the house. At first, he thought that the vision was over, but he saw Murielle and realized that he was still under the influence of this strange vision. Murielle was alone and pacing the floor. She did not acknowledge his presence. On her face she wore a look of consternation. She stopped her pacing and went to a window. She looked out briefly and then resumed her pacing.

"That is Murielle," he said aloud. She did not hear him, and she continued her pacing.

Yes, it is, he heard his own voice say from far away yet right inside his head.

"What is she doing?'

She is waiting.

"For whom is she waiting?" He heard himself ask the question although he already knew the answer.

She is waiting for he who will come, he who must come.

There was a sharp rap at the door and Murielle stopped her pacing with a horrified look on her face. Gilles held his breath, afraid to see he who must come. But before he could see his wife open the door, he found himself floating upon the comforting gray mist again.

Presently he came out of the mist and found himself beside a narrow road. He looked around at the trees reaching high up into the pale blue sky, obscuring the brilliant summer sun. Shadows fell across the road bathing him in green coolness. He heard the drumming of feet again. This time it was the quick, hard sound of horse's hooves. He knew where he was. He was on the Straight Road, the road to Darloque. A horse and rider raced around a bend, passed him without a glance, and raced up a hill and out of sight.

"That was Gilles and Cheval," he said as if pointing out a most ordinary thing.

Yes, it was.

"Where is he going?" he asked flatly. It seemed natural in this vision to refer to himself in the third person. The man who rode by seemed like someone else altogether.

To Darloque.

"Why is he going to Darloque?"

To see the Old King.

"What can he do?"

He can do much. He can save her.

"How can he do that?"

He can. He will. That is all you need to know.

Gilles wanted to ask more but he had the strongest feeling that the vision's time was over. Before he could consider any more, the gray mist surrounded him again. He was floating once more, and when he opened his eyes, he found himself back inside the house, kneeling in front of the altar. Murielle and Emmeline were still bickering. He found it a most welcome sound.

Alas, the joy he felt as he rose from the floor did not last long. But it was only now that Gilles realized that the vision he had seen this morning was the vision he had been longing for all his life. He had been so overjoyed that he had found a way out of this terrible business with the Prince that it had been completely lost on him that this was a vision from the Golden Child.

He thought now, his pacing forgotten, that the vision was odd in its own way. He did not actually see the Golden Child. And the voice he heard was his own. But he felt that the vision was from Lord Aufeese, and it was he who had spoken to him. It had to be from the Golden Child.

Faith, he thought to himself, *I have faith that it was Lord Aufeese who spoke to me.* It was that same faith that let him believe that Murielle had a vision and that vision—not the changing of the wind—told her of the impending storm.

It had seemed odd to him back then, but he had quickly dismissed it. Now with much time on his hands, he pondered what he had put aside long ago. Murielle was a city girl. Her manners, dress, and style were all that of the city. What did she know of the farm? How could she know what the changing of the wind foretold? But Murielle had a rational and scientific mind. To her there were no miracles, no signs, no visions. To her everything in nature had a logical explanation and in the case of the unexplainable it was up to man to seek out the reason. All could be determined by logic and reason. Certainly, that rational mind of hers had spent time analyzing the weather.

Enough of that, he scolded himself as he resumed his pacing, *you dwell on this far too much. In any matter, it was not science that aided her but the unsolicited help from a god.* He knew this, he knew it, and he believed it. He possessed the faith that she lacked.

It was Murielle's lack of faith that disturbed him the most nowadays. He could not even pretend anymore that she was simply disinterested in the gods. Her open hostility toward anything related to the gods revealed her true feelings. Her outburst today was long overdue. She had long since stopped trying to hide how she rolled her eyes when he spoke of Lord Aufeese–although he had seen it long before she thought he did. She had for some time though, been letting slip disparaging comments here and there. At first, he had reprimanded her when she spoke ill of the Golden Child, but he had become slack in his chastisement, and as a result she had become less fearful over time of offending him. That was very evident by her behavior today.

Her tirade today had more than offended him though. It had hurt him. It had cut him like a sword, swiftly and violently. He had known the weapon was there, yet he had refused to believe her capable of using it, capable of using it on him anyway. She had cut him so deeply that he still felt it even now. He had forgiven her that grievous injury for that is what he had been taught to do. Yet, it still hurt. He found it hard to shake off the feeling.

The worst part of this task in the effort to save Emmeline was the waiting. Waiting gave one time to think–too much time. And it gave one time to think about things that were better left alone. But those thoughts came uninvited into the mind, knocking down doors, barging into rooms, and announcing themselves loudly to those present. The hurt he felt was no less obnoxious than any other unwanted thought. Finally, he gave in and let the hurt have its way with him.

Je suis desolé, she had told him. She had been ashamed; he had seen it in her eyes. He knew that she dearly wished she had not said what she had said. She would pay any price to take back the words, to undo the effects of her unbridled rage and frustration. But there was another look in her eyes: relief. He saw it there underneath the shame. In a way, in a strange way, she seemed to be glad of that cathartic episode. It was the release of everything she had been thinking for a long time, thoughts building up inside of her, boiling and raging inside her, seeking release. This was the catalyst: when she saw that her only child was in danger—mortal danger Gilles reminded himself—the thoughts proved too much to contain. All the feelings she had been holding in, all the things never said, finally spilled out in a great flood of rage, and yes, hate.

Gilles saw all of this in his wife's eyes. He did not need a vision from Lord Aufeese to see this. He had been with her for so long that he could read every expression on her face. He knew what she was thinking before she even knew. He had watched as her patience with him deteriorated, and deep in the back of his mind he knew this day would come. Gilles stopped and ran his hands over his bald head. He truly wished she had more faith. *More faith?* he asked himself. He wished she had any faith at all.

An urgent banging brought Gilles back to his small farmhouse. He looked to the altar of the Lord Aufeese with the carved wooden likeness of the god standing over the offering bowl brimming with the sad fruits of his bitter harvest. He approached the altar and ran his hand over the statuette. He could see the flaws: the head that was not quite right, the feet that were a little too large. And was that the exact expression he had hoped to achieve on the god's face? He could still do better. There was much room for improvement. Perhaps he would carve a new likeness and eliminate those nagging flaws.

The banging came again, harder, more urgent. Gilles ignored it and continued to run his hand over the statue. But there would always be flaws. Deep down he knew this. No matter how many times he carved it there would still be flaws, he would always find them, and they would always nag at him. The god himself was flawed after all, but his flaws were not Gilles's flaws. Gilles was human and his imperfections grossly outweighed the few trivial blemishes of a god.

But Gilles could still not ignore the faults in his statue. He began to think—and not for the first time but certainly more clearly than before—that perhaps he had dedicated his life to the wrong god. Perhaps he had taken the wrong path altogether. He had made a choice when he was younger. When he came to a crossroads in his life with two clear, distinct, and viable paths, he had made a choice. Perhaps he had taken the wrong road. It occurred to him that had he taken the other road, chosen the other option, none of the present events would be taking place. His family would not be near ruin, his wife would not be out upon a fool's errand, and most importantly, his daughter would not be in grave danger.

"Please tell me I have made the right choice," he pleaded to the altar, his hand falling still upon its polished surface. No answer came. The statue only stared mutely and indifferently out into space.

The banging upon the door came even harder this time, shaking the door frame and causing a few strands of thatch to drift down from the ceiling. The doves fluttered about briefly before settling on a rafter again.

"Who could that be at such a time as this," Gilles spat and then cursed under his breath. Travelers spying their home from the main road were always stopping in for rest and refreshment. Murielle was always the gracious host, particularly to those who passed through on a regular basis. Although Gilles was the one who reminded her of the maxim of hospitality, deep inside he resented always playing the role of gracious host to yet another weary guest. *Non*, he thought, *I have made my choice and I must deal with what comes.*

"Whatever that may be," he finished aloud.

With that he took his hand from the altar and yanked open the door to see just who could be bothering him at such a time with such a crisis going on. He opened the door to see a pair of brilliant blue-green eyes staring back at him.

"Well, hello there!" the visitor exclaimed.

CHAPTER EIGHT

Emmeline screamed again and dragged herself back though the wheat, clawing the ground with her hands, kicking feebly with her feet, trying to put as much distance as she could between herself and the owner of those vivid blue-green eyes. She left a flattened trail of wheat as she backed further into the field. The trail she left would tell her pursuer exactly where to find her, but her strength finally left her, and she collapsed on the ground, uncaring. Her breath came in a rapid pant, her eyes bloomed with panic. She could think of nothing; the blind fear had stripped her of even the thought that she was going to die in this wheat field. She lay on flattened stalks of wheat, gazing up at the other stalks standing tall around her, but she was unaware of them. Her ears were full of the pounding of her heart and the quickening of her breath, but from somewhere far away she heard the rustling. She tilted her head up and thought she saw a few stalks of wheat move. Then again. Then she was sure of the movement. The rustling came louder, yet still muted by her extreme panic.

The Prince had finally caught her. The handsome prince had caught her and was going to take her away, far away from her home. She would never see Mama and Papa again. She did not understand how such a handsome man could do something so terrible and hurtful. Were not all beautiful things good? As she saw it in her immature mind, external beauty was the mirror of the soul. The beautiful outside reflected the good inside. It was crime against nature that a person of unquestionable beauty could be so ugly inside.

The stalks of wheat rustled loudly as her pursuer approached. Emmeline still could not see him, only the nearby wheat gently moving. She froze. Her flight had sapped her energy; she could not move any more even if she wanted. *This is it*, she thought. *He has caught me, and I am going away forever.* With a last great rustle, the wheat nearest her parted and the owner of the blue-green eyes came into the open area of flattened wheat Emmeline had created.

"Well, there you are!" her pursuer cried.

Emmeline sat up and screamed again. She had thought she did not have the breath to do it, but the scream came anyway: long, loud, and piercing.

"Indeed!" he said, looking offended, "Now that is quite rude of you. Have your mother and father taught you no manners?"

The scream tapered off slowly as Emmeline's eyes grew wider and wider. It was not the Prince after her in the wheat. It was...

"The Lord Aufeese," she said in a hoarse whisper.

"And a pleasure it must be for you to make my acquaintance," he replied as he extended a dainty paw.

Emmeline stared at the paw dumbly. She was not sure whether she should take it in her hand, or kneel before it, or whatever else. This was too much to take in. Only moments ago, she had been running from the Prince and now she was in a wheat field face to face with one of the gods. The Lord Aufeese withdrew his paw with a shrug. He looked at it if considering some aspect of its appearance and then gave it a brisk cleaning with his tongue.

"Oh, no!" Emmeline exclaimed as she scrambled to her knees. "The Prince!"

"Who?" asked Aufeese, cocking his head to one side, his ears askew.

"The Prince!" she said through clenched teeth. "He was chasing me, trying to take me away from my family. He chased me through that pasture and almost had caught me when I landed in this field of wheat." She looked up at the Lord Aufeese. "Down! Down! You must get down before he sees you!"

The god continued to look at Emmeline quizzically until a look of understanding dawned on his face. He put his paws to his mouth and giggled high and girlishly.

"Oh yes! Indeed!" He giggled again. "You mean Henri!"

"Yes, that is him," she hissed. "And if you do not duck down, he will see you, and he will find me."

Lord Aufeese smoothed the golden fur behind his ear with a forepaw and laughed again in that same annoying laugh.

"Why do you laugh?" Emmeline hissed again. "Get down now before he sees you!"

"Oh, human girl," Aufeese said, continuing to giggle, "that was not Henri."

"What do you mean? I heard him! He chased me into this wheat field!"

"Indeed!" The Golden Child continued to giggle with his high girlish laugh, which Emmeline was finding increasingly irritating. "That was not Henri pursuing you."

Emmeline looked at the god. A look of consternation crossed her face. This was not funny at all. "If it was not the Prince then who was it?"

Aufeese giggled even more with his paws pressed daintily to his lips. He tried to speak but could not form the words because of his laughter.

"Who was it then, tell me!"

"It was I!" Aufeese squealed with laughter, placing a delicate paw to his chest.

"What?" Emmeline cried incredulously. "What do you mean?"

"No one was pursuing you," he laughed. "I made you hear those sounds so that you would come here faster!"

"What!" she nearly screamed, the fear she had felt only moments ago melting away.

"Well, you must admit that you were moving quite slowly," Aufeese said, his laughter returning to the shrill giggle. "You clearly needed a little prodding."

Emmeline's fear had completely evaporated. Rage flared up in her like a flame. She had inherited her mother's temper and had used it with increasing frequency over the last two growing seasons. She shot to her feet. "I do not believe your nerve!" she growled.

Emmeline suddenly realized that she was now looking down at Lord Aufeese. He was sitting erect on his haunches, his head carried high, yet the top of his head did not even come close to her shoulders. Emmeline was not a tall girl by any standard, and she was accustomed to looking up at both her parents–and most people for that matter. Looking down at someone was unusual enough, but looking down at a god, this god in particular, took her breath away and left her slightly unsettled. "You are short," she said abruptly.

"Indeed!" replied Lord Aufeese, the smile fading from his lips as his ears lay down on his neck. "Well, you may be angry at my deception, but that is no cause to be insulting!" He craned his neck and pulled down an ear between his paws. He considered it carefully and gave it a careful couple of licks before letting it go.

Emmeline felt a slight twinge of regret at her outburst. This was a god she had been raging against after all. His frown and his blue-green stare cut through her, and she had to turn away. She looked at the circle of flattened wheat she had made when she had crashed into the field. She was even more sorry for that. It was a waste of a good crop and especially during this drought. Her father would chastise her for the waste. Her remorse heightened when she took in the sheer size of the damage.

Emmeline turned back to the Lord Aufeese. He was still frowning, but now he was craning his neck again trying to get at his left shoulder. He noticed Emmeline staring at him. His smile returned and his eyes became kind again, his ears erect again and attentive. His brilliant blue-green eyes were compelling, therefore she found it a struggle to keep her anger, but she had also inherited her mother's stubbornness and she fought hard to remain angry.

Lord Aufeese appeared as an ordinary rabbit, his blue-green eyes, golden fur, and his larger than normal size being the only qualities which betrayed his godly nature. In the bright light of the near noonday sun, his fur absolutely glowed with a surreal golden brilliance. His ears were relatively short when compared to the rest of his body but increased his overall height almost to her own. His head was full and rounded and his body the same, giving him a well-fed yet compact and muscular appearance. His body contained all that was beautiful in the wild rabbits Emmeline had seen, and that beauty was amplified even more by his godly qualities.

He sat up on his haunches, his front paws held in front of him close to his chest, his head cocked slightly to one side like a wild rabbit curiously examining a stranger. He did not blink. He watched her and smiled, silently. Emmeline watched his nose wriggle as he breathed and saw his whiskers twitch from time to time. He groomed himself as a normal rabbit would but with perhaps a little more frequency than a normal rabbit. Just as she considered this, the Golden Child stretched out a hind leg, splayed his toes, and cleaned them vigorously. He saw her watching him and put his leg down, a smile returning to his lips.

"It is just that..." she began, trying to collect her thoughts, "It is just that... *je ne sais pas*... I expected you to be... um... taller."

Aufeese began to frown. His nostrils flared slightly as he breathed, and his ears slowly tilted back.

"That is," she began again before he could say anything, "from all the stories my papa had told me, I always pictured you as a giant."

"Oh my," he said, waving a paw dismissively at her, his ears flushing a bright crimson underneath his golden fur. "Now, we all cannot be giants. We are each made to a proper size that suits our needs. But do not forget," the Golden Child said turning serious again, "It is not our stature which defines us, but our deeds."

Emmeline smiled inwardly. It was easy for one to dismiss the importance of height when one lacked that very quality. But she dared not say this.

A slight breeze had picked up causing the standing wheat to sway ever so slightly. She looked out over the field, watching the wheat move in its own eddies and currents. She imagined that this must what the sea must look like. And this was the closest she would ever get to the sea now. It seemed so long ago, an eternity since she was promised a trip to the sea by a handsome, charming prince. That had been a lie she supposed. Or maybe not. Perhaps she would have been able to stand on the edge of the sea and look out upon its magnificence, seeing what those people in the stories had seen. Perhaps she would be able to see that but never be able to return home.

She reached out to some of the wheat swaying at the edge of the large circle of destruction. The heads were full and ripe, golden with a touch of green still on them. Ready for harvest. The heads were big, bigger than she had ever seen and bigger than they should be considering the lack of rain this growing season.

Emmeline was marveling at this when Aufeese spoke up. "Yes, the wheat is ready for harvest." He clasped his paws together. "And what a harvest it shall be! Glorious, simply glorious!" He smoothed some ruffled fur on his paws.

But who shall receive the fruits of this harvest? she thought. *Who should feast so well on this grain while my family may very well starve?* Emmeline grew angry again, sinking deeper into that well of ire inherited from her mother. *Who has been more pious than my father? Who could be more deserving of this bounty than my father who has given everything to this god?*

Emmeline looked around at the great field of golden wheat that neither she nor her father nor her mother would ever taste. The wheat waved at her, tantalizing, taunting her, mocking her. Or did it? Eddies and currents flowed, beckoning her as the cool water of the lake beckons on a lazy summer day when all the chores are completed, and nothing remains to be done. The wheat waved to her seductively, enticing Emmeline, beckoning her to share its golden embrace. She felt sure that if she were to walk to the edge of the swaying wheat that she could dive in and swim in a great golden ocean more refreshing than any lake or sea could ever be.

Her head snapped around suddenly breaking the spell. This was not right. The area of flattened wheat was quite large. *I did not make this*, she thought, *this is far too large for me to have made.* And then, *What is happening here?*

A shrill whistle broke her from her thoughts. Emmeline looked around in near panic. It was a long continuous sound, like nothing she had heard before. She had lost all sense of direction. As she looked around all she saw was wheat, an endless ocean of wheat. The corn field she had emerged from was gone and nothing could be seen in any direction but wheat waving out to the horizon in all directions. The chariot of the sun rode in the center of the sky so she could not tell which direction she had come from nor which direction she should go. The shrill whistle continued, filling her mind, maddening with its sound.

"Indeed! Indeed!" Aufeese cried, clapping his forepaws together excitedly and bouncing on his haunches. "It is time! Oh joy!"

"What is that terrible noise!" Emmeline cried. "Make it stop!"

"Oh, you silly girl," the Golden Child said as he examined an ear. "What do you fear? Indeed."

The god of the harvest turned and walked over to a small stone hearth. Emmeline's eyes grew wide for it had not been there a moment ago. The hearth stood over to one side of the huge area of flattened wheat. It was small, perhaps only large enough to bake two loaves of bread at one time. Wood burned inside, sending out sparse gray smoke drifting straight into the air, undisturbed by whatever breeze stirred the sea of wheat. The top of the hearth was flat and upon this level surface sat a strange pot with steam pouring out of a spout at its side. The shrill whistle issued from the pot.

Lord Aufeese turned and walked toward the hearth. "Silly girl," he repeated, looking over his shoulder at her. "It is time for tea."

Emmeline's grew wide in amazement. Suddenly the god's ears shot up in alarm and his body went rigid. The Lord Aufeese quickly, awkwardly, maneuvered himself to the far side of the hearth so that it stood between them. A smile returned to his face, then he craned his head trying to get at his left shoulder. He returned his eyes to her and pretended that nothing had happened, but Emmeline still had seen. Still, she was more concerned about the strange shrieking pot upon the hearth which had appeared just moments ago.

"T?" Emmeline asked, not understanding what Lord Aufeese had said.

"Yes, tea."

"*Je ne comprends pas.*"

"Indeed. Surely you jest," he clucked as he reached for the pot. "Your parents have certainly served you tea."

The hearth was small, but the diminutive god had to reach up to grasp the wooden handle directly opposite the screaming spout. The shrill whistle began to die as soon as he removed the pot from the hearth and transferred it to a shorter stone table more suited to the god's small stature. On that table was a similar spouted pot but his one was made of fine silver. Emmeline looked at the second pot wondrously.

"Yes, I know. It should be made of gold, but it was a gift." The god paused. "Indeed."

The Golden Child picked up a small, perforated silver ball hanging from a fine silver chain and twisted it apart. He placed something dark that looked like leaves into one half and reassembled the ball. The god removed the lid from the silver pot and placed the curious silver ball inside. He then took the screaming pot and poured its contents into the silver pot. Steaming water poured into it. Plain, steaming water. Lord Aufeese worked at this endeavor with the casual air of someone who has performed such a task quite often, but Emmeline had never in her life seen such an operation. When he seemed satisfied that he had poured enough into the silver pot, Aufeese set down the screaming pot and took the silver chain, bobbing the ball in the steaming water one, two, three, four times.

Emmeline found all this too incredible to believe. Her father had told her many of the tales of the gods, particularly the Lord Aufeese. Most of them were stories of the gods and their interactions with man. But never in any of the tales of the gods had any of them, particularly the Lord Aufeese, made such a bizarre performance.

The god of the harvest stood before the two pots, steam drifting lazily up from them and dissipating into the air. He said nothing. Emmeline watched his nostrils move as he breathed. In, out, in, out. After a moment or two of this awkward silence he began to groom himself again, apparently finding minute imperfections only he could see. Emmeline began to wonder if she should say something if only to break the silence.

The Lord Aufeese looked up from his grooming and saw Emmeline staring at him. He cleared his throat and twitched his long whiskers. His eyes darted momentarily to his left as he seemed to want to crane over his left shoulder but instead, he gave a slight sigh and muttered "Indeed," more to himself than to his guest. He grasped the fine silver chain and after giving the ball a final dunk, seemed satisfied that it had completed whatever task he required of it. He laid it aside then placed a lid upon the silver pot which he in turn moved to a silver tray with two white porcelain cups and a variety of other items upon it.

"Come now," he said brightly, "let us enjoy tea."

The Golden Child, with the tray in his paws, sidled to the right. He kept his left shoulder always turned away from Emmeline as he approached a small table and two dainty chairs that she knew had not been there before. She was drawn away from thoughts of the god's left shoulder to the intricately carved furniture. The chairs were quite lovely, she thought. Lovely was an accurate description for them. Her father was particularly good at woodwork, but nothing he had made compared to the swirling, organic complexity of this beautiful table and these magnificent chairs.

The Lord Aufeese set the silver tray with strange pot on the table. Thin clouds of steam drifted lazily into the air, dissipating in the summer sun.

"Come, human child," he said, "sit and have tea before it grows cold." His smile was wide and pleasant, his blue-green eyes beckoning. His golden fur glowed in the bright sunlight.

Emmeline hesitated. She looked again into the vast wheat field. The wheat waved and flowed in the stillness. *So much like the sea,* she thought, *so welcoming and so comforting.* She turned back to the god of the harvest standing at the ornate furniture, smiling and patient, in the middle of an impossibly large clearing within this infinite wheat field. Even though he seemed concerned that the contents of his strange pot should get cold, he was perfectly willing to wait until she was ready to share his hospitality. The last of Emmeline's anger slipped away as she took a shuffling step across the stone floor toward the Golden Child.

Emmeline approached the small setting and stopped.

"Please," said the god in a civil tone, "be seated and I will serve."

Emmeline was not sure what he intended to serve but she nodded in agreement. She looked at the silver tray Lord Aufeese had set upon the table. In the center sat the silver pot, steaming slowly from its strange spout. Two silver spoons and two small white porcelain cups with dainty handles sat on small white saucers, one flanking each side of the pot. Surrounding them was a small array of lidded silver containers containing the gods only knew what.

"Please," he said again, but this time sounding just slightly impatient, "let us sit and have tea. It shall be quite splendid."

Nodding, only half aware of her surroundings, Emmeline sat in the chair to the right of Aufeese. Keeping his left shoulder always turned from her, the god poured dark liquid from the silver pot into the nearest cup and placed it, saucer and all, in front of her. He then filled his cup and sat down in the other chair. Emmeline stared mutely at the steaming cup in front of her. On his side of the table Lord Aufeese took one of the silver containers and poured a small quantity of milk into his cup. He made a couple of dainty stirs with a silver spoon and laid it upon the saucer. Seemingly satisfied that his tea was to his liking he took up the cup, his last claw–what would be a pinkie on a human–extended primly and took a dainty sip from his cup. He sighed contentedly. He took another demure sip then looked at Emmeline still staring at her cup on the table.

"Indeed!" he said, his head cocked to one side, "Is it not to your liking? It is my own personal blend: exceptionally fine indeed."

Emmeline said nothing and continued to stare at the cup.

The Golden Child's whiskers twitched. "If you do not like it black then you may add whatever you like to it. I promise I shall not be offended. I have seen some... *unique* items added to perfectly good tea. Indeed."

Emmeline did not respond. Her eyes did not move from the cup.

Lord Aufeese shifted in his chair, turning slightly more to his left. He took another sip from his cup and smiled.

"What do you like in your tea?"

Nothing.

A forlorn look crossed the god's face as he changed his glance from Emmeline to his teacup then back to Emmeline. He took another sip from his own cup. He smacked his lips with a quizzical look as if trying to detect something wrong with the tea which he knew to be perfect.

"Do you like milk? Do you care for honey? Some prefer sugar, but I do not. Indeed."

He rummaged through the containers on the tray. "Indeed! I know. Would you like some lemon?"

Emmeline snapped out of her torpor and stared at him dumbfounded. "*Le monde?*"

"Oh, yes! *Le monde*, indeed!" The Golden Child burst into his shrill girlish laughter. "No, no, silly girl! Not *the world*, only lemon!" He put his paw demurely over his mouth as he giggled.

Emmeline looked at him, baffled.

"Indeed!" the god said through his laughter. "That pun was

simply too witty. Oh, we are having such a splendid time! Indeed!" He took another sip, his final claw extended ever so daintily.

"But, oh!" said Lord Aufeese, his ears snapping to attention, "There is something I simply must share with you!" He leaned in toward Emmeline and began to speak in a hushed tone as someone sharing some particularly racy gossip.

"There will come a man, a storyteller, who tells the story of the world. He tells the tales others have told and also tells his own. One day he will die when others die, but he will continue to tell his tales."

The Golden Child leaned back in his chair, nodding his head knowingly, apparently certain that Emmeline knew what he was talking about. Emmeline had no idea.

Aufeese took another dainty sip of tea and exclaimed, "Oh yes, we are truly having a splendid time. Indeed!"

Non, Emmeline thought, *we are not having a splendid time.* This was becoming entirely too strange for her. *Perhaps I will just drink this "tea" or whatever it is, and everything will start to make sense somehow.* She took up the cup, still warm to the touch, and raised it to her lips, but she never had the chance to taste it.

High in the air before her, hung a stone archway. Stone by stone it was slowly weaving its way downward toward a stone floor she had not noticed before. Out in the distance beyond the archway the wheat continued to ripple in its eddies and currents. Emmeline glanced around her. In four directions archways hung high in the air, supported by nothing: one at each point of the compass. A shadow passed over her and she saw with great alarm that a rib-vault was forming above them, blotting out the sun as it wove down stone by stone to meet the archways. *Non*, she thought. She turned to the Lord Aufeese, panic rising inside her. But he merely looked contentedly at his cup of tea.

Stone by stone the rib-vault closed the gap to the archways which had now reached the floor. Through the each one of the archways she saw a stone corridor forming. Stone by stone the walls built up from the stone floor weaving steadily to meet long vaulted ceilings which wove their way down. The sun was now completely gone as the hall in which they sat completed itself. Yet, it was still rather bright. Emmeline saw multiple torches set in ornate gilded sconces regularly spaced on the walls of each corridor. Brighter than any of the torches though, was the golden glow which emanated from the Lord Aufeese. The glow from his fur was brilliant but not blinding. He was beautiful and radiant inside the dark stone hall. And although she could not see it anymore, she knew that the wheat was there outside the walls, flowing and eddying, rippling in its subtle currents.

"Non!" Emmeline cried as she stood up abruptly. She rose too quickly, and the chair clattered down on the stone floor. Even with the rushes spread around, the sound was quite loud in the large hall. She bumped her thigh against the table as her teacup fell from her hands and shattered on the surface, spilling unsampled tea everywhere. The silver tray slid across the table, sloshing the contents of the containers, and spilling some. Lord Aufeese snatched up his own teacup before any of his tea could be spilled and held it close to him, protectively, as one might hold a precious jewel. Emmeline's saucer rolled across the table and then off the edge. She watched it as it fell slowly, taking an eternity to travel the short space, tumbling over and over, then shattering on the floor with a bright sound that seemed to echo forever throughout the hall.

And then it was gone. The sun shone bright upon her again, the weight of the sunlight a heavy burden as it was before. The wheat had returned but it no longer waved to her. The air was still, and the wheat stood silently, mute and unassuming.

The table remained, and Emmeline's chair lay on the ground within the small circle of flattened wheat. Lord Aufeese still sat across from her clutching his teacup in a protective grip and looking at her with a look that could have been either amazement or horror.

"No," she said again, her voice sounding too loud in the still air. But she did not care. "No, we are not having a splendid time."

And there it was, spoken out loud, and it could not be taken back. The words gave her power. The words were like a magic incantation which broke the last remnants of the spell once and for all. Her rage welled up in her again, spreading through her like wildfire.

"We are not?" replied the god incredulously. "But we are having tea and pleasant conversation."

"No, we are not having a splendid time," she repeated. Her voice grew stronger, more confident. "And I do not understand why we are having "tea" when my parents are in such distress!"

Lord Aufeese was taken aback at this sudden outburst of anger. "Well... Ahh... Hmm..." His ears drooped slightly, and he looked forlornly into his cup. "Indeed."

Emmeline snatched up a handful of wheat stalks and shook them at him. "Just look at these! Full and ripe yet we have not had rain in ages!"

Lord Aufeese shifted slightly to his left in the chair.

She shook the stalks again. "These are perfect, yet my father's crops wither in the fields!"

"Well," replied the god haughtily, "this wheat is for a higher purpose that you simply do not understand."

"By the gods's ears, I do not understand," Emmeline shouted. "I do not understand how you can neglect a man like my father who is as faithful a man to you as you will ever find!"

"Indeed. True, indeed. But you still–"

"My father prays to you every day, several times a day. I remember when he carved that altar in our house. Mother thought it was a waste of time, but he spent so much time on it, working many late nights after long days in the field. I remember! He wanted it to be perfect. Perfect like you."

"Well, yes. It is a fine altar, and I think it is quite good. Indeed."

"But you are not perfect, are you?" Emmeline continued as though Aufeese had not spoken. "I know the truth my father refuses to admit."

Lord Aufeese again shifted ever more slightly to his left. The haughty look returned to his face. "You could not possibly know anything, human child."

"I know that you, the Golden Child, Mava's favorite son, bear a black mark upon your left shoulder. Mava put it there just out of your reach as punishment for your vanity!"

Lord Aufeese's blue-green eyes narrowed, his ears lay flat on his back and his nostrils flared angrily. "You impudent child!"

"Everyone knows it is there, and that Mava put it there because you are so obsessed with your own beauty. Everyone knows! Ha! Everyone has heard the story of how you got it." Emmeline stopped only long enough to draw a breath. "It is only foolish believers like my father who ignore it. And I have seen it now for myself, so I know. I know!"

Lord Aufeese seethed with rage. His lips parted slightly to reveal a glimpse of sharp white incisors. "You dreadful, dreadful girl," he hissed. "Why I should–"

"*Que?*" Emmeline asked with a haughtiness of her own. "What are you going to do? Blind me like you did Senus?"

The Golden Child, Mava's favorite son, the Lord Aufeese, shrank back suddenly at this. His eyes softened and became wide, his ears rose up slightly. "No!" he cried. He clutched his cup in his forepaws closely under his chin. "No!"

"*Oui,*" Emmeline said, her voice rising again. "Everyone knows that story as well."

Lord Aufeese sat rigid in his chair, his blue-green eyes wide and his mouth open slightly. His ears drooped limply.

His head drooped down. "I never..." he said quietly into his teacup.

"Oh yes you did!" Emmeline snapped back. "Everyone knows the story of how Senus stayed with you, writing your story, then one day he saw that infernal spot of yours and spoke of it. And in your arrogance, you blinded him simply because he saw your flaw. That infernal spot!"

"Infernal, indeed."

There was a long moment of silence. An eternity as the Lord

Aufeese stared into his teacup and Emmeline fumed across the table from him.

"I am finished with you," she said flatly.

Before Lord Aufeese could reply, Emmeline turned and walked away from the table. She found her paquet at the edge of the flattened wheat. She slung the bundle over her shoulder and marched off into the wheat toward the East, tying her hair back in a ponytail as she did. The Lord Aufeese watched her go. He sat, holding his teacup forlornly and watched her grow smaller in the distance.

With a start the Golden Child jumped up and trotted to the edge of the flattened wheat. "No! Wait!" he cried out to her. "You must come back!" He stood up on his toes to see her better as she disappeared into the golden distance. "I must..." he tapered off.

He groomed some mussed fur on the back of his paw then craned his neck over his left shoulder trying to get at that cursed black mark. He looked at his empty teacup still clutched in his paws. His ears drooping sadly, he let out a frustrated sigh and turned back to the small table. He poured himself another cup of tea.

It was cold.

CHAPTER NINE

MURIELLE APPROACHED the South Gates of Darloque, the sun well into its westward descent from the meridian, keeping Cheval at a full gallop. He was sweaty, foaming, and tired, but in great spirits. Murielle reined the horse back as she approached the gates and, although nearly exhausted, the animal seemed reluctant to slow. The handful of guards watched her approach with languid interest. As Murielle slowed the horse to a trot, they gripped their weapons tighter out of habit rather than from any perceived threat. *Such is the way of soldiers during peacetime*, Murielle thought idly.

She sighed. Father would be appalled at the lax behavior of these guards. A couple of young faces stood at the post. These boys certainly had never experienced real battle. She snapped a very proper military salute as she approached the gates. The older guards snapped to attention and returned her salute automatically, while the younger ones responded with half-hearted waves. These younger guards looked at her curiously, obviously wondering why a simple country woman would be saluting them. Murielle smiled at them, glad that her father was not here to see them. Glad for them anyhow.

The South Gates were not as massive as the great Eastern Gates, but they were still quite impressive. Great oak beams reinforced with iron kept this end of the city protected from attackers. There was only the one set of gates here, and given the difficulty–nay, impossibility–of moving a large army up the Straight Road and given the fact that the castle was at the opposite end of the city in the northwest corner, the South Gates were generally considered safe. These facts and the long-standing peace certainly contributed to the lackadaisical attitude of the guards here.

Cheval ambled gently through the gates. Murielle noticed that the guards had quickly forgotten her, engaged in some benign conversation. Knowing what she knew about guards and soldiers, she was sure that their talk was limited to drinking, women, or gambling. Or perhaps a combination of all three.

Murielle reined Cheval toward a stable not far from the gates. Stables near the gates were typically more expensive than those deeper inside the city, but she knew the horse was tired from his run, even though he did not seem to think so.

She patted his neck. "You have done well today my friend. Let us get you to this place so you can have water and hay. And perhaps a handful of oats if I can negotiate it."

The stable owner greeted Murielle warmly. "*Bonjour, madame*, welcome to my humble stable." He swept a hand toward his stable in which only a few horses were kept. A stable boy was offering a bucket of water to a sorrel mare. He was an older man, heavyset but not what she would call fat. His head was clean shaven as was his face, and when he turned to greet her, she saw that the entire right side of his face was covered in scars. He wore an eyepatch over his right eye. His appearance was hideous, but Murielle had seen enough disfigurements as result of the wars to render her immune to any show of revulsion.

"Good sir, I wish to keep my horse in your stable for a short while and retrieve him before the day is gone," Murielle said quickly.

The stableman nodded and gave his going rate for a day's board.

Murielle nodded. "Not much business today I see, so I can expect a better rate to keep a tired horse who will not trouble you for the entire day." Murielle cut through the polite formalities and drove straight into bargaining. She was on a mission, with no time for civilities.

The stableman replied, ready to bargain. "I do have overhead nevertheless and when business is slow, I need the money ever so more."

"If you wish to turn away business when you are in such need, that is your prerogative," she replied coldly.

The stableman looked at her quizzically. "*Excusez-moi*, madame, but I feel I should know you."

Murielle's face remained placid but inside she clenched. "*Non*," she said calmly, shaking her head, "I do not believe so. I have not been to the city in a long time. I am but a poor farm woman who wishes to stable her horse at a fair price."

The stableman nodded his head slowly. Murielle saw a light of recognition dawn in his eyes. "*Oui*, I see." He was silent for a time, too long a time to suit her. Just when the silence was becoming uncomfortable the stableman spoke again.

"*Oui*, a poor farm woman certainly would want a fair price. However, if you are who my eye believes you to be, then you should not be asking for a fair price under that condition." He crossed his arms over his broad chest and looked down at Murielle.

"Surely your eye deceives you," she replied, her placid face a mask covering a growing discomfort. She did not recognize the stableman at all, but he surely knew her. "I *am* but a *poor* farm woman, and I do not have much money, so I merely ask for a fair price, especially since my horse shall not require a full day's board." Murielle's placidity finally broke and she glared critically at the stableman.

"*Non*, my eye..." The stableman trailed off then quickly changed his approach. "*Non, non*. I will charge you half my normal rate to stable your horse today. For if you are who my eye says you are then consider it as gratitude for a past business relationship. If by some chance my eye deceives me," he shrugged, "then enjoy the benefits of an old stableman's foolish mistake." He snapped his fingers, and the boy took the horse back into the stables.

Murielle could not find the words to reply. Her face returned to an impassive expression, and she stared blankly at the stableman. Finally, she handed him coins with a low *"Merci beaucoup."* She saw the boy had already removed Cheval's saddle and was giving him a rubdown.

Murielle turned and walked solemnly toward the street, but the stableman called her back. In a low voice he said, "The city is different in these dark times than you may remember, my *poor farm woman.* Caution is advisable and discretion most necessary."

With those final words floating in her head, Murielle turned up the street, making her way toward the castle. Once out of sight of the stables, she cursed herself. "Fool!" Realizing she had spoken aloud she cursed herself again. A man walking in the other direction looked at her strangely and increased his pace. Murielle cursed herself a third time, this time only in her head.

Blest be Mava's many litters, she cursed, *why did I need to try to bargain with that stableman?* Murielle wished she had brought a head scarf or some other covering with her. She had not thought about being recognized. The imminent crisis had pushed that thought from her head, and her greatest concern had been that the Old King would *not* recognize her. Murielle calmed herself. She needed to remain calm. She would need a clear head to get into the castle and to the Old King. Of greater concern: will the Old King recognize her? If he did not, then this trip was for naught and Gilles was right after all. *And I may very well lose what is most precious to me in the whole world.*

An old woman came down the street pulling a small cart filled with clayware jugs. Murielle guessed the jugs were empty by the easy manner in which she pulled the cart down the cobbled street. The woman wore a glum expression, but when she passed, she offered Murielle a wan smile. It occurred to Murielle suddenly that she had only seen four people since entering the city. Darloque was a large city and even inside the South Gates, the streets should be bustling with activity. She looked back down the street. The old woman had disappeared, and Murielle was alone again.

Darloque was not simply an old city, it was an ancient city. The city is mentioned in some of the oldest records known to exist. And even in those the city is called ancient. Not even the most expert scholars knew how old it was. "This city has always been," they said with finality. Hence, we call it The Eternal City. The people said, "It has always been and will always be." Murielle was not sure of that assessment. She had seen a lot of changes in her life and the destruction of many things people had thought immutable. Things changed, people died, cities fell.

The great walled city of Darloque possessed four gates, one at each point of the compass. Being that the South Gates were fed by the Straight Road, which was not conducive to heavy cartage traffic, the southern end of the city was not a hub of business activity. Small dwellings lined the streets interspersed with small businesses providing necessities for the people who lived here. It was not a wealthy neighborhood but certainly not poor. One could feel reasonably safe walking down these streets. Murielle had not been to this part of the city in an exceedingly long time, but it seemed as though there were more pubs here than she remembered and the buildings looked a little grubbier. Perhaps she should amend "reasonably safe" to "questionably safe."

Just then, she passed a pub on her side of the street. From the open doorway came the sounds of merriment. Murielle frowned. It was far too early for decent people to be engaged at a pub. A man's voice rose above the rest as he broke into a popular song about returning home after a long journey. She had heard it before from travelers who stopped at her farm from time to time. It was a merry song, and it usually made her smile when guests sang it to her, but now it gave her a chill. Further up the street she heard young voices shouting. Two boys emerged from a side street arguing. "Go home now!" one shouted angrily to the other. Still further along she came upon a young man standing at the door of a dwelling, a large sack at his feet. A young woman opened the door. With a squeal she leapt into his arms. "I am so happy you are home!" she cried.

If Gilles were here, she thought, *he would think these events to be signs.* "Signs from the gods," she said aloud, looking around to make sure no one had heard. *Coincidence*, Murielle thought. Her father had taught her to see the world for what it really was: rational and ordered. He shunned superstitious worship of the gods and instead followed the doctrines of science and reason. Although a knight in the service of the Old King, he was of a rare breed. He was an educated knight. He read the classic masters, Dulco, Sergius, and Marcellus, as well as modern thinkers Lucien de Frévent, Geffroi de La Chapelle-d'Angillon, and Theodose de Boiscommun.

"Nonsense," she said aloud, thinking of Gilles's propensity for reading signs into ordinary activity. Murielle slammed her fist into her thigh. She must cease talking to herself out loud. If someone thought her mad, or just peculiar, she would never get in to see the Old King.

In Murielle's childhood home her father did keep the customary images of the war god. He was a soldier after all. An altar stood by the door, used more by guests than by the man of the house. A bronze relief of Bellicor hung on the wall of the great hall, and a few other pieces were placed in conspicuous places around the manor. Affectations of a pious soldier in the Old King's service.

Yet they were not completely hollow gestures. Richard knew the power of the war god's image. It motivated men, gave them focus in war. Dulco said as much in his writings. Theodose de Boiscommun elaborated more on the subject in his famous treatise "On Gods and Men". Boiscommun wrote that it was not the gods themselves that gave a man courage, or strength, or wisdom, but the belief in the gods which gave him the focus to find those qualities within himself. All good qualities resided naturally in each man, Boiscommun reasoned, hidden beneath layers of unreason built up by society through religious repression of man's reason. Ironically, at a critical juncture in a man's life, focus upon a particular god caused him to temporarily break through the layers of unreason and to find the reason hidden within. Boiscommun further stated that if completely freed from the oppression of religion and its trivial ceremonies, a man could once and for all strip away all unreason and live a life of reason, as it is his natural state. If all men shook off the chains of religious oppression, and embraced their true natures of reason, society would become the peaceful, ordered state it was meant to be.

Many thought that Boiscommun's concept of the "critical juncture of religion" came directly from the writings of Peter l'Agnostique. A controversial figure, Peter wavered throughout his life between a reluctant belief in the gods and faith in pure godless reason. Boiscommun for his part, called Peter "a dated relic of weak religion" and "a coward in philosopher's garb." But even he could acquiesce that Peter's crowning achievement of reason was his oft-quoted statement, "*Si les dieux n'existaient pas, il faudrait les inventer.*" "If the gods did not exist, it would be necessary to invent them" was a phrase that guided Richard's dealing with men whether he was conscious of it or not.

Richard de Conquil preached such ideas to his daughter from an early age. They did not pray in their home, nor did they pray in the temples. However, the business of war took Richard quite often to the Temple of Bellicor. Murielle accompanied him many times. She did not find the business of war boring at all. *Au contraire*, she found the whole business of stratagems, weapons, and tactics quite fascinating.

One day however, as they were departing, she saw a knight in the group pause. He knelt before the marble altar and began to pray. The great marble statue of the war god loomed behind the altar casting a heavy shadow across the penitent knight. In Bellicor's outstretched paw, a sword extended out above them. The god's look was severe; the look of a warrior about to go into battle. Everything about him suggested strength: the weight of his ears, the cut of his jaw line, his powerful hind legs bulging with lapine muscularity.

The statue entranced Murielle. It was like she was seeing it for the first time. But the knight kneeling before the statue fascinated her even more. He knelt, eyes shut, fingertips pressed firmly and reverently to his forehead, as he spoke in a low tone, his voice barely audible. He seemed truly penitent, asking the god's favor, or begging his forgiveness. She could not determine which. She had never seen her father in such a position, either in their home or in the temple. She had never seen her father even acknowledge the god. The knight seemed at peace as he knelt praying. Something about him suggested contentment and wholeness. A feeling of want came over her. Murielle wanted what the knight had.

She began praying at the perfunctory altar in their home when she was certain no one was looking. Unsure how to pray to the war god, she began with simple praises of his prowess in war. She soon found it difficult to keep up. Kneeling upon the stone floor hurt her knees. Keeping her fingertips pressed to her forehead for an extended length of time was difficult to maintain. The worst part was that her mind would begin to wander after only a few moments of prayer. She had no idea how long one was required to pray to a god, and she exhausted her supply of praises in a short time. Certain that one needed to pray for a lengthy time in order to appease the god, she tried to devise lengthy praises only to wander off the subject and begin thinking about the weather, what the ladies of the court were wearing, the latest tale of adventure circulating around, and so forth.

It seemed that she would never attain what the knight in the temple had found. Murielle fixed upon an idea after she and her father visited the Temple of Bellicor on another occasion. As he engaged in conversation with his fellow knights, she stared at the mute marble stature behind the altar. *I want to meet you*, she thought suddenly. *If I can meet you, prayer will come easier, for I will believe.* And thus, she prayed. She found easy to focus on this simple prayer, this one simple request. Time flew by as she knelt before the home altar asking to meet the war god. She lost track of the time and was nearly caught by her father on several occasions. But it did not matter to her if he should catch her. With her one simple prayer, Murielle began to feel some of the peace she had seen in the penitent knight.

"I want to meet you," Murielle said aloud. Outside the castle gates she found herself standing before a colossal stature of Bellicor. This statue was different than the one inside the temple. This one, cast entirely in bronze, was said to be as old as the city itself. Once, they said, the bronze statue gleamed as bright as the sun, as bright as the Lord Aufeese, but now it was dull and dusky colored, green corrosion spotted it here and there along the seams. It towered above her on a stone pedestal, blocking out the sun. Bellicor, the God of War, clad in plate armor of the ancient style, sat astride a massive war horse. He was bare headed, his ears stood alert above his head. He held aloft a long lance in his right paw: a war lance, not a jousting lance with a blunt coronal as used in the tourneys, but a lance with a savage point used for grave business. In his left, the god held close to his body an enormous round shield of the same ancient style as the armor.

But Bellicor's expression differed greatly from that on the statue in the temple. Whereas the expression on the marble statue exuded a fierceness and a fearsome quality, the bronze displayed a calm nobility. Whereas the marble statue expressed "woe to enemies," the bronze spoke of "honor in battle." Here, towering above Murielle, was the true face of chivalry. All the codes her father had taught her of the behavior befitting a knight resided here in this statue.

Murielle closed her eyes. She could see her father in the jousting lists behind their country estate, astride his own charger. He held his blunted lance, the butt planted on the ground at the horse's feet as he explained to her the Laws of Chivalry. "A knight must fight only for the honorable cause. He must never fight selfishly or for revenge. He must defend the defenseless, protect widows and orphans." He gave Murielle a wry smile and added, "He must also protect the honor of ladies."

Murielle smiled herself at the memory. The smile faded from her lips as she came back to herself at the base of the statue. A base knight had attacked the defenseless and threatened the honor of a lady. Knights of the Prince's ilk roamed the land attacking and pillaging the weak. They killed innocent men and raped defenseless ladies, taking whatever they pleased from whomever they could most easily wrest it. Chivalry and honor were dead. And the war god had performed a poor job of defending the defenseless from the onslaught of immorality. He was as ineffective as the god of the harvest to whom Gilles prayed so fervently. Murielle shook her head angrily and moved on to the gates of the castle.

As Murielle had traversed through the streets from the south end of the city, she had noticed a gradual increase in the amount of foot traffic. Now as she entered the castle gates, quite a few people entered along with her. The thick, imposing gates, like the city gates, each bore the crest of Lord Portiscule, asking the god's protection of the castle. Guards positioned themselves on both sides of the gates, on the ground and also atop the high parapet of the solid stone walls. These men appeared tougher and of a graver demeanor than the guards she had met at the South Gates. They stopped no one but watched everyone with suspicion. Many people had business in the castle, but to stop everyone entering the courtyard would be time consuming. Instead, keen-eyed and experienced guards were placed here to check for any suspect behavior. Murielle kept her eyes forward, walking with purpose. There would be no flippancy here with these guards. If she gave these men any reason to doubt her harmlessness, her mission ended here.

On the other side of the gates, the castle courtyard teemed with life. In spite of the searing heat, a panoply of figures dressed in all their finery circled the courtyard, conversing and socializing, all set on the serious business of courtly affairs. At once Murielle felt a twinge of self-consciousness stab at her. She had been at the normal chores of the farm when this grave business was thrust upon her. She had had no time to change, no time to *think* about changing out of her simple country attire to suit the graceful etiquette of the king's court.

She fretted over this a moment then remembered something her father had told her.

"There are those," Richard de Conquil had said, "attending the court who are dressed the finest, richest clothes money can buy. These are the least important in the court. They wish to impress others and pretend they are important. Some of the least impressive looking people have true importance. They have true power. It is your name and your connections which matter here. Without those, you are nothing."

Murielle nodded to herself. This is why she had fought so hard with Gilles to come here herself. She had a name and she had connections. With these she would gain admittance to places these fancy petitioners could only dream of attaining.

Guards were everywhere. This she thought odd. When she was younger and attending court, there were far fewer guards than were present now, even during the height of the war with Ocosse. The main castle doors stood open and a few people stood inside, conversing leisurely in the cool shade. The castle loomed high above her. If she had the time, Murielle could walk around the castle's perimeter and see the centuries pass in this one building. The legend told that Lord Daedemus himself built the original castle long ago with his own paws as a gift to humans. On the West side one could see portions of that original structure: rough-hewn stones unknown to any quarry in the kingdom.

The doorway at which Murielle stood was part of the newest addition to the castle. This was where the Old King and his son kept their residences and held court. Murielle passed through the wide doorway into the hall whereupon she began to shiver at the sudden drop in temperature. Rushes lined the floor and angry red coals glowed in braziers spaced at regular intervals which broke the chill not in the least. It was a marvel how on such a blistering day even a single brazier would be necessary. The massive stone structure of the castle seemed to draw all the warmth out of the air itself.

Murielle's eyes adjusted slowly to the gloom. She made out the shapes of sconces lining the walls, their fires burning lazily, black smoke drifting in a slow rotation to the distant ceiling. Figures soon became apparent in the dark room: petitioners to the Old King. In here the clothing was not as fine as in the courtyard. While those people outside had come to impress others, the people in here had come to petition the Old King in hopes that he might grant a humble request.

Doorways on either side of the hall led to other rooms of the castle. Occasionally, a person or persons would exit though one of these doors. However, the door at the end of the hall was the one for which she had come. Summoning her courage, Murielle set off purposefully for the door at the end of the hall. Instantly people began to take notice. They whispered behind hands to each other. She did not need to hear to know what they said. By her grubby countenance, dirty and sweaty clothes, and the firm set of her jaw as she strode intently toward the door, the strange woman summoned all sorts of discussion from the waiting petitioners over who she might be.

The door opened just before Murielle reached it. She had made no attempt to knock as this is what she had expected. She was however, surprised by the man who opened the door. He was not a *secretaire* or footman, but a burly guard, and not a palace guard at all.

The guard stood blocking the entire doorway with his body, his silent glare more powerful than any gruff words with which he could have rebuked her. He offered no greeting, no rebuff, nor any words at all. His close-cropped hair capped a rough-hewn face possessing a single long scar running raggedly from his temple, down his cheek, and disappearing into a gnarly beard. An ordinary guard Murielle could contend with, but this thug and the stony stare offered by his cold iron eyes was almost too much to bear.

Murielle set her resolve firmly, lifted her chin which had sagged a little, and made her request which came in a voice which wavered only slightly, but still more than she would have liked.

"I am her to see the O–" was all she got out before the guard finally spoke in a deep voice, heavy with a low country drawl.

"No one sees the Old King."

Murielle fired back haughtily with her well-rehearsed response to the expected initial rebuff. "I am Murielle, daughter of Richard de Conquil, and I demand to see the Old King!"

The guard leaned forward. Murielle fought against violent nausea from the foul breath which stunk of ale and rot as he spoke through blackened teeth.

"Never heard of him," he said slowly, deliberately.

Murielle gasped audibly then choked on the stench of body odor coming off the guard which was mercifully cut off when he slammed the door in her face. Those cold, hard eyes offered not a trace recognition of the name she had given. What castle guard, or soldier in the army did not know the name of Richard de Conquil? That certainly was no castle guard nor any soldier of the Old King. He was of the cut of the rough men, the thugs, who had accompanied the Prince on his fateful visit to her home.

Murielle's head spun in a whirlwind of maniacal thought. The very reason she had fought so hard with Gilles to embark on this journey, on this desperate plan, was because of her name which had just failed her. She had to think, to recoup her reason and her mind. *Mais réfléchis donc un peu!*

She was aware of whispering behind her. Murielle turned her head slightly to see out of the corner of her eye the other petitioners speaking to each other behind hands. She could hear what they said, her ears, trained by life in the country, being more sensitive to the quiet sounds of crickets at night, the rustle of wind through rows of corn, the weight of predatory feet upon dry grasses. Even if she could not hear their words, she would know what they were saying, nevertheless.

Murielle had thrown out the name Richard de Conquil. These other petitioners were of an age that they would have either known her father or were aware of his renown. They were saying that if the daughter of that great soldier, a pillar of the Old King's army, could not get in to see the Old King, then their petitions would go unheard as well.

The whirlwind in her head grew into a violent storm, blowing about rational thoughts and thrashing them to kindling. She had to leave, to go someplace to reassemble her thoughts. Murielle walked purposefully, her head held high, toward the entryway. The storm raging in her head broke down her reason against her futile efforts to hold it together, so that by the time she reached the entry to the hall she was running, her head hung in desperation.

Murielle burst into the bright sunlight and the blistering heat. Immediately a fresh sweat broke out all over her body. Her mind was a ruin, her reason a mere shell. This was not the plan. Her father's name had opened so many doors in the city so long ago, and to find a door which could not be opened with that particular key was simply unfathomable.

Murielle's breathing came in rapid pants. The wall of hot air hit her, and the full force of the sun bore its full weight upon her as she staggered blindly into the courtyard. The heat did nothing to ease her growing panic. It made it even more difficult for her to recapture her lost reason. Then, a voice boomed out from somewhere behind her.

"Well, well! By the gods's ears, it has been ages since I have seen the form of Guillaume de Marschal inside these blessed walls!"

Despite the heat, a chill raced down Murielle's spine causing gooseflesh to break out all over her, and her eyes grew wide in the brilliant sunlight. Fresh panic broke in her. It had been ages since she had heard that forgotten name.

CHAPTER TEN

EMMELINE WANTED to put as much distance between herself and the Golden Child as possible. She stomped through the wheat field rumbling about conceited gods and their fickle ways. The wheat soon gave way to pasture, and her mood calmed. If she had spared a glance back, she would have seen the shimmering golden wheat evaporate into nothing.

Emmeline stepped up her pace in the low fescue of the pasture as her mind returned to the dire circumstances which had led her to embark on this fateful journey. She walked, lost in thought, not even aware when the pasture gave way to low foothills dotted with sporadic young pines and the occasional oak and hickory. As the foothills steepened, Emmeline might have pondered–were she not so otherwise occupied with other thoughts–why she was climbing a mountain in the middle of the flat Eastern Plains. It was as she climbed into thicker growths of taller pines and older hardwoods that a memory came to her unbidden:

———

The last time Emmeline's father had taken her to the Market had been two harvests previous. Her father had never given an adequate explanation as to why he had not taken her with him since. But that was something else entirely. At the last Market she had attended, they had found themselves wandering through the stalls in the streets of Darloque, all the fruits of their labor sold after a brisk second day of trade. Emmeline recalled one man—who looked vaguely familiar—buying up much of what they had to sell. As with Market Days past, they stayed in the city for the remainder of the festival and perused the vendors, seeking small luxuries on which to spend their excess coin.

Her father paused at a vendor selling woodworking tools and wooden crafts. A variety of chisels lay on a table in neat rows. He picked up a small, scalloped chisel used for fine detail work and inquired about it. As he and the vendor conversed about woodwork, Emmeline looked around for something more interesting. Across the street, an armorer had set up two massive tents to show his wares. Two men and one young woman stood in one of the tents speaking to a group of young noblemen about the ornate tournament armor for sale. Every piece of armor in the booth shone with the brilliance of highly polished steel. Leather belts hung in even rows in the back of the tent. Even across the street, the air was heavy with the smell of leather and oil. Emmeline looked up the cobblestone street at the throng of busy pedestrians inspecting the wares of the various vendors there. Back at the woodworking tent, her father and the woodcarver had transitioned from pleasant conversation into deep negotiations. A variety of other figures milled around the booth.

One in particular caught Emmeline's attention. He was large fellow, wearing a brown, hooded cloak. Although now past the harvest, it was still warm enough to make such clothing impractical, if not outright uncomfortable. He walked slowly around the booth holding a quarterstaff in one gloved hand and picking up tools at random with the other. He examined each tool closely then moved on to another. Before she knew it, the hooded stranger was standing next to her at a table filled with small wooden statuettes.

"What ho!?" he cried, in a deep but boisterous voice as he picked up a small wooden figurine. "'Tis this not as fine a carving as mine eyes have laid sight upon at this Market in many a season?"

The fellow turned to Emmeline, although she could still not discern a face under the hood.

"What thinkest thou my young lass? 'Tis this not a magnificent piece?" He let out a merry guffaw.

Emmeline wanted to tell him that she had no real interest in wood carving. She thought that he would find better conversation talking to her father.

But before she could say anything, the stranger leaned down level to her ear. Emmeline noticed his smell at once. It was not unpleasant, nay, it was quite pleasant. Familiar and comforting, like something of home, she could not place it. And it was wholly unexpected from the likes of this hooded stranger.

"My young lass," he whispered in a calm, soothing voice, "to dream above thine standing is a pleasant diversion, but to reach beyond is not without its own peril."

Up close, Emmeline saw that he wore the rough cloak of a woodsman. His face remained hidden beneath the hood, but she thought she could discern brown eyes, deep and kindly. At once it seemed prudent, nay *nécessaire*, that she remain at the wood carver's booth. She looked hard at the woodsman, trying to read the face she could not see. Then as suddenly as it came upon her, the feeling passed.

Emmeline turned suddenly and without a word, walked quickly up the street, wanting to put as much distance between herself and the woodsman as possible. She walked past a few booths of little interest to her and a few more that were so packed with people that she could not even determine if the merchandise interested her. Only once did she glance back over her shoulder, but the woodcarver's booth and the strange woodsman had disappeared behind the crowd.

At a corner which the booths stood mostly in the cool shade of the surrounding buildings, Emmeline noticed a greater concentration of nobles engaged in browsing and shopping. Although a few people of the lower class scudded about, it was largely the beautiful people in their finery milling about here. And the booths reflected the tastes of their noble clientele.

Emmeline was taking in all the items for sale: gold and silver jewelry, fine crystal, and precious gemstones. Then she spied something in a booth a short way up the side street. Clothing filled the booth–the finest clothing she had ever seen in her life. She went immediately to a chemise of such fine material that it was like air. She gazed longingly at an exquisite *pelice* with a shining silver clasp. She was then drawn to a beautiful woman's *bliaut* with such elaborate *orfois* that she could not help but run her hands over its embroidered surface. Emmeline stopped at a cloak made of exceptionally fine *esscarlet* in a deep blue-green. She opened it to reveal a fur lining of the softest miniver. She stroked the soft fur. She had never felt the like even on a live animal.

A noise brought Emmeline back to herself. In the deep shadows of the booth an old man sat on a small stool. Instinctively, Emmeline snatched her hands back from the cloak and looked away. The man made a clucking noise and Emmeline looked at him again, but warily. He remained seated on the stool, but his face opened into a broad, friendly smile. His eyes sparkled in the gloom. She could not help but to return the smile. He said not a word but nodded his head once and motioned toward the cloak. Emmeline looked around, sure that he had not meant for her to touch the fine garment. He repeated his gesture toward the cloak. She returned his smile once more and tentatively began to stroke the softest fur she had ever felt. *Would I not look fine in this?* she asked herself. She looked back at the man with the sparkling eyes who continued to smile.

Emmeline returned to the chemise. The cloth was like gossamer. And then the *bliaut*. The embroidery was the most detailed she had ever seen. Complex patterns of organic swirls encircled the collar and sleeves. As she lightly traced the patterns with her fingers, she realized that the embroidery was of gold thread. The ornate detail captured her so thoroughly that she became lost in it. *I would look most fine in this, I believe!* She imagined herself walking into the court of the Old King wearing this *bliaut*, all eyes on her, the most beautiful girl there. The other girls would be so jealous for they would not look even half as beautiful as she–

"*Allez! Allez!*" a voice shouted from somewhere. Emmeline's head jerked up as she looked around to find the source of the disturbance. Her eyes fell upon the old man with the sparkling eyes who was now staring down at his hands laying limp in his lap, the smile gone from his face. "*Allez!*" the voice shouted again and then a slender rod of ash rapped down hard on her knuckles where she touched the *bliaut*. Wrinkled and bespeckled hands shoved Emmeline rudely away as she pulled her own stinging hands to her body.

"*Allez!*" A face appeared close to Emmeline's. A hooked nose, more than resembling a beak, very nearly touched her own. Harsh lines carved themselves into sallow, sagging skin around keen hazel eyes and thin lips pursed into a permanent frown. Shimmering white hair, perhaps the old crone's only pleasant feature, framed her haggard face, then cascaded down over her thin shoulders, coming to a neat end past her waist.

"Are you deaf as well as dumb, you filth!"

Emmeline stared back in horror at the woman shouting at her. She could not speak. All she could do was rub her hands where the old woman had hit them.

"I say begone!" the woman shouted anew. "How dare you put your filthy peasant hands on these fine pieces of clothing! Begone!"

Emmeline turned back to the man with the sparkling eyes. He avoided her gaze, his disgust with his wife and himself evident. Finding no protection there, she turned back to the old woman who glared back with an inconceivable malevolence.

The old woman turned to the man in the booth, jabbing the ash rod savagely at him. "And how could you let this peasant filth touch our fine things?" He gave no response to the woman and continued to stare at his feet.

The old woman reeled back on Emmeline. "You must be a simpleton as well as a peasant." She shook her head in disgust, her sleek white hair flowing around her as she moved. "It is astonishing to me to find someone even more simple than he," she added, jabbing the rod again at the man.

Emmeline continued to stare at the old woman as she rubbed her sore knuckles. She could feel the welts rising on them. Never in her life had she been so abused. The sting of her knuckles was painful, but not as painful as the woman's acerbic tongue. The words stung her to her core. She was not filthy. She was not a peasant, her family lived quite well, or so she believed. She wanted to tell the woman these things. Slowly, as if awaking from a deep sleep, she came back to herself as the initial shock wore off. She wanted to tell the old woman that the clothing she made was incredibly beautiful. She knew that it must be well beyond her means, but she wanted to tell the woman how dearly she wished she could afford them. She wanted to tell the woman that these clothes would make some girl very happy.

Emmeline opened her mouth to say these things when renewed fury passed over the old woman's face. "Simpleton!" she shouted, a brilliant red flush filling her pale face all the way to her white hairline. "How dare you put those filthy peasant hands on my fine things! Begone now!"

Emmeline opened her mouth again wanting to explain herself but before she could utter a sound, the old woman's hands thrust forward with an incredible youthful speed that defied her apparent age and shoved Emmeline back with violent force. Emmeline went sprawling on the cobblestones in the middle of the street. A small crowd had begun to gather on the street when the old woman began shouting at Emmeline. The crowd was made of mostly nobles, although a few common folk stared meekly from the fringe. A few of the nobles began to speak amongst themselves loud enough for Emmeline to hear.

"Serves her right," said one.

"What nerve," said a high-toned woman. "That simple peasant thinking she could touch those clothes."

"She's obviously not right in the head," chuckled a fat nobleman to another.

"The sheriff should lock her away," a man with a pointed goatee said nasally.

Tears welled in Emmeline's eyes. She was no longer aware of the pain in her knuckles nor of the new pain in her elbow and hip from where she had landed on the rough cobblestones. She looked at the man with the sparkling eyes one last time. He still stared at his feet. His head arced back and forth slowly as he rubbed the back of his neck and let out a pained sigh. The old woman stared down at her from her position in front of the booth. She stood there haughtily, protectively, spindly hands balled into fists set firmly on her narrow hips, and ready to strike again should the presumptuous peasant girl attempt to profane her fine clothing once more. Emmeline looked to the crowd gathered around her, a crowd which had grown considerably in the short time that this exchange had taken place. Eerily silent now, no help would be found there. A few of the common farm folk on the fringes stared and shifted uncomfortably on their feet, not daring to come to her aid amongst these nobles. "Simpleton," a man's voice shouted from somewhere in the crowd, breaking the silence.

Something broke inside her. Emmeline's lip began to quiver, and rivers of tears began to flow freely down her face. She scrambled to her feet, banging her knee hard on the cobblestones as she did. The pain did not matter, she would not feel it for some time. She got to her feet, forced her way past the uncaring spectators, and ran. Destination did not matter. She ran. She ran down the streets of Darloque, the tears flowing freely, moving her mouth ineffectively, wanting to cry out but unable to make any sound whatsoever. She ran. It could have been an eternity, or it could have been only a few moments. She did not know, and she did not care. Time was inconsequential. As was direction. She turned a few times without knowing what she was doing or where she was going, driven by the pain and the primal need to escape it. All she knew was the hurt, the indelible hurt of the old woman's abusive tongue, the insults of the crowd, the passive stares of the commoners. She ran. She ran, trying to escape the pain, but she could not.

After a time, which seemed like an eternity, measured in the acid burn of the old woman's unbridled hatred, Emmeline slowed to a stagger. She had no more to give. Her energy was spent. She limped up several stone steps to the entrance of a large building. Instinctively, as a wounded animal seeks refuge in a dark hole, she sought refuge in a shadowed corner of the entryway. Here she could hide away from prying eyes. She fell to the cool stone in the dark. She could not see the street from her hiding place, and therefore the street could not see her. She sat, sniffling, staring at her feet but not seeing them. She soon found herself sliding down the wall to the stone floor of the entryway, then curling into a ball on her side. She lay that way for some time sniffling and wiping her eyes with her sleeves. The trembling started first, then her lip began to quiver again. A low whimper started deep inside her, building slowly. Just as the bells began to chime for vespers, she released everything inside her with a deep, loud howl.

Two nuns, dressed in the gray habits of their vocation, found Emmeline in this state outside the East entrance of the temple. Gently, the two helped Emmeline to her feet and led the sobbing girl into the temple. Through the massive nave they went, through the transept, and out the North entrance which led to the temple's adjoining nunnery. Once inside, the nuns laid the girl on an empty pallet. The older nun fetched a cloth soaked with cool water from the well and began to wipe the girl's forehead and cheeks in an effort to calm her. The girl's sobbing slowed, then eventually stopped altogether.

The older nun turned to the other. "Someone is surely seeking this girl. Go now, find her family, and bring them here. Turn over the entire city if you must, but do not return without whomever claims her."

The other nun, a young novice, did as she was told, running from the room with clear urgency.

"Now, my girl," the older nun began, her voice soft, calm, and soothing. "Would you care to tell me what has made you so over-wrought? This behavior is certainly not just the result of being lost during the Market Days. You are safe in this place and my novice has gone to find your family. Tell me, have you been abused?"

Emmeline turned her head away from the kind nun without a word.

Sitting on the edge of the pallet, the nun swallowed hard. Truly, she had spent her entire life within the confines of the cloister, but she was aware of the ways of the evil world outside. She swallowed again. Despite being aware of the evils of the outside world, the words came with great difficulty. "Has anyone touched you... improperly?"

Fresh tears began to roll down the girl's cheeks. She buried her face in the pallet.

The nun clenched her hands into tight fists; her eyes slammed shut against the rage welling inside her, the rage against the sins so prevalent in the evil world. Slowly, it subsided, and she was able to speak again.

"You must tell me my dear, tell me how you were...abused. Tell me so that healing may begin within you."

Emmeline shook her head slowly, her face remained buried in the pallet. She fought back the sobs welling up inside her. She did not want to speak. She had used up all her strength running and now only wanted to hide in a cool dark place far away from all the cruel, heartless people.

But this nun, she was different from the mocking nobles. She was a kindly woman, someone Emmeline felt was deserving of trust. She felt she should be able to tell this woman anything without fear of condemnation. She slowly turned her face to the old nun and told her tale of woe. The old nun tensed as she began, then a look of great relief spread across her face as Emmeline finished her tale.

The nun took a deep breath and released it slowly. "My girl," she said, with the strange look of relief still on her face, "I am sorry that you were wronged so. Clearly you meant no harm."

Emmeline shook her head slowly.

"It is a sad situation when people value their possessions over another human's well-being.

Emmeline nodded.

"Do you feel that you can walk, my dear?" asked the nun. "I wish to show you something."

Emmeline nodded again and began to rise from the pallet. The old nun helped her up and led her slowly into the temple. They stopped before the altar near the West end of the nave. The light of the lowering afternoon sun straining through the enormous rose window revealed a plain but functional altar made of rough-hewn stone. The diffuse light from the rose window, and the lancet windows on either side in the high clerestory combined to bathe the lustrous white statues behind the simple altar in a glorious palette of color. Emmeline found it hard to believe there was enough white marble in the world to have carved the massive statues which towered above her.

"Among their other attributes, The Sisters teach women strength and independence," the nun began, gazing devotedly at the statues. "We learn from them that a woman can perform any task a man can. We learn that in this ability, this equality, there is a strength within us that cannot be broken."

The nun took a breath and continued. "When others attack us, even other women, we must draw upon the strength of The Sisters to empower us. Those who wish to break women, to prevent us from displaying wills of our own cannot succeed if we have sought strength from The Sisters."

Her head dropped, heavy with sorrowfulness. "It is a shame

when women attack other women, for it shows their weakness. The women who attack, in truth, lack the strength of The Sisters in their lives. Their attacks are in fact desperate attempts to force you into submission, and therefore make you weaker than themselves. This is how they attempt to empower themselves. Sadly however, this ploy is nothing more than a pitiable self-deceit, for they are empowered only briefly before slipping once again into despair."

Emmeline pondered this. Her eyes followed the lines of the immense white marble towering above her. The Inseparable Sisters they were called; the only gods to share a temple. Calapine, the goddess of steel, leaned over the altar, her hammer held upright in her massive paw. She was a stout and strong looking rabbit, her scowl a greater warning to others than her hammer. Felapine stood beside her, as stout, strong, and imposing as her sister. She held nothing in her paws for she was the digger, the goddess of iron who mined ores and minerals from the ground from which Calapine forged her works. The two goddesses were identical save for Felapine's right ear which hung down the side of her head. The reason for the deformity escaped Emmeline.

A loud clamor arose from the East entrance of the temple as several dirty, rough-looking men entered with shouts of obscenities. A couple of them carrying large sacks slung over their shoulders straggled behind the main group while the others walked with cocky swagger up through the long nave toward the altar.

The nun frowned. She pulled herself upright and turned to face the approaching group. She took a half step, placing herself in front of Emmeline and smoothed her habit.

"*Bonjour, monsieurs!* Welcome, welcome!" Her voice echoed though the mostly empty temple. "How may I, a humble nun in service to The Inseparable Sisters, be of service to you this day?"

A tall man approached, of stout build and no cleaner than the rest of his crew, but not yet hunched over by the nature of his profession. He did not remove his cap, nor did he offer a respectful bow to the nun.

"*Bonjour*, sister. If it pleases you," he said with a tone of indifference, "we have come from the mines to make our offering to The Sisters."

The nun observed a couple of the men eyeing Emmeline hungrily. She straightened a little more and smoothed her habit again.

"Come, bring your offering to the altar," she said with as pleasant a voice as she could muster, yet her words came out with a certain stiffness.

The leader of the mining crew motioned to the men carrying the sacks who dutifully laid them at the base of the stone altar without, however, a break in their conversation.

The nun stole a quick glance at the open sacks which contained their humble offerings. Humble was an appropriate word as the sacks held only common ores, nothing of real value. It was a perfunctory offering made in vain hope of appeasing the gods who watched over their work.

Her eyes returned to the rough crew. The men stood waiting. Apparently, they expected some sort of blessing for their great offering. The nun hoped this was the case. She did not like the way three of the men in the back of the group eyed the girl behind her. One of the three made a movement with his hands which brought great laughter from the whole group. The nun caught this and frowned.

"My *good* men," the nun said at last, praying that all they wanted was a blessing. "Bow your heads and receive the blessing of The Sisters." All bowed their heads. A few even stopped talking while a couple more made a good show of properly pressing their fingertips to their foreheads.

"Goddess of Iron, Goddess of Steel, accept the *gracious* offering of these men, protect them in their work, and watch over them in *all* their endeavors."

A few of the men turned their eyes up warily to the statues looming over them. The leader of the group removed his fingertips from his forehead and looked at the nun. His eyes flashed briefly at

Emmeline then back. "Thank you, sister," he said after a moment with the same indifferent tone as before. Low, obscenity laced conversation resumed in the background.

The leader stood silently, staring at the nun. The conversation grew louder behind him. The nun was growing uncomfortable when the bang of the East entry doors broke the awkward moment.

"Sister, sister!" a voice shouted. The nun looked up, recognizing the voice of her novice.

The young nun led a large man with a bald head up the nave toward the altar. By his stocky build, the older nun guessed him to be a freeman farmer. The young girl behind the nun peered around her cautiously. Apparently recognizing the man as someone she knew, she broke out in a run to him. The man rushed up to meet her. As the two embraced in a storm of joyful tears, the miners stared disconsolately at the stone floor. One let out a low curse in language unsuitable in the presence of nuns.

The older nun gave the speaker a stony glare of contempt and walked over to the reunited couple. They stood hand in hand as the nun greeted them. She stared a moment at the large hand, calloused from his lifetime of manual labor, tenderly holding the small soft hand of the girl the nun guessed to be his daughter.

"I am so grateful to you sisters for finding my Emmeline," the man cried. "Words cannot express my gratitude."

The nun offered a polite bow, touching her fingertips lightly to her forehead. "Your gratitude is appreciated but not necessary, my good freeman. As nuns in service of The Sisters, it is our solemn duty to render aid to women in distress, and we do so both willingly and joyfully."

"I am grateful nevertheless that you found her."

"And to be perfectly honest, my good freeman—"

"Gilles, please."

"To be perfectly honest, Gilles, it was she who found us." The nun glanced at her novice. "We simply provided aid to a girl in distress."

"Your humility, my dear sister, is refreshing. However, it may have come to pass," Gilles said with a sigh, "I am grateful that Emmeline found you two dutiful sisters and not..."

Gilles trailed off. The nun saw the farmer's eyes flit quickly to the miners and back to her.

The nun cleared her throat and smoothed her habit.

"Well then," Gilles said, "I am grateful to The Sisters for leading my Emmeline to their temple so that their dutiful servants might give her aid and comfort." He lifted his eyes upward. "I am also grateful for the Lord Aufeese, Mava's glorious Golden Child, leading me in the proper direction so that I might be found by the servant of The Sisters."

"Blest be Mava and her many litters, blest be Lady Calapine and Lady Felapine, blest be the Lord Aufeese." The nun bowed and touched her fingertips to her forehead. The novice followed suit as did Gilles. Emmeline performed a perfunctory bow. Out of the corner of her eye the nun watched the group of miners slowly slide toward the entrance. They left with nary a word and hardly a glance back at the penitent group. Emmeline glanced up at the silent statues looming over them, wondering what they had done to help her.

———

Nothing, she thought as she climbed the steepening terrain. *They were as ineffective to me that day as that silly golden rabbit has been to me this day.*

It was the kind actions of that nun and her pupil, she thought as she scrambled around a rocky outcropping. The tiny ember of rage still smoldering inside her flared brightly.

If the Sisters had really wanted to help me, she mused, *Calapine would have smashed that vicious old woman with her hammer, and Felapine would have pelted the mocking nobles with stones cast from her sling*. The thought brought a brief savage smile to her face.

The nun spoke of The Sisters giving strength to women. What

strength she would have had in the street that day with The Inseparable Sisters looming behind her. Yes, Calapine would have smashed
the old woman, Felapine would have stoned the mocking nobles, and
the kind old man would have given her all the fine clothes she wanted
as a gift for freeing him from the vicious woman's tyranny.

Emmeline smiled. Sweat poured anew down her face as she used
the trunk of a sapling to heave herself over a small ledge. She paused
a moment, gazing up the slope at the old growth hardwoods: ash,
maple, oak. The massive trees covered the mountainside with a cool
shade. Low grasses intermingled with old leaves from autumns past.
Grey rocky outcroppings jutted out here and there, and somewhere
in the distance Emmeline could hear the babbling of a waterfall.

She was now incredibly grateful her mother had made her
change into breeches as climbing this mountain would have been
exceedingly difficult in a dress, although she would never admit it to
her. She also would not admit that putting her hair up into a bun had
been a wise idea as well. Emmeline had reluctantly pulled her hair
back into a ponytail when the climbing had become arduous: it was as
far as she could go toward admitting her mother was correct on that
point.

Two things occurred to her at once: the realization that this
mountain should not be here in the flat Eastern Plains, and the sound
of a rhythmic noise coming down from the mountain directly ahead
of her. Bang, bam-bam! Bang, bam-bam! Bang, bam-bam. A bright
metallic noise followed by two rapid dull thuds. The sound repeated
several times, paused briefly, then resumed. Emmeline listened for
some time at this cycle of noise.

She looked back down the mountain. Regardless of whether this
mountain should be here or not, she did not want to go back the way
she came. Emmeline looked up the mountain again and listened
again as the noise made a few more cycles. She sighed, then took a
deep breath and released it. Up the mountain she climbed. Whatever
was ahead of her had to be better than what she had left behind.

CHAPTER ELEVEN

MURIELLE TURNED SLOWLY, stiffly, toward the sound of the voice. An older man wearing the uniform of a castle guard stood at another doorway in the courtyard. His gray hair hung long to his shoulders, in the bygone style of a knight of the Old King.

"Well, well, well," said the old knight, stepping out into the daylight. "Time has done its work to my eyes and my faculties, but I would recognize the daughter of my good friend Richard de Conquil anywhere."

Murielle stared quizzically at the old man. She took a cautious step toward him, squinting in the savage daylight.

"But I see that recognition cannot be reciprocated. By the gods's ears! How can it be that an old man can have a sharper memory than a young woman in her—"

"Frédéric!" Murielle cried. She ran to the old knight and embraced him tightly.

"Gently, gently, my lass," he gasped. "My memory may be strong; however, my bones are not. Use more care!"

Murielle loosened her grip. "Oh, this is wonderful! To see you after all this time!"

"To see you again, Murielle, brings such great joy to this old man's feeble heart." Frédéric looked into her eyes. "You have your father's eyes. Gazing upon you is like seeing my old friend again."

"The similarities do not stop with the eyes," she laughed. "It is said that I share my father's temperament. There is more of your old friend here than you might believe."

The old knight laughed. "If you mean that you are as independent and willful as he, then you truly are your father's daughter!"

The old knight's laughter trailed off. His eyes stared off blankly into the distance.

"Richard, my old friend," he said to no one, "independent and willful you were. Difficult and frustrating as well. Oh, how sometimes I wished to throttle you, however you were still my friend. My best friend. Oh, how I still miss your company after all this time!"

A single tear welled at the corner of the old knight's eye and rolled slowly down his wrinkled, sun-burnt cheek.

He awoke from his reverie, turning to Murielle with a broad smile. "It has been too long, my dear, far too long. How have you fared? I hope you have been living well. You must tell me everything!"

Murielle returned Frédéric's smile. "Oh yes, I have fared quite well."

"Come," said Frédéric, leading Murielle to a recently vacated bench in the shade of a large sycamore tree. "You must tell me all that has happened to you since I last saw you. Leave out nothing!"

As they sat in the cool shade, the purpose for journeying to the castle slowly slipped from Murielle's mind, pushed out by the flood of nostalgia flowing through her. She ran her hand over the peeling bark of the tree trunk. Absently, she pulled off a long sliver of the mottled bark, exposing the brown beneath it. She turned the bark over in her hands, examining it, yet not really seeing it.

Murielle's eyes followed the trunk upward. The springtime blossoms, long since gone, had been replaced with the developing fruits of this tree. Greenish-brown seed balls, each suspended from a long, slender stalk, hung throughout the branches. As the air turned cool, they would reach maturity, turning a deep brown. Then, as winter progressed, each ball would drop from its withered stalk to the snowy ground and open to reveal a multitude of gossamer nuts inside. As these scattered across the ground, blown about by chilly northern winds, birds–goldfinches, nuthatches, cardinals–would congregate under and around this tree to gather a bountiful winter meal.

Time. Time passes. It more than simply passes. *Tempus fugit,* the scholars say, Time flees. As if sensing her temporal introspection, Frédéric sighed as he turned his own eyes up to the sycamore tree.

"Where has the time gone, my girl? Where has it gone?" He shook his head ruefully. "Ah, there I go, caught in the past again. My eyes, clouded by remembrance, see you differently than you are here now. You are no girl, a woman now. No longer the child I remember, daughter of my dear friend, scurrying about with a doll or some other toy clutched tightly in your tiny arms, asking a thousand questions, and waiting not a moment for the answers.

"You, I see now, my vision unclouded briefly from the mists of remembrance, a woman now, with your own small, precocious bundle scurrying about underfoot, no doubt asking her own myriad enquiries and yet still too absorbed in the serious business of play to wait for even one answer. You, another man in your world to replace the one you first knew: teacher, counselor, father. That man, long since gone, replaced with another. A man who stands not above you, but alongside you. Partner, lover, husband, a man you cherish dearly, but in not quite the same manner as the one he replaced."

Murielle let wave after wave of memory wash over her. Yes, it was as Frédéric imagined it. Emmeline had always been underfoot, asking questions and never waiting for the answers, but instead choosing to make up her own. Murielle smiled thinking of her precocious daughter, far more similar to herself than she had ever chosen to believe. Richard de Conquil would have had a good laugh at his granddaughter.

As for Richard de Conquil himself. At one time long past,

Murielle could have never believed she could find anyone to replace her father. He doted on her, and she idolized him. Frédéric was correct. As a child Murielle had asked endless chains of questions without waiting for the answers. But her father could remember her questions and answer them all later when she was ready to listen. He always had the answers, and he always had time for Murielle. In an age when children were handed off to servants to be raised, Richard de Conquil preferred to do the majority of the paternal chores himself. It seemed prudent to hire a nurse to help raise her and to teach Murielle about "female matters," as he put it. Angélique helped her in that respect, but Murielle found her frustrating on any other matter. So, she gravitated to her father. There was never any business so pressing in Richard's busy schedule that he would not stop to tend to one of his daughter's needs. He brought Murielle with him to meetings of state. There was but only a few official proceedings that he attended without his daughter. And woe to him that dared question Richard de Conquil on her right to be there.

Murielle's mother had died in childbirth, so Richard de Conquil was the only parent she had ever known. She knew extraordinarily little about the woman who had died bringing her to life. Nothing was ever said about her. Early on, when Murielle had begun to have such thoughts, she reasoned that her father was simply too grief stricken over her death to speak of her. She held this idea for a long time. But then, on rare occasion, particularly when he had imbibed too much, he would speak of her. Not very much, of course, but just enough to give Murielle a sense of his feelings for his dead wife.

"Your mother..." he slurred angrily on one such occasion and said no more. It was the tone in his voice and the fire in his eyes which spoke more to Murielle than the two words. For a time, she could pretend that he was simply angry at her for leaving him. She tried at any rate. But she could not escape the memory of his face at that moment. His bleary eyes, bloodshot from the overindulgence of drink, became clear for a moment, his lips quivered then turned down to a scowl. "Your mother..." was all he said. Two words. But the manner in which he said it, and the rage which had suddenly bloomed in his eyes led Murielle to believe that all had not been well in the kingdom of their marriage. It was on another occasion, after an exceptionally good day at the lists, that Murielle heard enough to finally convince her that her father's wife, her mother, had been a source of great strife in their marriage.

On one wall in their manor house hung the portrait of a woman. Nothing surrounded this portrait; it hung alone just as the perfunctory altar to the god of war hung alone on a wall in another room. And it served a similar function to that altar. Murielle had come to learn that Richard de Conquil was a man of appearances. Not that he was a vain man who sought only to impress others, *au contraire*, he had no desire to impress others. However, as a student of the human condition, he understood the irrational passions and compulsions which sometimes governed men. As he understood that in his age soldiers would neither trust nor follow a man with little faith in the god of war, he understood men would think ill of one who did not properly mourn his deceased wife who died while bearing his child. Richard de Conquil understood that men's perceptions of him affected his ability to lead. To that end, the single portrait hung alone on one wall, a testament to the love he felt for his wife and mother of his child.

Richard had been drinking in celebration of their progress, as Murielle's skill with the lance had improved tremendously. He turned to that portrait, staggering slightly from the effects of his celebration and raised his goblet. "Cheers!" he cried. "Here's to your daughter who has accomplished what you could not! She has broken the chains; she has gained her freedom from the oppression of this *grande société* which enslaved your mind all your wretched life!"

Murielle's own goblet slipped from her lips. She had never heard her father speak so about his wife. She looked at the portrait. To her, in that moment, it was as though she had never seen it before. Murielle had never known her mother, never seen her, and her mother had never seen Murielle. The birth was said to be difficult.

There was a lot of blood. The woman had lost consciousness without seeing the fruit of her labor before the Lord Noirceur had taken her.

The solitary portrait was the only image Murielle had of that woman, that stranger. She had looked it over a few times in her short life, mildly curious about this unknown woman. But at that moment, watching her father sway angrily before it, Murielle was certain she knew the passions in that woman that the artist had captured so well. The woman's dark, almost raven black hair hung free, cascading over her shoulders, nearly touching her knees. It hung unrestrained, not as a married woman should wear it, but as a maiden might. Ornate embroidery embellished the sleeves and collar of her silken dress. A costly dress, Murielle thought. Drawn then to the woman's eyes, dark and cold, set above high, haughty cheek-bones, she shivered. There was no sternness there, only self-absorption.

No one had ever spoken to Murielle about the woman who had brought her into the world. None of the servants would speak to her about the woman. Direct questions were ignored.

She had assumed, naively, that it was out of respect and from overwhelming sorrow that they would not speak of her. Gazing at her father wavering before the aloof figure in the portrait, Murielle realized it was out of fear of Richard de Conquil's wrath that they remained silent. Gazing at that portrait, Murielle felt that she finally knew that woman she might have called Mother in another life.

"Your mother would not have approved of the path upon which your father took you." Frédéric continued to stare blindly into the distance, the veil of the past thoroughly covering his eyes. Murielle gave the old soldier a hard stare. He had a knack for tapping into her thoughts.

"*La gentille femme*. That was the woman's role in the *grande société*." Frédéric turned and looked at Murielle with a wan smile. He gave a short chuckle. "She would have never approved." He paused for a considerable time before he resumed, speaking more to his feet than to Murielle. "I must admit I agreed with your mother. At the time, I thought what he taught you could only bring anguish." Frédéric smiled to himself. "But I did not know everything, it seems."

Frédéric snapped from his reverie and clasped his hands warmly on her shoulders. "Enough of the past! It depresses me! What brings you to the city after so long an absence?"

Murielle was lost in her own *rêverie*, the veil of the past now covering her eyes. Knowing that the woman she might have called Mother had died in childbirth made Murielle all the more anxious when she learned she herself was with child. Her fears, however, were for naught. The midwife in fact, spent more time calming her than delivering the baby. After applying cool compresses, she spoke soothing words in Murielle's ear as she held her hand, working to keep her calm only to find that the baby had already come. Murielle was hardly aware of the fact.

"Well," the old woman cried, "I have never seen a first-time mother deliver so quickly and so easily! Truly you have been blessed by Mava the great mother herself!"

Murielle held her daughter, the pain, fear, and exhaustion all washed away by the love she felt for the little bundle she held to her breast. And Gilles was there, smiling down at her as she lay on the pallet. She returned his smile. The love she felt for him at that moment could not have been greater.

Frédéric shook her back to the present. "Something troubles you my dear. Does grave business bring you to the city?"

Grave business indeed. *The gravest business of all*, she thought. And then, Murielle's eyes opened wide for she suddenly saw what had been in front of her all this time. Frédéric was a castle guard. A castle guard and former knight in service of the Old King. If anyone could grant her access to the old King, it was Frédéric.

"Yes, Frédéric, my business is grave." Murielle swallowed hard. "I have come to entreat the Old King. You must take me too him! You must!"

Murielle had turned to face the old knight and seized his shoulders in a death grip. Frédéric pried her hands from him and shook his head sadly. She looked at him strangely for his expression had changed to one of desperate sadness. As sad as he had been remembering his good friend Richard, he now looked absolutely morose and inconsolable.

"Alas my girl, it is not possible." Frédéric shook his head. "Much has changed since you were here last. The kingdom is not what it once was. The Old King has been ill, terribly ill. It has been a long lingering malady, one which has weakened him little by little, day by day. And as he has weakened, Prince Henri has grown stronger. He has slowly wrested power from his father. He has driven out his father's supporters and replaced them with his own lackeys."

Frédéric swept his hands over his own uniform. "I, once a knight and trusted advisor to the Old King, am relegated to the position of castle guard. A position which is a mere joke. I wear the uniform but am allowed no access to the important parts of the castle. Henri and his "advisors" cut me off from the Old King." He leaned in close to Murielle and lowered his voice. "But I have influence they do not know about. Servants loyal to me tell me he is far from well. His breathing is labored; he cannot rise from his bed. More recently, he has not even been able to be aroused from a deathly sleep. I fear that the Dark One awaits in the wings for him. But more dreadful than his impending demise is the loss of his power before it."

Murielle walked a short distance and turned her head to the sky. *All for naught*, she thought, *this journey has been all for naught*.

Frédéric rose stiffly and approached Murielle. "But do not despair," he said, a hoarse whisper in her ear. "There are those of us who have not abandoned our king. We merely wait, gathering evidence against Prince Henri. We wait for the truth to be revealed. We wait for a sign to be revealed, by the gods's ears, we wait a sign which will damn the mutinous son!"

Murielle hung her head in dejection and exasperation. Her brilliant plan had failed her. Her reason was spent, she could think no more. All her father's teachings were for naught. She wrung her hands as two castle guards passed by, engaged in light conversation.

They stopped ahead of her and Frédéric at a little distance away, and they could hear their words.

"I had a most peculiar experience this morning," said the first guard to the second.

"Peculiar?" his companion replied.

"Yes peculiar. Well, perhaps that is not the word I wish to use. Weird may be a better word for it. Or perhaps merely odd–"

"At any matter, this peculiar, weird, or odd experience you had-"

"Yes, well, it was unusual."

"So now it is unusual," replied the listener with a look of annoyance. "Get on with it."

"Well, it was that this morning I had a... a... swoon, I suppose one might call it." The first guard let this out haltingly.

"A *swoon*?"

"Yes, a swoon."

"As a woman has a swoon?"

"Yes, just as a woman has a swoon." The first guard paused then added, "Just as your wife had a swoon when she saw me and realized she could have no other."

The second held up his fist. "You are about to swoon again, my friend."

"Peace, peace." The first held up his hands. "I shall recount to you my tale. As it was, I was making my rounds near the Old King's chambers when I felt faint. I sat down on a nearby chair, then all was black."

"Peculiar, indeed."

"But that was not the odd part—"

"Now we are back to odd," the second sighed.

"Perhaps it was merely unusual."

"Get on with it."

"Well, out of the black came the form of a man. I could see him clearly, just as I see you now."

"Curious," replied the second.

"Perhaps that is just the word to describe this experience," said the first thoughtfully, "Curious."

"Get on with it."

"Well, behind the man stood another figure, but I could not make out this second man's face, if he were a man, that is. He was as indistinct as a mountain in a fog. Presently, he spoke to me."

"The man?"

"No, the indistinct figure behind him was the one who spoke." The first paused for a moment, deep in thought. "What was unusual was that the indistinct figure spoke in my own voice."

"Peculiar," replied the second. "You mean to say that it was high-pitched and very annoying?"

The first raised his fist. "You, my friend, are very close to having a swoon yourself."

"Peace," responded the second, shaking his head. "Continue with your curious tale. What did the indistinct figure say to you?"

"He said, and I remember the words exactly, 'This man, who stands before you, will come to see the Old King this very day. You will take him to the Old King immediately, without hesitation.'"

"Very odd," said the second. "What else did he say?"

"That and nothing more. I awoke thereafter and continued my rounds."

"Peculiar." The second furrowed his brow in consternation. "Do you remember the appearance of this man you saw?"

"Oh, most definitely. His image is burned into my mind. I feel as though an entire lifetime could pass, and I would yet know him. Even as an old and feeble man, if I had not my senses, I would still know him if nothing else."

The second chuckled. "Old and feeble. Those conditions are in you now!"

The first raised his fist.

"Peace. Describe this unusual fellow then."

"Oh, there was nothing unusual about him at all. He was, in fact, quite ordinary in appearance. He was a big fellow, not fat, but solid and muscular. He had the countenance of a man who has worked all his days. A farmer perhaps. His hands were large and strong, his head bald, and his eyes were a kindly brown. He seemed a good peaceable fellow. I think I would lead him to the Old King even if I were not compelled to do so."

"Compelled?"

"Why yes," said the first, frowning. "That is the most unusual part of this entire tale. I feel an intense compulsion to take this man to Old King, through no will of my own. I cannot resist even if my life depended on it. And further, I feel, nay I *know*, for reasons I cannot ascertain, that when I take this man, the Old King will instantly awake and greet this fellow warmly as he has not done to anyone else in many a day."

"Very odd indeed, this tale of yours." The second began to walk. "Come, let us go down the pub. I will buy you a drink for such a peculiar and entertaining tale."

"I hope you are as generous as your wife. She always buys me the best when we are at the pub."

The second raised his fist.

"Peace."

The old knight followed the pair with his eyes as they walked out of sight. "What people will say in these times," he said, shaking his head. "What make you of that preposterous tale, Murielle?"

He turned his head to her and was greeted with a horrific sight. Murielle stood trembling, her face white, and beginning to turn a pale shade of blue. She was not breathing. Her mouth worked, as a fish on a riverbank. No breath came, and neither came words.

Frédéric held his hands out to her. "Murielle! Whatsoever is the matter? Has an illness come over you? A seizure? By the gods's ears, what is the matter?"

Murielle's mouth still worked feebly, her color changing to a light blue. Presently, Frédéric became aware of a noise emanating from Murielle's throat. She began to shake her head back and forth. The noise became louder and Murielle's face turned bluer until suddenly–

"Wrong!" she gasped out. She took a shuddering breath, then another. "Wrong!" she gasped again, this time more clearly.

"What say you?" asked Frédéric, relieved that Murielle's face although still pale was no longer any shade of blue.

"Wrong, wrong, wrong, all wrong," she cried as she swung her head in rapid arcs.

"I do not understand."

Murielle looked at him, but her eyes did not see. "This is all wrong! This is all wrong!"

Frédéric took up her hands into his. "Whatsoever is wrong, all wrong, my dear?"

Murielle locked onto his eyes as if seeing him for the first time. "Oh, I have made a terrible mistake. Terrible! Terrible!"

"But whatsoever is the matter, dear?"

Murielle brushed her hair back from her face, taking two deep, but ragged breaths as she did. "I never should have come. I never was meant to come."

"My dear, I do not understand."

"I must go! I must return home and try to repair my mistake!" Murielle began to walk briskly toward the castle gates. It was all Frédéric could do to keep up with her.

"I do not understand!" he said in exasperation. "Whatsoever is the matter? Why must you return home?"

When Murielle reached the gates, she broke into a run and Frédéric had to stop for he had not the energy to follow any further. "You must return again and visit with me again, Murielle!" he cried out to her as she wove through the thickening crowd.

Murielle paused long enough to turn and call back to him through the crowd. "I will Frédéric, I will if I am able!"

"You will always find me here, my lady," he said with a formal bow, "where one will find any loyal subject of the Old King."

"I will, I will!" Murielle promised, and somehow, she felt certain that she would keep that promise.

Murielle broke into run, racing back through the streets of the Eternal City. Although pushing her way through thicker crowds than she had encountered on her way to the castle, she arrived at the stable in short order. She ran into the stableman standing in the entryway.

"I need my horse immediately!" she cried gruffly.

The stableman looked at her calmly. "I suspected as much. Your horse has been going mad in here, tearing up the stall, frantic to leave this place. He knows something is afoot."

Murielle tossed the stableman a small bag of coins. "Take this for the trouble and the damage. Now saddle my horse and bring him to me."

The stableman let out a low chuckle. "He awaits ready for you now." He called to the stable boy who brought Cheval saddled and ready to ride. "He ceased his destructive behavior as soon as I showed him the saddle."

Murielle mounted up and reined Cheval toward the street. The stableman stopped her and tossed back the bag as well as the coins she had given him earlier. "I return these to you, for if you are who I believe you to be, then consider my service as minuscule repayment of a great debt I owe you."

Murielle looked at him and said nothing. After a moment of silence, she nodded her head at the man and kicked Cheval into a gallop. The stableman watched her disappear down the street and toward the gates. Much had happened to change the stableman's appearance, so he was not surprised Murielle did not recognize him. But he recognized her. Étienne, as Richard de Conquil's reeve, had recognized her right away despite the long interval of time since he had last seen Murielle. Or Guillaume de Marschal for that matter.

Cheval raced back down the Straight Road at a pace which Murielle never would have believed possible from the horse. He galloped as if the Demon itself were on his tail. Once Murielle looked back to check with nearly disastrous results. Cheval was reckless. He slowed not one bit for blind curves or hanging limbs. For a while Murielle wondered at what possessed the horse, attempting to slow him to no avail. Finally, she resolved herself to the animal's madness and held on for the ride.

In far less time than it had taken them to reach Darloque, Murielle and Cheval had returned to their home. Thick foam flew from the horse's lips. His sides slick and dripping with sweat, his eyes wide and wild, he seemed neither willing nor able to stop. Fearful that Cheval might speed past the farmhouse in his madness, Murielle gripped the reins tightly in her hands and pulled back with all her strength and then some. The horse, awakening from his trance, stopped immediately, leaving long skid marks in the dirt leading up to the open front door.

Murielle threw herself from the saddle and rushed into the farmhouse, finding it empty. Not even the doves were there. Across the open room, the door to the barnyard stood wide open. She did not call out, for she already knew there was no one to hear her voice. Murielle walked out the other door to the empty barnyard where long shadows stretched across the dirt. The barn only contained animals at rest, hiding from the heat. Leaving the barn, Murielle walked to the edge of the drought-ravaged cornfield, searching futilely for whom she knew deep in her heart was not to be found.

Cheval stood in the open front doorway of the farmhouse as Murielle returned from the barnyard. The horse panted heavily, dripping foam onto the dirt floor, a look of pain and desperation in his eyes. Murielle wrung her hands in her own desperation. Where could Gilles have gone? He would not have left–or would he have? In her mind she could see her husband on his way to Darloque, convinced that he was the only one destined to see the Old King. Similarly, she could see him running after Emmeline to escort her to safety beyond The Wild Hare.

Murielle hung her head in her hands. Reason had left her entirely. She could not think. The plan was askew, as she had heard her father say, and she had no idea how to get it back on track. The

Prince would be coming soon to retrieve his bride. Murielle shivered at this thought. What should he tell him? Should she keep to the plan? What if Gilles had changed the plan, and she sent the Prince straight to her husband and daughter. She could not think.

Cheval's labored breathing filled the room with white noise. Murielle could not think. "Reason, sweet reason, why have you failed me now?" she cried out through her hands.

She ran her hands through her hair, Cheval's heavy panting echoed though her head. Eyes shut tight, she cried out against Reason's fickle nature. When she opened her eyes again, she knew in an instant that it was too late, far too late. She knew that Gilles had not left for the reasons she had suspected. The plan was more than askew, it was obliterated. Murielle opened her eyes and gazing at the floor, she saw, she saw.

Blood.

CHAPTER TWELVE

EMMELINE CLIMBED. As the terrain became increasingly steep and rocky, the sporadic young hardwoods and occasional pines had become a coniferous forest of massive, old-growth pines and firs. She wove in between the trunks, climbed over boulders, and scrambled up rockslides, all to the beat of the never-ending pounding from somewhere up the mountain. Bang, bam-bam. Bang, bam-bam. There was a rhythmic cycle to the noise. Sixteen sets and then a short pause. Emmeline had plenty of time to mark the pattern as the mountain seemed to reach into infinity. When the sixteenth set finished, she held her breath as she counted to four and the cycle repeated itself again.

Emmeline continued her climb. As annoying as the noise was, the rhythm let her set a good pace and helped take her mind off her dilemma. It was during the normal break in the cycle as she wiped sweat from her brow, that she looked up the mountain and thought the ground did not look as steep as it had before. She paused as the pounding began a new cycle. *No, it is not as steep now*, she thought. The ground was not as rocky, and she saw that the massive trunks of the trees stood far apart, yet the sun did not reach the ground here. Emmeline turned her eyes upward. Tree trunks which two grown men together could not reach around climbed into the sky. Great green boughs stretched out from the trunks at a height which made Emmeline's head spin. The boughs joined with those of neighboring trees to create a great green canopy providing a cool, shady area far beneath them.

A thick bed of needles crunched beneath her feet as she continued up the mountain. Here and there large cones–some as large as her head–littered the ground, presumably dropped from the massive trees. Emmeline looked up again to the distant boughs and shivered. If one of those giant cones were to fall and hit her, she might very well be killed.

The pounding noise had increased in intensity as she climbed the mountain, but now it seemed very close. Emmeline looked at small outcropping near her and saw the loose stones tremble with each hit. Presently, a handful of them rolled free and tumbled through the needles and down the mountain. *Awfully close*, she thought.

She struggled over the last major outcropping and began walking uphill at a leisurely pace. "Blest be Mava's many litters," Emmeline said aloud. She kicked a few of the cones she came across, watching them roll leisurely down the mountain. She shifted her paquet from one shoulder to another. It was when she came upon a great, flat boulder set into the ground that her stomach released a low rumble.

Emmeline looked to the sky. The canopy was so thick and green that it was impossible to determine the place of the sun in the sky. Regardless of its position, it had been a long time since she had eaten. Her parents's rules for the morning routine were simple: awake, chores, then eat. And in the mad rush of the morning's events, Emmeline had not taken her morning meal. It came upon her suddenly that she was famished.

The boulder's level surface made a perfect table upon which to spread open her paquet. Emmeline laid out the contents in an orderly manner, dragged a fallen log over to sit upon, and began her repast.

She forsook the prayer her father offered up before every meal, not because he was absent, but simply because she was too hungry to wait even the moment it would take to offer the short prayer of thanks. Devouring the food as a starving animal would, she soon found herself slowing her pace, chewing to the rhythm of the ever-present pounding. At one of the breaks in the cycle, Emmeline was taking a sip from her flask when she heard a voice speaking.

The pounding resumed. Emmeline swallowed with difficulty, her eyes growing wide. She held her breath until the next break in the cycle. She heard it again, not the particular words, but it was definitely someone speaking somewhere up the mountain. At the next break she corrected herself: somewhere *close* up the mountain. Emmeline began to eat again, slowly, and determinedly, in arrhythmic measure to the noise up the mountain, willing herself not to choke.

At the next break Emmeline listened carefully to the sound of the voice, hoping to discern the words of the speaker. Nothing came to her. So as the pounding resumed, she took a sip from her flask, then rose from her seat and walked slowly up slight grade, leaving her paquet and the remains of her meal spread out upon the flat boulder. She crept up slowly, moving from tree trunk to tree trunk, being careful to remain out of sight of whomever was up ahead. Shortly, she came over a rise, and as the pounding took its accustomed break, she stepped onto a wide plateau, upon which she was greeted by an incredible sight.

The trunks of the mountain trees were spaced out farther here, allowing the sunlight in its steep angle to touch the bare, dusty ground. The air itself seemed to shimmer in the light, dancing in the faint breeze that whirled across the plateau. Emmeline thought the place must be filled with some kind of magic until she turned to her right and beheld the massive forge with its immense bed of angry coals pouring out smoke and turbulence into the sky.

In the brief pause between cycles of the pounding, Emmeline took in the scene on the plateau. Before the forge stood a huge figure covered in dark brown fur, its back turned to her. Its long ears tilted back from its head. The figure held aloft a steaming sword in its paw, turning it over, examining it carefully before tossing it carelessly into great pile of blades on the ground beside the forge. The figure grasped a bar of steel with the tongs it held, plunged the cold steel into the angry coals, then pulled another bar of glowing red steel from the coals, and laying it upon a great anvil, proceeded to pound it in that all too familiar rhythm with a great, lethal looking hammer.

Emmeline jumped as the pounding resumed. On the plateau the noise was beyond deafening–she felt it in her teeth. The figure pounded out the rhythm. One hit on the steel, followed by two on the anvil. Sixteen sets and the hunk of steel was transformed into a sword. Emmeline counted as she had all the way up the mountain. In a great fluid motion, the figure plunged the sword into a cask of water, held it aloft to examine it, tossed it into the pile, buried a bar of steel in the angry coals, pulled a bright red bar out from the coals and resumed the hammering.

Mouth agape, Emmeline stood out in the open, watching the incredible process occurring before her eyes. She dashed behind the nearest tree trunk when she realized she had been standing out in the open for too long. Emmeline, wincing with each blow of the hammer, watched the cycle repeat again and again with the same rhythmic fluidity. Calapine, the goddess of steel, continued at her work in perfect rhythm, forging steel into blades and tossing them into an ever-growing pile.

From her hiding place Emmeline looked around the plateau. *She must be here somewhere*, she thought to herself, *they are called The Inseparable Sisters*. Then she spied an opening in the side of the mountain. She heard great cursing emanating from it. It was the foulest language she had heard in her life. A few of the words she did not even know. Presently, a giant figure emerged from the cave, shaking great clouds of dust and dirt from its massive furry body.

The pounding stopped. "What in the name of hell are you

complaining about now, Sister?" screeched Calapine. "You had better be making me more steel, damn you!"

Felapine, the goddess of iron, offered an obscene gesture to her sister, then threw a large, featureless black rock almost the size of Emmeline's head at Calapine. She ducked the rock, and it smashed through the trunk of a nearby tree.

"Beware, Sister! You almost hit me!"

"Believe me, Sister, if I had wanted to hit you, I would have."

Calapine raised her hammer. "I will hit you and not miss, Sister."

"Never mind all that," screeched Felapine. "All I can dig out of this hole is this idiotic pitchblende. Useless it is. The iron is gone in this hole."

Felapine picked up another of the featureless black rocks lying at the cave entrance and examined it thoughtfully. "As useless as pitchblende is though, it will one day cause the humans a great amount of suffering."

Calapine pumped the bellows under the forge with her foot. *Her crooked foot*, Emmeline noted. The goddess of steel set down her tongs and her hammer, then wiped her paws casually on her blacksmith's apron. Taking up her hammer again, she limped over to where her sister stood at the entrance of the cave.

"You will find more iron, Sister," she said calmly. "We have too many weapons to produce in too short a time."

Felapine straightened, the ear which did not lay flat on the side of her head perked up. "I told you, the iron is gone in this hole."

Calapine scowled. "We must make more weapons. If there is no more iron in that hole, then you will dig another."

"I will not dig another hole, Sister. This entire endeavor is a fool's errand."

"That may be so, Sister." Calapine's eyes narrowed. "But we have been given a task, and this is what we must do."

"Who says we must finish this task? Bellicor! Bahhh!" Felapine held her paw in front of her, holding a pair of imaginary reins. She pranced around the plateau. "Hear ye! Hear ye! It is I, Lord Bellicor!

I will give you all tasks to perform and not tell you the purpose while I sit on my bum and bask in my own glory!"

"Quiet, Sister!"

Felapine pranced in circles around her sister on her imaginary horse crying over and over: "Hear ye! Hear ye! All is mum while I sit on my bum!"

"Silence, Sister!" shouted Calapine angrily. But her twitching whiskers betrayed her. In another moment she bent over double, cackling laughter.

Felapine continued to prance around her sister, singing her song, but her voice began to waver.

"Hilarious, Sister!" Calapine stood again, tears streaming from her eyes as she cackled. "You have captured him completely!"

Felapine came to a stumbling halt, bent over double herself, and roared with laughter at her own humor. After a few moments, Felapine righted herself and staggered over to Calapine. Throwing a paw around her sister, she wiped her eyes with her other paw as they cackled in unison.

Emmeline watched this display, unsure what to make of it. The Sisters's lack of respect, nay, their outright mockery of the god of war, disturbed Emmeline in a way she could not fully explain to herself. She was certain this behavior was not of the sort that the nun in the Temple of the Sisters expected of her gods.

The goddesses separated with a hearty slap on each other's backs. Felapine walked over to a great furnace, wiping her eyes, and issuing a few staccato cackles. She peered into a large stone cauldron sitting upon the smoking furnace. Her one good ear laid back a little as she frowned. She pumped the bellows a few times, then seemingly satisfied with what was happening in the cauldron, turned back toward her hole.

Calapine had returned to her forge. She pumped its bellows as she cackled to herself a few times. She grasped a new bar of steel from the coals and seemed ready to shape it into another sword, however, her eyes were not on the task at hand. Emmeline watched curiously as Calapine held the glowing steel over the massive anvil. Calapine's eyes were on her sister as she inspected the cauldron. She held her hammer over the anvil as if ready to strike yet did not make the first blow to start the rhythm anew. Calapine's eyes followed her sister as she made her way across the plateau and back down into the gaping hole.

Emmeline's eyes remained set upon Calapine, watching her as she set her hammer on the ground and the glowing bar back into the coals. Wiping her paws deliberately on her apron as she went, the goddess limped around to the back side of the forge and picked up an object. The forge blocked Emmeline's view of the object Calapine held, but whatever it was brought a smile to the goddess's face. Emmeline did not dare move from her position behind the tree to try to see the object more clearly. For the moment she was content to simply watch the goddess of steel admiring this object which lit up her face–especially the white mark on her lip–with a diffuse golden glow.

Renewed cursing from the hole in the side of the mountain made her look up. Calapine shifted the object quickly behind her back as her sister emerged from the hole carrying a pile of stones in her paws. She looked around, saw Calapine standing behind the forge and walked over to her, grumbling as she made her way.

Felapine dropped her load unceremoniously on the ground in front of the forge. "Pitchblende is all I can find in that hole!" she screeched. "There is no more iron!"

Calapine kept the object behind her back, hidden from her sister. A scowl formed on the goddess's lips; her whiskers twitched in annoyance. She opened her mouth to say something then she paused. Her scowl turned pensive; her eyes became distant as she stared at the dark pile of black stones.

"Pitchblende is commonly found among silver deposits, is it not, Sister?" she said, tilting her head slightly.

Felapine stared at the rocks and furrowed her brow. "Yes, it is, Sister. There is quite a good amount of silver down there." Her eyes returned to her sister. "Why do you ask? Silver is not iron, and the iron is tapped out."

Calapine started. "Oh, I wish to wrap some of the handles with silver wire," she blurted out. She became contemplative again. "I also wish to decorate the swords with silver ornamentation."

"Bahh!" grunted Felapine. "A waste! Those swords will not be used long enough for anyone to care how pretty they look!"

Calapine's thoughtful look evaporated, and the scowl returned. "Do not tell me how to make weapons, Sister."

"I will tell you if what you plan is foolish and wasteful."

Calapine's ears tilted back. "I am the goddess of steel, *I* make the weapons, and *I* will make them with whatever metals I choose!"

Felapine's whiskers twitched, and her one erect ear laid back. "*I* am the goddess of iron, *I* dig out the ores, and you will make the weapons with whatever metals *I* provide!" She paused a moment; her ear rose slightly. Her head tilted slightly to the left and then to the right.

Calapine's eyes grew wary. She watched her sister's eyes as she tried to see what Calapine held behind her back.

"What did you do with the last batch of silver I found for you?" she asked, her eyes narrowing.

The goddess of steel straightened and adjusted the object minutely behind her back. "I used it on a weapon of course."

"What weapon, Sister." Felapine tilted her head again.

Calapine flustered. "Well, umm... it was umm..."

"Yes, Sister?"

"Fergu's axe!" she blurted out.

"Fergu's axe?" Felapine tilted her head, scratching her head.

"Why yes, Sister. You know how particular he is about his weapons."

"Ahh, yes." Felapine nodded. "I recall that one." She waved her paw as if trying to shake the memory out of the air. "He made you rework the silver at least three times before it was to his liking."

"A damn waste of silver," Calapine replied with a growl.

Felapine gave her sister a curious look for another moment before she spoke again. "Very well," she said with a grunt, "I will retrieve silver for your swords, if that is what you wish." With that, Felapine crossed the plateau and disappeared down the hole.

Still standing behind the forge, Calapine gazed upon the mysterious object once more with a winsome smile before returning it to its hiding place. Emmeline shrunk back behind her hiding place as the goddess of steel came out from behind the forge and limped over to the pile of swords.

Calapine looked over the swords, thrown carelessly into an irregular pile on the ground. Selecting one at random, she held the blade aloft, turned it around in the slanting sunlight and nodded what might have been an affirmation. She tossed it back into the pile and ticked off a count on her paw. She frowned and counted again. She planted her paws on her hips and shook her head with a grunt.

"Sister!" she screeched. "Sister!"

A great cursing again welled up from the hole and Felapine emerged carrying a load of silver ore in her paws. "What do you want now?"

"I require more iron, Sister! I do not have nearly enough swords!"

"What? Just how many do you think you require?"

"Many more than I have."

"I see plenty in that pile," Felapine screeched back, pointing at the dull blades on the ground.

"Not enough!" Calapine crossed her paws over her chest. "And besides the swords, I need iron for axes, armor, pommels, and–"

"No, no, no!" Felapine crossed the distance to the furnace in a few rapid steps. "I told you before. The iron is tapped out in this hole! No iron, no steel, no swords. *Fini!*"

"Then dig another hole," Calapine said flatly.

The goddess of iron dropped the load of silver ore on the ground before the furnace with a loud thud. One stone rolled over to Calapine, stopping next to her crooked foot. She kicked it roughly out of the way. It tumbled erratically across the plateau and came to rest next to the tree behind which Emmeline hid.

"NO!" Felapine roared. "I have said it before, and it is as true now as it was when I first said it. This is a fool's errand and a complete waste of our time!" She peered into the cauldron and pumped the bellows with her foot then loaded several pieces of the silver into the great stone pot.

Felapine spat into the fire. "That cursed Bellicor, always thinking he can teach the humans some great noble lesson. Bahh! We do the work, and they learn nothing. I am disgusted with him and his great nonsense!"

"Nevertheless, Sister," Calapine replied coolly as her ears tilted slowly back, "We have a task to perform. Ours is not to question the reasons, only to dig and to forge."

Felapine dropped another piece of silver ore into the pot then turned her head slowly. Her dark brown eyes, cool and brooding, met those of her mirror image.

"I said no," she growled softly over her shoulder. "And you will drop the matter now, or this silver goes back into the ground."

Calapine's own dark brown eyes grew large. Her ears flattened against the back of her neck. Her whiskers twitched in agitation. Her brown fur prickled up her back.

"You will smelt that silver," she hissed, "and then you will dig another hole for the iron that I require to make weapons of steel."

As her right eye began to twitch, Felapine's nostrils flared with tense, rapid breath. "Very well," she said tersely, and in one swift motion she dumped the contents of the stone cauldron into the pile at her feet. She scooped the entire load up in her paws and stomped back to the hole.

Emmeline glanced nervously at the stray lump of silver ore so very close to her hiding place.

Despite her debility, Calapine rapidly covered the distance between the forge and the hole and easily caught her sister before she disappeared within. She seized Felapine by the shoulder with an iron grip and spun her quickly around to face her.

"Put those back!" she screeched into Felapine's face, spittle flying wildly.

The goddess of iron dropped the load at her feet, then wiped her face with her paws. Her eye continued to twitch, perhaps even more fiercely than before.

"I will not, Sister." Felapine spoke with surprising calm in her voice, however, her twitching eye betrayed her true inner tension. She glanced stonily at her sister's paw on her shoulder. "Remove your paw."

The scowl deepened across Calapine's face. "Put the ore back into the smelter, Sister." She spoke in a smooth tone which was anything but calm. Deep tension roiled in her voice.

"Remove your paw," Felapine repeated smoothly. "Or I will remove it for you."

Slowly, Calapine released her sister's shoulder. She raised her hammer in her right paw and brought the head down into the free paw with a hard thud. Her scowl deepened. "You will pick up this silver ore on the ground and put it into the smelter, and then you will dig another hole for iron."

Felapine leaned forward slightly, her eye twitching maniacally. "Who says?" she replied, slowly and deliberately.

"I say," Calapine replied, lifting her hammer again. "And so does my hammer."

Felapine pressed closer to her sister, her ear tilted back slowly as she scowled. Her right eye slowed its twitching minutely. "You just try it, Sister. I will feed you that hammer."

"You will not be feeding anything to anyone after I shove this hammer up your arse."

The two goddesses stood *vis-à-vis*, nose to nose, whisker to whisker, each tensed and ready to strike should the other merely flinch.

After a long, indeterminable time of charged silence, during which Emmeline began to seriously fear for her safety, Felapine brayed laughter, a high-pitched cackle sounding more sinister than joyous. Calapine joined in with her own wicked screech and dropped her hammer. The two goddesses embraced roughly.

"Oh, Sister," Felapine sighed when she had finished laughing. "What is another hole in this great mountain? I can easily find another vein of iron." She tapped the side of her nose as she nodded.

Calapine chuckled in low series of grunts. "I hate this as much as you do." She eyed the pile of silver ore. "I have better things to do than to make weapons for soon to be dead men."

"Perhaps, Sister," Felapine said with a hoarse chuckle, "now that we have come to an agreement, Emmeline will come out from behind that tree and we can complete our other task."

Tingles raced up Emmeline's spine at the mention of her name.

Calapine casually spun the head of her hammer in the dirt. "Hmmpf," she grunted. "Come, Emmeline," she said with a sidelong glance to the tree behind which the girl hid. "Come out now and let us do this business."

Behind the tree Emmeline began to shiver. How did they know she was hiding here? How did they know her name? She slapped her forehead with her palm. *Idiot!* she muttered under her breath, *They are gods! Of course they know who you are and where you are hiding!*

Emmeline took a deep, shuddering breath and peered out cautiously from behind the tree. Calapine and Felapine looked at her expectantly. She ducked back behind the tree and leaned heavily on the trunk for support. Her heart raced, and her breath came fast. Taking a deep, cleansing breath, she collected herself. The stray lump of silver ore still lay next to the trunk where it had come to rest. Emmeline picked it up and slowly turned over the rough stone in her hands. Its solidity gave her focus. She breathed deeply again and peered out once more. The Sisters still stood by the hole, staring at her. Calapine crossed her forepaws over her apron and tapped her good foot impatiently.

"Come. Now." grunted Felapine, sounding as impatient as her sister appeared.

Emmeline came out from behind the tree slowly, walking toward the Sisters, her head down, still turning the ore over in her hands. It was not a particularly pretty stone. It had a face only a mother could love. She chuckled to herself at her wit.

Emmeline stopped next to another, even larger tree a short distance from the goddesses. She felt safer to be near something large and solid. The trunk was so large that ten Emmelines might have been just able to join hands and encircle it. It rose majestically, disappearing into the sky above the mountain. High above, branches spread out over her, touching no other tree. A few cones littered a bed of old needles. The tree gave her a feeling of safety, and the silver ore gave her focus.

"It is about time," said Calapine, the scowl still impressed on her face, her forepaws still crossed imposingly over her blacksmith's apron.

"Good," said Felapine with a sigh of indifference.

"Good," said Calapine.

Emmeline could feel the heat emanating from the forge and the smelting furnace next to it. Emmeline began to sweat from the combination of heat and stress. Except for the maddening tap of Calapine's foot on the ground, the awkward silence continued unabated for some time. Emmeline stared at her own feet, markedly diminutive when compared to the giant rabbit feet before her. She stared at Calapine's foot, tamping the ground at a regular pace, but with no break in the rhythm as there had been with her hammer. Desperate for something, anything, to happen, she let her eyes drift from the rock in her hands over to Calapine's crooked leg. It was not hideous, or even what she would call ugly. It was covered in the same dark brown fur which covered much of the goddess's body. The only sign of any real deformity was the odd angle it took relative to the other. That and Calapine's pronounced limp when she walked.

Emmeline let her eyes follow the leg up to the body of the

goddess. Her blacksmith's apron hid much of her furry body, but one only had to look at Felapine to know that the brown fur turned to a creamy white on her underbelly. Up and up her eyes rose, higher and higher, just as she had followed the impossibly tall trees up into the sky. The paws crossed at her chest were massive, unquestionably designed for the chores of the blacksmith, and decidedly capable of handling the massive hammer which rested beside her. Her head was large, erect ears long and thickset; her long whiskers, stiff and straight, could easily impale a human. A permanent scowl etched itself across her face.

And there was the curiosity of the Sisters. The entire head was covered on dark brown fur, except for a spot on her upper lip which was pure white. Emmeline's eyes turned casually to Felapine. She possessed an identical white spot on her upper lip. Emmeline tried to recall the story. One of the regular travelers who often stopped by their farmhouse had told it to her. Julien was his name, but Emmeline for the life of her could not remember the story. Something about drinking forbidden milk.

Felapine looked identical to her sister. She possessed the same features as Calapine, save for her right ear which lay flat against the side of her head, hanging down past her shoulder. Her paws hung at her side, just as large and threatening as her sister's, for they were designed to dig through the toughest rock the ground had to offer. Felapine's feet both stood straight and motionless on the ground. Emmeline's eyes returned to her own feet. And the tapping went on.

A new noise made Emmeline look up. Felapine was staring hard at her sister. The goddess of iron cleared her throat again.

"Will you cease tapping your damned foot, Sister!" She spat out a couple of more obscenities which caused Emmeline to blush.

Calapine merely turned to her sister, and as her scowl deepened across her face, she began tapping her foot more intensely. Emmeline could feel the ground shaking beneath her feet.

Felapine balled her paws into fists and let loose a torrent of obscenities at her sister. The ones that Emmeline knew made her eyes bulge; the ones she did not made her cringe for she was sure they were very bad words indeed.

Calapine returned her sister's vitriol with a half scowl, half smirk, then concluded her tapping with one final stamp of her foot which shook the ground so hard it made Emmeline jump.

"Better, Sister?" purred Calapine though a smirk.

Another torrent of obscenities followed; all the words which Emmeline knew and wished she did not. Calapine continued to smirk.

The goddess of steel picked up her hammer and smacked it hard into her left paw. "Are you quite finished, Sister?"

"I will be finished, Sister, when I have caved in your damnable skull with that infernal hammer of yours!"

The smirk quickly melted into a scowl. "You will not lay a paw on my hammer, Sister," she replied coolly.

Felapine straightened. She crossed her forepaws over her chest. Her left ear stood straight and alert.

"If I wish to touch that hammer, Sister, I will touch it. And there is nothing you can do to stop me." Felapine cracked her neck with a grimace and added smoothly: "Bitch."

"If you lay one claw on this hammer–" Calapine's eyes grew wide, "What did you call me?!"

A smug smile formed under the white patch on Felapine's upper lip. "Bitch."

Calapine's brown eyes bulged in their sockets, the fur stood up along the ridge of her back. She began to tremble all over.

Felapine slowly stretched out her right paw and tapped the head of the hammer with her index claw. "Bitch," she repeated in the same smooth tone.

Calapine's hammer flashed out in a wide arc, a mere blur of turbulence in the hot air. Felapine's head bobbed down, and Emmeline saw the hammer momentarily as it connected with the tree next to her. The trunk exploded in a cloud of chips, splinters, and sawdust. From somewhere far away Emmeline heard the tree groan and felt the rumble beneath her feet as the trunk toppled. It hit the ground with a deafening crash, jolting her into the air. When the dust settled, the giant tree lay less than an arm's length from her. Emmeline looked up at the massive trunk now on its side, and she began to shiver violently. Sawdust swirled to the ground like snow, falling in her hair and covering her clothes.

The voices of the screeching Sisters came to her from a muffled distance, her ears still full of the tree's violent demise. Emmeline stared at the gigantic trunk, still impossibly huge, even lying on its side. Her shaking would not stop. The tree, that impossibly huge tree, now lay half-way across the plateau, its shattered trunk broken and hanging some distance down the mountainside.

Emmeline turned to the goddesses, disbelieving. This tree could have very well killed her. No, not just killed her but smashed her into nothingness. There would have been nothing left for the Lord Noirceur to take to the afterlife. Yet, these two ill-mannered sisters squabbled as if nothing had happened. As if they had not nearly obliterated Emmeline completely.

"Now see what you have done, Sister," huffed Felapine finally. "You and your temper."

Emmeline stared down at the lump of silver ore in her still shaking hands. It was dirty, covered in a dusting of fine sawdust. She brushed the offending dust from its surface. It had given her focus before. She turned it over in her hands, tracing the ridges and crevices with her fingers, seeking that focus again.

Shouting began anew between the Sisters, an argument heavily-laden with obscenities. Emmeline turned the stone over and over in her hands. Slowly the focus returned. The stone's solidity, calmed her fear, cleared her mind. She lifted her head and shouted in a strong, resounding voice.

"STOP!!!"

The Sisters fell silent, mouths frozen in mid argument. Slowly they turned to stare at the human girl. They cocked their heads toward each other in amazement.

"What?" they asked in unison.

"Stop this senseless quarreling!" Emmeline shouted.

"Why?" asked Calapine.

Emmeline ignored the question. "You two nearly killed me, and all you care about is your selfish wants!"

"Well, you are not dead, so I do not see your problem," replied Felapine with a nod.

Emmeline's jaw dropped. She waved her arms erratically at the massive trunk lying next to her.

"Use your words," Felapine said with a frustrated sigh.

Calapine planted her paws on her hips with a huff. "You seem to believe," she interjected, "that I cannot fell a tree without killing someone."

Emmeline's mouth worked uselessly; only weak squeaking noises came out. "You nearly killed me!" she spat out finally.

"I believe you have said that before," sighed Felapine again as she shook her head slowly. "You are not dead."

Calapine scratched her chin. "Your problem is that you are obsessed with things that did not happen."

Felapine nodded. "Yes, if we had wanted you dead, you would most definitely be dead now." She pointed at her sister. "She is very good at that sort of thing."

Calapine nodded smugly. "Most definitely. I am exceptionally good at that. Better than her, in fact."

Felapine gave Calapine a sidelong glance. "I think not!"

"As with most things, Sister, you are wrong again."

Felapine turned to her sister; her eye began its spasmodic twitching anew. "I have *by far* killed more humans than you have!"

Calapine bristled as she hefted her hammer. "Anyone can throw stones randomly on a battlefield and hit something. I have killed more humans with this hammer than you have with that ridiculous sling and looked them dead in the eye as I killed them."

"Liar!" Felapine screeched. "I can load my sling and dispatch ten men in the time it takes you to swing that pathetic hammer at just one!"

Calapine slammed the hammer into her free paw. "The Battle of Chauvency! Twenty men with a single blow!"

Felapine's eye twitched faster. "That was a tournament, not a battle, and wiping out spectators when that damnable hammer slips from your grip does not count!"

Calapine growled as she raised the hammer to swing it at her sister again.

"You just try it, bitch."

"STOP IT! STOP IT! STOP IT!"

The goddesses paused their bickering and stared at the human girl.

Emmeline panted rapidly, her chest heaving in frustration and rage. Her eyes shut tight; she wished these two selfish goddesses to be gone. This was not what she imagined; this was not what she wanted. The old nun was wrong. These goddesses only wanted to tear down and destroy, not support and uplift. They had no interest in building strength in women, their only concern was their selfish desires. Emmeline regretted ever wanting to see them.

Slowly she opened her eyes. She still held the silver ore in her hand. She turned it over, tracing the ridges with her fingers. Sunlight, angling steep through the trees, reflected off the shiny specks on its surface. Silver ore. Silver.

Emmeline raised her head to look at the goddess of steel, her hammer still raised, ready to strike at her sister. Suddenly, it came to her, clearly. She had not made the connection before, but it was obvious now. She saw it clearly.

"You made the silver tea service," she said smoothly.

Calapine's hammer sank a little. "Wha-wha-what?"

"It was you who made the silver tea service," Emmeline said confidently.

Calapine's eyes grew wide, and the hammer fell to the ground with a loud thud that shook the ground.

"What silver tea service?" Felapine asked, eyeing her sister suspiciously."

"Never mind," said Calapine a little too loudly. "The mortal girl does not know what she is saying."

"What silver tea service?" Felapine asked again. "Tell me girl."

"Forget it, Sister." Calapine laughed nervously. "The girl does not know anything."

Emmeline turned to the goddess of iron. "Why the silver tea service she made for Lord Aufeese, of course."

Felapine screeched hideous laughter. "I knew it! I knew it! You and Aufeese! I knew it!"

"You know nothing!" screeched back Calapine, but with a slight tremble in her voice. "And neither does this ridiculous girl!"

Felapine screeched more laughter, then began making sloppy kissing sounds at her sister.

Calapine began to tremble in anger. "Cease that, Sister!"

Felapine strutted around the plateau, lifting her tail, and shaking her rear-end as she made more of the sloppy kissing sounds.

Calapine scowled. "Stop!"

"The Lord Aufeese gave her a gift as well," continued Emmeline. "I have not seen it, but it glows with a golden light."

Calapine shook her head violently. "No!"

"Really?" cried Felapine, ceasing her strutting to focus on the girl. "Where is it? I want to see it."

"No," repeated Calapine. "No one gave me anything."

"She has it hidden behind the forge," stated Emmeline matter-of-factly.

"I want to see this gift!" screeched Felapine. She dashed in the direction of the forge.

"No!" cried Calapine, and despite her crippled leg, she tackled her sister before she could reach the forge. They both rolled violently in the dirt, punching, kicking, and clawing each other.

"I want to see it!"

"No, you will not!"

Emmeline turned over the lump of silver ore in her hands once more and tossed it aside. She crossed the plateau briskly, passing the open maw of the mine, and walked calmly, head held high, down the opposite side of the mountain. She left the Sisters there on the plateau as they fought and cursed each other in the dust.

CHAPTER THIRTEEN

THE HORSE LURCHED ONCE MORE, throwing Henri forward in the saddle. He cursed loudly, reined his mount to a stop and cursed again. The members of his party all looked away, each finding something more interesting than what they knew was about to happen. The Prince threw his leg over the back of the horse and jumped down, raising a cloud of dust on the dry road. He walked back slowly, watching the dust drift lazily across the wide North/South road as he slid his hand loosely down the rope tied to the rear of his saddle. When he reached the end, he grasped it in a tight grip and snatched up the man tied to it in a single quick movement. The man had no choice but to rise to his feet, although he had no desire to do so.

"Why is it so difficult for you to keep up!" Henri shouted into the man's bruised and battered face.

The man at whom he shouted bore little resemblance to the one he had found alone back at the farmhouse. The damage was hideous. His entire face was colored in varying shades of red and purple. The nose was broken and sat at a most unnatural angle. Both eyes were swollen, the left more completely than the right. Missing teeth were evident through his broken and bleeding lips as he panted heavily. Blood had stopped flowing as freely as it had been before, clotted briefly by the dirt he had picked up when he fell this last time.

"Tell me, Gilles," he said, snatching firmly on the rope for emphasis. "Why must you be so difficult? Why must it be this way with you?" Henri snatched the rope again. It bit into Gilles's swollen wrists, making fresh blood flow from the wounds. "It is far too hot for these games of yours!"

The Prince closed his eyes, shaking his head. "If only," he said. "If only you had given me what I wanted instead of playing games with me. Perhaps..." He trailed off.

He snatched on the rope again, bringing Gilles's face closer to his own. "The quicker we make it to The Wild Hare, the quicker this will be over for you." He reached up with his free hand, and grabbed Gilles by the back of the neck, drawing him even closer, looking hard into the eye that was not swollen completely shut. "If you drag this out, I will make the pain linger. And not just for you. *Comprends?*"

A single tear rolled from that eye, glistening in the savage sunlight, cutting through the blood and dirt on the left side of Gilles's face. He gave no other affirmation, but the Prince saw that he understood. He released the farmer with a rough shove and walked back to his horse, his hand dancing playfully up the rope as he did. Gaining his mount, he glanced back to ensure the man was still standing, then he addressed his companion.

"That is why they are farmers, Philippe. Dumb as posts. Not smart enough for anything else but digging in the dirt and feeding animals. Men of his ilk only learn respect through fear and intimidation."

Philippe nodded ruefully, giving no other affirmation.

Henri gazed around at his party. No one dared look at him.

"Move out men!" he shouted angrily. "We have much ground to cover before nightfall!" He kicked his horse forward at a good walk, and the others followed suit.

After a good distance, Henri slowed his horse and fell to the back of the group. Presently, Philippe joined him in the rear. The other men relaxed a little and began to engage in casual conversation on the subjects of whores, drink, and gambling. And the preference for all three in conjunction.

Philippe rode silently alongside the Prince. He knew Henri all too well.

"You do not approve," Henri said at last.

Philippe noted a rider some distance up the road approaching them on a dark horse. "It is not for me to approve or disapprove of your actions, my Prince," he said indifferently. "I only obey your orders."

"Nonsense. I know you all too well, Philippe. You do not approve of this entire endeavor. I can read it in your face." Henri looked his lieutenant in the eye. Philippe's long blond hair curved around his sad face making it look even longer and sadder. The Prince ran a hand over his own closely cropped blond hair.

"What I think privately does not matter," Philippe said flatly. "I am here to serve my captain and take his orders as a loyal knight of the Old King should." His eyes flit briefly to the approaching horseman. He was still some distance away, but Philippe could discern that he was shrouded in a dark, hooded cloak.

Henri kept his eyes on his lieutenant.

"Perhaps," Philippe said idly, "and I say *perhaps*, I only question the logic of such an endeavor." His eyes flitted forward again and then back to the Prince. "Perhaps I merely question the timing of such an endeavor."

Henri looked him narrowly. "Logic? Timing? What mean you by these words?"

"Perhaps, and I say only perhaps, *bien sûr*. Your father is old, and it is only a matter of time before his appointment with Lord Noirceur. Therefore, one might have a more constructive use of one's time."

Henri considered this. "You mean to say that I should be making preparations for the inevitable."

Philippe's eyes flitted forward again. The rider was close enough to make out the rough woven fabric of the dark cloak: the beggarly fabric of a palmer's cloak. That was all he could make out. The face was still hidden. Philippe wondered how a man could wear such clothing in this brutal heat, but palmers were generally an odd lot anyway.

"One might take the time to consolidate one's power."

Henri laughed. "My power is secure. The only son and heir to the Old King has the certainty of the throne."

Philippe said nothing.

"Unless," Henri said with a note of suspicion in his voice, "you are aware of a plot. Perhaps?"

"I am aware of no plot, my Prince." Philippe eyed the approaching palmer. The hood of his cloak covered his face. Long sleeves covered the hands which held the reins. Nothing visible to identify him as anything other than a nameless religious pilgrim.

"Well then?" replied Henri.

"I have eyes and ears in the streets and throughout the country-side, my Prince. There are no reports of subversion against you."

The palmer began to pass on the right of their party. The men at the head of their group paid him no attention, being fully engaged in their essential conversation. Philippe noted suddenly that the palmer's horse was a far larger animal than any poor pilgrim should have. It was a healthy, broad-chested heavy horse, easily eighteen hands high. It held its head low, as a well-worn animal might, but its dead-eyed gaze betrayed its true demeanor. Philippe glanced at Henri. The Prince was speaking but he did not hear the words. Philippe rode on Henri's right meaning the palmer would pass close to him. Slowly, subtly, Philippe loosened his right hand from the reins, ready to draw his sword.

Philippe tensed as the palmer approached ever closer. Henri prattled on, unfazed neither by the palmer nor by his companion's lack of response. As the palmer passed within an arm's length of him, Philippe let his hand drop down and grip the handle of his sword. He could still not see the palmer's face even though the palmer was upon him.

Philippe heard it. The low sound, like a cool, faint autumn breeze, drifted across the short gap between he and the palmer, but at the same moment it resounded inside his head like a clap of thunder from a violent spring storm. Three languages at once in one utterance, in one sound.

"*Verbi.*"

"*Paroles.*"

"*Words.*"

And the palmer was gone, passed behind them, traveling down the road to destinations unknown.

"Are you listening?" Henri's voice came to him suddenly.

"*Oui, oui,*" Philippe replied shakily, placing his right hand back on the reins. "Yes."

Henri shook his head sullenly.

A sudden compulsion seized Philippe and would not let go. He feared his nerves would betray him, that the Prince would see his uncertainty and question him further before denying his request. But when he opened his mouth, the words flowed out naturally, they sounded normal; the request sounded perfectly plausible and reasonable.

"That palmer did not acknowledge you, my Prince. Give me your permission to pursue him and teach him proper manners."

Perplexed, Henri looked around him, then looked behind to see the palmer disappearing into the distance. "By the gods's ears, he did not."

"It is this very sort of thing I referred to earlier," continued Philippe, amazed at the words coming from his mouth. "After the long reign of your father, there are those who may 'disregard' you in your reign. You must consolidate your power now and show all in this kingdom that you will not be dismissed as a mere replacement for your father."

Henri tapped his lip thoughtfully. "I see your point, Philippe. He was only a palmer. No one important, but it must start with someone." He glanced back at the farmer in tow. "As I am otherwise engaged, go teach him that I will not be disregarded."

"Yes, my Prince."

Philippe began to rein his horse around when Henri reached out and grasped his arm. "However, be quick about it. I wish to make it to the Wild Hare before sundown, and I *will* need you there."

"Yes, my Prince."

Philippe's eyes fell upon the farmer trudging behind the Prince's horse. The man kept his head up, even when the severity of his treatment and the blight of the sun should make him hang it in despair. Philippe held his pity. Henri had not broken him yet.

Kicking his charger into a gallop, Philippe hastened back down the dusty road after the palmer. He gained a small rise and saw the palmer only a short distance away, his horse set at the same easy walking pace he had passed them with earlier. Philippe kicked his horse harder. His horse, a well-trained war horse, was known as one of the fastest horses in the kingdom, if not the fastest. It was even said by some to be the fastest horse ever known to man, although Philippe would balk at such talk. Nevertheless, Philippe's horse was a very swift horse, yet he could not catch the palmer. Faster and faster he pushed his horse, and he came no closer the palmer's horse with its easy walking gait.

Frustrated that he could not catch the palmer he finally cried out in a loud resounding voice: "By the gods's ears, and in the name of the lord I truly serve! Halt!"

The palmer stopped his horse immediately, and Philippe had to pull hard on his reins to keep from colliding with him. His horse's hooves carved deep grooves in the dirt as he slid to a stop only a hair's-breadth from the palmer's horse. Philippe's hand automatically dropped to his sword as the palmer slowly reined his horse around to face his pursuer. Philippe still could not see the face underneath the hood.

"In the name of the lord you truly serve," said the palmer slowly in a deep, resonant voice. It was a voice full of strength and power. "*Cui tu servis?*"

Silence seized Philippe as anger welled up inside him at the arrogance of this palmer. Who was he to address him in this manner?

"I ask you again, knight," said the palmer measuredly. "Who do you serve?"

Philippe shook his head at the question. "I serve the right and true king of Darloque."

The palmer's voice rose in volume and severity. "I ask you once more, knight. WHO DO YOU SERVE?!"

The palmer threw off his cloak; it slid to the ground, falling in a black pile on the dusty road.

Philippe's eyes grew wide, almost to the point of bulging out of his head. He immediately threw himself from his horse, pressing his hand firmly to his forehead as he groveled in the dust.

"Forgive me, my Lord, forgive me!" he moaned, tears flowing freely down his face. "I serve you and you alone! Please forgive me, please!"

"Regain your mount, then and let us converse as knights."

Slowly, Philippe rose from the road and pulled himself weakly into the saddle. It was a few moments before his heart slowed its pounding in his chest, and he could look at the rider he had once mistaken for a simple palmer. He lifted his eyes reluctantly to the rider opposite him.

The Lord Bellicor, the god of war, sat tall in the saddle of the immense, dead-eyed charger. Severe eyes, deep and brown, glared back at Philippe. He was large and solid; a hardness dwelled beneath the short, soft fur of his body, suggesting nothing less than formidable strength. Lord Bellicor's fur was pure white, except for red spots the color of blood which played across his snout, blending into solid red on the top of his head capped with long, solid red ears. Spots of red continued down his back to his white tail.

Philippe said nothing. He could say nothing at all; he had no words. He took in the war god, seeing him now, for the first time. All the years he spent praying, making offerings, living in devotion to him, and the war god sat before him at last. All the things he had wanted to say, all the things he had dreamed of saying. Those thoughts were gone now, washed away in the shadow of the war god's magnificent glory. His eyes dropped to the belt at Lord Bellicor's waist. An impressive leather belt exquisitely trimmed in gold held a scabbard which in turn held the sword which all warriors dreamed of one day holding.

Lord Bellicor shook his head slowly. "Do not dwell on it, knight. No human shall ever hold Viresdefeu save for the one who shall fight the final battle, and his day has not yet arrived."

Lord Bellicor reined his horse back in the direction they had been traveling. He motioned for Philippe. "Come, knight. There is much to say and little time."

They rode together at a leisurely pace, side by side and slowly, Philippe began to relax. A calm passed over him. It was as though he were riding with another knight. There was the feeling of mutual respect: the mutual respect between honorable knights which bonds them all.

Lord Bellicor spoke again. "Prince Henri has a plan to regain the territories lost to Ocosse."

Philippe started at this. "The very same territories surrendered in the treaty his father organized?"

"The treaty *you* and his father organized," Lord Bellicor corrected. "Do not understate your role in that vital peace deal. It was you who proposed the surrender of the disputed lands to keep the peace."

Philippe nodded his head begrudgingly. "I merely made a suggestion to the Old King."

"I recall the events differently." The war god kept his eyes forward as he spoke. "Believe what you wish, knight, but one cannot hide from the truth forever."

"The war over those territories lasted too long and cost many lives," Philippe said with a sigh.

"*Vero*. Even the war god knows the waste and futility of a senseless war."

"But a plan to take back the territories cannot be implemented as long as his father is alive," Philippe replied with a tilt of his head. "The Old King would not stand for it."

The Lord Bellicor remained silent for a moment. "Henri's time rapidly approaches," he said at last.

Philippe hung his head. He knew the Old King could not live forever, yet every fiber of his being denied it strenuously. Nothing grieved him more than the thought of the Old King's death. Many others would grieve his death simply because of the length of his reign and his renown for benevolence. To Philippe, however, the Old King was a dear friend. The Old King had taken to Philippe when he had been knighted. Later, when the war with Ocosse had continued without end in sight, it was Philippe to whom the Old King listened when he would hear no talk of compromise. It was Philippe who insisted that the treaty be constructed so that the Old King would not lose face.

Lord Bellicor reined his charger to a stop in the road, and Philippe stopped alongside him. The violent sun in its steep western angle beat down on both of them. The war god looked directly into his companion's eyes.

"I *have* heard your prayers, Philippe," he said, addressing his companion by name for the first time. "The war god is not without pity for your struggle."

Philippe dropped his head with a sigh, searching for the words. He lifted his eyes to those of Lord Bellicor. He opened his mouth to speak when two ordinary brown rabbits hopped out of the tall grass onto the edge of the road. They both sat up on their haunches, their heads bobbing and dipping before Lord Bellicor. He nodded at them appropriately, responding to the silent language of the common rabbit.

"*Vero,*" he spoke aloud to them. "This news is well met."

With a final bob from the rabbits, they turned and disappeared back into the tall grass. Philippe turned to the war god, the question forming on his face. Before he could speak though, a shadow passed over him as a hawk dove out of the sun toward the direction in which the rabbits had gone. The war god's eyes shot up to the hawk which dropped from the sky with a strangled squawk and hit the ground with a thud. Two sets of ears popped up over the grass some distance away. The rabbits looked around frantically then spied Lord Bellicor. They dipped and bobbed again. The war god responded with a single nod, and the rabbits disappeared into the grass again.

Lord Bellicor turned to face Philippe. "Those under the protection of the war god shall not be harmed."

Philippe swallowed hard. His mouth was incredibly dry.

"Unless," the war god added, "they refuse to follow his guidance."

Philippe looked down at the water skin hanging from his saddle. Lord Bellicor motioned for him to drink. When Philippe had his fill, the war god continued.

"*Tempus fugit,* knight. Time is short and there is much to tell you. Ride with me a moment longer then return to your party."

———

Philippe came fast upon the Prince. He slowed his horse as he passed the farmer, who was keeping up a good pace and still held his head high. The unmerciful sun beat down on the poor man, highlighting his wounds. The dried blood on his face and hands stood out in dirty crimson. *Henri will not break him,* Philippe thought. *No matter what he does to this man, Henri will not break his spirit.* Philippe fell in alongside the Prince. The other men ahead of them looked back at him curiously. Henri gave him a narrow look.

"It took you long enough to discipline that palmer, Jean-Louis."

Philippe smiled, dismissing the comment. "You know how pietistic palmers can be. It took a little extra time to make him understand that he must acknowledge his terrestrial master."

Henri continued to look at Philippe narrowly. His eyes slipped down to Philippe's hands holding the reins. The knuckles on both hands were scuffed and bloody. "Is that so?"

Philippe laughed. "Yes, my Prince."

Henri raised an eyebrow. "How goes it with you now?" asked Henri, still giving Philippe a narrow look. A few of the men looked back with concern. They did not like the tone of the conversation behind them.

Philippe continued to smile. "My Prince, the priests tell us that our actions shape our hearts. It is through our actions that we learn to change our hearts and learn true devotion. That is why they often give us tasks to perform as penitence for our transgressions."

"I see." The narrow look persisted.

"It was while I was disciplining the palmer that I felt my heart change, my Prince. I have found my true devotion, my Prince."

Henri smiled, then let out a hearty laugh. "Very good, Philippe!" All the men ahead of them turned and smiled warily.

"Yes, it is, my Prince."

Henri laughed again. "This business with the palmer has turned out very well then!"

"Yes, it has, my Prince. Yes, it has." Philippe joined the Prince laughing. The other men joined them, all thankful the awkward tension had dissipated.

They rode along, the horses kicking up dust from the road in little puffs gathering into a great cloud behind them. The farmer kept up the pace, his head still high. Philippe looked around at the wide open plain, the scrub grass standing straight in the hot, still air. He looked for hawks or wild rabbits, but none appeared. The low conversation ahead and the beat of hoofs on the hard-packed dirt were the only sounds. He looked to the sun, steep in its westerly descent, the Wild Hares now charging hard for the horizon.

"It grows late, my Prince," Philippe said at last. "We have not made the pace we have needed to make our rendezvous."

Henri looked nonchalantly toward the sun. He seemed unconcerned with the time. "Do not fear, Philippe. We will keep our appointment. I have made sure of that."

CHAPTER FOURTEEN

THE WILD HARE bustled with activity which Arnaud thought odd with it not yet evening still. Of course, the tavern being at the cross of the two great roads–the North/South road from Darloque to Sassan and the East/West road from Ocosse to *La Mer d'Ouest*–meant that it always bustled with activity. Yet, there were times when business was less brisk and one–especially a young boy who perhaps should not be working in a tavern at all–could find a little rest with a peaceful group of patrons.

The heat drove them in, Arnaud supposed. The Wild Hare was an old tavern with thick walls made of rough-cut stone and a high thatched roof. Even on a day such as today, when even the oldest patrons could not remember it being so hot before, the tavern remained quite cool inside. It made for a comfortable place for one to escape the heat outside and the boredom in one's own home. The cellar beneath the wooden floor remained absolutely frigid year-round, providing patrons with an additional incentive of a cold drink. Or two. Or three.

Therein lay Arnaud's main concern. The house was packed;

everyone had been drinking for quite some time, and it was still a long time before evening. When night fell on any normal day, the tavern became a madhouse. Arnaud prayed to any god who would listen that it would not become anymore mad than it already was.

A packed house ordinarily would not concern him greatly. Arnaud had been practically born in this place and had seen ten harvests here so far. He had seen a lot, so he had a great deal of experience for a boy his age. He had perhaps seen more than a man thrice his age. What did concern him though was that Margaret was missing and he had not seen his master Chrétien in a long while. Granted, he did not terribly miss his master: he was an abusive lout who had beat Arnaud countless times for minor transgressions and many more times just for good measure. Margaret, however, made a good serving wench—when she was not chatting up the male patrons. So here he was, a young boy, alone in a busy tavern already full and more patrons streaming in through the door. And it was not yet evening. "J'aime ma vie," he sighed.

Fortunately for him there were plenty of ale casks stacked behind the bar. The delay of retrieving a heavy cask from the cellar would most certainly complicate things. Patrons were generally congenial when the ale flowed cold and quick, but any delay and that same congeniality evaporated like morning fog on a sunny day. Yes, he thought with a contented sigh, so far things were going well. A large table of patrons continued to settle arguments by buying more rounds of ale. They had money; Arnaud had seen it. A dart game in the corner became sloppier as the players drank more, but it was still friendly, with hearty slaps on backs and congratulations for well-placed throws. Several patrons danced to the tunes the musicians played. The fiddle player was in particularly fine form today, leading the other musicians in a spirited set. Several patrons sang along to the more popular tunes and repeatedly shouted out requests for others. Hopefully, the general good mood would last well into the night.

Arnaud looked across the dark room to a small table by the door.

Any potential for trouble sat there. Two large men, not a particularly friendly looking pair, sat quietly, whiling away the time with the two cups of weak ale they had purchased without asking for a tab. Arnaud knew the manner of men who awaited something, or someone. He admitted to himself that there was nothing wrong with waiting in a cool tavern, out of the heat, yet his finely honed instinct developed over the time working in this place told him there was something not right about the pair. He hoped that whoever or whatever the two men awaited came soon, and they left without disruption.

"Boy, boy!" The shouts of a man at the large table brought Arnaud out of his thoughts.

The man stood and threw down a bag of coins. "Another round of ale for my friends!" Shouts of joy rose up from around him.

The dart players paused their game and turned to Arnaud. "More ale for us as well!" cried out one.

Several dancers cried out for ale and soon the whole tavern was filled with chants of "Ale! Ale! Ale!" All to the beat of fists on tables. Arnaud noted that the pair near the door remained silent, staring somberly into their cups.

Arnaud grumbled as his peaceful mood evaporated. He really needed Margaret here now. He would even welcome Chrétien's help. Arnaud cursed to himself, grabbed a serving tray, and began loading it up with cups. He started to fill them from the tap on the first cask when he sensed the stranger sidle up to the packed bar behind him.

Over the course of time Arnaud had been working in The Wild Hare, he had developed an innate sense about what was happening around him. He had "eyes in the back of his head" as his mother might have said, if he had known her. In a rough environment such as tavern, it paid to be vigilant. Reprobates, miscreants, and other ne'er-do-wells always looked for an opportunity to steal, sneak out without paying, or start some sort of trouble. You may not have your eyes upon everyone, but one needed be especially aware when someone approached from behind.

Arnaud sensed him coming up to the bar, wedging himself in among the other patrons there. He heard the stranger prop something up against the wooden bar. Arnaud split his attention between the cups of ale and the stranger as he began to speak.

"Aye, lad," the stranger said in a thick brogue. "Looks a mighty craic here alright."

"That it is, stranger," Arnaud replied flatly. He finished filling a cup with ale, set it on the tray balanced on his left hand and held an empty cup under the tap.

"Aye lad, 'tis it always this great?"

Arnaud frowned at this stranger's attempts at conversation while he was busy. "Yes stranger, as it *always* is. Sitting as we are at the main crossroad." He set the full cup on the tray and held another empty one under the tap.

"Aye, aye."

Arnaud thought the conversation was finished. He set a full cup on the tray and held an empty one under the tap. The tray was becoming heavy and awkward to hold, but he was determined to serve the large table in one trip before the chants of "Ale! Ale! Ale!" started up again.

"So, lad," the stranger began again in his thick brogue, "gi' me a mug o' the black stuff."

Arnaud grumbled. The stranger apparently did not understand that he was already engaged with another patron. "Yes, *monsieur*. As soon as I serve that large table, I will serve you a stout." Another full cup went on the tray.

"No lad. *Now.*" The stranger spoke calmly, yet forcefully.

Arnaud released a low growl. "It will be only a moment, *monsieur*, and then I shall pour you a stout." Another full cup on the increasingly heavy tray.

"No! Black stuff! NOW!" All pretense of civility had vanished from the stranger's voice. Arnaud had been here before. Some people believed they were the most important patrons in the tavern. It was best to let them hold that belief, especially when he was still but a young boy and said patrons usually weighed five stone or more than he.

Placing another cup on the awkwardly balanced tray, Arnaud reached up and took a mug from the shelf above him. The cask of stout was on the far side of the ale cask. He kicked the tap with his foot, causing the tray to lean heavily to one side. He corrected it and thrust the mug under to flow of the dark, foamy liquid. The mug filled to brim, he kicked the tap shut, balanced the tray again, and reached back to set the mug on the bar without looking at the stranger.

At once the shouts of "Ale! Ale! Ale!" resumed as patrons beat their fists on the tables. Arnaud was sure the pair at the door were still silent.

"Bloody 'ell, lad," said the stranger calmly over the din. "Not in that mug. *That* mug."

Arnaud fumed. He did not need to look at the stranger to know to which mug he referred. Every so often, some drunk *benêt* came into the tavern and asked for a drink served in *that mug* just to see if he could get it. Every tavern had that same mug set aside. There was only one patron who could drink out of it; it was kept cleaned and ready for him should he ever bless the tavern with his presence.

Arnaud spun to face the presumptuous stranger, the tray listing dangerously in his left hand. His eyes met the stranger's deep brown eyes; he was still pointing to the great crested mug high on the shelf. The stranger looked back at Arnaud, smiling broadly.

"By the gods's ears! It... is... you!" The tray tipped hard and slid off Arnaud's hand, hitting the floor with a loud crash and clatter of cups on the planks. A foaming tidal wave of ale surged across the floor behind the bar.

Chrétien rushed out of a doorway behind the bar, adjusting his breeches and buckling his belt as he came. Margaret followed, adjusting her dress, and crying out "Wha' happen'd?"

Chrétien immediately spotted the cups and in particular, the spilled ale on the floor. "Damn you, boy! Wasting all this precious ale!" He balled his fist and punched Arnaud hard in the ear, knocking him sprawling into the foamy mess on the floor.

Arnaud immediately jumped back to his feet, holding his right ear. He pointed to the stranger at the bar, stuttering excitedly. "But, but, but, Master! It... is... HE!"

Chrétien turned to face the stranger. Color drained from his face, his knees buckled, and he grasped the edge of the bar for support.

"Lord Portiscule!" he managed breathlessly.

The entire tavern fell silent as all eyes fell upon the god.

The rabbit standing at the bar, took up the spear he had propped there and gave a slight bow. Not counting his ears, Portiscule was at least as tall as Chrétien—who was a tall man himself. The great marble statue of Lord Portiscule in his temple gave no hint of the black and white markings of his fur. The markings on his head appeared as a mask. Black encircled both sides of his face from the top of his head down to each side his lower jaw. The two halves met at the top of his head where the white of his nose and whiskers ended in a point. His ears were solid black. The upper half of his body and his forepaws were pure white, while the lower half of his body and hind legs were solid black, giving the impression he wore black breeches. The tips of his hind feet ended in white, looking altogether like short stockings. His build was solid, his rounded head and body looking muscular and quick. His physical appearance left no doubt that the gatekeeper of Mava's palace could effectively use the great spear he held.

"Bloody 'ell!" cried the gatekeeper, his ears splaying in frustration. "What must a god do 'round here to get a mug o' stout?"

Chrétien punched Arnaud in the ear, knocking him down again. "Damn you, boy! Get that mug for Lord Portiscule and fill it! Now!"

Arnaud pulled himself up again. He did not mind Chrétien's abuse, being so captivated by the appearance of the god. He climbed up the shelf and pulled down the giant mug—larger than his own head—and began to fill it from the tap. Arnaud placed the heavy, laden mug on the bar, the god's crest facing toward Lord Portiscule.

"I can pay. I have gold." Portiscule opened his free paw and several gold coins clattered onto the bar. He picked one up and turned his face to match his profile on the coin. "It has me face on it!" He broke into a grin.

Chrétien eyed the gold coins as a starving man might stare at a chicken strutting around a barnyard.

Portiscule easily lifted the mug with his free paw and nodded to the barkeep and his boy. "*Sláinte.*"

But before the gatekeeper could take a draught, a voice rang from entryway: "I would not take coin from that one, barkeep. For he is a rascal and a rogue, and no doubt he came about those coins by some unscrupulous means."

Portiscule's ears laid back. He lowered the mug slightly as he gripped his spear tighter. "Wha? Who the bloody 'ell says this!"

The entire room fell silent as the speaker entered. Another large rabbit casually strolled in the room. He was the same size and build as Portiscule and marked in the same manner. However, wherever the gatekeeper was black, this god was a grayish slate. In the dim light of the tavern, he appeared blue.

Portiscule threw both his forepaws open, dousing a man behind him with the mug of stout. "Brother!" He ran and embraced the other god.

The entire tavern broke out in a loud roar. Daedemus, Portiscule's "twin" brother had arrived. Everyone knew the stories. Whenever Portiscule and Daedemus were together, the festivities would last for days. Arnaud smiled broadly as he looked around the room, then his face fell slightly. The pair at the door did not join in the revelry. Arnaud thought they looked worried.

Portiscule looked glumly into the mug then slammed it down on the bar. "Aye. I seem to have lost me stout. More, barkeep!"

Chrétien held his fist up at Arnaud who immediately filled the mug and set it heavily on the bar. Portiscule drained the mug in one draught and slammed it onto the bar. He motioned to Arnaud who happily filled it again. Portiscule opened his paw and threw more gold on the bar as the mug returned. Portiscule drained it again and returned it once more to the bar with a bang.

"Brother," spoke Daedemus. "Will you only stand there and drink? Will we have no music, singing, or dancing?"

Portiscule wiped the foam from his lip with the back of his paw. "Well bloody 'ell, Brother. I think we have it all covered. Those lads in the corner there will handle the music, I have the singin', and you take on the dancin'."

"That shall very well do, Brother!"

"Lads!" Portiscule cried, pointing his spear at the musicians. "Play a tune, a jig, or a reel. I do not care which. Play it, an' I will find the words."

The musicians stared mutely at their instruments. No doubt, there was not a more intimidating audience than Portiscule and Daedemus. They all would have more likely played for the most demanding king in all the lands than risk a bad set for these two gods.

Portiscule drained the refilled mug and slammed it back onto the bar again. He wiped his lip with a sigh. "Bloody 'ell. It seems I will have to 'prime the pump' so to speak. An' as my pump is well primed now, I will begin."

A wave of laughter rolled though the tavern.

Portiscule propped his spear against the bar and strolled to the center of the room. He broke into "The Wild Rover." The lute player forgot his nervousness first and jumped into the tune with a grin. Soon the drummer joined, followed by the piper, and finally the fiddler jumped in.

By the third chorus, the entire house had joined in the singing. Seeing the song was going well, Portiscule motioned to the musicians, then added a new verse followed by a couple more sets of the chorus. The song finished with a great roar.

"Bloody 'ell, after that, I am dry!"

The room filled with laughter as Portiscule drained the mug again. Another slam of the empty mug and more gold on the bar.

The gatekeeper stepped back to the center of the room and

addressed the musicians. "Aye lads, now that you are primed, I will gi' ye a new one. Jump in when you have the tune."

And he sang:

When I was but a wee young lad, I told me ma so long,
I set out on that lonesome road to find adventures new,
I traveled far and traveled wide, I traveled north and south,
I traveled east and traveled west, to see all I could see.

"Now the chorus, lads!"

OH! Gi' me another drink, lads, gi' me another drink,
For I have traveled a thousand miles, so gi' me another drink.
Gi' me another drink, lads, gi' me another drink,
My throat is dry from a many a mile so gi' me another drink!

Portiscule sang two more verses then sang the song again and again until everyone had learned it. When he finished, the whole tavern broke out in cheers.

Portiscule continued with the singing. He sang songs of drinking and fighting. He sang songs of leaving home and of returning home. He sang songs of the long road and of the rocky road. He sang songs of Finnegan and Lannigan, and of Molly and Jenny.

Daedemus, the architect, the builder of Mava's palace, walked to the center of the room and held up his forepaws. The tavern soon quieted.

"My brother promised we would also have dancing."

A few cries of approval went up at this announcement.

"Thank you," Daedemus said with a bow. "Now," he said addressing the musicians, "play a spritely number, a jig or a reel, something to which the Lord of Dance may demonstrate his talent!"

The fiddler started into a fast reel and the other musicians recognizing it, jumped in. Daedemus walked over to Margaret, bowed, and politely held out his right paw. Margaret immediately flushed a bright red at the great architect's offer.

"Ahhh!" cried out someone in the crowd. "Look at ol' Maggie blushin'! Who wuda thot there was anytin' that wud make 'er blush!"

Margaret scowled in the direction of the speaker. "Shut up, eh! I will box yer ears like yer ol' mum used to, I will!"

Margaret turned back to Daedemus, her cheeks turning red again, and took his paw. The great architect, the Lord of Dance spun her around the room to the fast reel, the claws on his hind feet ticking across the wooden floor. The pace was swift, but in the god's capable paws, they twirled and swept about the room. The crowd kept time clapping and stomping to the beat of the reel. Portiscule banged his empty mug on the bar to the beat of the music–when it was empty, that is.

Daedemus took Margaret around the room to another, slightly slower tune, then danced in turn with all the ladies in the tavern. Margaret leaned hard against Chrétien, fanning herself and staring dreamily at Daedemus as he worked his way around the room.

When all the ladies had danced, the crowd broke into groups as day wore down toward evening. Ale flowed freely. Arnaud found himself busier even with Chrétien's and Margaret's help than he had been when he was alone. Lord Portiscule insisted on buying for the whole tavern, as much as they wanted, whatever they wanted. And he had gold. Gold flowed as freely as the ale.

Yet, Arnaud kept turning to the pair by door. They sat quietly, appearing increasingly nervous as evening approached. They continued to nurse their cups of weak ale. They had engaged in none of the revelry, none of the singing, none of the dancing. Arnaud was no less concerned about them than he had been earlier. With the great mood created by Portiscule and Daedemus, he did not under-stand how the two men could not help but be drawn into the two gods's infectious good humor.

Two fellows were dividing up darts, about to start a new game when Portiscule came upon them.

"Darts! Bloody 'ell! I love a good game o' darts!"

One fellow smiled slyly. "Ahh, do you? Well, we only play for coin around here."

Portiscule drained his mug and motioned for Arnaud. "Wha?! D'ye not think I have gold?" He opened his paw and cast several coins on the floor. "There is nary a wager I cannot cover!"

Suddenly Daedemus appeared between them, his ears perked at attention. "Did I hear someone speak of a wager?"

"Maybe, you did," said the other fellow smiling widely.

"I will give you odds," said Daedemus with a confident smile. "Two to one that you cannot defeat my brother."

"Make it three to one, and you have a wager," responded the first fellow, the sly smile still on his face.

"Done," said Daedemus and they shook on it. "In fact," he said, addressing the whole tavern, "I will give the same odds to anyone who here who is willing to take them."

A great cry came up as several men approached Daedemus with handfuls of coins, eager to take those odds.

Arnaud brought Portiscule the refilled mug, shaking his head as he handed it to the god. *How fools will line up to lose a wager*, he thought to himself. Portiscule drained the mug and handed it back to Arnaud. *However*, he thought again, *there was that one time Daedemus did lose if I remember my stories correctly.* He shook his head. Best not to think of such things.

"Aye now, lads," Portiscule said seriously. "I am ready to start the game; however, I have one condition."

The two fellows frowned, apparently suspicious of some trickery. "Eh? What condition, then?"

"Aye, aye, lads. Keep yer heads." Portiscule gave a congenial smile. "I just prefer to use me own dart." With a grin the god pulled out his spear, thumping the butt on the floor.

The two dart players broke into riotous laughter as Portiscule crossed his eyes, splayed his ears, stuck his tongue out of the side of his mouth, and aimed the spear at the dartboard. Arnaud giggled as

195

he returned with the foamy mug. The spear flew from the gatekeeper's paw and struck the wall behind the pair sitting by the door, the spear landing next to the ear of one. He was looking down at his hairs falling to his sleeve when Daedemus suddenly appeared at his other ear.

"Oh, I must heartfully apologize for my brother's dreadful aim," he whispered. "You see, he cannot hit the side of a barn when he has been drinking."

The man looked to Portiscule. Intense brown eyes met his. The gatekeeper stared fiercely over the rim of his mug as he slowly drank.

He looked to Daedemus. The god smiled congenially.

"Perhaps it would be advisable that you move."

The man with the spear next to his head got up and moved over to the next empty chair at the table.

Daedemus was at his ear in an instant. "Not far enough I believe."

The man looked to Portiscule again. The god had handed the mug back to the boy, keeping that fiercely intense stare on the stranger as he wiped his lip slowly and deliberately with the back of his paw.

The man looked to his associate. They got up abruptly, each knocking down his chair with a clatter, and fled the tavern as quickly as they could run. They ran outside into the deeply slanting daylight, making haste toward the stable as the sounds of loud revelry dwindled behind them. After paying the stable boy, the pair mounted their horses without a word. When they had turned onto the road, one addressed the other.

"The Prince will not be pleased that we have abandoned our post."

"We must report back to him," the second replied with a shrug. "Tell him what we saw."

"Do you think he will believe us?"

"I do not care. I would rather deal with the Prince than take the gatekeeper's spear to my head." The second kicked his horse into a gallop.

The first kicked his horse and caught up to the other. "Yes, if he wants that girl so badly, then let him deal with those two gods."

"And let *him* take a spear to the head if he so desires."

CHAPTER FIFTEEN

EMMELINE WAS LOST.

———

Her journey down the other side of the mountain proved easy and uneventful. She listened to the commotion of The Sisters's fight for some time as she grumbled to herself about rude and disruptive gods. Emmeline realized too late that she had left her paquet on the flat rock. She certainly did not want to see The Sisters again to retrieve it, convincing herself she would be fine until she reached The Wild Hare. The fact that she had no money, no food, and no water did not concern her greatly. She was still too angry at the meddlesome gods who had interfered with her on this journey.

The foothills with their random outcroppings of gray rock and variously spaced young trees gradually gave way to the flat plain to which Emmeline was accustomed. As she trudged through the scrub grass of the open prairie, watching her long shadow precede her, she took a brief glance over her shoulder to see the great mountain of the Sisters shimmer in the slanting light and evaporate into nothing.

Emmeline stopped and turned around, futilely searching the wide plain for the great mountain that never should have been. Her heart sank a little. *Why?* She could not discern.

Traveling across the prairie was easy enough. As long as Emmeline kept her shadow pointing straight ahead of her, she knew she was going in the right direction. *Bien sûr*, she thought to herself, *if the Wild Hares decide to take the chariot of the sun on some random course away from the West, then I am in serious trouble.* She decided not to think about that.

Emmeline's shadow led her to a wood. She paused at the edge, patting the trunk of a young yew tree. At first, she thought it odd, but reminded herself that she had never traveled cross-country before, and therefore she did not know what existed off the course of the main road East. She thought of trying to go around it, keeping out in the open where she could see her shadow and better keep her direction. But the wood was wide, and the chariot of the sun was rapidly chasing the horizon. She risked running out of daylight by attempting to circumvent the wood, and that was not desirable. She patted the yew again. It seemed a normal tree, and the wood seemed a normal wood.

The young trees tightly spaced on the edge of the wood gave way quickly to a larger, older growth of oaks, maples, and hickories. A few pines fought for space here and there, but the wood was largely made up of hardwoods. She took a few steps in, looking up at the larger trees as she did. They were ordinary looking trees, large as most people would define them, but to Emmeline they looked quite small compared to the immense trees on The Sisters's mountain. Woven upon the ground amongst the trees, faint trails left by wild animals lay about the wood. In a wood such as this, there were most certainly deer, birds, and rabbits–hopefully only rabbits of the ordinary variety.

After a lengthy examination, Emmeline decided the wood really was just a normal wood. She took a few steps back, marking the direction of her shadow on the grass. Once she had marked due East, she started into the wood, making sure she continued in as straight of a line as possible. She soon discovered a wide trail, presumably made by deer and other larger wildlife, tracking due East.

The trail was well worn. Animals, like humans tended to follow trails that many others had followed before them. Cut down to the bare dirt of the forest floor, the trail continued straight for the most part, weaving around large trees here and there, and then resuming its path due East. Lush grasses flourished in the shade of the hardwood canopy. A few tracks of flattened grass turned off the main trail at periodic intervals. Emmeline walked slowly down the wide trail at first, wary of any animal of the carnivorous type which might be lurking behind the trees, then settled into a steady walking pace as she became more comfortable with the direction of the trail and confident of the absence of the aforementioned carnivorous animals.

The sun disappeared behind a canopy of leaves so thick that not even one ray of the steeply slanting western light made it through. Emmeline still felt confident of her direction. The trail kept its straight eastern track as she noted the moss growing at the northern side of the large hardwoods. Emmeline's pace picked up as her confidence rose, but deep inside she wished to be out of the wood as quickly as possible. The journey had not been going as planned, and she did not want yet another interruption. She had begun to whistle a tune when the two rabbits standing in the middle of the trail brought her to a sudden halt.

Emmeline released a small squeak. It was another moment before she realized that these were not gods, but two ordinary wild rabbits. The pair sat up on their haunches, ears erect, and forepaws held neatly at their chests, apparently just as surprised to see her. They did not run from her though. Emmeline had learned that wild rabbits generally did not fear humans. In her life she had seen a few passing through the farm. *We are taught to respect the wild rabbit*, her father had told her once, *for they are corporeal representatives of the gods*. It was forbidden to interfere with wild rabbits. One was to allow them safe passage when met. It was considered a blessing when a wild rabbit ate out of one's garden. Hunting or killing a wild rabbit was punishable by death.

The two ordinary sleek brown rabbits standing before Emmeline on the trail stared at her. They turned to one other, whiskers twitching, and turned back to her. The one on the right began to bob its head. It turned to its companion who dipped its head once, and then a second time. Emmeline frowned. The wild rabbits Emmeline had seen before did not do anything; they nonchalantly passed her on their way to their destination, disregarding her presence entirely. The two rabbits before her tilted their heads curiously at Emmeline, then with another bob and a dip, the rabbits dashed off the trail, rushing though untouched grass in a northerly direction.

The cool shade of the wood made for a pleasant journey. The absence of the scorching sun lifted Emmeline's spirits some. The compacted dirt of the trail stretching out before her was smooth and flat, which made for the easiest walking on the entire journey. She soon forgot about the rabbits on the trail, the gods, and the Prince. Emmeline began to whistle again when she once again came to a halt.

The trail ended abruptly at a thicket. A dense undergrowth of brush stretched across the trail in either direction as far as she could see. Emmeline stood before it, blinking, befuddled by the obstruction. Flattened grass marked where animals had gone around it, but neither track was as heavily traveled as the main trail. She assumed a deer would have simply leapt over the obstruction. Emmeline jumped up in place, hoping to get a glimpse of the other side of the thicket, which proved futile. She attempted to push through, but with the dense foliage and thorny brambles she discovered painfully that only the smallest travelers could have made it through. Emmeline looked up, but the deep green canopy offered her no suggestions. Aware of the dwindling day, she turned left and followed the edge of the thicket, hoping to pick up the trail on the other side.

———

That was some time ago. Emmeline leaned against the trunk of a hornbeam; a tree she was certain she had passed at least three times. The previous time she had marked the bark with a stone. She lifted her head and looked at the mark. She was walking in circles now. Moss grew on all sides of the trees in this dark part of the wood as the thick canopy blocked all but the faintest light, giving her no clue as to direction. Panic began to slowly rise in her, but Emmeline fought it back down. *I cannot lose myself. Not now*, she thought to herself. *There must be an answer somewhere.*

Emmeline pushed herself from the hornbeam and took a deep breath. She had come too far and experienced too much to fall apart now. But she was tired. This long and arduous journey was becoming too much for her. She wanted to go home. She did not want the Prince; she did not want the gods. She wanted home. She wanted her mother and father. She wanted the crops, and Cheval, and even that temperamental donkey Jacques. She wanted to be where everything was, most importantly, normal.

A rustle came from far behind her. Emmeline hung her head with a sigh. She was simply too tired and frustrated to deal with another meddlesome god. That of course was what it had to be. She had dealt with enough of them by now.

Another rustle. The noise was quite a ways distant, but she was certain it was closer than the last. Or perhaps it was her imagination. It did not matter to her. Emmeline began walking, ignoring paths, tracks, and trails, instead taking a new direction across the low grassy floor of the wood. She walked, keeping as straight a line as she could manage. Certainly, this wood did not go on forever, and when she had found the end, she could work out her bearings and get to The Wild Hare from there. Once at The Wild Hare, she would embrace her father, and everything would be set right.

She set a brisk pace, her feet swishing through the thick grass. Concentration was the key. She had let her mind wander after she had passed the thicket. If she could plough and plant straight rows by herself, why could she not walk a straight line? No distractions. She must remain focused.

Another rustle behind her broke her concentration momentarily. "Blest be Mava's many litters," she cursed under her breath. The noise was definitely closer. Still quite a ways behind her but just a little closer to her. Perhaps it was only a wild animal.

Emmeline wished she had not let that thought into her mind. Images of wolves, bears, and other creatures with savage teeth and equally savage appetites, blossomed in her mind. Some of the travelers who stopped at her farmhouse told fantastical tales of horrific creatures who hunted and devoured humans. Lions and tigers stalked humans on distant plains. Some said that if one sailed far enough, there was a land inhabited by giant dragons. These great ferocious reptiles devoured humans after tearing them apart with their razor-sharp claws and teeth. After hearing such stories, Emmeline found it difficult to sleep. Her mother told her that those were just the tales told by simple men, and it was not reasonable to believe that such creatures could exist. Her father told her that the gods could not and would not let such creatures exist and torment the humans in their care.

Today Emmeline had discovered two falsehoods told to her by her mother and father. The first is that reason holds rule over life. It is not reasonable for the Prince to want to marry her. It is not reasonable to be required to run from the Prince who wants to marry her. It is not reasonable to be lost in the woods because of the Prince. The second falsehood is that the gods care about the well-being of humans. They are vain and self-centered, and as long as the lions, tigers, and dragons do not interrupt their teatime or get in the middle of their disputes, then the gods are happy enough to let them go about doing whatever they please. If given a choice of meeting a dragon or a god in this wood, Emmeline could not say for sure which would be worse. At the moment, she preferred to meet neither.

Leaves and branches rustled again from behind. The noise came from somewhere up high and still closer than before. Emmeline glanced back over her shoulder but saw nothing in the canopy. Dragons could fly, it was said. They perched like birds while waiting for their prey, it was said. She increased her pace.

She knew she was being silly. There were no such things as dragons. Nevertheless, the light in the wood had become subtly darker and she did not wish to be in it when full dark came. Whether she were near The Wild Hare or not, Emmeline wanted out of this wood quickly.

The rustle came again, this time from a great White Oak behind her. Emmeline stopped and turned. Her eyes tracked carefully up the massive trunk then roamed all over the limbs, searching through the leaves for a glimpse of whatever had made the noise. She could see nothing. She resumed her course at a brisk pace, carefully plotting her direction, concentrating on the task at hand. All distractions banished. When she heard something large land lightly on the grassy floor of the wood directly behind her, she broke into a run.

There was no panic in Emmeline. Tired, frustrated, and angry, yes. Panicked, no. Direction ceased to be important. All she wanted was to get away from meddling gods and escape from this wood. Emmeline pushed herself hard with an energy she did not know she had, sidestepping trees and small patches of brambles, leaping over fallen logs, ducking under low branches. At one point she encountered a thicket, although not as wide and dense as the first one. Not wanting to stop or slow to circumvent it, she leapt blindly through it, the thorny bramble tearing at her clothes, scratching her skin, and pulling her hair. She was not immediately aware of the pain, although she did notice blood trickling down her right arm through the tears in her sleeve.

The sound of her footfalls on the grassy floor of the wood resounded in Emmeline's head. She chanced a look back over her shoulder hoping not to see anyone–particularly any god–following her. She saw no one, but in taking a look back, she nearly ran into the broad, swift moving river directly in her path.

Emmeline stopped with a splash as she slipped off the riverbank into the water of a small tidal pool at the river's edge. *"Merde!"* she cursed out loud as she climbed back onto the bank. She looked back and listened. There was no noise behind her. Hopefully, whoever was pursuing her finally understood that she did not want to be bothered. Satisfied that she was alone, Emmeline turned to face her new problem.

The river, at least one hundred furrows wide, flowed swiftly, forming white crests which lapped the banks. The smooth, flat water in the center indicated a pronounced depth. The gap in the leafy canopy over the river showed a blue/gray sky, darkening as the Wild Hares approached the horizon. If this river was the one she thought it was, then she was far South of where she should be. Getting back on track would mean arriving at The Wild Hare long after nightfall. Traveling in the dark bothered her somewhat, but her father worrying when he arrived and did not find her already there concerned her greatly. She wiped the sweat from her brow with her tattered sleeve, smearing blood on her forehead in the process. Emmeline growled. She squatted down to wash her face in the small tidal pool.

Rising, she looked upon the river before her. Emmeline thought it sad that her family's crops were dying from drought and yet this river, fed by the great northern mountains, flowed strong and swift with more than enough water for their parched crops. At the very least, Emmeline had direction again. She merely needed to follow the river North until she exited the wood then backtrack to The Wild Hare. Yes, she would arrive well after the chariot of the sun had passed beyond the horizon. Yes, her father would be worried, but he would wait. Father would wait as long as it took, for he believed in *the plan*.

Emmeline followed the river upstream. The grassy bank was as firm and easy to walk upon as the rest of the wood. Listening for her mysterious pursuer, then satisfied he was gone, Emmeline picked up the pace. She wanted, needed, to be out of this wood as quickly as possible. Walking was generally easy, small fallen limbs in her path disrupted her pace, but overall, she kept up a steady fast walk. It was when she stepped over a sizeable log and a small branch broke under her foot with a percussive snap that she heard the voices.

They came from behind her, but not from exactly the same direction as the mysterious pursuer. This was not he. Emmeline remained motionless as she listened carefully. The voices were too far away to distinguish the words. She paused without daring to move, without daring to breathe. Emmeline listened. Two distinct voices. She could not discern the words, but she could discern the deep male voices.

Mindful of where she stepped, Emmeline increased her pace on the riverbank. Whoever these people might be, she surely did not want to see them or be seen by them. She hoped they were not traveling toward the river. However, the voices were becoming louder and more distinct. She broke into a trot, soberly wishing to get past the owners of the voices before they arrived at the river. Emmeline's blood froze at the first words she could hear distinctly: "My Prince."

A long moment passed before she could breathe again. She only thought she had known panic before. Emmeline took a ragged and awkward breath, trying to remain as silent as possible. The voices were getting closer, coming toward the river. Heart beating out of her chest, she looked up and down the bank. Across the river was the only escape. She searched frantically for some place she might cross. There was none. Emmeline could swim, she swam very well in fact, yet she was not strong enough to fight the current of this great river.

Beads of sweat popped out on Emmeline's forehead. She wiped her brow out of habit before she realized too late that blood still flowed freely on her arm. Growling softly, she squatted on the bank—a good idea anyway she thought to herself—and held her hands in the current, silently washing her face and arm. Emmeline exhaled slowly, listening to the voices approach, and staring into to the clear, swift running water. She suddenly realized with alarm that someone was staring back at her. There was a face in the water, and it was not her own reflection. She sat back with a gasp louder than she intended as a figure rose slowly out of the river.

The rabbit lifted itself chest high out of the river and placed its forepaws on the surface of the water as she might place her hands on a table. Below the surface, its long wool ebbed and flowed in the current, waving hypnotically in the clear water. Above the surface, the rabbit was perfectly dry, his long white angora wool standing out from his ears, head, and body like a halo. The rabbit's face, however, was a mask of black wool, making it difficult to see its eyes.

"Greetings, young human girl." Then after the briefest of pauses: "Forgive me, Emmeline. I should and must address you by your given name."

Emmeline jumped at the mention of her name, then began looking frantically around. "Shhhh! The Prince will hear you, and then I am caught!"

"Oh no," the rabbit said calmly, "the Prince and his party cannot hear us now. That may change in a few moments, but for now, we speak privately."

His voice was gentle and soothing, but Emmeline looked at the wooly rabbit uncertainly.

The rabbit's tone became grave; its eyes were still difficult to discern though. "I can keep you hidden for the moment, but if we do not act quickly, that *will* change."

Emmeline swallowed, but said nothing.

"Do you know me?" asked the rabbit, his gentle tone returning.

Emmeline shook her head timidly.

"You surprise me," he replied brightly. "I was certain you would. Perhaps you know my two sisters."

Emmeline shook her head again.

"Hmmm," he said, tapping his chin with a paw. "My brother?"

Emmeline's eyes lit up with the recollection. "Your brother is the god of the sea!"

"Ah yes," the rabbit nodded. "My brother's reputation precedes him. Everyone knows Merinwar, the god of the sea. Most tend to forget his brother though."

Emmeline's mouth twisted as she tried to remember the rabbit's name.

"Fleuvenar at your service," he offered with a bow.

"Can you take me to see you brother, the god of the sea?" Emmeline cried. She looked around cautiously, still unsure if she were truly safe.

"Well," Fleuvenar said with a shrug, "he does not particularly care for humans, so I do not believe that would be a wise idea."

Emmeline frowned.

"Although," Fleuvenar continued, "there is one human with whom he will work closely." He took a long pause. "But I do not believe that human is you."

"Surely the god of the sea would find no fault in me," Emmeline said, hopefully.

Fleuvenar shrugged again. "The fact that you are human is the only fault he requires."

"But I have done him no harm," Emmeline said, shaking her head. "I have done no harm to anyone!"

Again, Fleuvenar shrugged. His dark eyes, hidden behind the mask of long black wool, betrayed nothing.

Emmeline was becoming exasperated. She had forgotten the approaching Prince and was solely focused on the god of the sea. "I merely wish to visit the sea! I have never seen it before. Surely the god of the sea would grant me that single wish."

The River Rabbit chuckled pleasantly. "If you only wish to visit the sea, then I have the power to grant your wish. This river follows a long winding course, eventually flowing into the sea. I will gladly take you to the sea, and we need not involve my brother."

Emmeline beamed. "Truly? You will?"

The River Rabbit bowed slightly. "Yes, I will. But we must make haste. The Prince and his party approach even now, and if they see you, I can no longer assist you."

"Yes," said Emmeline with a great smile. "Let us go to the sea. How shall I travel though? I cannot swim in this river."

Fleuvenar offered a friendly smile. "Climb on my back. I shall carry you, and so long as you stay with me you shall be safe in the river."

Emmeline turned toward the sound of the Prince and his party. Voices, several of them now, were very close. The time grew short. She turned back to the god who waited patiently in the river. She looked up to the slowly darkening sky over the river.

"Yes," she said, her voice barely a whisper. "Let us go to the sea."

———

"Well?!" shouted the Prince. "Where is she?"

"I do not know, my lord."

"What do you mean, 'I do not know, my lord.' You are the best–or alleged to be the best–tracker in the land. You tracked her to this river. Now where has she gone?"

Gautier scratched his head. "I do not know my lord."

"You keep saying that!" The Prince's face flushed a bright crimson. "Where has she gone?!" the Prince said, growling through his teeth.

"I... I... I... do not know, m-m-m-my lord!" stuttered the tracker. When he saw the Prince reach for his sword, he quickly composed himself and explained. "We followed the trail through the wood, lost it, then picked it up again near the river. At the bank, the trail turned north, following the river upstream. And then... well... the trail just ceases."

"Ceases?" Prince Henri eased his sword back into its scabbard.

"Yes," Gautier said with a sigh. "The tracks just stop."

"You lost her before, did she backtrack her steps?"

"That is an *impossibilité*. Before, I picked up her tracks after a short space. Now there is nothing. Nothing as far as I can see in any direction. Backtrack? She could not have do so without me knowing. She could try, but I know the tricks."

"Then she must have swum across the river."

"Another *impossibilité*, my lord. This river is too wide, deep, and swift for a young girl to swim across. Even I, an experienced swimmer, would have great difficulty swimming across. *Non*, if she attempted to swim across this river then she is—"

A cry went up somewhere down river. The tracker took off down the riverbank. Henri kicked his horse in the same direction with Gilles in tow. Philippe's chest tightened, fearful that they had found the girl. After a moment, he too kicked his horse in that direction. Following behind the Prince's horse Philippe remarked to himself how after the torture the farmer had endured, he still possessed the energy to keep up with the horse. Barely, though.

The Prince arrived at the source of the cry first. Others rode up out of the wood from different directions. Philippe saw Gautier dash around Henri's horse just as the Prince dismounted. The others began to dismount and form a semicircle on the edge of the river as Philippe rode up behind them. He leapt from his mount, rushed over to the crowd, and roughly shoved a couple of men out of the way as he forced himself through.

Henri stood rigidly at the riverbank next to a tidal pool. Philippe looked at him curiously. The Prince's face was drawn tight, his jaw clenched, his lips stretched thin. His eyes were huge, bulging with rage. Philippe had seen this before, many times in fact. Slowly, he turned his eyes to what the Prince fixated upon. Dominic and Sébastien knelt by the tidal pool with gloomy looks upon their faces. The looked up at the fierce visage of the Prince, clearly concerned at how he would cope with their discovery. Philippe did not see at first what the pair had found which had sent up the cry. Perhaps he did not want to see. But soon his eyes turned toward the tidal pool, the wide cutout in the bank into which water from the river entered and swirled around at a much slower pace than the swift river. Dominic spoke, his voice barely above a whisper: "The Dark One has been here."

Emmeline's dark, unseeing eyes stared back at Philippe from under the water of the shallow pool. Her long chestnut hair flowed around her head like a halo while her arms lay straight and still at her sides. Philippe could not help but gasp out loud. He covered his mouth too late to suppress the sound. Only Dominic and another man whose name Philippe could not recall paid him any attention. All others were focused on the Prince.

Henri waved his arm frantically at Dominic and Sébastien. "Pull her out of there," he roared.

The two did as ordered and pulled the girl's body from the water then placed it gently on the grassy bank. All eyes remained on the Prince. He did not speak for a long time. Presently, Henri knelt and took the girl's pale face in his hand. He turned her head side to side, clinically, as if examining her. He said nothing, but the intense look remained on his face.

Everyone started as the Prince leapt to his feet with a roar and pushed roughly through the group of men gathered behind him. He returned momentarily, dragging the farmer Gilles with him. The Prince threw him roughly onto the ground next to the body of the girl. Philippe could not help but gasp out loud again. He did not want to watch anymore. He wanted to leave, but if he did not stay, Henri would castigate him beyond all measure later.

"LOOK WHAT YOU HAVE DONE!" roared the Prince. "Look what your foolishness has cost me!"

The farmer knelt on the bank, face to face with his daughter. The one good eye welling with tears as his broken lips quivered in ultimate sorrow. He reached out to his daughter with his bound hands, trembling violently as he caressed her wet face.

Low moaning escaped him as he began to tremble all over.

All the Prince's men shifted uncomfortably on their feet. Philippe valiantly fought back tears and trembling of his own. Of all the men here, only he understood the farmer's loss. He willed himself not to think of his own sweet, beloved Claire. If he allowed himself to do that, he would most assuredly lose his fragile self-control.

The Prince yanked the farmer to his feet and spun him around to face him. Philippe could no longer bear to watch. The farmer's sorrowful expression on his ruined face broke him.

"Do you see what your foolishness has done?!" the Prince roared into his face. "Do you?!"

The farmer only trembled and moaned.

The Prince raged. "It was so simple. You only had to hand her over to me, and all would have been well. But you had to try to trick me, to try this foolishness. AND LOOK WHAT IT HAS COST!"

The Prince grabbed the farmer by the back of the neck and thrust his face into the cold, pale countenance of his daughter. "DO YOU SEE WHAT YOU HAVE DONE?!"

Violently pulling the farmer up once more, Henri spun him around again to face him. This time the Prince pulled his arm back and drove his fist into the farmer's face with a loud crunch. The farmer spun and landed upon his daughter's body, once again coming vis-á-vis to the pale face and unseeing eyes. Blood flowing freely from his face, the farmer began to sob loudly.

Henri snatched up the farmer one more time and started to drag him back through the crowd.

"My lord?" asked Sébastien cautiously. "What shall we do with the body?"

Henri stopped and turned, his face still a mask of rage.

"I do not care! Do with it as you wish!" He turned and dragged the farmer through the cluster of his men.

Sébastien looked at the dead girl. Her soft, smooth skin gleamed in the fading light. He raised an eyebrow at Dominic. Dominic grinned back wickedly.

CHAPTER SIXTEEN

MURIELLE JUMPED as the door flew open with a loud crash, revealing a large and dark figure framed in the doorway by the pre-dawn light streaming into the barn from behind him.

"Your father would not appreciate the sight of you praying before an altar of one of the gods, I believe," said Étienne with a scowl.

Young Murielle stammered without producing a coherent word.

Étienne stepped into the room. "And why have you dared enter into the court of Étienne without the lord Étienne present." the reeve placed his hands on his hips. "This is a grave offence my young lass."

Murielle struggled to rise from the feed sack. She stammered again, still unable to produce a coherent word.

"Well?!" the large man bellowed, causing the thatched roof to quiver. "What do you have to say for yourself?!"

Murielle failed to utter a word. She struggled to rise and instead fell from the feed sack, landing flat on her back on the floor.

Étienne bellowed again, this time with laughter. He watched Murielle flop like a fish on the floor of the barn, struggling to rise but failing miserably.

The reeve held out a large, calloused hand. "Come lass, let me help you." He chuckled merrily.

Murielle took his hand and Étienne pulled her effortlessly to her feet. She hung her head in shame, fearful of some punishment for violating the reeve's personal space.

Étienne chuckled again. "No fear, lass."

Keeping her head down, Murielle turned up her eyes to him uncertainly. Étienne was a large and powerful man. Any punishment he dealt to her would certainly be painful and memorable. Her father's only response would be that she had deserved it.

Étienne shook his head. "I only jest with you, my lass." He held his hands up in a gesture of peace. "No fear."

Murielle turned her head up with a sigh of relief. She looked at her father's reeve framed by the golden morning light shining through the open end of the barn. He was a large man, taller and wider than her father, or any man she knew for that matter. His long shaggy hair and equally long and shaggy beard gave the impression of a wilderness man. His countenance and his size combined to make him a very imposing fellow. However, his genial nature, kind heart, and jolly spirit–only seen by people who knew him well–countered that image. Murielle glanced back at the altar. A true human representation of Lord Arbrinner, that was Étienne.

"I have no quarrel with you, my lass," said Étienne with a smile. "You are my good friend and welcome here anytime, whether I am present or not. I do not afford that privilege to anyone else."

Murielle gave him a shy smile.

"However," he continued, frowning as his tone turned serious, "I do not jest when I say that your father would not approve of your prayers before my altar, or any altar in fact."

Murielle dropped her eyes. Slowly she shook her head. "No, he would not," she whispered.

"I will make a bargain with you. I will not tell him I saw you praying before my altar if you will not tell him that I allow you to come in here and pray before it any time you wish."

Murielle looked at him questioningly.

Étienne placed a finger to his lips and looked around as if checking for anyone watching. "Any time you wish."

Murielle's face sobered. She nodded somberly and placed a finger to her lips.

"Agreed," he said.

They both broke into smiles.

"Well, my lass," Étienne said after a moment, "would you care to assist me in leading the animals out to pasture before we milk the cows?"

Murielle's face brightened. "Yes! Very much so!"

Étienne's face broke into a broad smile. "Come then, let us go. I am quite certain they are all very hungry."

The reeve walked toward the front part of the barn. He had just passed outside the doorway to his "court" when he realized the girl was not following him.

Murielle stood staring at Étienne's altar. "How do you do it?" she asked.

"I presume you do not mean how do we get animals to pasture, but I do not know of what else you could be asking."

Murielle shifted uncomfortably, picking randomly at her cloak. "Pray," she said eventually.

Étienne stepped back into the doorway. "Pray?" he repeated, scratching his head. "Well, one just... just... prays."

"But how?" She looked at him with that expression children have when they wish you to explain something overly complex in one brief statement.

"Well... ahh... hmmm..." The reeve scratched his head again.

"One just prays, is all."

"How?"

"Well... ummm... there are many stock prayers the priests use. My father never taught me those. I simply kneel before the altar and say whatever is on my mind."

"How?"

This is why I have never had children, Étienne thought to himself. "I do not have a plan. I tell the god whatever I am thinking at the moment."

"Show me."

Étienne took a deep breath and released it slowly. He motioned Murielle aside and lowered himself slowly onto the feed sack. The ends bulged with the displacement of feed from his great mass. After placing his fingertips on his forehead, he closed his eyes and took a deep breath.

"Ahem." He collected his thoughts for a moment and then began. "Lord Arbrinner, thank you for this lovely day you have provided for us. May you bless us and watch over us and protect us from all harm." He turned to Murielle and shrugged. "Just so."

Murielle nodded somberly.

It was Étienne's turn to ask questions. "I know your father keeps the altar to Bellicor in the manor house only for affect, but has he not at least shown you how to pray for the same purpose."

Murielle shook her head somberly.

Étienne looked down to the altar with a sigh.

"Why is he not happy?" Murielle asked suddenly.

Étienne looked around the room then his eyes fell upon the altar again. "Lord Arbrinner?"

"Yes," she said in a glum voice. "I thought he was always happy."

The reeve let out another sigh. "He was at one time past."

"Why is he not now?"

"No one believes any longer."

"Why?"

"Most people in these times only believe what they can see."

"Why?"

Étienne looked the girl up and down. He looked out the doorway and then back to Murielle. He shifted uncomfortably on the feed sack. "I should not say," he replied haltingly.

"Why?"

Rising stiffly to his feet, the reeve walked to the doorway. "Come, we must lead the animals out to pasture."

Murielle stood in place, looking at the altar. "If I pray to Lord Arbrinner, will that make him happy again?"

Étienne smiled wanly. "Perhaps." Then his face brightened. "Yes, perhaps it will."

Murielle kneeled on the feed sack and pressed her fingers to her forehead. "Lord Arbrinner, do not be sad. I believe in you even if I cannot see you." She paused, looked at her father's reeve and bowed her head again. "Thank you for Étienne. He is nice."

She smiled at him. He returned it.

Murielle looked thoughtful. "May I ask him for something?"

"Certainly, anything you wish."

She bowed her head once more, pressing her fingers to her forehead. "Lord Arbinner, I wish to meet Lord Bellicor. Please tell him. Thank you."

Étienne could not help but smile a genuine smile at the prayer of a small child. So innocent and believing. He made a silent prayer to Lord Arbrinner that she hold on to that innocent faith into adulthood. If she could hold onto that innocent faith and more besides her could do so as well, then perhaps this bleak world could truly change for the better.

"Was that good enough?" Murielle asked.

"Yes, it was," he said. "It was a fine prayer, as fine a prayer as I have ever heard." He turned again to the door. "Now let us go lead the animals to pasture, they are certainly hungry by now."

"Yes!" she said, jumping up from the feed sack and running after the reeve.

The two walked back up the barn, the sun already shining in a steep angle through the large doors at the end. Their breath came in clouds: a great one for Étienne, and a smaller one for Murielle. The reeve came to the first animal pen and opened the gate. The sheep looked at him as if he had lost his senses. Murielle held the gate as Étienne tried to encourage them out.

"Have you ever seen one of the gods, Étienne?"

"I have not," he said as he pushed one particularly stubborn ewe through the gate. "No one has that I know. My father never saw a god, nor did his father, nor his father before him."

They moved on to the next pen. Fortunately, the goats were easier to work with.

Murielle held the gate again. "If no one has seen the gods, then how do we believe in them?"

"We have the tales. Others before us have seen them."

"As Senus did?"

"Yes, lass." Étienne watched the goats leave the barn. He shook his head as the sheep stood at the door looking back at him as if he were mad. "Senus was the most fortunate human ever in that respect. He not only met the Lord Aufeese but was able to live with him for a time."

"But the Lord Aufeese blinded him."

Étienne paused at the next pen. A cow inside nudged him encouragingly. "We shall milk the cows later," he said before answering the girl's question. "I would gladly give my sight and more to meet Lord Arbrinner. Senus wrote: 'To gaze upon that beauty for such a short time and to be able to hold that memory with me, is apt reward for a life of darkness.' I believe that with all my heart, lass."

Murielle dropped her hand from the gate. "Is that what is required to meet a god?"

The reeve started at the girl's voice, brought back to reality from his reverie. "Oh, certainly not, lass," he said as he opened the gate for the cattle. "There are many, many tales of men and women who have had encounters with the gods. Senus was but one, the most fortunate of them all, but merely one of many."

Murielle nodded somberly as she took hold of the gate again. "But it has been a very long time since anyone has encountered a god, has it not?"

The cattle exited the barn. The sheep still stood at the door staring at Étienne. He shook his head and moved on to the next pen.

The pigs appeared to share with the sheep the same belief as to Étienne's sanity. He entered the pen and tried to encourage them, but they refused entirely. The reeve sighed heavily.

"Yes, lass, it has been a long time, but the tales encourage us." He gave one large sow a shove with no success.

Murielle rested her chin on one of the rungs of the gate. "Are the gods dead?"

Étienne stopped pushing the pig and looked up in alarm. "Do not say such a thing, lass! The gods are alive, indeed, but they choose in their own time when to reveal themselves, and to whom!"

"But how do we know for certain?"

The reeve left the pig and straightened. "Faith, lass, faith. We hear the tales and believe in the gods. We live by faith that they will reveal themselves to each of us one day in their own time. We each can pray that we will one day meet a god. Some will, many will not, and those who do meet a god may be required to make a great sacrifice for the privilege."

"As was Senus."

"As was Senus."

The large sow Étienne had been working on suddenly decided she wanted out of the pen. The others followed, oinking happily all the way out of the barn and into the bright sunlight. The sheep, seeing the pigs leave, apparently decided it was time to leave as well.

"Lord Arbrinner at work," Étienne cried, turning his face upward in exaltation.

Murielle looked around frantically. "Where? Where?"

Étienne laughed heartily. "No lass, no lass. That is the other part." He leaned down, placing his large hands on the gate, and putting his face close to hers. The great white clouds of his breath combined with hers in the frigid air. "The gods work in our lives without us seeing them. They make things happen that we do not see; without our knowledge, they make things happen for our benefit."

Murielle frowned. "Lord Arbrinner moved the pigs?"

"Yes, lass, I believe so. I prayed for it and he granted it."

Murielle continued to frown. "I did not hear you pray."

"One more piece to the puzzle of faith, lass. Prayers begin in one's heart," he said, pointing to her chest. "One need not say a prayer out loud for a god to hear it. Likewise, one may speak a prayer as much as he or she likes, but if it originates not from the heart, no god will ever hear it."

"So, the prayer I said at your altar must come from my heart if Lord Arbrinner is to hear it."

"Yes, lass, yes. If you wish it to come true, you must believe it with all your heart."

Murielle nodded her head slowly. She thought of the altar to Lord Bellicor in the manor house. That was the source of her problem with her prayers to the war god. Her prayers did not originate from her heart. Étienne was correct. Once she learned to pray from her heart, her wish would be granted.

"Come lass," said Étienne as he walked toward the barn door. "The animals are out of the barn and in the courtyard. We must lead them to pasture and return before your father leaves this day."

Murielle grumbled as she caught up with Étienne. She had forgotten that Father was to return to the front today. "Must he go, Étienne?"

"Yes, lass, he must. He leads an army against Ocosse and must be with them."

Murielle growled. "I do so hate war."

"Do not fret, lass," Étienne said with a smile as he looked around the courtyard. Sheep, goats, cows, and pigs nosed around the drifts of pure white snow. "Deeper snow lays outside the gates. It is an answer to another prayer."

Murielle looked at the reeve curiously.

"Although Richard must return to his army, there will be no battle today; the deep snow prevents it. If the snow continues–and the low, dark clouds moving in from the West say it will–there will be no battle for the foreseeable future."

Murielle smiled.

––––––

Murielle jumped as the door flew open with a loud crash, revealing a large and dark figure framed in the doorway by the bright light of multiple torches streaming into the house from behind him.

She sat on the floor, in the dirt, next to the stain of Gilles's blood as she had sat since she returned home. The blood, fresh and red in the dirt when she first discovered it, was now a faded rusty brown stain. Murielle was so fearful it would fade away into nothing. She wanted it to stay; it was all she had. Cheval had stayed in the doorway, watching, waiting for a long time before he had eventually wandered off. Murielle sat, sometimes rocking back and forth, sometimes still, always praying. She prayed until she thought she could pray no more, and then continued to pray. She was sure there was a permanent dent in her forehead from her fingers being pressed there so hard for so long. She prayed to every god on the list–even Lord Merinwar, who was not known to do anything for humans, except quickly end their brief lives–at least three times and was working on the fourth round of prayers when the door crashed open. She did not even remember closing it. Cheval must have closed it when he left. He was always such a polite horse.

The figure rushed forward into the room and collapsed before her in a heap. It was not Cheval, Murielle was sure, almost sure at any rate. The figure's face was difficult to discern as it was black, blue, red, and many other colors of the rainbow. Murielle felt sure it was not a horse's face, no matter what the color. Then she realized someone was laughing. Cheval? Why would he laugh? It must be a particularly good joke. Cheval never laughs at anything.

She realized the laughing came from the men standing at the door. Murielle shook her head, clearing it from the fog which had cloaked her mind. She looked again at the figure before her. "Gilles!" she cried.

Gilles's face was a bloodied, multicolor ruin. "By the gods's ears! What has happened to you!"

This brought intensified laughter form the men assembled outside. One of them strolled leisurely into the room, sauntering up next to where Murielle sat on the dirt floor. She turned her eyes up to the man. Prince Henri sneered down at her.

"Believe me, lady, no matter how hideous your husband looks now, he has fared far better than your daughter." Henri's laughter drowned out that of the others outside.

Murielle puzzled this as she watched Henri leave. He did not bother to close the door. The sound of many hooves receded into the distance.

Murielle looked down at Gilles. She spoke, more to herself than her husband. "What did he mean by tha—"

She gripped Gilles tightly by the shoulders and shook him violently. "What did he mean by that Gilles?! What did he mean?! Where is Emmeline?! Where is Emmeline?!"

Gilles opened one eye, the only one he could open. Tears would have flowed from that eye if there were any more tears to shed. He began to moan, weak and low, as a man might who has very little left in him. He reached up, his hands still bound by a length of rope, and gently took his wife's face. Murielle did not mind the blood on them. Such things did not matter to her any longer.

Gilles spoke, his voice so low and weak she could barely hear it at first.

"I... I... h-h-h-ave f-f-f-ailed us."

"*Non*, Gilles, *non*," wept Murielle as she pulled his head into her lap. "You have not failed us. It is I who failed us. If I had—"

"*Non, ma cherie*, I... I... f-f-f-ailed us. It... it... is m-m-my fault."

"No, Gilles, no." Murielle's tears ran down her face in a great flood. "Never mind the blame, where is our daughter? Where is Emmeline?"

Gilles began to blubber. Blood ran thickly from between his lips causing a coughing fit. When it had subsided, he spoke again.

"It w-w-w-as m-m-my plan, and it f-f-f-ailed. I f-f-f-ailed you, and I f-f-f-ailed E-E-E-Emmeline most of a-a-a-ll."

Murielle shook her husband again. "Where is she Gilles?! Where is she?!"

Murielle's shaking brought on another, more violent coughing fit. Blood flew from Gilles's mouth in great clots, splattering the front of Murielle's dress with gore.

Gilles's face became a pathetic mask of misery. He blubbered and coughed again in a great bloody fit, spraying even more gore on Murielle's dress, before he could finally speak again.

"Dead," he said in a voice that was more a passing of air than actual speech.

He spoke so low that Murielle could not be sure what her husband had said. Surely it could not be what she thought she had heard. She shook him again. "Where is Emmeline, Gilles?! Where is our little girl?!"

Gilles's head lolled in Murielle's lap. He moaned and blubbered again, and then, in a voice clear and strong, he spoke his last: "Dead. Our little girl is dead."

Murielle let loose a long, wretched, guttural scream and shook Gilles's lifeless body. "NO! NO! NO! NOOOOOOOOOOOO-OOOO!"

The doves flew around the rafters madly. Murielle screamed, wept, screamed again. She held Gilles close to her, stroking his ruined face and battered head. Murielle wept, and wept, and wept.

At some point Cheval appeared in the doorway looking as wretched and miserable as any animal possibly could.

CHAPTER SEVENTEEN

As they left the farmhouse, the sounds of the wailing woman echoing in the warm night air, Philippe drifted back as far to the rear of group as he dared. He lost sight of the others, following the clopping of hooves on the packed dirt road. He knew that once they arrived back at the Eternal City, Henri would remember him and this rare opportunity to himself would end. He offered up a silent prayer that Henri would stay to the main road rather than taking the more direct Straight Road. He offered up thanks when the party passed the Straight road without turning. Philippe could now spend time with his memories.

———

"You bear his mark; blest from birth by the god, his purpose for you awaits to be revealed," Laurent de Lois had told Philippe long ago. Philippe's hand absently stole up to his chest, at the center of which lay the small, crimson birthmark.

Although much time had passed since he had last seen the High Priest, his image was as clear in Philippe's mind as if he had last seen him only this morning. Laurent de Lois was a tall man, with long red hair and a neatly trimmed beard, not impressive looking in the least, yet he possessed a strength which defied his lean stature. Laurent had hit Philippe many times over the years in his training, and although they fought with crowned lances and blunted training swords to minimize injury, Philippe had, more often than not, crumpled behind his shield from the power of his master's blows.

It was his eyes which Philippe remembered the most, and the meeting with Lord Bellicor brought that back to him. The god's dark brown eyes, peaceful enough, were filled with a watchful calculation. As with Laurent de Lois, it was not unsettling, only curious. He knew Philippe's responses to his statements even before Philippe had known them, the same way Lord Bellicor seemed to know how their entire conversation would play out even before it had taken place.

Many of the brothers of the *Confrérie du Chêne* commented—when Laurent could not hear—that he looked as much like the god as any human could, giving him special right to the position of High Priest. Philippe had not entirely concurred with that assessment, but this day, having met the war god, gazed upon him, and spoken with him at length, found the comparison startlingly more accurate than the brothers had likely ever imagined.

Laurent de Lois was as close to a father as Philippe had ever known. His own father and mother had been killed in a wagon accident at the edge of the great lake when Philippe was only an infant. Brother Valentin, a good monk and knight, had found him and brought him back to the monastery. A search went out and finding no one who would claim the child or the parents, the consensus of knights of the *Confrérie du Chêne* was to raise the boy as one of their own.

Philippe grew and thrived on the order's studious worship of the war god, and the rigorous training as a squire. Philippe eventually reached the proper stage in his training when he could be knighted. In those days, The Old King alone knighted those who had met the requirements. Philippe had decided to petition the king at the grand

Eglinton tournament being staged by Renaud, the new Earl of Forcalquier. The Eglinton tournament was intended to be the grandest tourney ever held. Philippe felt that if he were to be knighted at this tourney and then compete well, he could only bring honor to the *Confrérie du Chêne*. Laurent could find no fault with Philippe's logic, and although there was no rule against a Knight of the Oak competing in a tournament, it was generally discouraged as such competition aroused vanity and braggadocio. However, Laurent felt that if any knight could resist those temptations, it was Philippe. The other knights of the monastery approved of the decision by consensus.

So, Philippe set out on a warm spring day, the tall green grass of the adjoining meadow waving in the slight breeze, and the few white clouds drifting lazily in a bright azure sky. He was given a fresh young charger, enough arms and armor for multiple contests, and letters of recommendation. With the permission of the Knights of the Oak, Philippe took the oak leaf as his herald. It seemed to take an eternity to arrive at Eglinton, but he eventually crested the hill over the town. He paused to take in the panoply of knights in their spectacular armor. He was awed beyond words. He met The Old King, was knighted, and although he performed well, he did not win a single event. Two knights divided most of the honors: a mysterious figure only known as The Black Knight and another who went by the name of Guillaume de Marschal. Nevertheless, The Old King was impressed with Philippe's performance and thus began their friendship.

Philippe learned the art of war on the fields, fighting against the armies of Ocosse. He proved himself time and time again, advancing in the ranks quickly. He and The Old King grew ever closer as he rose in rank. Eventually he was given his own command.

It was during this time that Philippe became acquainted with the Old King's son Henri. The Prince was pleasant enough to Philippe, at first. Philippe was older, but their ages close enough that they could easily find common ground. However, there was a certain undertone in Henri's attitude toward him that bothered Philippe. He could not place it, and it was not until the Old King named Henri captain of the armies to replace the deceased Richard de Conquil, that Philippe finally was able to put a name to it. *Jalousie*. Henri was captain of the armies, yet Philippe was the Old King's closest confidant. Henri envied Philippe's close relationship with the Old King. However, Henri never had a kind word to say about his father, and some of the things he said to his friends made Philippe flush with anger. This perplexed Philippe for some time. When Philippe finally convinced the Old King of the futility of the war with Ocosse, Henri bristled. When Philippe helped forge the treaty which turned over the disputed territories to Ocosse, Henri was silent with him for some time and retreated to the companionship of his friends.

Another issue was that Henri's "friends" were some of the most artless and uncultured individuals Philippe had ever met. They were not the sort of men with whom a man of Henri's position should be associating. They were of the ilk that slithered down dark, dank alleyways, infinitely searching for the next opportunity to fill their bottomless pit of boredom. Quite simply, Henri surrounded himself with cheap, vacuous thugs.

The Old King was completely oblivious to his son's behavior. He believed his angelic son could do no wrong. Philippe found himself in an awkward position. He felt he could say nothing of what he knew without embarrassing the Old King or even angering him. Yet, Philippe mused as he rode along in the dark under the bright points of light in the heavens, if he had shown the Old King the truth, certain events would not have occurred. He shook off that thought. *The past cannot be undone*, Laurent had said many times.

———

A shiver ran through Philippe. In the long time he had spent with the Prince, Philippe had watched his behavior shift from eccentric, to unsettling, to disturbing. He looked back over his shoulder at a great stone fortress, a relic of the wars with Ocosse, its dark shape looming in the night and blocking out many of the stars. It was there that Philippe had witnessed the Prince make the shift from unsettling into truly disturbing behavior. After Henri had promised to marry the Jocelyn girl, Philippe saw him do things far worse than he could have ever imagined the Prince capable. Henri had come to the fortress with his fiancé and several of his close associates for a private engagement feast, far away from the prying public eyes. Philippe had been compelled to attend, and he went, even though he knew what would happen. As it turned out, Philippe did not know anything.

He shivered violently, hard enough to force a muted neigh of concern from his charger. He patted the horse's neck and shivered again. He would not think of it. He could not think of it. He forced the memories out of his mind. Philippe had become quite skilled at that over the time he had spent with the Prince. He turned his mind instead to the war god. Lord Bellicor. The god of war. The memory of his meeting this afternoon brought a small smile to his face. Not one of the knights of the *Confrérie du Chêne* had ever seen him. Philippe was the first. He let his mind drift around that pleasant meeting for the remainder of the journey.

At last, they came to the great walls of Darloque. *The Eternal City*, Philippe thought to himself, *the city that has always been and shall always be.* He caught up with the rest of the party as someone called out to the guards. "Open the gates, Prince Henri approaches!" The three sets of gates, one by one opened, and they rode into the city. As the last set of gates closed behind them, Henri gathered his men for a parting message.

"Events did not come out as planned this day, men," he said with no less energy than he had possessed in the morning. "It is late. Go rest and meet me tomorrow evening in the old banquet hall. The great news I wanted to share today shall wait until the morrow."

The group was tired, yet abuzz with expectation. Philippe nodded solemnly.

"I hope you enjoyed you time alone, Jean-Louis," Henri said, directing his attention to his lieutenant. His eyes flamed in the dark street. "I expect to see you there as well."

Philippe frowned inside, revealing nothing in his face. There seemed to be extraordinarily little he could hide from the Prince. He hoped at least to hide just one secret for a time. "As you wish, my Prince," he replied with a nod.

The party broke apart, some going off alone, others in pairs or threes. Philippe followed a northerly street toward the castle. The apartments he kept in Darloque were east of the castle, close enough for him to be summoned quickly should the need arise. *And close enough so that Henri can keep an eye on you*, he thought to himself.

She was waiting up for him, of course. Sophie sat by the low fire, working on her embroidery. Philippe came up behind his wife and watched her push the needle through the fabric. It was a pastoral scene, a *cocque* and a hen standing together in a grassy area surrounded by a few flowers of blue and yellow.

"That progresses nicely," he said, "but you shall go blind doing such work in this low light."

"I am fine," Sophie said without looking up from her work.

Philippe watched silently as she worked, pushing the needle through the fabric, the yellow thread trailing behind.

"How went the hunt?" she asked without missing a stitch.

Philippe hesitated, choosing his words carefully. "Unsuccessful," he replied at last.

"Ahh."

"The drought I suppose."

"Yes, the drought certainly made it more difficult." he bent down and kissed her cheek. "That is quite good," he said, examining his wife's embroidery more closely.

Philippe realized that the flower she was working on was in reality a downy yellow chick pecking in the grass between the *cocque* and the hen. The *cocque* and hen both looked over the chick with watchful, protective eyes.

He straightened and walked toward the bed chamber. "It has been a long day, I am exhausted. Will you come to bed soon?"

Sophie stopped in mid-stitch, the needle and bright yellow thread hanging in the air and looked up at her husband. She smiled the sweet little smile which had drawn him to her so long ago. "Soon. I wish to finish this one part before bed."

"Very well."

Philippe stopped by Claire's bed chamber and looked in on her. She lay in her bed, sleeping soundly, her nose wrinkling in her sleep as she did when she was dreaming. *Whatever do you dream, ma petite fleur?* he thought wistfully.

Philippe stripped the dirty, sweaty clothes from his body and deposited them in the corner of the chamber for the servants to take care of later. He went to the basin and splashed water on his face, and he wondered if he would be able to get to sleep at all, with the day's events buzzing around his brain like a swarm of angry wasps. However, as soon as he lay down, he fell into a deep sleep.

Philippe sat up suddenly in bed, his ephemeral dreams evaporating quickly. The room was dark. He felt around on the other side of the bed, and Sophie was not there. He figured he must have been asleep only a few moments for Sophie had not yet come to bed. He sighed. The door opened and Sophie entered with a lantern.

"Ah. Awake finally, I see," she said with a glum smile as she sat on the bed next to him.

"Awake? Finally? Whatever do you mean by that? I have only just gone to bed."

"Oh no," she said with the same glum smile and set the lantern on the bedside table. "That was last night. You slept all night and all this day. It is night again. It must have been a grueling trip with the Prince for you to have slept this long."

Philippe stared back at his wife incredulously, believing this to be some jest of hers.

"No, husband," she said, reading his thoughts, "this is no jest. You have slept all day."

He took this in and lay back down. "I must have been more exhausted than I believed."

"Perhaps," she replied.

Philippe turned to his wife. The glum smile returned. She suspected things.

"You frightened your daughter terribly." Sophie frowned. "It is not normal for you to sleep for so long, and she has been concerned for you all day."

Philippe smiled as he lay back down. "I will see her and show her I am well. That will comfort her."

"Yes, that will do." Sophie pressed her lips together tightly. She took a long pause then spoke. "I am still quite surprised the Prince has left you alone this long."

Philippe sat up with a start, then lay back with a groan. "I am to meet with him and his men this evening. He has an important announcement."

Sophie could not hide the look of distaste. "Very well," she replied, and left the room.

Philippe dressed in a fresh uniform. Out in the main hall Sophie sat working at her embroidery. Claire sat at a desk a little distance from her, writing thoughtfully. Philippe had insisted early on that their daughter be taught to read and write. Although Sophie could do neither, she had embraced the idea. It was not uncommon for Philippe to come home to find Claire reading to her mother one of the latest stories of knightly romance.

Claire looked up from her parchment. She dropped her quill at the sight of her father and ran to him, embracing him tightly. "Father! I am so glad you are well!"

Philippe embraced her. "Of course I am well. How could I be otherwise?"

Claire looked up at him with her big brown eyes so exactly like her mother's. "I was so worried. You slept for so long!"

Philippe looked down at his daughter, her silken blonde hair hanging down to her waist, a single braid at each temple as was the fashion nowadays of the ladies of the court. Claire knew all the current fashions of the ladies of the court. This thought made Philippe a little sad, but he kept the smile.

"*Ma petite fleur*," he said as he stroked her hair, "I went on an exceptionally long ride with the Prince and was very tired afterward." Philippe paused a moment then added, "Additionally, the goddess of dreams decided to visit me with very strange and wondrous dreams."

"Truly?" Claire's expression perked up. Her rosy cheeks bloomed. "What dreams did the goddess give you?"

Philippe became thoughtful. "Well, I dreamt that you did not practice your writing and had to go live with a witch." Philippe tapped his chin. "And then the dream turned very bad."

Claire hung on his words, engrossed by the story. "Oh no! How terrible! How could it become worse?!"

"The witch brought you back."

"Father! You are silly!" Claire cried with a big smile.

Philippe laughed. "Now go back to your writing. I must go meet with the Prince on important business."

Claire flounced halfway to the desk, turned, then flounced back to her father and embraced him again.

"Father, may I go with you to court one day?"

Philippe stiffened. He looked at his daughter, somewhere in the strange position between girl and woman. She was still so innocent. He longed to keep her like this, to keep Claire from ever experiencing all the evil he had seen. He loved her so much. It pained him to think that evil might touch her. He suppressed a shiver.

"One day, I promise." He gave her a kiss.

Claire squeezed him tightly and flounced back to the desk, taking Philippe's heart with her.

Philippe glanced over at Sophie. She remained focused on her embroidery, the needle with its yellow tail flashing behind it, working diligently. She had heard but gave no sign. He kissed his wife on the cheek then went to the stable where the stable hand held his charger at the ready. His wife had taken care of his needs.

The castle stable hand took Philippe's charger with a yawn, and Philippe made his way to the old banquet hall which Henri had taken over when the new hall was completed. He wove through the labyrinth of dim corridors in the heart of the castle–the castle built by Lord Daedemus himself after he constructed the protective labyrinth around Mava's palace. He finally arrived at the grand entry doors of the old hall. By the sound emanating from behind them, the festivities were well under way. Philippe laid his hand on a door just as Sébastien rounded the corner from another direction.

"Ah! Jean-Louis!" he cried drunkenly. "We feared you would miss all the fun!"

Philippe scowled, not caring if the drunken lout could see him in the low light or not. "Of course not, Sébastien. My Prince summoned me, and I came."

"*Oui, oui*, quite so."

Philippe thought for a moment. "Has the Prince made his announcement yet?"

Sébastien smiled and put an arm around Philippe. "No, no, Jean-Louis." His face became clear for a moment. "No, he has not given his announcement, but he is in an extremely good mood."

Philippe tried to pull away, but Sébastien held firm.

"The Prince is in a good mood, and you know what that means? Eh, Jean-Louis?"

"When the Prince is in a good mood, we are all in a good mood."

"*Exactement*, Jean-Louis! *Exactement!*" Sébastien laughed long and loud in Philippe's face.

Philippe finally wrestled himself away from the drunkard's grip. *Call me Jean-Louis one more time,* he muttered to himself, *and I shall kill you with my bare hands.*

"What was that, Jean-Louis?"

"Nothing, Sébastien. Let us go in."

"*Oui, oui.*"

Philippe pushed open the doors to find the old hall filled with people. Torches hung from sconces at regular intervals on the walls, providing more than sufficient light by which he could see throughout the room. He stood in the doorway, mouth slightly agape, stunned by the sight. In the old days, the hall would have held perhaps five hundred people comfortably during a feast. There were at least that many here now, and probably a lot more. Most were men whom Philippe had never seen before. Several risqué, painted women of a decidedly ill reputation roamed around the room as well.

"Let me by, Jean-Louis," cried Sébastien as he shoved past Philippe. He spied a woman who had cried out his name, and with a shout, he disappeared into the crowd.

The room was a cacophony of voices. A group of musicians played somewhere in the room, a loud raucous song with bawdy lyrics. Mindful of the noise, Philippe closed the doors behind him. Philippe was aware that Prince had associates he had not met; however, he did not realize they numbered so many. He looked around the room. So few faces he recognized, but the ones he knew, particularly the ones of the hunting party, appeared to intimately know the others. Philippe was aghast. Who were these people and how could he have missed them?

A glassy eyed trollop with gaudy splashes of bright rouge on her cheeks accosted him drunkenly.

"Sayyyy," she slurred, "I knowwww yyyyou." She ran a finger seductively down the front of his tunic.

"I think not," Philippe replied flatly. He began searching the room for the Prince.

"Yesss I do. You are Michel. I would rec... rec... recognize you anywhere." She began to play with his hair, then burped.

Philippe swatted her hand away. "You are mistaken, now go."

He caught sight of the Prince sitting on the dais at the head of the hall, sitting in the very throne the Old King had used when this hall was the main banquet hall. Henri had been leaning over, speaking to someone off the dais. He sat back in the chair, then leaned to his right and began to speak into the ear of the person sitting in the chair next to his—

Philippe's heart stopped completely and leapt into his throat.

"I dooo know you, Miiichel. I-I-I would rec... rec... recognize you aaanywhere."

Philippe's eyes grew large, swelling in their sockets. His mouth dropped open, a great yawning cavern. He made no sound, no breath issued from him.

"Yesss," the painted woman slurred, "Michel, Michel, Michel." She walked her fingers down his tunic to his belt.

Philippe began to tremble, minutely at first, then gradually building to a violent seism, a spasmodic seizure. In one great convulsive effusion he choked out a single word.

"Claire!"

"*Que?!*" cried out the trollop as she swayed back dangerously on her heels and somehow kept her balance. She lost the slur in her speech as her eyes flashed angrily. "Who is this Claire, Michel? I am Marie! Who is Claire?!"

Philippe stepped forward, brushing the painted woman aside roughly without a thought. He was only aware of the young girl on the dais next to the Prince.

"Claire!" cried the woman. "Youuu are soooo fickle, Michel! Very wellll then! Yyyou have your pre... pre... precious Claire!" The trollop turned and ran into a man passing by. "Sayyyy," she slurred, "I knowwww yyyyou."

Henri whispered in the ear of the young girl seated next to him. She was a noticeably young girl; certainly, she had only seen twelve seasons. Blonde and pretty with rosy cheeks. And from the side as Philippe saw her, a braid at her temple, as was currently the fashion with the ladies of the court.

Philippe ran a hand through his hair, his breath came in rapid pants. His head devoid of thoughts, filled only with raw, rabid panic. And then the girl turned, looking around the room nervously, clearly uncertain about the proceedings. Even from across the room Philippe could see the timidity in her ice blue eyes.

Blue eyes. Philippe's heart began to slow, but it was far from a normal pace. He covered his mouth and nose with his hands, breathing in heavy pants and tried to recover himself. *Not Claire! Not Claire!* he repeated over and over. He needed air.

He fled the room, running blindly through the maze of the corridors, turning randomly in the dimness. He raced up a flight of stairs, taking the steps two at a time. He slipped once, striking his shin sharply, but continued his climb with no loss of momentum. He eventually found himself on the roof of the northern tower overlooking the wall of the city.

With nowhere higher to go, Philippe paced around the roof, panting through his teeth, and running his hands through his hair. His mind was a jumble. Confused thoughts raced inside his head, colliding with each other, scrambling anything which might become something resembling coherent. Finally, exhausted by the maelstrom in his head, he propped his elbows upon the parapet and held his head in his hands.

Philippe did not know how long he stood there that way. At one point he turned to the sky, massaging his face and neck, and stared blankly at the constellation of Bellicor directly overhead, the bright red star at its heart gleaming brightly. When he turned his face to the heavens again, the constellation was far down in the western sky.

He stood at the parapet, propped up on his elbows, head in his hands, contemplating the thick, impenetrable city wall, when he heard the door open behind him. A few cautious footfalls on the stone and then a voice.

"Ah, Jean-Louis, there you are."

Philippe remained in his position, unmoved by the sound of Sébastien's voice.

"Jean-Louis?"

No response.

"Jean-Louis?"

Philippe heard tentative footsteps behind him, approaching. Sébastien came up and laid a hand on Philippe's shoulder.

"Jean-Louis, are you well?"

Philippe spun around quickly, startling Sébastien.

Sébastien looked at Philippe narrowly in the darkness, swaying slightly. "You are well? *Oui?*"

Philippe looked into glazed, bloodshot eyes. "Oh yes," he replied, trying to put on a good face. "It gets stuffy in that old hall, always has, and I came up here for some air."

"Ah, yes." Sébastien looked around. He gazed over the parapet at the city wall below. "I have never been up here before. *Très bonne.*"

"Yes, it is," Philippe replied, trying to keep appearances as normal as possible. "It is quite beautiful up here."

Sébastien slapped the parapet with a loud smack and turned clumsily to face Philippe. "Say, you should have stayed around a bit longer."

"Well..." Philippe shrugged. "I am not the one for feasts and drinking." He began to almost believe that he felt normal.

Sébastien laughed, blowing foul alcoholic breath in Philippe's face. "Well, you should try it more, Jean-Louis! This feast was an incredibly good one, probably the best the Prince has ever had!"

Philippe chuckled, intending to tell him he would endeavor to participate more at the next feast when Sébastien broke in.

"That blonde girl the Prince brought," he laughed, shaking his head. "She was so sweet." He chuckled again. "Even though there were at least a score of men ahead of me."

Philippe's face dropped.

"Probably was still sweet after a hundred, I would say," Sébastien said matter-of-factly.

The world tilted sideways. Everything lost focus, Sébastien became nothing but a vague shape in the night.

"Are you sure you are well, Jean-Louis? You do not look well."

Without thinking, without a single thought in his head, without anything inside his head but pure, blind rage, Philippe lunged forward, seized Sébastien, and even though the drunken lout weighed at least four stone more than himself, lifted him easily over his head, and in one smooth motion, pitched him headlong over the parapet to the rocks below.

Philippe propped his elbows on the parapet, head in his hands, and stared off at nothing.

———

He did not remember coming down from the tower. He did not remember leaving the castle. Yet, he found himself standing before his apartments. His horse was nowhere around, and the stable hand stared out from the open doorway with a puzzled look on his face. It was dark, but a dim gray glowed in the East. Philippe signaled to the stable hand that all was well and watched him disappear into the stables.

Philippe entered the dark dwelling and moved, guiding himself by memory, through the front room and down the hallway. He stopped automatically and turned toward the door he knew was there. His hand hovered over the latch. He released it and slowly pushed open the door which emitted a small squeak. The sound did not even cause the sleeper within to stir.

Claire's bed chamber possessed one East facing window. She was at an age where she had begun to hate the early morning sunlight of summer for it awakened her too early. Of course, she would be happy if the sun did not rise until midday. The night was hot, so the heavy curtains were parted to allow the faint breeze inside.

The dim, gray light illuminated the room enough. Philippe saw his daughter lying on her back in the bed, blooms on her cheeks just visible in the early light, the braids at her temples lay crossed on her small, developing bosom. Her nose wrinkled; her breath came in slow, easy movements. She looked so peaceful there, so far away from the hideous world which encircled her, threatening her. Philippe ran a hand through his hair and thought.

Tonight was a warning. The Prince did not make eye contact, did not acknowledge Philippe's presence. He did not need to see a confirmation in Philippe's eyes to know the message was delivered and understood. Philippe thought at first that Sèbastien had been sent as an unwitting messenger, but that was so unlike Henri. Henri delivered the message and knew that it was understood. Sèbastien simply stumbled in by accident. Philippe understood the message. His daughter was not safe. His family was not safe.

The task Lord Bellicor had given him was daunting. Philippe could pretend otherwise, but the war god would not accept anything less than full compliance. And now Philippe saw the other side of the coin. Lord Bellicor could only protect Philippe's family by his strict adherence to the god's instructions. His family would never be safe unless he took the difficult path. The choice was difficult, and Philippe was afraid.

Two arms slipped around his waist.

"Philippe?"

Sophie leaned into him, pressing her cheek to his back. "I am so sorry."

Philippe nodded once and gave no more.

"The messenger came only a short while ago and told me the Old King has died this night."

Philippe nodded again. Under any other circumstances he would have been grief stricken beyond measure at such news. However, the situation was different now. Events were unfolding as Lord Bellicor had told him they would.

The sky outside the window took on a distinctly crepuscular tone. Claire stirred in her sleep, her nose wrinkling. He knew she loved him, but her love was nowhere near as great as his for her. Philippe felt the soft press of Sophie's body against his; he felt her love. He knew she depended on him, knew she needed him.

Philippe knew what he must do.

CHAPTER EIGHTEEN

THE RIDER SAT upon a despondent horse. Moving at an easy walking pace, the horse hung his head low, staring only at the ground directly before him, but he kept a straight track on the road, nevertheless. The rider stared straight ahead, yet she saw nothing before her. The great clouds of inky black smoke billowing up some distance behind the horse and rider signaled that no matter what lay ahead of them, they could never return to the place they had departed.

The rider held her back straight, her head high. Sticky, black pitch stained her hands and dress, but she seemed not to notice. All she was aware of were the plumes of black thoughts billowing around in her head. If she felt the burning sun, it did not register on her face. Nothing, in fact, registered on her expressionless face.

A mental communion of sorts bound them together, horse and rider, which bound them not by mutual need, but by mutual loss. In the course of one day, that had lost not everything they had known, but everything for which they had both cared. What lay ahead was known and familiar, but in this case the known and familiar could be no comfort to either. What lay ahead could only serve as a painful reminder of the great loss they left behind. So, they rode on, horse and rider, guided by mutual communal instinct, knowing together, deep in some shared connatural knowledge, that the road they took was the only one available to them. There were no turns; there were no options. There was only forward to their singular destination.

———

Julien watched the horse and rider slowly approach. At first, he ignored them. It was the time of the harvest and he was far too busy to concern himself with random passers-by. But his eyes kept returning to them; something about the pair drew his attention. The horse walked steadily and purposefully, the dust kicked up by its hooves clouded around its feet, dissipating slowly in the still, hot air. The rider seemed either content with, or indifferent to, the lethargic pace of the horse. As they drew closer, Julien suspected the latter.

It soon became clear to him that the destination of the horse and rider was the manor itself. Julien set the lid onto the barrel with a heavy sigh. He simply did not have the patience for travelers at this time. Harvest was such a busy time, what with coordinating all the men working the fields, sorting the crops, filling the storehouse, and keeping the house in order, he had no time to tend to a stranger's needs. Additionally, he must make his report to–

A random breeze rose up, moving gently across the plain, briefly fluttering the rider's dress and tossing about her long chestnut hair.

"Lady Murielle!" he cried as he clamped a hand to his mouth. Julien grabbed the two servants closest to him and dragged them, stumbling, up the road to intercept the horse and rider. The Lady had paid an unexpected visit, and the manor was in complete disarray. The women he had appropriated turned to upbraid him for his rude behavior, then they saw who Julien had dragged them to meet and bowed as she approached.

"Greetings, my Lady," Julien said. "What brings you–"

Lady Murielle continued past them without a word, her eyes forward, staring off into the distance.

"Marked you her appearance?" asked one of the women.

"Why yes!" exclaimed the other. "The stains on her dress and hands, and her face smeared with soot!"

"She appeared so disheveled; her hair so disarrayed." The first paused a moment, shaking her head as she searched for the words. "By the gods's ears, she has experienced something frightfully evil."

Julien continued to stare blankly into the air where Lady Murielle had recently passed. He came to himself with a start and turned on the two servants.

"Cease your chattering!" Julien cried, startling them. "Come! We must catch Lady Murielle and discover what has happened to her." He grabbed the two servants again and led them roughly down the road, back to the manor. "Pray to every god you can name that some dire circumstance has not befallen our Lady!"

Murielle passed through the gates to the stares of numerous servants inside and outside of the courtyard. She reined her horse to a stop at the main door of the manor house and dismounted.

Julien and the two servants ran through the gates as Lady Murielle disappeared into the manor house. Panting, Julien held up a hand, snapping his fingers at everyone. He caught the attention of a young boy, the son of one of the two women servants he had dragged with him.

"Boy! Boy!" he cried out hoarsely. "Take Cheval to the stables. Feed and water! Rub him down! Now!"

The boy did as he was ordered. Cheval came willingly enough as the boy took the reins, although the horse still hung his head dejectedly, and he followed along with no enthusiasm.

Julien rushed into the house, leaving the two women servants still gasping for breath in the courtyard. Inside, it was a madhouse. Servants who had been rushing about at harvest work now rushed about two and even thrice times more quickly when they saw the Lady had arrived. Moreover, Lady Murielle's appalling appearance caused an additional uproar. No one had ever seen her in such a state. It was more than unseemly for her to appear filthy and disheveled; it was unnatural. Immediately Julien was mobbed by the house servants.

"Did you see Lady Murielle?"

"What has happened to her?"

"Who has done this to her?"

Julien gritted his teeth. "Silence!" he hissed.

The servants hushed.

"I do not know what has happened to our mistress, but I will endeavor to discover it. Did anyone see where she has gone?"

A dozen voices rose up, each attempting to speak over the next. A dozen hands went into the air, each pointing in a different direction.

"Silence, all of you!" Julien hissed again. He calmed himself. "Who actually saw where Lady Murielle went?"

A young maiden raised her hand timidly.

"Ahh, *très bonne!*" he exclaimed, clapping his hands together. "Now, where did Lady Murielle go?"

The young maiden looked around with uncertainty then pointed to a closed door off the main hall.

Julien looked at the door with vexation. He stared at it for a few moments then turned back to the servants.

"All of you, go!" he clapped his hands sharply. "We still have a manor and a harvest which to attend. I will speak with Lady Murielle alone and inform you of what I discover."

The household servants hesitated. Julien clapped his hands sharply again and they scattered to their chores. He turned and walked briskly to the door. His right hand paused in midair before it. He brushed his hair away from his face with a trembling left hand. Julien took a deep breath and closed his eyes. He knocked gently and entered the room.

At one time in the past, the room had been the office of Richard de Conquil. A large desk still stood in the center of the room upon which countless charts and maps had been laid out for important men who had pored over them and conducted war stratagems. The room also contained a pair of chests and a few other furnishings of little consequence. Two large portraits dominated one wall. One, commissioned shortly after his death, depicted Richard de Conquil arrayed in his splendid uniform as the captain of the armies. His expression was as severe as Julien remembered it. Although he was a benevolent master, Richard's cold piercing eyes made many a man tremble in his boots.

The other portrait Julien knew little about. The woman, as he had been told, was Lady Murielle's mother. The woman, like her husband, wore a severe look. However, whereas Richard's eyes pierced one with an intense gaze which commanded respect, the lady's frigid gaze and high cheekbones only communicated aloofness.

Her ornate dress suggested a woman of privilege, yet Julien had learned that it was an arranged marriage. Her family, seeking to rise higher in the ranks of society, married her off to a young knight who was already quite connected to higher nobles. Julien could only guess as to how their marriage played out, but he suspected that two intense looking people such as these did not fare well together. Regardless, it was perhaps just as well that Lady Murielle's mother had died in childbirth. Julien supposed that a woman such as the one in the portrait would not have passively accepted Richard's odd–to say the least–views on how to properly raise a daughter.

Julien turned his eyes from the portrait and found his mistress sitting on a low bench near the window. Her back was to him and her long chestnut hair cascaded down her back, spilling onto the bench. Even in its unkempt state, Julien thought it was still as beautiful–he suppressed that thought. She stared out the window, at what, he could not guess. He cleared his throat and waited. When she gave no response, no indication she had heard him, he cleared his throat again. There was still no response.

"My Lady..." Julien could not suppress the tremble in his voice.

"*Les cahiers*," she said without turning her head. Her voice was a dry rasp, barely recognizable, the sound of the wind whipping up chaff in the fields after harvest. The sound was terrible, yet it still made Julien's heart beat faster, nevertheless.

"Yes, my Lady, I will bring the books," he said, attempting to keep his voice level. "The estate has done quite well this season despite the drought. I believe we shall have more than enough to supplement your husband's farm again. I will have the house servants bring you food, water, and clean clothes–"

"*Non*," she rasped again, her back still to Julien. "*Les cahiers.*" A short pause then, "*Allez!*"

Although it pained him to do so, Julien bowed and left the room. Closing the door, he turned to see the expectant faces of several servants in the main hall.

"The Lady has told me nothing," Julien said with a sigh, answering the question on all their faces. Julien could not look at the servants. To see Lady Murielle in such a state was excruciating. Julien fought back tears. He could not, would not, allow them to see him weakened. He spied two young men in the group and seized upon an idea.

"Antoine, Matthieu," he said, gathering himself. "Get the two fastest horses in the stable and ride swiftly to her husband's farm. Discover what has happened."

Antoine and Matthieu dashed from the manor house without a word.

"As for the rest of you," Julien said with a scowl, looking into each of their eyes in turn. "I have told you all to get to work. Regardless of Lady Murielle's state, we still have a harvest to carry out."

They stared blankly at him.

"*Allez! Allez!*" Julien clapped his hands sharply and the servants scattered once more. He turned back to the closed door and brushed the hair from his face with a trembling hand.

Sometime later, Julien entered through that same door with a knock, carrying the estate's inventory and transaction books.

"My Lady," he said cautiously as he entered. Lady Murielle sat in the same position next to the window, her back to him and still staring out the window. He stepped further into the room and cleared his throat.

"Leave them on the desk," she ordered with the same dry, hoarse voice as before.

"Yes, my Lady."

Julien turned to desk and saw the food and decanter of wine a servant had left for her some time ago. The food was untouched and the wine unopened. He stared at them a moment and set the books down next to the tray. He turned back to Lady Murielle and opened his mouth to speak when her hoarse voice came again.

"Leave me."

Julien bowed silently and left the room.

Night fell and the sun rose again. Lady Murielle remained unmoving in her seat by the window. Food and wine were repeatedly brought and later taken away untouched. Julien met a servant as she exited the room with another tray of untouched food. He shook his head sadly at the sight, and the maiden burst into tears as the door latched behind her.

"What is the matter with Lady Murielle?" she cried.

Julien tried to speak, but his voice failed him.

The tray slipped in the girl's trembling hands. Julien took it from her before she dropped it. The serving girl ran from the hall, sobbing loudly.

As night began to fall, Julien quietly entered the room. Although sconces lined the walls, none of the candles were lit. Lady Murielle sat in the fading light by the window, staring out emotionlessly, her back to the door. Julien crept to the desk. A tray of food and wine remained untouched, but the books lay opened. He felt this was a good sign. At the very least she was moving about. He squinted in the weakening light to see what she had been reading. The books were opened, but not to the entries of the current season. Lady Murielle had been examining the inventory and finances of twelve seasons previous.

Julien turned to her. He cleared his throat. "Lady Murielle," he said as a bright tone as he could muster, "allow me to light some–"

"*Non.*"

Julien's heart sank. "Madame, if you do not like the food the servants bring you, I will gladly—"

"*Non.*"

He closed his eyes. The rough rasp of her voice sliced through him. "My Lady," he said, fighting to keep the tremble from his voice. "Please, you must eat something, or at the very least drink something. I fear..."

Lady Murielle turned her head slightly toward Julien. In the low gray light straining through the window, he saw the black stains on her cheek and forehead.

"Do not concern yourself with me, Julien," she rasped. "Leave me." She closed her eyes and swallowed with great difficulty. "Please."

Julien fled the room, barely able to contain his sobs.

Early in the afternoon of the next day, Julien stood in the courtyard checking off items in a book. He had found the books on the floor outside Lady Murielle's door. He realized that not only was Lady Murielle finished with her inspection of the books, but she also was sending the message that she did not want to be disturbed. With a heavy sigh, Julien scooped the books up in his arms and carried them away. He needed them to do his work on the harvest anyway.

All the men had returned to the field to continue with the harvest. The women busied themselves shucking fat ears of corn. The harvest was in full swing, and Julien was glad for this as it kept his mind occupied. Two riders barreled through the open courtyard gates and slid their horses to a stop before Julien. He looked up from his book curiously to see Antoine and Matthieu dismounting. They rushed up speaking hurriedly over one another.

Julien set the book down on a nearby bench. "You have returned! What did you find?"

Antoine and Matthieu spoke so rapidly over each other that Julien could not understand a word either of them said.

Julien raised a hand and shushed them. "Only one of you. What did you find?"

The two looked at each other, then Antoine spoke.

"The farmhouse," he began, still gasping for breath. "Burned to the ground. The barn and other buildings burned as well."

Julien's hand went to his mouth.

Matthieu continued. "The fire had spread to the fields. When we arrived, we encountered several neighboring farmers battling the blaze. We worked with them for some time to extinguish the fire. The farm is a total loss."

"After we had extinguished the fire," Antoine resumed, "we made a search of the place. The fire had been intentionally set. Pitch was used."

Julien nodded grimly.

Matthieu continued. "In our search we found a single grave near the corn field."

Julien gasped. "Did it bear a mark?"

"Yes," said Antoine. "A single small stone. Upon it was carved a name: 'Gilles'."

Julien hung his head in his hands.

"Was that her husband, Julien?" asked Matthieu.

Julien nodded, his head still in his hands.

Antoine and Matthieu stood silently, staring at the ground, their feet nervously kicking up small clouds of dust.

Julien looked up at them. He shed no tears yet, but his eyes were red and swollen. "They had a daughter," he said with a tone of desperation. "Was there any sign of her?"

Antoine and Matthieu exchanged glances and shook their heads.

Julien looked to the sky and ran both hands through his hair. "If Lady Murielle is here then we can only assume that her daughter has encountered some evil. Oh! By the gods's ears! How could this have happened to Lady Murielle? Why, oh why? How could any of the gods have allowed evil to touch such a saintly woman?"

Antoine and Matthieu stared at the ground.

"*Monsieur*," said Matthieu, turning his face to Julien, "there is more."

"More?!" he cried. "How is it there can be more? Has not Lady Murielle suffered enough? Has she not been ravaged enough by these crimes? How many more ghastly and beastly injustices must our Lady endure before whatever force that has perpetrated them against her has deemed it sufficient?"

Antoine spoke. "After we helped the neighboring farmers extinguish the fire, they told us of some most grievous news from Darloque."

"Tell me, though I am loath to hear it," cried Julien, his face in his hands.

———

Julien entered the room with a light knock on the door. Everything was as it had been for the last three days. A tray of food and wine sat untouched on the desk. Lady Murielle sat at the window, her back to the door. Julien did not have time even to clear his throat before Lady Murielle spoke.

"Julien," she said, her voice more dry and rasping than ever. "Leave me." A pause. "I do not want anything but to be left alone."

Julien nodded silently, gathering his thoughts.

"My Lady," he began. "I will leave you if you wish, but I must speak before I leave. I do not know what evil has befallen you. It is within your right and privilege not to tell me. It is also within your right and privilege to refuse food and drink. I find no fault. But it is within *my* right and *my* privilege to show concern for my Lady whom I so devotedly serve. I will be concerned for your welfare, and you cannot stop me from showing it.

"That said, I feel I must tell you something which may change your perspective on recent events. I have received word that the Old King died three days ago. His son Henri has been crowned king in the Temple of Bellicor. His first official act was to declare war on Ocosse to force them to relinquish the disputed territories which his father surrendered to them."

Julien fell silent. Lady Murielle said nothing. He waited for what seemed an eternity, then made to leave. Lady Murielle turned toward him, stopping Julien with a cold stare.

"You have been *truly* concerned for my welfare?" she asked.

Julien could only nod.

Lady Murielle rose and approached the desk. She took up the decanter of wine, removed the cork, and drank. She swallowed with a pained grimace. She took another drink. Another grimace, but not as pained.

Julien stared at the Lady of the manor. Her features were gaunt. Where there was not black soot on her face, the skin glowed red with the exposure to the chariot of the sun. Her dirty and sweaty chestnut hair hung wildly about her face, its luster all but gone. A black hand, stained and sticky with pitch, held the wine carafe to her pale, cracked lips. Julien willed himself to maintain composure in the face of her ghastly appearance. He would have cried out if not for Lady Murielle's eyes. Whereas her features painted a portrait of a destitute woman, a woman with nothing left to lose, her eyes painted a different picture. Though surrounded with dark circles, her brown eyes were keen and sharp; there were plans and deep calculations behind them. The Lady Murielle Julien knew was not lost, only hidden beneath a facade of mourning.

Lady Murielle took another drink—this one went down much more smoothly—and turned away from Julien. She walked across the room and stood before the two portraits. She looked at them in turn, pausing a moment before each one as if considering. She turned to the portrait of her father once again and stared at it for a long time.

"You have been *truly* concerned for my welfare?" she asked again.

Julien started, as if awakened from a dream. "Yes, my Lady." Then he added, "We all have been."

Lady Murielle continued to stare at her father's portrait, her back to Julien. "You would do anything I ask?"

"Well... yes my Lady."

"You would do anything I asked of you, Julien, my ever-faithful reeve?"

"Yes, my Lady. I–what is it you get at my Lady?"

Lady Murielle turned abruptly to face him, and in that moment, Julien saw it. Standing before the two portraits, he saw what he had never seen before. There was nothing in her features of the woman who had given birth to her. It was all her father. The firmly set jaw and thin, pressed lips. The almost hawkish nose and high set cheekbones gave them both a simultaneously aristocratic and predatory look. But it was the eyes, both so keen, both so calculating, both so obstinate; their eyes showed the real resemblance. It was a resemblance so remarkable, so uncanny, that one must wonder if the mother really had anything to do with the birth of the child.

"You would do anything I ask of you," she said distractedly. Not a question, but a statement of fact.

"Yes, my Lady," said Julien quietly.

Lady Murielle approached the desk again. She spoke bluntly and purposefully. "You will deliver a message for me."

"A message, my Lady."

"You will find Frédéric, he was most recently a castle guard, and deliver this message: 'My dear friend, whatever your thoughts are on the new king, I am of a like mind.'"

"I will do that immediately, my Lady."

"Deliver that message to no one but Frédéric."

"Yes, my Lady. It will be as you wish."

"You will do something else for me as well." Lady Murielle set the carafe on the desk and walked to a chest in one corner. She kicked it open to reveal several pieces of armor. They had been oiled for long term storage, but spots of dark rust dotted them in places.

Julien looked at her incredulously.

"You will have this armor cleaned and repaired. Be certain it is in perfect condition."

"As you wish, my Lady."

"And this as well." She crossed the room to the opposite wall where a sword and shield hung in solitude. She pulled down the sword and crossed back to Julien, the hem of her dress swishing around her ankles. She drew the sword a short way from the scabbard and stared at the blade for a long time. She slammed the blade home and handed it to him.

"Have this cleaned and sharpened. Have the blade burnished to the light." Lady Murielle glared directly into Julien's eyes, her own eyes burning fiercely.

"I will do as you wish, my Lady. Always. But what does this all mean?" The tiny bright point of hope which had flared up in his heart upon learning of her husband's terrible fate began to fade, extinguished in the flames of those fierce, burning eyes.

"What it means, my dear, faithful reeve..." she said coolly, her eyes locked with his. "What it means is that Guillaume de Marschal rides one last time."

CHAPTER NINETEEN

"It need not be this way," the King of Ocosse stated grimly. "We need not go to war."

The King sat upon his war horse, surrounded by a small entourage, in the center of a level valley with gently sloping hills rising all around. The low grass was surprisingly green despite the heat and lack of rain. Before the day was out, though most of the green in the small valley would be red.

"I wear the kilt of war," continued the King, his sweeping hand indicating his array, "but I would gladly change into a dress kilt and feast alongside you, Henri, if we could but put a rest to this dispute peaceably."

Henri shifted in the saddle. His dark war horse stamped the ground anxiously, chomping at the bit, as intent on getting on to the battle as his master. Henri held the reins tightly with one hand, his helm balanced upon the saddle's pommel. With his free hand he touched the crown upon his head. He was still becoming accustomed to the feel of it there. He liked the feel of the crown upon his head.

"I demand the return of the lands my father gave away," Henri said flatly. "I want *all* the lands I am entitled to in my birthright."

The King of Ocosse sighed. "This dispute has raged between our two kingdoms far longer than either you or I have been alive. I have grown accustomed to peace in the short time we have been blest with it, but our claim is stronger, and I will defend our right to those lands with my life, if necessary."

"I will have those lands," Henri snorted, "and I will take your life to get them, if necessary."

The King sighed again. He passed his eyes over the thugs in Henri's entourage, then settled them upon Philippe who sat calmly upon a placid mount.

"Philippe," he said fiercely, "you played a major role in the treaty. Is this your mind as well?"

Henri's eyes flamed at the snub. A brief look of satisfaction flashed upon the King's face.

"I have the mind of my King in this matter," Philippe replied coolly.

"Very well!" cried the King of Ocosse. "If it is war you desire, Henri, then you shall have it!"

"Oh yes," said Henri with a savage smile, "I *shall* have it." He paused a moment then added: "Prepare yourself for your destruction." With that he and his entourage turned and galloped back to their end of the field where the rest of Henri's armies awaited.

———

"What is the condition of their armies?" the King of Ocosse inquired of the spotter atop the tower.

"Not good," he called down. "Not good for our armies, that is to say."

"What have they?"

Heavy cavalry in the front. The *échelle* is in the wedge formation. I see a few light cavalry behind, but it is largely heavily armored."

"They mean to break our line with brute force," said the King in a low voice.

"I see infantry behind," called down the spotter. "From the looks of it, I believe Henri intends to send out cavalry and infantry all at once."

The King turned to his captain of the armies. "MacTavish" he growled, "ensure the schiltron is strengthened. Pikemen with added shields and archers in support. Tell them to hold no matter what. Let Henri wear himself out against them, then send out our cavalry."

"Wise plan, sire," agreed MacTavish.

"Where is Henri?" called up the King. "Do you see him?"

"He leads the center phalanx," replied the spotter. After a moment he called down again. "I see the red oak leaf of Philippe. He leads the right flank."

"Ahh," cried the King. "Then we shall–"

"By the gods's ears!" cried out the spotter sharply.

"What see you?" cried the King.

"Behind Philippe, near the rear with the other light cavalry. 'Tis The Black Knight!"

The King's eyes grew large. "The same from the Eglinton Tournament?"

"If I had not been there to witness his might, I would not believe it, but it is that very same knight!"

The King looked to MacTavish with concern. "This bodes not well for us. A knight of his caliber fighting for Henri–"

"Blest be Mava's many litters!" cried the spotter.

"What see you now!" cried the King and MacTavish in unison.

"On the left flank! Not in front, but in the rear with the light cavalry is Guillaume de Marschal!"

The King held his head in his hands. "Philippe is enough. But to have the two best knights from the Eglinton Tourney fighting on Henri's side... I do not know what our chances are."

"They are but three men in a massive battle," replied MacTavish. "They can be undone." He said this, though he did not have much faith in his statement.

The spotter called down another report. "Henri has archers on the hill behind his infantry."

The King opened his mouth, but MacTavish spoke first. "I shall order the men not to be drawn by a false retreat. We shall keep the battle on this end of the field, far out of the archers's range."

"I must fight," the King of Ocosse said determinedly.

The King's aide spoke up. "My Lord, no! You cannot go into battle at your age!"

"I may be gray," the King retorted, "but I can match anyone on that field!"

MacTavish took a diplomatic approach. "My King, Henri said he would kill you if he could. If you should die on the field, it would be disastrous for morale. We would lose the battle immediately."

The King grimaced. He knew the days had long since passed when he could hold his own on the battlefield. He scowled at his aide, nevertheless.

"There seems to be something going on up on the hill with the archers," called down the spotter. "I cannot see what it is for the sun reflects strongly off something there."

————

"What a pathetic lot of putrescent filth I have been given for archers!" shouted the sergeant as he walked down the line. The archers stood in straight formation as he dressed them down, each fearful to even take a breath.

"I doubt any of you can take a piss by yourselves, much less pull back a bow." He stopped at one trembling archer and glared into his eyes. "How 'bout it, boy?! Do you still need your mother to wipe your ass for you?!

Someone tapped the sergeant on the back. "Ahem. *Excusez-moi.*"

"Who dares?!" He reeled to face the insolent swine who dared interrupt him as he addressed his men. He saw no one. He then looked down, sucked in wind, and fell to the ground, groveling. "*Excusez-moi*, my Lord. *Excusez-moi*."

The Lord Aufeese waved him off with a delicate paw. "Oh, never mind all that. Get in line. There has been a change of plan."

The sergeant immediately squeezed into the line and snapped a salute. The others followed suit.

"Oh, stop," said Lord Aufeese. "Stand down men."

They stood down.

The Lord Aufeese stood before the archers, his golden glow, diffused somewhat by the light leather armor he wore, brightened as he removed the archer's coif and his ears raised above his head. A magnificent long bow suited to his stature hung over his shoulder. A quiver of arrows was slung across his back. The arrows were not ordinary issue. Instead of feathers, heads of living wheat grew out of the shafts at the ends to form the flights. The wheat waved slightly in the hot, still air.

"Ahem," the Lord Aufeese began. "As I said before, there has been a change of plan. I shall give you new instructions which should make this battle go much more quickly."

The archers nodded hesitantly.

"And then we shall all have tea!" The Lord Aufeese jumped up and down excitedly, clapping his forepaws together.

The archers glanced at each other uncertainly.

———

Lord Portiscule leaned against a tree, whistling a jig as he twirled his spear around his free paw, a pikeman's helm cocked jauntily between his ears. Lord Daedemus approached from the woods carrying a sword and a shield. Portiscule smiled broadly and brought the butt of his spear down with a thud.

"Bloody 'ell, Brother! Ye 'ave come!"

"Aye, Brother," Daedemus replied smoothly. "I am not much of a fighter, but I shall do my part."

"Aye! Aye!" Portiscule cried. "I dona think this will take very long." He looked over his brother, then added, "Bloody nice armor, Brother. I like the small metal plates worked inna the leather."

"I like it as well." Daedemus flexed. "It has a good fit and is quite stylish."

Portiscule nodded in agreement.

"No armor for you, Brother?"

"Bloody 'ell no." Portiscule shook his head, tossing the helm aside. "Slows me down. Me spear is enough."

"Very well, then," Daedemus said with a bow. "Shall we get to it?"

"Aye Brother, let us go."

They had walked a little way toward the battlefield when Portiscule spoke again.

"Brother, di' ye know that Felapine and Calapine have a wager goin?"

Daedemus's ears perked up. "A wager?" His whiskers twitched with great interest.

"Aye. 'Tis over which one of them shall kill the most men."

"Well, that is a splendid wager. I should like to get in on that one."

Portiscule laughed loudly. "Bloody 'ell yes! Just so long as ye share wi' me yer thoughts on the winner."

They walked on to the battle and discussed it further.

———

Deeper into the woods, three mercenaries in the employ of the new King of Darloque came upon a small encampment. In the center burned a fire over which nothing cooked, and nothing would ever cook. Three figures sat around the fire, unmindful of it, silently sharpening weapons.

"Well, well," said the largest of the mercenaries with a savage grin, "what do we have here?"

The three figures continued to sharpen their weapons, as oblivious to the mercenaries as they were to the fire. The red-orange firelight reflected in their brightly polished chain mail shirts.

The mercenaries stood their ground, waiting. The largest one spoke again presently. "I have come this day to do battle for the King of Darloque. I would not mind a preliminary match before the main event."

The three figures looked up disinterestedly at the mercenary, but they dropped their sharpening stones and stood with their weapons and shields. They towered above the intruders.

"Espin, Tybalt, Fergu. I challenge one of you to single combat!" cried the lead mercenary. "Which one shall it be?"

The Three Heroes exchanged silent glances with one another. Tybalt and Fergu stepped back and stood down. Espin stepped forward, holding his sword and shield at the ready, his large, muscular body an impassive wall. His red-brown ears stood erect and unmoving on his head. His whiskers stuck out rigidly. He held his massive round shield before him and gripped his sword tightly in his forepaw.

"I am Gudbanamadr, son of Brynjarr," began the mercenary. "My name means 'slayer of the gods' and I have—"

Espin rushed forward with the speed of a lightning bolt. Gudbanamadr was just able to raise his shield as Espin collided solidly with his own. The mercenary staggered backward, attempting to hold his balance, when Espin's sword whipped forward, hammering four solid blows on his challenger's shield. The shield split in two, each half falling on either side of Gudbanamadr as his back hit the ground with a heavy thud. In one fluid motion, Espin spun the sword to an underpawed grip and drove the blade to the hilt into the mercenary's chest, the blade piercing deeply into the ground beneath.

Espin rose and pulled his bloody blade out of the dead man's chest with a wet sucking sound. He stared mutely at the remaining mercenaries, his calm brown eyes betraying no emotion.

The other two mercenaries stared wide-eyed at the god. Silently agreeing they wanted no more of battle this day, they took off through the wood in the opposite direction of the battlefield.

Tybalt and Fergu looked at Espin with a nod, and the Three Heroes broke camp.

———

Murielle's hand tightened around her lance. The time grew near. Beneath her, Cheval pawed the ground anxiously and chomped at the bit.

There was quite a lot of muttering amongst the ranks when she rode out alongside Frédéric. No one approached her. The older knights stayed away out of respect of the champion of the Eglinton Tournament, and the younger knights avoided her out of fear of the mighty warrior of which the older knights spoke so highly. Despite the lengthy time out of sight, the name Guillaume de Marschal still commanded much respect.

She hung her shield on the saddle and ran her hand over the left side of her great helm. The repair was so well performed that she could not tell where it had been damaged. Many of the knights were wearing more open helmets because of the heat. She scanned the sky. Clouds drifted in slowly from the West. Perhaps they would bring a break from the heat.

Murielle's great helm had originally been chosen for concealment rather than comfort or protection, she wore it for that reason this day. The heat was already growing under the helm, but it did not matter. She turned her eyes to the center phalanx. Somewhere over there was her target. When the time came, soon enough, she would go for him. No one would stand in her way. She would unhorse anyone between her and her target.

A rumble of voices rolled through the ranks. Another participant from the Eglinton Tournament was here: The Black Knight. Her famous adversary had also not been seen since the tourney. He was somewhere in the right flank, which meant that he was in on the plan. Guillaume de Marschal and The Black Knight on the same side of the battle. Their chances appeared good.

Murielle felt Cheval breathing beneath her. His breath came steady, if not a little quickly, anxiously, like her own. Horse and rider were bonded, bonded together as one. Their bond was far deeper than ordinary horse and rider, far deeper than her father could have ever imagined. Their shared experience made them one. One heart, one mind, one soul, united in tragedy.

When the horn blared, calling the charge, Cheval leapt forward without a prod from Murielle's spurs. Murielle leaned forward in the saddle at the same instant, as two limbs on one body might move in perfect synchronicity. Murielle and Cheval were of one body, and together, the one body would have its revenge.

———

"Here they come, sire!" the spotter cried down.

The King paced back and forth. MacTavish had gone down to give the last orders to his lieutenants, then had joined the cavalry to await Henri's charge. As predicted, Henri charged cavalry and infantry at once. He obviously expected his heavy cavalry to break the schiltron easily, allowing his light cavalry and infantry to lay waste to the armies of Ocosse. The King hated to admit it, being as stubborn as both his father and mother combined, but now that scenario seemed a likelihood.

"Hold! Hold!" he growled through gritted teeth. "By the gods's ears, hold!"

The thunder of hooves grew louder. The King held his clenched fists tightly before him, his eyes clamped shut, his teeth gritted. "Sire–" his aide began, but the King unclenched a fist long enough hold up a hand to silence him. The King's eyes popped open in surprise when a second horn sounded from across the field with four bright, brassy blasts.

"By the gods's ears! By the gods's ears!" cried out the spotter.

"What see you?!" cried the King, but he had climbed halfway up the tower before he had finished the question, much to his aide's horror.

What he saw was the left and right flanks of both Henri's cavalry and infantry rapidly drawing back from the center.

———

"ARCHERS! LOOOOOOSE!" bellowed the Golden Child, the Lord of the Archers. And the archers rained hell down upon the center phalanx, the Lord Aufeese firing four arrows from his quiver before any of the archers could pluck one from the ground before him.

———

All was silence. Not a man spoke, not horse neighed. No breeze fluttered the flags or ruffled clothing. The armies of Ocosse watched purblind as both flanks of Henri's cavalry made new formations and charged the center. They watched, equally baffled as the archers on the hill slaughtered the center phalanx of the infantry while the flanks held positions and took down the fleeing survivors.

It was the King who broke the silence. He hung from the tower, as awestruck as the others, then started and leapt to the ground with a youthful exuberance.

"It is a rebellion! Sound the charge! Sound the charge!" he cried. He seized his aide by the ears and screamed into his face. "SOUND THE CHARGE!"

His aide cried out, hands fluttering wildly as he ran in circles. "Sound the charge! Sound the charge!"

Behind them, the war pipes started up, deafening the hill with their call. All was madness then. MacTavish, as stunned to silence as the rest, quickly rallied the cavalry which had not anticipated such an early involvement. They streamed around the schiltron, the pikemen and archers at a complete loss as to their next move. The men at arms behind them surged ahead, forcing the pikemen forward as the archers scattered in the confusion.

The King of Ocosse raised his fist high in the air. "This is Philippe's doing! I know it!" He grinned with satisfaction. "See how you like that, Henri!"

———

Madness surrounded him. Before Henri, his heavy cavalry faced a new obstacle as the Ocossian heavy cavalry streamed around their defensive lines onto the battlefield. The news came hot and fast, shouted over the din, spread from knight to knight. The cavalry flanks had pulled back and were now attacking the rear of the main body. Further back, the main body of infantry was being cut down by the archers on the hill while both infantry flanks assailed it on the sides.

King Henri bellowed with rage. "I know this treachery is your doing, Philippe! I will take your head for this myself, but only after I have taken other parts of your body first!"

Henri lowered his lance, kicked his mount harder, and charged through the heavy cavalry to engage the enemy.

———

The Three Heroes stood on the edge of the battlefield, watching impassively. The battle was engaged, and the time had come to fulfill their oaths. Each hefted his massive round shield and pulled his weapon from the belt at his waist. They exchanged silent, passionless glances and charged onto the battlefield in three different directions.

———

Murielle had never killed a man before. The Tourney was about domination by skill and technique. On the battlefield the game was life and death. If one lost this joust, one lost his life. As it had been in the Eglinton Tourney, Murielle had no intention of losing.

As the knights of the main phalanx turned to face their attackers, Murielle leveled her lance at the nearest. By the look of surprise in his eyes, he clearly understood he was being challenged by Guillaume de Marschal, Champion of the Eglinton Tournament. Nevertheless, he lowered his lance and took his chances. Cheval surged on without encouragement. As they closed, Murielle pressed her thigh into Cheval's right side, but the horse was already drifting slightly to the right before the fatal contact with the opponent who was easily unhorsed, never to arise again.

Murielle's blood ran hot, not with excitement, but with burning hatred. She banked to find another opponent. She recognized a pair of eyes behind a visor. A pair of eyes which she recognized from that fateful day. That one was dispatched easily. Hatred burning hot and white within her, she sought out every pair of eyes she knew from that dreadful day.

———

Calapine swung her hammer upward connecting with the unfortunate soldier who believed he could challenge her. He flew quite a distance away before coming to rest in a heap. He did not arise.

The goddess of steel nodded smugly at her sister. "Another one, Sister."

Felapine fumed. She loaded her sling with a stone from the pouch slung over her shoulder. She spun it over her head, the sling whipping the air loudly. She released the stone which connected with the helm of one of Henri's men at arms. He fell into a heap some distance away, never to arise.

"Oh wait, Sister," the goddess of iron said primly. "Watch this."

Felapine loaded two stones into the sling and whipped it over her head. She released the stones, each connecting with the helm of a soldier. Neither soldier arose.

"Show off," Calapine growled.

Felapine threw her head back with a wicked cackle.

"Sister," called Calapine excitedly. "Come here. I wish to show you something!"

Felapine obliged, smashing a soldier in the head with her bare paw as she walked over. "What?"

Calapine indicated a man a short distance away standing behind a line of Henri's men engaged in a fierce fight with some Ocossian men at arms. "See him there?"

Felapine cocked her head. "Yes. What of him? He appears to be a cowardly commander hiding behind his men."

"Exactly!" cried Calapine. "Now watch."

She raised her hammer and pointed it at the commander. "You!" she screeched. "You will answer the call of the hammer!"

His face flushed with abject terror. He froze in place for a few moments then stumbled backwards again and again in an attempt to hide himself behind the line.

The Sisters fell over each other in laughter. After a few moments they calmed themselves. Felapine wiped the tears from her eyes and asked, "So, can I kill him now?"

Calapine straightened and scratched her head. "What?" A befuddled look crossed her face. "No!"

"Why not?"

"He is mine, that is why not!"

"Well," replied Felapine, scratching her head, "let me kill him anyway."

"No!" Calapine shook her head in consternation. "I marked him. Now he will be in terror until I have had enough fun and decide to kill him."

"Well...." Felapine looked thoughtful. "Let me kill him now anyway."

"No! That is not how the game is played."

A light appeared in Felapine's eyes. "Ahhh! This is not about a game; this is about the wager."

Calapine crossed her paws over her chest. "No, it is not."

Felapine wagged a claw at her sister. "That is cheating, Sister! You cannot mark soldiers so I cannot kill them!"

"That is not so."

"Cheating bitch!"

Calapine's eyes grew wide. "What did you call me?!"

"A lying, cheating bitch," replied Felapine smugly.

The goddess of steel raised her hammer. "Sister, I would–"

Before Calapine could say anymore, Felapine loaded a stone into her sling and flung it at the cowardly commander, killing him.

"Sister! He was mine!"

"Not anymore."

Calapine swung her hammer, but when Felapine ducked, it slipped from her grip and wiped out a band of Henri's soldiers coming to aid their brothers.

———

A group of weeping women huddled together on a hill overlooking the battle below. They wept for their husbands, sons, and lovers, all fighting valiantly for the good cause. Amongst them stood the Lady Blanchefleur, the beautiful, pure white, goddess of love. Her brilliant blue eyes gleamed with pity for the women.

On this day, her long white ears were held back with a delicate netting of fine silver. Around her waist she wore an exquisite belt of equally fine silver links. There was no one who would say that she was not the most beautiful creature in the world.

"*Aimons*, ladies, *aimons!*" Blanchefleur told them. "Think of the love you hold for your men. Love shall keep them safe, *n'est-ce pas?*

A young maiden cried out. Below, her lover had been fighting fiercely, but he had tripped and now lay sprawled on the ground, his sword and shield out of reach. One of Henri's soldiers went in for the kill.

"Remember your love! Remember your love!" Blanchefleur cried to her.

The young maiden bowed her head and shut her eyes tightly. She muttered words of prayer rapidly.

Suddenly, Henri's soldier was seized by a spasm. He dropped his sword which fell within his opponent's reach. The young maiden's lover grabbed it and thrust upward. The maiden cried with relief.

"See what love can do?" the goddess of love cooed. She looked over to the part of the field where Daedemus was engaged in battle with another of Henri's men.

"Ahh! It is such a thrill to see your love fighting, knowing that your love keeps him strong, *nest-ce pas?*

The weeping women all wiped their eyes and nodded in agreement.

Blanchefleur's eyes strayed to another part of the field. Abruptly, she raised up onto her toes.

"Yes, yes!" she screamed. "Kill the filth! Kill him! Kill him! Oh, how I hate that detestable creature! Kill him!"

The women dabbed their tears and looked at each other.

———

Two score of Henri's men formed a circle around The Gatekeeper. He fought them all, his spearhead flashing in the bright sunlight. He cut, slashed, and smashed, yet they still kept coming. For every opponent he killed, two replaced him.

"Oh, Brother!" he called out, spinning the deadly spear at his ever-increasing opponents. "D'ye think ye could gi' me some bloody assistance here!"

Daedemus looked up from the single mercenary he battled in a most lackadaisical manner. "Nonsense, Brother. You are doing quite well. A smashing job in fact."

Two score men had become four score. "Bloody 'ell! I am over-whelmed!"

Daedemus's opponent traded casual blows with him. "I believe you should help your brother. He does look overwhelmed."

"Oh, not at all," replied The Great Architect, "he is doing quite well." He looked over at his brother again. "He has had worse."

Four score men had become eight score. Portiscule's spear became a blur.

"Nonsense, I say," said the mercenary, driving his sword into the ground and leaning on it. "I will even wager he does not survive."

Daedemus's ears perked and his whiskers twitched with interest. He lowered his own sword. "Did you say *wager?*"

"Your Brother is grossly outnumbered. Not even a god can beat those odds."

"Care to back your words with your purse?"

The mercenary looked over at the men encircling Portiscule. It seemed another score of men had arrived since he and Daedemus had paused their battle. "Yes, I will wager you five crowns he will not make it."

"Pshhh," replied Daedemus, waving a paw in the air. "So much confidence you have in your position. Do not waste my time with such a paltry wager."

"Brother!" shouted Portiscule.

"Fifty, then."

"Hmmm," Daedemus said, stroking his chin. "That is better, but I still do not think you have much faith in your position."

"What would you suggest them?"

"Brother!" shouted Portiscule again. He was a blur within the circle.

"Five-hundred crowns I believe would prove your worth."

"Five-hundred crowns?!" The mercenary looked over at The Gatekeeper and the ever-increasing circle of opponents. He stroked his long blond beard thoughtfully. "Yes."

"You have the coin?" Daedemus asked.

The mercenary reached into his jerkin, pulled out a fat purse and shook it. The coins inside jingled. "Do not worry about me, worry about yourself when you lose."

"AAAARRRRGGGGHHH!!!!"

Then suddenly, Henri's men surged forward, tackling Portiscule, grabbing him by his forepaws and hind feet. The mob dragged him backwards and wrestled him to the ground. Soon Portiscule disappeared under an immense mound of men all punching and kicking.

The mercenary smiled. "I told you. He is done."

"I am afraid you do not know my brother very well."

In a great fountain of blood, the head of Portiscule's spear thrust up through the mountain of men. With a roar, the god burst through the pile, scattering men–and pieces of men–across the field.

Daedemus smiled smugly, the mercenary stared, his mouth agape in disbelief.

The Great Architect held out a paw. "Pay up, my good man."

Without taking his eyes off Portiscule, he slapped the purse into the god's paw with a grunt.

Portiscule spun around slashing and thrusting his spear long after all his opponents had been dispatched. Soon, realizing they were all gone, The Gatekeeper stopped and hung his head with a great sigh. He was covered head to toe in blood. He raised his head again, a scowl crossed his face, his ears laid back, and he threw his spear onto the bloody ground.

"BLOODY 'ELL, DAEDEMUS!" he bellowed with rage. "WHY D'YE NOT ASSIST ME?!"

"You were doing quite well on your own, Brother," he replied nonchalantly. "And besides," he continued, ticking off on his claws, "I believe with this single fight, you have surpassed both Calapine and Felapine."

Portiscule wiped his face with his forepaws, his rage unabated. "An' what the bloody 'ell 'bout him, eh?" He pointed to the mercenary. "I took care of this lot, the least ye ken do is finish 'im."

The mercenary turned to Daedemus scratching his head. "Wha?"

Daedemus nodded his head. "My brother is quite correct, old chap." He picked up his sword. "'Tis war, you know." The Great Architect spun his blade to an underpawed position and side armed it through the mercenary's chest. He fell to the ground with a groan.

"Bloody 'ell! 'Tis more like it, Brother." Portiscule had cleaned the blood from his fur. "Let us go finish this, eh? Then go down the pub?"

"Aye, Brother," he replied, jingling the purse in his paw. "But this time, I am buying."

————

Espin stood at the center of a circle of men. His chainmail shirt gleamed brightly in the brilliant sunlight. He held his sword down, casually, as if he anticipated no violence. However, he held his shield before him at the ready. Upon his shield, a massive round shield of ancient times, was a relief depicting the first of three scenes of dire prophecy: two men engaged in a fierce battle, the final battle between the Far Traveler and the Great Seer, the battle which decides the fate of mankind.

Espin slowly turned his head, looking over the circle of Henri's men who had gathered to challenge the god. His ears rose high above his head, erect and alert. His whiskers moved not at all. His head stopped. Slowly he slipped the strap loose and let the shield fall heavily to the ground. Next to it lay a discarded broadsword. The god picked it up in an underpawed grip in his left paw. He raised both swords slightly. Henri's men began to shift on their feet and sway with anticipation. This day Espin would teach them a lesson: the lesson of Combat with Two Swords.

————

Murielle looked up at the clouds piling up on the Western horizon, then turned back to the battlefield to see her target. He had just unhorsed a knight across the field. Nothing lay between her and Henri. Cheval saw him as well. He started into a gallop before Murielle had a chance to kick him. They closed in. Henri turned to see Guillaume de Marschal closing in on him. He lowered his lance and kicked his charger. Murielle lowered her head and braced for impact when the Black Knight cut her off. She lost her target; Henri had disappeared into the throng. She cursed the Black Knight as she watched him lower his lance and unhorse one of Henri's knights. Murielle felt certain his action was unintentional, a simple consequence of the chaos of battle, nevertheless, if he got in the way again, she would take care of him as well.

————

Calapine screamed again as she obliterated another soldier with her hammer.

"What is your problem?" Felapine called from across the field as she loaded another stone into her sling.

"It is that damnable Arbrinner, Sister," she called back as she took a swing at another soldier.

Felapine spun her sling and let loose the stone which connected solidly and deadly with her target. "I do not understand, Sister."

A voice echoed clearly across the battlefield. "What ho?! Dost thou challenge me, knave?!"

"ARGH!" shouted the goddess of steel. "Someone tell him to cease!"

The goddess of iron spun up her sling again and released another deadly missile. "I pay him no mind, Sister. You would do well to do the same."

"His voice annoys me. He makes it exceedingly difficult to enjoy this battle." With a grunt, Calapine dispatched another soldier with a swing of her hammer.

"What ho?!" Arbrinner's jolly voice came across the field again. "Knowest thou that mine staff is named 'Wasp'? Now thou shalt feel its sting!" A loud thud resounded.

Calapine growled loudly and missed an attacking mercenary. He landed a blow harmlessly on her leather armor. She swatted him across the field with her left paw. "I wish he would fight silently!"

Felapine unleashed another stone upon its deadly course. "Sister, you need to worry less about Arbrinner and more about the fact that I have surpassed you in kills again."

"Hmmpf. A lot of good that does when Portiscule has surpassed you by at least a hundred." Calapine drew her hammer back and set upon a small group of Henri's soldiers.

"What?! Portiscule?!" The stone flew off errantly, completely missing its target.

"What ho?!" cried the merry woodsman again.

———

Tybalt turned; his fawn-colored fur shone in the unrelenting sun. Behind him a new challenger fast approached as he dealt with a mercenary before him. He drove the mercenary back then turned to quickly deal with the charging soldier behind him who was followed a short distance behind by a large group. Flipping his sword into the air, he caught it by the blade and threw it. The blade sunk deep into the charging man's chest, throwing him backwards to the ground, never to arise under his own power.

Tybalt returned to the mercenary who was being joined by reinforcements. The hero loosened the strap of his shield, the shield which bore an engraving of the Second Dire Prophecy. The image was of a lady with long flowing hair. This was the Lady of the Stars. She was the mistress of all the stars in the heavens, but one in particular, a dread star of destruction, aligned with her. Because of her alignment with this dread star, she would suffer greatly, even as she brought untold suffering upon the world.

Tybalt loosened the strap on his shield and prepared to give a lesson to the challengers who approached on both sides: the lesson of Combat with Shield as Offensive Weapon.

———

Murielle found her target once more. Horses and riders in the maelstrom of battle parted suddenly to reveal the object of her revenge. Cheval saw him as well. As before, he started into a gallop without Murielle's prodding. Henri's back was to her, having just unhorsed a knight from the rebel group. Cheval gained speed, but Henri had not turned to see their approach. Murielle wanted him to see her approach, she needed him to see her. She wished the most foul and loathsome creature that had ever come into existence to see just who was ending his existence.

Murielle focused on him, willed him to turn. He seemed to be speaking to the knight he had just unhorsed. She gave the poor knight a casual glance, and her eyes grew wide. Frédéric lay on the ground, his helm removed. He bled profusely from a wound in his chest. Blood flowed freely from his mouth as he spoke words Murielle could not hear. Then, Henri placed the tip of his bloody lance over Frédéric's exposed throat and thrust downward, ending her friend's life. Murielle, enraged, kicked Cheval on faster toward their target. She did not care if he saw her. She lowered her lance and braced for impact.

Beneath her, Cheval let out a low grunt then she and the horse heeled to the left. Murielle lost sight of her target as the ground came up quickly. A sharp pain flared in her left shoulder and then in her hip and leg. Her lance flew from her hand. As they slid along the ground, Cheval attempted to regain his feet, but he could not and fell back heavily onto Murielle. She grimaced with the pain.

When they came to a stop on the bloody ground, Murielle searched vainly for her lance. A knight came into her field of vision. One of Henri's knights, one she did not recognize stopped before her holding a broken lance. At more than half of it was missing. This caused Murielle great concern. Another concern was that Cheval was not attempting to rise. She felt him breathing, the rapid rise and fall of his of his side on her leg. He was panting, panting too fast.

The knight approached. He held just enough of a lance to do mortal damage to the helpless Guillaume de Marschal and seemed quite intent on doing so. Murielle struggled. She was pinned beneath Cheval, and her sword beneath herself. The sound of hooves rapidly approached from behind her, and the knight turned, raising the broken lance to defend himself. But the short piece of ash proved insufficient to protect him, and he was unhorsed, never to rise again.

Murielle turned her head to see this new player in the game. The Black Knight reined his charger around, coming to a stop near Murielle and Cheval. He said nothing, but it was clear by his stance that he was guarding his former foe, now ally, Guillaume de Marschal, until he could free himself.

"One last time, Cheval," Murielle whispered into the horse's ear. "Lift enough to release me so I may finish our work."

With a great groan, Cheval lifted himself and Murielle wriggled out from under him. He neighed in pain and fell back to the ground, panting.

Murielle checked her sword then turned to The Black Knight. He appeared to her just as he had at the Eglinton Tourney. Black, helm, black armor, and a black shield with no heraldry upon it. He held a black lance upright in his black gloved hand. He even appeared to ride the same large, black charger he had ridden back then. He was an entity of solid black, seeming to draw the light out of the air itself.

"*Merci*," Murielle said with a nod.

The Black Knight returned a single nod, then reined his charger around and rode off quickly.

Murielle walked around her fallen mount, pulling off her helm as she did. Her vision unobstructed by the narrow slits of the great helm, she now saw the problem with Cheval. A short, broken end of a lance stuck out from Cheval's side. The point extended out from his chest at the base of his neck. Cheval's wide staring eye looked up at her. Blood and foam sprayed from the panting animal's mouth.

Murielle removed the sweaty coif, allowing her dark ponytail to slide down her back. She kneeled and embraced the horse.

"I am so sorry, Cheval," she cried into his neck.

Julien had acquiesced to each one of her requests, yet when she had told him to outfit Cheval for battle, he had balked. "We have solid war horses in the stable, Madame. Much more suitable than a simple farm horse." Murielle had grimaced. "I would have no other. He has been through much with me, and he deserves this." In the end, Julien sighed and did as he was told.

Now Cheval would not have his revenge. "I am so sorry, Cheval," she said again into his ear. Murielle rose to her feet.

She pulled out her sword and placed the tip of the blade over the horse's heart. Murielle turned her eyes upward to the growing wall of black clouds streaking across the sky. "I will at least not let you suffer," she said.

She thrust downward with both hands.

CHAPTER TWENTY

FERGU PUSHED BACK the opponent with his great round shield upon which was engraved the Third Dire Prophecy. The city of Darloque was set upon the shield. Flames roared from her towers and from the castle, spewing great plumes of black smoke and soot into the sky. Foreign armies attacked her at every gate, their great siege machines pummeled her walls. The Eternal City was falling, dying. Above her in the sky, a mysterious star descended, signaling the end of an age.

Fergu drove the mercenary back. The force of the hero's battle-axe proved too fierce for him to withstand, and the mercenary fell, never to rise again. Fergu looked around. He had encountered a small group of challengers and had conquered them all. Yet, the enemy still fought mightily, therefore his work was not completed. The hero turned, his dark charcoal fur contrasting with his shining mail shirt in the dimming daylight as he sought more opponents. He spied a group of Henri's men-at-arms moving toward him when something on the ground caught his heroic eye.

Fergu's eyes grew wide, his mouth opened a little. He crouched on the ground, hooked his axe into his belt, and carefully picked up the sword. He tenderly cradled the two-handed sword, a claymore. It had been most certainly lost by a fallen soldier of Ocosse. The god turned the sword over in his paws, struck by the exquisite–as exquisite as a human-made weapon could be–craftsmanship. His ears turned back, hearing the rapidly approaching footfalls behind him. Quickly he loosened the strap on his shield, slipped it over his ears, and onto his back. Blows rained down upon the shield, and still in a crouch, the hero spun the sword into an underpawed grip and thrust it behind him to the screams of his new opponent. The hero spun, rising as he did, and swung the claymore in a wide arc with a single paw, taking the head of another opponent. A new group of challengers approached. Thus, began the new lesson: Combat with Two-Handed Sword.

———

The King of Ocosse became increasing agitated as the spotter called down the events of the battle.

"You must remain behind the lines, sire," his aide whined, "and allow MacTavish to direct the battle."

The King paced in circles, waving his hands in the air, shouting, "The gods! The gods!" over and over.

Suddenly the spotter cried out. "Look sire! To the North!"

The King had climbed halfway up the tower before his aide could utter a word of protest. Upon the hill to the north stood a great band of knights, all arrayed in red armor, each bearing the heraldry of the white oak.

"The Knights of the Oak!" cried the King.

"Now we shall see this battle finished!" shouted the spotter.

The Knights of the Oak, however, remained motionless on the hill.

"No," replied the King. "They will not engage."

"But why not?" called down the spotter. "This is most certainly a 'Bataille Juste', is it not?"

"Aye, it is," replied the King, "but this is Philippe's battle, his to win or lose. Laurent will not steal away Philippe's moment to prove himself. They merely watch their son's progress."

"Yes, my King," said the spotter, "that is most wise."

The King began to climb down the tower–much to his aide's relief–when the entire tower shook with a great thud.

"Aye! What has happened!" cried up the King.

The spotter did not reply. The King called up again, now concerned the man had been struck. He began to climb up again–as his aide tried in vain to pull him back down–when the spotter leaned precariously over the side of the platform, gasping, and pointing.

"What is it," cried the King again.

"The... the... the... Black! Knight!" he finally spat out.

———

The Black Knight unhorsed yet another of Henri's knights. He reined his charger around and looked out upon the field. The rebel line had broken, across the battlefield skirmishes large and small raged. The rebels were scattered and spread out too far, although the archers kept back the occasional breakthrough of Henri's men. The armies of Ocosse were in better condition, but their line was ragged and haphazard. It was time to rally Philippe's armies and finish what had begun long ago.

The Black Knight reined his charger around again, and holding his lance aloft, galloped back into the range of the archers. He reined his charger around once more and spinning the lance around, he then stabbed it deep into the hard ground. A red banner unfurled from the end, waving in the gentle breeze which had sprung up. The Black Knight removed his helm and cast it to the ground. Long red ears rose high above the red spotted fur of his noble head.

The war god cried out in a deep, rich voice which resonated across the battlefield. "All knights, all soldiers, all men of valor loyal to the true King of Darloque! Rally to this banner!"

Bellicor pulled back on the reins, rearing the charger. He pulled forth the sword Viresdefeu, thrusting it high into the sky. The blade flashed as lightning cracked the blackened sky.

————

The King of Ocosse leapt from the tower and ran to his horse, his great kilt billowing behind him, and his aide rushing frantically to catch him. He leapt into the saddle like a man half, nay, a quarter his age. The King reined the horse around, seized up a lance from a nearby rack, and took up the shield which hung on the saddle. His aide was upon him as he turned again.

"But sire! Your age! The danger!" The aide pulled at the King's boot. "You must remain here out of harm's way!"

The king of Ocosse gripped the lance tightly. "What?!" he cried. "And miss the chance to fight alongside Lord Bellicor and the gods themselves? Are ye daft, man?!"

With a great shout the King kicked the horse into a gallop, charging down the hill. His aide grabbed the King's helm, then chased down the hill after him.

"But sire," he whined. "Your helm! You must have your helm!"

————

MacTavish had watched the gods enter the fray, and as many did that day, he disbelieved what he witnessed at first. No one had seen the gods in generations, a fact which fueled the current disturbing trend of atheistic thought. But now, they were here, on this battlefield, fighting on Philippe's side. As a boy he had cherished the tales of The Three Heroes–as all young boys did–and now he was witnessing a living tale unfold. Then it occurred to him as he drove his lance into another of Henri's knights that he himself was part of the tale.

He scolded himself for engaging in boyhood fantasy. Then the Black Knight removed his helm and revealed himself as Lord Bellicor. MacTavish pulled his charger to a stop. His kilt fluttered in the strengthening breeze. The Black Knight, mysterious combatant in the Eglinton Tournament, if he were in reality Lord Bellicor, then who was the knight who had defeated him? Who was Guillaume de Marschal that he could defeat a god? He had little time to ponder it for one of Henri's knights came upon him fast. He couched his lance and set upon the challenger.

―――――

Murielle ran across the field taking on any of Henri's soldiers. Many knights on both sides had lost their horses and fought on foot. She saw it in her opponent's eyes as she challenged each man. There was the initial surprise as the woman charged, then the shock at the ferocity at which she fought, and then no more thought as he fell to the ground, never to arise again.

She heard the cry from the rear and understood its meaning. The rebels had become too scattered. They needed to pull back and reform the line under the protection of the archers. If the captain of the Ocossian armies—MacTavish was his name, she believed—if he understood, then he should push his line harder and close the gap on Henri's dwindling forces.

Murielle pulled back, aiming for the red banner. Several members of the rebel army looked upon her in confusion seeing a woman dressed the armor of Guillaume de Marschal. Nevertheless, they pulled back with her, leading Henri's soldiers along. Murielle brought her sword down upon a fast and aggressive man, ending his role in the play. She jogged backwards, watching them come when she ran into something hard and unyielding. She spun quickly, bringing her sword around in an automatic gesture of defense, and her eyes fell upon the forms of Espin, Tybalt, and Fergu. Murielle stopped the sword short of Espin. Her eyes grew wide, her heart skipped. What she saw stood in stark opposition to what her father had taught her and what she had come to believe—or disbelieve.

"We witnessed your performance at the Eglinton tournament,"

said Espin in a cool voice after a brief silence. His eyes registered no emotion.

"You performed quite well for a human," added Tybalt in a similar cool voice.

"Yes," added Fergu with a nod. Murielle noticed that the axe the tales told of hung from his belt, and he held an Ocossian claymore in his paws.

And then The Three Heroes did something Murielle had never once dared imagine possible. Espin bumped his shield with hers in a sign of soldiers's solidarity. Tybalt followed suit, and Fergu tapped the pommel of his sword on her shield.

And then they were gone, lost somewhere in the battle. Murielle staggered. If only her father were here now to see this. The Three Heroes, long in receiving praise and short on giving it, had given her a grand compliment. She looked around the battlefield. She was alone in this part of the bloody field, neither ally nor foe nearby. She could see the rebels drawing half of Henri's troops ever back as the Ocossian armies drove the other half before them. It would be over soon, and she was trying to comprehend what had just happened to her.

"What ho?!" a voice cried from behind, startling her from her stupor. Murielle swung around, brandishing her sword.

"Guillaume de Marschal! Well met!" cried the merry woodsman.

The Lord Arbrinner stood before Murielle. Immediately, a flood of memories came to her, memories of Étienne, his small altar, and their conversation so long ago. The god stood now in the same pose Étienne had conceived. His deep brown fur was the same color as the dark wood of the altar. He stood with his quarter staff planted solidly on the ground, his foot propped up upon a log. He wore simple leather armor, and a satchel hung at his right hip from a strap slung over his opposite shoulder. The greatest difference between the conception of Étienne and the god which stood before her though, was that his broad head, prominent brow, and lop ears framed bright, shining eyes and a mirthful smile.

"Well met, Lord Arbrinner," Murielle replied meekly. She could not help but stare at the beaming face so different from Étienne's figure.

The god's face began to sink. He let out a pained sigh. There was the face with which Murielle was familiar. "Thine husband," he said, "he wast a good, faithful man."

Murielle hung her head. "*Oui*. Yes, he was."

"Methinks he wast a tad misguided though."

Murielle raised her head a little. Her eyes slowly opened, wider and wider. In those days it was the custom that when a soldier entered battle, he wore an emblem with the image of a person for whom he fought, whether it be for revenge or for inspiration. Many wore the image of a person who had been wronged, others, an image of a father, brother, wife, or other who inspired the soldier to fight his best. Lord Arbrinner wore such an emblem on his chest. The image was of a man, a large-framed man with a bald head and kindly eyes.

Murielle released a ragged breath. Gilles was no farmer. Together they had struggled as Gilles worked the farm with never any improvement. For so long she had secretly supplemented their storehouse with crops from her estate. Gilles was, however, brilliant with wood. He had to think long and carefully about the crops and still he fared poorly every season. But wood? He was a natural master. He would take merely one look at a piece of wood, envision the finished product, and execute it exactly as he saw it in his mind. If she were–had been–a religious person, she would have thought him divinely inspired not by the Lord Aufeese, but by the Lord Arbrinner. And by this emblem on the god's chest, Murielle knew that although her husband had offered up prayers to one god, another had listened, and blessed him.

The smile returned to Lord Arbrinner's face. He leaned down and whispered in her ear. "Marry, I givest thou a piece of advice. If thou doth wish to move pigs, thou must promise them the cob, for of that part of the corn, therein lies their greatest desire."

Murielle smiled at the memory of she and Étienne trying to move the animals out of the barn on that long-ago frigid morning.

She blinked and the god was gone. She heard his voice far across the battlefield, laughing merrily at his challengers. Murielle was alone again on the field. The battle seemed so far away. Likewise, her pain, her anger, her hatred. And in the light of this new dawn in her life, her desire for revenge felt ever so distant.

But not completely banished, however. Slowly, as she gave it more leeway, it began to creep back upon her, stealthily, on silent dark paws, creeping closer, advancing slowly on the unsuspecting victim to pounce, attack, and devour. She felt its dark shadow upon her, cooling her heart and heating her blood. She waited, wanting its attack, desiring the feel of its claws on her skin, tearing into her, tearing her apart.

Murielle was barely aware of the sound of hooves approaching her from behind. The sound of the single heavy horse on the hard-packed ground was like thunder. When the horse stopped, she did not even turn. After a long moment of silence, the rider spoke.

"Guillaume de Marschal." The rider's voice was full of strength and power. Murielle closed her eyes and said nothing. She tightened her grip on her sword, pressed her shield closer to her body. She knew what stood behind her, who stood behind her, yet she stared out into the distance, looking at nothing, the distant crash of battle a world away from her. Murielle waited, gathering her thoughts, and preparing for what was to come. And then–

Murielle turned slowly, a new idea blossoming in her head. She turned and looked up into the dark, fearsome eyes of the noble war god. He sat astride a massive, high-headed charger as black as the armor he wore–the same armor he wore at that long-ago tournament.

"No," the war god replied to the question burning in her mind. "Unbeknownst to you, your prayer was answered long ago."

Murielle could say nothing as she basked in the glory of the magnificent Lord Bellicor, the god to whom she once had prayed so fervently.

"When a god answers a prayer," the war god continued, "he does so in his own time and in his own manner."

Murielle let this sink in. Étienne had told her that prayer required patience. Soon another question flared in her mind.

"Did I..."

Lord Bellicor gave a single somber nod. "Richard taught you well. However, had he not been given a medium of exceptional quality, his art would not have been as successful." He tilted his head slightly. "*Vero.* You did defeat the war god in honorable competition."

Murielle's breath quickened as her world spun around her.

"Although," Lord Bellicor added, "it was written long ago that no man shall defeat the war god in honorable combat."

"And that tenet still holds," quipped Murielle as she looked up at the war god, a smile spreading across her face, "for no *man* has defeated the war god in honorable combat."

Something that might have been a smile played across Lord Bellicor's lips. His whiskers gave a twitch, and his dark eyes sparkled briefly. "*Vero.*"

Murielle's head still spun with this new realization. She thought of her father. What would he say at this moment? He only believed in what could be observed and proved through reason. Surely, he could not deny the existence of the gods–as she now could not–with them standing before his very eyes. Yet, this revelation would have flown in the face of everything, every code, by which he had lived his life. All the philosophies denying the gods were shattered now, with no more meaning than a fairy tale. Murielle wanted to ask Lord Bellicor why he did not reveal himself to her, to her father, and make him realize the error of his atheism.

Again, the war god answered the unspoken question. "*Magna fides omnibus hominibus reperiendae sunt.* One must discover his faith within his own heart, for there is where it truly lives."

Murielle hung her head. Étienne had tried to tell her that the essence of faith is in the heart, not the eye.

The war god then addressed the dark passion burning inside her.

"The revenge you seek is not yours to have." Lord Bellicor's face was firm and grim, his eyes cool and hard.

The hatred in her heart flared up mightily, offended at the denial of its fulfillment. It turned on the war god, angry at his suggestion that Murielle cease her pursuit.

"Although the completion of your quest would produce the same result, there is another who would reap a greater benefit."

Murielle's face flushed. The idea that the war god was dismissing her loss, angered her. "You mean Philippe."

The war god nodded somberly. "I do not dismiss your loss nor your pain, but Philippe, and the whole kingdom as well, stand much to gain from the completion of a stratagem set in motion long ago."

Murielle clenched her jaw.

"Understand one thing, honorable knight," Lord Bellicor said. "Sometimes the best revenge against a base opponent is to keep one's honor and hold to the noble path, even if it leads one away from that same opponent."

Murielle turned her eyes away from Lord Bellicor. Her heart longed for blood, but at the same time she knew she could not have it. Her father had taught her as much. Although an atheist, he did preach the litany of honor. *A knight follows the code of honor*, he had told her on many occasions. *Hold yourself to a high standard regardless of those base knights who may goad you to do otherwise. Such is the path of honor.* Murielle closed her eyes and sighed. She pushed away the desire for revenge from her heart and banished it forever.

The war god spoke again. "Richard told you that revenge destroys the practitioner more completely than the object, did he not?"

"*Oui*," she replied, her head down and eyes still shut. He had said that, but in her lust for revenge it had slipped from her memory. Such was the way that the desire for revenge worked.

"Look upon me now," Lord Bellicor said. "Look upon me as one honorable knight looks upon another."

Murielle looked up into his eyes.

"There is still much work to do on this battlefield. If you so desire, I shall give you a horse and equip you afresh for cavalry."

"No, thank you," Murielle replied. "I did quite well in the man-at-arms competition at Eglinton as you may recall."

This time Lord Bellicor gave a true smile. "And so, you did, Guil-laume de Marschal, and so you did." With that, the war god reined his mount around and charged back into the heart of the battle.

The sounds of battle came back to Murielle. She looked around blankly, as someone awaking from a dream. The armies of Ocosse had pushed Henri's front line back so far that she was now behind the Ocossian line. Philippe's reorganized army was fighting hard, although subtly drawing the Henri's rear line ever back. Murielle saw they were nearly within range of the archers. She smiled. Guillaume de Marschal had no opposition to fighting alongside Ocossian soldiers.

———

Philippe took a breath and looked around. All was going according to plan. Had anyone but Lord Bellicor told him this strategy would work against Henri, he would have thought him daft. Of course, the participation of the gods on his side had greatly increased their chances for success. Up on a hill, Laurent and the *Confrérie du Chêne* waited. Philippe did not feel slighted. He knew they awaited the outcome of this test. He felt confident. He felt they would not be disappointed.

He turned suddenly–something inside him made him turn. He saw Henri unhorse one of the rebel knights. The King turned. He paused a moment then slowly removed his helm. His eyes swelled large in his face. A scowl turned into a sneer.

"You! Traitor!" Henri shouted across the field as he raised his lance, pointing it at Philippe. "I will have your head!"

King Henri thrust his helm upon his head, leveled his lance and charged Philippe. Without hesitation, or thought, Philippe kicked his own charger to a gallop and leveled his lance. The two combatants met with a great crash; their lances exploded into a storm of splinters. Each had hit the center of the other's shield. Henri lurched in the saddle but managed to remain. Philippe, however, rolled over the back of his charger and hit the ground. He quickly scrambled to his feet knowing full well Henri would not waste a moment. Philippe pulled off his helm to give himself an unobstructed view. His shield was shattered. He drew his sword and swung around in a circle, panting, and searching for Henri.

The shouting, screaming, and other sounds of battle filled his ears. He could neither see nor hear his enemy. And then, a single set of hoofbeats, a horse approaching from somewhere at a hard gallop. Philippe turned and saw Henri approaching, the shattered remains of his shield dropping as he raised his sword high in the air to strike Philippe down. Henri unleashed a wild animal roar as he bore down on Philippe who raised his own sword in a futile effort of defense.

And then four bright flashes, four shrill streaks breaking the air from behind Philippe, four metallic thuds. Henri fell from his horse, crashing hard onto the ground. He rolled a short distance from Philippe. He did not rise as quickly as Philippe, nevertheless, Philippe approached slowly, as one might approach any dangerous, wounded predator. He saw the King rise slowly to his knees and remove his helm. Henri's back was to Philippe, and he circled slowly around Henri's side at a safe distance, wary of any deception. Henri looked around in disbelief, panting heavily. Philippe came around in front of Henri as the King looked down at his chest to see what lay there. Philippe saw blood running down Henri's armor from four wounds in his chest and abdomen. Henri looked down at his own blood, touched it with his hands. He held them up and looked at them, uncomprehending. Philippe stared at Henri, and Henri stared down at the source of his wounds. They both saw four arrows imbedded in Henri's body. The end of each shaft possessed a glimmering golden flight, made not of feathers, but of the heads of living golden wheat growing from the shafts themselves.

Philippe turned to the West, to the hill upon which a magnificent glow resided, not of the setting sun but of the Great Archer himself, the benevolent god of the Harvest, the Lord Aufeese. The Golden Child of Mava held his bow down a bit, waiting for Philippe put an to end a life-time of madness. Even at the distance, Philippe could see with clarity the emblem which the Lord Aufeese wore upon his armor. It was an image of a young girl with long chestnut hair. The girl Emmeline.

Henri began to laugh. He looked at the arrows and laughed, he looked around to the battle still playing out and laughed. He looked at Philippe and laughed.

"So, Jean-Louis, you believe you have won?" Henri let out a chuckle which clearly pained him. He looked up at Philippe. "You cannot defeat me. You do not have it in you. Perhaps once, you could have, but not now, Jean-Louis. Not now. I have broken you. What-ever was in you before is gone."

Philippe stared at his King, his perennial melancholic appearance still on his face. He said nothing; he did nothing.

"These wounds are nothing, Jean-Louis." Henri coughed. "I shall recover. I shall rally my armies, overwhelm your pathetic rebellion, and repay Ocosse for its treachery. And when I am done, I shall punish you. Your wife, and your pretty little daughter first shall pay dearly for your daring to defy me. And after it is all finished, you shall thank me for it. Yes Jean-Louis, you shall."

Philippe drew in a deep breath. His brow furrowed and his eyes lit up with smoldering fire. "You are such a fool, Henri," he growled. "Are you so feebleminded that you never understood a simple child's tale? Did you never understand that Jean-Louis, that unassuming donkey, he learned courage, and in the end was finally able to undo his tormentors?"

A look of surprise flashed onto Henri's face.

Philippe raised his sword in both hands. The blade gleamed in the sunlight straining through the cloud cover. "I take the name given to me in ridicule. I am Jean-Louis."

For the first time, fear crept into Henri's face.

"And I, Jean-Louis, swear now that you will never harm another innocent again!" He swung down the sword, Henri's head separated from his body and rolled across the battlefield.

––––––

Murielle felt her hot blood coursing through her body. She felt alive. Although she mourned for Cheval and missed their connection, she fought on foot as fiercely as they had together. One by one her opponents fell, no match for her ferocity and superior fighting skills. The lessons her father had taught her in her younger days had not diminished in her memory. Although Richard had not taught her how to kill, she found it easier to do it, especially when there were so many people who deserved to die.

At one point she looked up from the heat of combat to see the object of her revenge charging across the field, his lance lowered, and preparing to engage an opponent. The once hot lust for revenge which had resided in her on this day had cooled and dissipated into nothing. She felt nothing at the sight of Henri. Lord Bellicor said he had his reward coming. Murielle felt a warm glow of satisfaction at that knowledge.

She pushed back an opponent–another mercenary–and beat him down unmercifully. She turned again and saw Henri and the knight Philippe coming together in a great crash. Murielle gasped when she saw Philippe fall from his horse. Doubt and worry raced through her. What if Lord Bellicor had it wrong? What if Henri was too strong for Philippe. He had looked so sad and frail that day, and Henri had seemed so powerful.

Instinct pushed her toward Philippe, she did not know whether it was to aid a fallen ally, or because of the connection she felt toward him, or whether it was simply to intercede for the one who might have actually ended the life of the hideous creature which had destroyed her life. Murielle stopped again as she watched the events unfold.

Then it was over. Oddly, she felt nothing as she watched Henri's head roll across the field and his lifeless body slump to the ground. Philippe's eyes remained on Henri's body for some time before he let out a deep sigh, and a look of resigned satisfaction came over him. She felt nothing as she stared at him, and this was good.

Murielle realized too late that she had spent too much time staring. The sounds of the battle still raging around her had faded from Murielle's ears as she stared at Philippe, but raged it had, and it would be some time before all the combatants realized that the King of Darloque was dead. It was her father's voice that came to her, his voice commanding her to pay attention, for in the tournament everything happens too quickly to allow oneself the luxury of idle thought. In the tourney such a mistake might cost one the match, in war, something far more dear.

Something struck Murielle in the back. There was no pain, only a brief pressure. She put her hand reflexively to her abdomen. When she held it up again, she saw bright red blood covering it. Mystified at this phenomenon, she looked down and saw the end of a sword protruding from her abdomen. There was a tug, and the sword end was gone.

Slowly Murielle turned, still in a trance, and still in no pain. Slowly her shield slipped from her arm and fell to the ground with a soft thud. She turned to face a soldier holding a bloody sword before him. *My blood?* Murielle thought idly from what felt like a long distance away. The soldier wore battered armor, chinked and dented from perilous battle. His shield, as his armor, had taken gratuitous abuse this day and would like likely not see another battle. Blood, both dried and fresh covered this soldier from head to toe. He had lost his helm, or simply discarded it, at some point in the battle. Murielle looked at his face, his wide-open face, recognition dawning in it, a memory registering in those familiar eyes.

Murielle's eyes opened wide, she snapped from her trance. A

large burly fellow stood before her, not a particularly bright looking fellow, but all too familiar. He was the fellow who had knocked upon the farmhouse door so long ago, bringing pain and death into her life. She knew him and he knew her. As he stood before her clearly unmanned to see the lady of the house here of all places. Murielle acted out of reflex, her mind still a long way away, bringing up her sword and connecting the blade with the burly man's head. Blood sprayed and he fell to the ground never to arise again. Murielle felt no satisfaction.

The pain was upon her at once, a fire in her belly causing her to bend over double and lean upon her sword for support. She gripped the pommel, handle, and cross, driving the blade into the hard ground with her weight. She attempted to walk that way, using the sword as a crutch, trying to make it off the battlefield. But she could not. Murielle stumbled and fell to the ground.

———

Philippe dropped to his knees. A wave of relief passed through him. It was over, finally. All the pain he had endured, all the pain anyone had endured. Over. Healing could begin.

But it was not over yet, and deep inside the experienced knight knew the battle still raged. The head had been removed, yet the dragon was still dangerous. Philippe raised his head. The armies of Ocosse had pushed Henri's remaining troops back into the range of the archers who were raining hell upon them once more. His own regrouped and revitalized troops fought on the other side, confining Henri's men into an ever-smaller space from which there would be no escape. There was only one thing left to do. Philippe rose to his feet and raised his voice.

"The King is dead!" he cried in a loud, booming voice which resounded across the field. "King Henri is dead!"

The reaction was instantaneous. Many of Henri's men began to signal for surrender. Others began to flee the field. The few who chose to continue fighting found they had fewer and fewer allies. Those who surrendered were taken from the field, those who fled were chased down and slain mercilessly, as were those who had chosen to continue the foolish endeavor of battle. In a short matter of time, the rebellion was complete.

Philippe became aware of riders approaching him from behind. He turned to see Laurent and the *Confrérie du Chêne*. The brothers surrounded him in a protective position, swords and lances at the ready for any treachery against the leader of the rebellion. Soon, another rider approached, the one Philippe awaited. He had fulfilled his promise to the war god. The base knight and faithless king had been defeated according to plan–as much of the plan as had been revealed to Philippe. Darloque now had no king. The time had come to reveal the final phase of Lord Bellicor's stratagem.

The war god reined his charger to a stop before Philippe. He knelt before the war god, pressing his fingers to his forehead. The Knights of the Oak dismounted and knelt in veneration as well.

"Arise, knight," commanded the war god. Philippe rose to his feet and Lord Bellicor commanded Laurent and his knights to regain their mounts.

A crowd had gathered around them. Philippe saw his own followers, battle weary knights and soldiers, aware of the dilemma of Henri's demise, looking upon Lord Bellicor expectantly. Philippe saw the King of Ocosse and his captain of the armies–MacTavish, Philippe believed his name to be–grow grim as they too realized the plight Darloque now faced.

"The evil is destroyed," boomed Lord Bellicor across the field. "Now harken all present to a truth which had been lost, an incontestable truth which I now reveal to all these witnesses present."

Over the hill, over the archers, a form leapt in a great long arc, landing delicately on the ground, then running on all fours down the hill and across the field. A great silver rabbit ran swiftly toward them. He wore an open-faced battle helm with an opening on the left side through which a long silver ear protruded. The right side of the helm was enclosed for there was no ear on that side.

The King of Ocosse leaned over to MacTavish. "One ear. This *must* be good news."

The messenger god of good news stopped before Lord Bellicor, rose up on his hind feet and bowed. Lord Bellicor acknowledged him.

"Greetings, Bonveritas."

Lord Bonveritas silently handed the war god a letter with an intact wax seal upon it. Lord Bellicor took it and raised it in his white paw.

"Behold! A letter, the contents of which shall reveal the truth of which I have spoken!" Lord Bellicor reined his charger around as he addressed the growing crowd. "The first wife of the Old King of Darloque bore him a son, which is known to all men present. That Queen Hélène and her newborn son died by treachery of traitors within The Old King's guard is also known to all present. However, at that point man's knowledge and truth part from one another.

"The letter I hold, a letter penned by Queen Hélène herself and sealed with her royal mark, lost for all this time and only recently recovered, tells a different story from the one men believe to be truth. Hélène became aware of the traitors's plans to kidnap the Old King's newborn son to force an end to the war with Ocosse. Privately, Hélène conceived a plan with Onfroy, the captain of the King's guard—a true and trustworthy man—to switch the boy child with another then secret him to a safehouse.

"Onfroy selected his son and a nurse to transport the infant son and true heir to the throne to the safehouse. Meanwhile, Onfroy, Queen Hélène, and the imposter were killed in an attack by the traitors. In a sad twist of Fate, Onfroy's son and the nurse met with a terrible accident, killing them both, but leaving the true heir of The Old King alive. The child was found by a band of monks, but the letter of his origins was lost, and no one remained alive who knew the infant's true identity"

The Knights of the Oak began to whisper amongst themselves.

Laurent de Lois raised his hand for silence, a look of consternation crossing his face.

Lord Bellicor continued. "This letter tells of the plot, asking the members of the safehouse to guard the infant prince with their lives until such time as the threat should be contained. It also gives a description of the infant, including a particular mark, the best means by which to identify the true prince. That mark was, and still is, a single blood red birthmark on his chest, over his heart."

Philippe's hand went to his chest. He drew a stuttering breath.

Lord Bellicor looked down at Philippe. "Raise your shirt."

Philippe grasped the edge of his mail shirt and the gambeson underneath and lifted them. A loud gasp came from the crowd as he turned in a circle, showing all present the mark over his heart, a mark as red as the spots across the war god's face.

Lord Bellicor beckoned Laurent. "I turn over this letter to you, Laurent de Lois, High Priest of the *Confrérie du Chêne*. The word of the war god is irrefutable, yet this letter must be reviewed by the Council of Priests as is the law."

Laurent bowed, pressing his fingers to his forehead. "It will be done, my Lord."

The King of Ocosse raised his fist into the air. "All hail the true King of Darloque! All hail King Philippe!"

The crowd began to chant. "All hail King Philippe! All hail King Philippe!"

————

From where Murielle lay, she could hear what had transpired. That careworn and beaten horseman she had seen at her husband's farmhouse had come to orchestrate her revenge, and now was proved to be the eldest son of The Old King and heir to the throne. Underneath the pain, her heart swelled with joy. She began to cough up fresh blood into her hand.

As she lay and listened to Lord Bellicor reveal the truth of

Philippe, she warily watched as a small black figure flitted about the bloody battlefield, darting amongst the dead and dying. Murielle had retrieved her shield and propped her head upon it so she could listen and carefully watch the small, black figure. It pained her to lay her head so, but she needed to keep her eye on that small, black figure.

When Lord Bellicor had finished speaking, and the cheers of the men had diminished, the moment she dreaded had arrived. The small, black figure stopped before her. The tiny black rabbit, perhaps small enough to fit cozily in her cupped hands, raised up on his hind feet and took a formal bow.

"Greetings, m'Lady," he said.

Murielle took a quivering breath.

"Or perhaps: 'Greetings, sir knight!' Which do you prefer?"

Murielle closed her eyes and swallowed. She said nothing.

"Ahh. I see. One of those types." He tapped his chin with his paw. "You do know who I am, correct?"

Murielle trembled. "Lord Noirceur, god of the dead," she managed.

"Well, you need not say it like that!" Lord Noirceur chuckled to himself, his short, pert ears twitching slightly. "Say, would you like to hear a joke? That usually mellows the mood, and I have a lot of new ones."

Before Murielle could respond the god of the dead began to tell a joke.

"Why is there a fence around the cemetery?"

Murielle said nothing.

"Because people are dying to get in!"

Lord Noirceur burst into laughter, bending over double and clutching his middle. Murielle looked glumly at him.

The god of the dead wiped his eyes. "Did not like that one, eh? Hmmm." He tapped his chin again. "Ahh! Here is one you shall like. Are you ready?"

Murielle nodded.

"Knock, knock."

Murielle closed her eyes and followed along. "Who is there?"

"Orange."

"Orange who?"

Lord Noirceur began to chuckle. "Orange you glad to see me?!" He rolled onto his back, roaring with laughter.

Murielle frowned, but slowly a smile crept onto her face. Her mouth contorted as she fought the urge, but she finally succumbed and broke into laughter. The pain in her belly was horrendous, but she could not stop laughing. A coughing fit came upon her, producing fresh blood on her lips, and she slowly regained her composure.

The god of the dead stood and wiped his eyes. "Oh, I do so love that one." He looked at Murielle, pale and wan, but she wore a smile, nevertheless. "Ahh, that is how I like to see them. None of that moaning and wailing."

Murielle wiped her eyes with her sleeve.

"One last joke. Aufeese just recently told me this one. He was having tea with a human female, and so asks if she would like anything in her tea. 'Would you like some sugar with your tea?' he asks, and she says, 'No, thank you.' 'Would you like some milk with your tea?' he asks, and she says, 'No, thank you.' Then he asks, 'Would you like some lemon with your tea?' and she says, 'What? *Le monde?*' And he says, 'No! Lemon, not the world!'"

Lord Noirceur rolled on the ground laughing at this, but Murielle only stared blankly at him. When he rose again, he looked at her with a sigh.

"Well, I thought it was funny."

Murielle began to cough again. When she had stopped, she looked into the darkening sky, black clouds rolling thick across to the horizon. She turned back to Lord Noirceur. "I do not wish to go with you. I–I have found something for which to live."

Scattered about the field had been the truth she had been denying all her adult life. The Three Heroes, Lord Arbrinner, and Lord Bellicor fighting on the field. Upon the hill with the archers, the Lord Aufeese himself glowed brightly, rivaling the sun. Upon another hill, the Lady Blanchefleur consoling the women. She had allowed her father's disbelief to permeate her. Despite her desire and her need for faith, she had given up on it too easily. Through the process of losing everything for which she cared, she had finally learned faith.

Lord Noirceur looked upon her compassionately. "I am so sorry, but there are no bargains with the god of death. Those who are summoned must go."

"Not even if I told a really good joke?"

The god of the dead tapped his chin. "I might be willing to consider breaking the rules if it is an exceptionally good joke. What is it?"

Murielle turned away sadly. "I do not know any."

"I am sorry for that." The god of the dead considered. "There is, however, something I can offer you."

Murielle turned back to face him. She coughed weakly. What is that?" she whispered hoarsely.

Lord Noiceur stepped closer as thunder rumbled in the distance. He leaned in and whispered in her ear.

"Reunion."

Murielle smiled, the light fading from her eyes, realizing she was finally at peace with her faith and with herself. Turning back to Lord Noirceur once more, she nodded, closed her eyes, and went with him.

The rain began to fall.

EPILOGUE

MY FATHER, not an ignorant man himself, insisting that all his children, whether boy or girl, be schooled in letters, in the arts and sciences, in mathematics, in philosophy, and in all those subjects in which intellectual men converse, and I, being his only offspring, was therefore schooled in all the aforementioned subjects. And I, not wishing to waste his good judgment and effort, therefore use my hard-earned skills, given by the gods and nurtured by my father's good diligence, to come to his defense.

For time is as a river, and as the river god Lord Fleuvenar is harsh and heedless, sweeping aside anything or anyone within his reach, regardless of its importance, or lack thereof, so also does time sweep away with a careless arm the great and the small so that many are forgotten in its wake.

I readily use my talents, both god-given and human nurtured, to compose the account of my father's fall and rise to the crown so that no detail may be forgotten, and nothing may fall into conjecture. The text I have composed reads both true and accurate, and as a rampart against the flood of time, let no one cast doubt upon the story of my father, King Philippe.

Anna-Claire de la Province
Regina Nova Darlocum

NOTES ON THE TRANSLATION

I wish to thank the faculty of the History and English departments of MacClelland College, University of New Darlo for their support and assistance on this new translation of Queen Claire's text.

I also wish to thank Dr. Gregory MacDonald for his invaluable assistance in my updated translation, especially on "the parts that just never felt right," as he put it, in his original translation of nearly fifty years ago.

I also wish to thank the staff of University of New Darlo library for their invaluable assistance and especially for suggesting texts to me that I might have overlooked otherwise.

This new translation of Queen Claire's account of her father represents hundreds of hours of diligent research and includes information from many sources not available to Dr. MacDonald when he composed his original translation. I believe this work represents the most accurate translation to date, providing what Dr. MacDonald himself has called "the most accurate representation of Queen Claire's original intent we have today."

Jules Lauwry, PhD
MacClelland College, University of New Darlo

Dear reader,

We hope you enjoyed reading *By The God's Ears*. Please take a moment to leave a review, even if it's a short one. Your opinion is important to us.

Discover more books by Christopher Fly at https://www.nextchapter.pub/authors/christopher-fly

Want to know when one of our books is free or discounted? Join the newsletter at http://eepurl.com/bqqB3H

Best regards,

Christopher Fly and the Next Chapter Team

ABOUT THE AUTHOR

My father had a PhD in Music and a strong interest in literature while my mother a master's degree in English Literature, so my house was filled with books of a variety of genres. It was not unusual for me to read Edgar Allan Poe one day and Norman Mailer the next.

As I got older, I was drawn to science fiction and horror. I was the guy who carried a copy of Stephen King's "Christine" around my entire senior year of high school.

In college my interests turned to Medieval literature and history. I soaked up the works of Thomas Malory and Chrétien de Troyes. In graduate school I branched out into Shakespeare and modern literature. I also took creative writing courses when I could. Post graduate work has included studies in World War I, World War II, and various 20th century conflicts.

In college I also met a special woman who would become my wife. I had come to class wearing my kilt, and she had to meet me. She came with three wonderful children whom I am proud to have had a hand in raising. My wife and I became involved Scottish Heritage Festivals, donning kilts and dragging the children all over the Southeast United States. We also started a not-for-profit organization bringing internationally known Celtic music artists to our area. We also raised pedigree show rabbits and traveled around the Southeast to various rabbit shows. When the children became adults and moved out to begin their own lives, my wife and I started a small farm. In addition to the rabbits, we added sheep, chickens, and a couple of Great Pyrenees dogs with a lot of personality.

Having been exposed to literature from an early age, it was natural for me to compose my own stories. I have always written stories for myself, but when the kids moved out, I finally decided it was time to get these stories out into the world. I hope you like what I have to offer.

Lightning Source UK Ltd.
Milton Keynes UK
UKHW011859120221
378724UK00001B/102